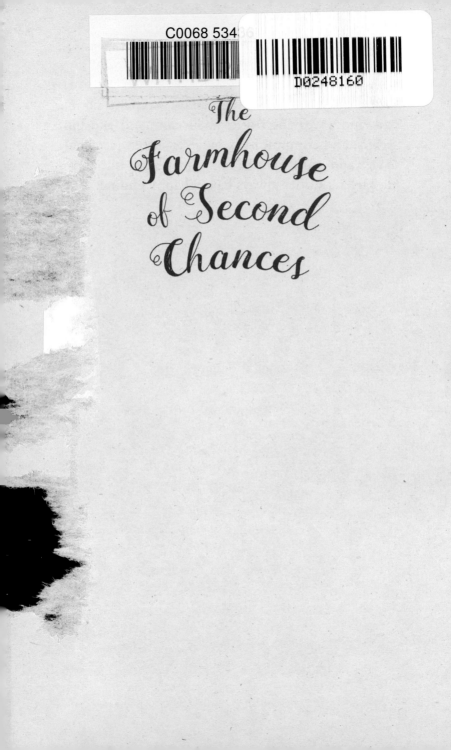

The
Farmhouse
of Second
Chances

Helen Rolfe writes contemporary women's fiction and enjoys weaving stories about family, friendship, secrets, and community. Characters often face challenges and must fight to overcome them, but above all, Helen's stories always have a happy ending.

The Farmhouse of Second Chances

HELEN ROLFE

ORION

An Orion paperback

First published in Great Britain in 2022 by Orion Fiction,
an imprint of The Orion Publishing Group Ltd
Carmelite House, 50 Victoria Embankment,
London EC4Y 0DZ

An Hachette UK company

1 3 5 7 9 10 8 6 4 2

A CIP catalogue record for this book is
available from the British Library.

ISBN (Mass Market Paperback) 978 1 3987 0030 7
ISBN (cBook) 978 1 3987 0031 4

Typeset by Input Data Services Ltd, Somerset

Printed in Great Britain by Clays Ltd, Elcograf S.p.A.

www.orionbooks.co.uk

For my family & friends

Chapter One

Joy

It was late June and the magnolia flowers on the bush by the main gates to The Old Dairy were showing off their creamy pink petals at long last. It would only be a matter of weeks before those petals fell and withered and the cycle started all over again.

Such was life. And Joy had grown to love the seasons, all of them. She welcomed the sun, the rain, the chill of an icy winter in Bramleywood, she watched the colours and the appearance of the village, her front garden and surrounding land change with them, but everything else remain constant. It had taken a long time to realise no matter the cyclical nature of the weather, the trees and the flowers, her place in the world remained the same. And she was content at long last, the shadows of her past fading gradually.

She sat by the open window at the front of the farm-house that had been her home for twenty-five years and tore open the envelope that had landed on the mat almost half an hour ago. Whenever she got a letter from her niece Libby, she did this; she relished it, wanting to savour every second of a rare moment of contact with a member of her biological family, which often meant waiting for the madhouse to quieten down before she could enjoy it in this exact same spot on the armchair next to the open window, a mug of tea beside her. Not that she minded the madhouse, it was the home she'd built and she wouldn't have it any other way.

She didn't get to read the letter as planned, at least not yet, because she saw Drew's jeep bounce in through the open metal gates at the front of the farm, crunch over the gravel and disappear down the side of the house where he'd be parking out back near the old cowshed. And despite spoiling her immediate plans, Joy never turned anyone away, she always had time for anyone who ever needed her, especially Drew who had no idea what it meant to her having him in her life. Drew, for reasons he didn't yet know, was the person she'd most wanted to see make something of his life; he was the person she'd most wanted to help, to give him something back, in some way. It could never make up for what he no longer had, but she hoped that somebody somewhere was looking down on her telling her she'd done good at long last.

Joy put down the letter, picked up her mug of tea and made her way from the front of the farmhouse, along the hallway where she straightened the painting of sunflowers opposite the stairs that promptly dropped at the corner again the second she took her hand away, cut through the kitchen and headed on out to the adjoining utility room at the end. She threw her head back laughing the moment she stepped outside where a makeshift pen kept six lively Labrador puppies from running out into the fifty acres of land she owned, and saw Drew doing his best to fuss each of them. All six, three golden, two black and one chocolate, wanted to be first in line and they'd somehow managed to get Drew to the ground and were tugging at his shorts, his T-shirt and one was licking at his face with him laughing his head off but telling them to stop.

'I think you're protesting too much,' Joy grinned, sipping her tea as though she were watching an elaborate performance. 'And finding it funny as well as talking in a higher pitch is never going to make them behave. It seems to me you're enjoying every second of the attention.'

Drew didn't deny it. And it was moments like these, the mayhem, that had filled Joy's house with the love she'd had to search for for so long. It had given her another sort of family, the sort you built around you and had nothing to do with genetic building blocks. She'd had the same sense of grounding and belonging with Ted and Marjory, the farm's previous owners, when they took her in all those years ago and now she'd found it again she didn't ever want it to change. Some folks around here assumed it would, thought that she'd get too old to be taking in waifs and strays, but Joy and what she did running a halfway house of sorts were as much a part of The Old Dairy now as the solid oak tree that stood next to the old cowshed and had grown wide enough to provide plenty of shade that reached part of the puppies' pen.

As Drew continued to protest but love every moment with the six little rascals, Joy looked up at the cobalt blue sky until the sun peeped out from behind a cloud making it impossible to keep looking in that direction. She never took this open space for granted, she never grew tired of the freedom she felt out here. Smiling and content she moved to the shade herself to enjoy the light breeze from the mighty oak's branches stretching up into the sky. She'd planted this very tree from a single acorn she found walking past the village pub one day. She'd brought it back here, planted it in a flowerpot filled with compost, nurtured it before transferring it outside, and slowly it had been turned from something someone might step on or kick across the street, into an impressive tree that now looked as though it had always been a part of the landscape with its deeply ridged bark and abundant burst of leaves. She knew without being able to see, that its roots would stretch way down through the earth, reaching as far as they could to claim this part of the village as their own, a place to belong, settle, and a place to grow old.

Drew finally got up and the puppies did their best to grab anything at ankle level, one of them catching the end of the lace on his trainers and pulling it the best he could until Drew escaped out of the pen, across the pavers and onto the flagstone floor once again. When Joy went over to join him he bent his head to kiss her on the cheek. 'How are you today?'

'Better thanks to this sunshine.' She'd been feeling sorry for herself yesterday, her knees sore and her hip a little uncomfortable, and it was too hot to soak in the bath, so she'd had to go and lie on the sofa rather than helping get the chickens in to their coop at the end of the day. And now it seemed someone had got Drew all worried. 'Might I assume you only heard about my knees because Lauren told you.'

'Not Lauren.'

'Cameron?'

Glossy eyes as brown as mocha caught the sunlight before Drew followed her inside for some respite. Despite only being June, it had been unusually dry and hot across the whole of the West Country and they were desperate for some rain. 'I don't think Cameron speaks to many of us yet does he? At least not unless it's after he's run off again and we try to find out why. I think we've got a way to go before he's talking about anyone's ailments.'

'Then it would have to be Freddie,' she guessed.

'Got it in one.'

She supposed it was good that he cared. Freddie had urged her more than once to consider taking it a bit easier than she usually did.

Ted and Marjory had been like parents to Joy. She'd even taken their last name, feeling safe and secure after so long of being adrift, a moment she knew they'd been as touched by as she was. Taking Ted and Marjory's surname of Browne had given her a sense of belonging, but more than that, it had given her a fresh start as someone else. It had marked a real new beginning. She'd never thought about the farm and what would happen to it when Ted and then Marjory passed away. She'd learned not to look that far into the future in case she didn't like what she saw, but The Old Dairy had become hers to do with as she pleased.

When Joy learned she had been left the farm, she had no intention of doing anything major with the home or the land. The Old Dairy hadn't operated as an actual dairy farm for quite some time and so Joy was content to live there and do what she could with the chickens, and she began to think about maybe growing produce, perhaps becoming self-sufficient if she could manage it. She didn't have a whole lot going on in her personal life after all, so a project was perhaps what she needed to get her through the days, past her grief at losing Ted and Marjory. Her personal life consisted of day-to-day hellos to locals, but not much more and other than that it was the letters from her niece Libby that kept her going.

Libby was the one member of family Joy had left who was willing to be a part of her life. And it was the farm and Libby that had given her focus from one day to the next until she'd taken Drew in and helped him get his life back on track, setting him off in a direction that could only mean good things for him. She'd opened her house and her heart to him, and once he seemed to turn a corner and go from a troubled man angry at everything and everyone around him, it kickstarted something in Joy. She wanted to do it again. It was her way of giving something to people who were as desperate as she'd once been, a way to pay it forwards.

For more than a decade now, Joy had been running The Old Dairy as a halfway house, helping young adults mostly, who'd fallen on hard times and didn't know which way to turn. Over the years she'd taken in countless people. Some lasted, others didn't, and went back to their old ways, as though bad habits were so entrenched there was no alternative. Some people who came to her moved on but stayed in touch, others naturally drifted away, some sent the odd Christmas card but had put this part of their lives behind them, and that was fair enough. Drew, Lauren, and Freddie, at various points, had all lived at The Old Dairy, in need of a roof over their head, desperate to find a way to reinvent themselves or get their lives back on an even keel. Each of them had yearned for family comfort and found it right here and Joy couldn't be happier that their ties remained strong. Despite moving into their own homes, Drew and Lauren were still a part of her life, and Freddie still lived here, something she was more than happy about.

'Cameron's a quiet soul,' Joy confirmed as she made Drew a mug of tea in the farmhouse kitchen. Cameron was the latest stray to cross paths with Joy. She'd caught him attempting to break into her car one day and had seen something in his eyes, something that begged for another chance. And so the eighteen-year-old, who looked a good few years younger than that with his vulnerability, was now living under her roof in exchange for helping out around the place. Not that he'd managed much of that yet. But Joy had recognised when to push and when to ease off, because she'd learned it from Ted and Marjory who'd been strangers to her when she first arrived in Bramleywood. Her own flesh and blood hadn't wanted to know, they hadn't been interested in giving her a second chance, but somehow Ted and Marjory, although knowing the bad in her – she'd never been anything other than honest with the people who'd given her a home – had also managed to see the good. And Joy was under no illusions that at times they'd had to dig pretty deep to get any sort of a hint of it, especially when she was having a bad day, wallowing in self-pity that would change nothing.

'Let's hope he comes out of his shell soon,' said Drew, knowing full well he'd been the same when he first arrived.

They watched the puppies from the window. Bisto, the only chocolate lab of the litter was chasing his own tail; Buttercup, one of the golden Labs, had taken to tearing apart an old shoe Joy had lobbed in there; a couple of the others were play-fighting in the corner of the pen, and their mum, black Labrador Luna, finally got up from her sunny sleeping spot to have a drink from her bowl of water and give a cursory glance to her babies. They chatted about the puppies and their personalities, how much they'd changed since the day they were born in early May, and it got Joy thinking about how much she'd changed herself since she turned up here in Bramleywood.

'You having an easy day today?' Joy, a good few inches shorter than six-foot-three Drew, reached up and brushed a small twig from his dark hair that had curled behind his ears. When he'd first come to The Old Dairy those curls had been wild, but over the years his hair and Drew himself had been tamed into a better version of the man who'd always been hiding underneath. She'd never doubted he could do it. And it gave her a slight sense of peace.

'I've had a pretty busy morning and thought I'd head out here for lunch.' He cradled his mug of tea in his hands as he leaned against the kitchen bench.

'I knew it, your heart is in your stomach.'

'Guilty,' he admitted. 'But I will offer to be the chef if it helps.'

'Go for it, you know where everything is.'

He tilted his head in the direction of the wire egg storage basket in the shape of a chicken. 'French toast, omelette or scrambled eggs? And how many am I catering for?'

'Let's have scrambled eggs and it's just me and you. Cameron has only just made a toasted sandwich.'

He spied the sandwich maker still in need of a bit of attention. 'Want me to go ask him to clean up.'

'No need, he'll come out of his room soon enough.'

'He's still not helping out around here?' Drew raised his hands when she shot him a look. 'I know, it takes some longer than others.'

It was what she told Drew, Lauren and Freddie when they got too protective. They looked out for her and, never imagining anyone would ever again, it was a feeling she valued.

Last year they'd had Gill, nicknamed Rapunzel because of her hair that was so long she sat on it, until she got so angry one night she hacked it all off. She'd been someone Joy had never quite been able to help, and nobody had any idea where she'd gone off to. All Joy or the others knew was that one minute Joy was trying to coax her into helping with the chickens and the next, she'd taken money from Joy along with her credit card and they hadn't heard a word since. Joy had cancelled the credit card and there hadn't been too much financial damage, but it was losing out on helping her that had hit Joy the hardest. She hated failing Gill. She hated failing anyone. She'd done that too much for her liking and it was a part of her personality she wanted to beat with a stick whenever it came calling.

Drew wasn't bad in the kitchen, and over soft and creamy scrambled eggs served with generous doorsteps of buttered toast, he told her all about his morning. It was what she loved, hearing voices fill the walls of the farmhouse, knowing the minutiae of the lives that had at one time had way too much drama. Hearing about the normal day-to-day stuff was like music to her ears.

'I taught a group of school kids basic kayaking techniques,' Drew shared, 'and all of them took to it straight away. I'm already looking forward to the next session. I'll lead a bit of a tour, they'll love it.' He tucked heartily into his food, always good to see from someone Joy looked out for. Cooking brought everyone together in this place she called home.

'I'll bet you're a good teacher, you have patience, not something everyone is good at.'

'Maybe I learned it from you,' he grinned. 'And I've needed patience, especially at the start when the business first launched. It's hard to believe I've gone from leaflet drops to drum up business and operating from my jeep at random places, to buying my own premises by the River Brue.'

'I always knew you could do it.'

'Not without your help I couldn't.' He winked, this man, this proud owner of a kayaking enterprise that took people out on guided tours along the river soaking in the Somerset countryside or provided kayaks for people to take out privately. A man who'd been totally lost when Joy first welcomed him in to The Old Dairy, he'd found his footing not on dry land, but on the water.

Joy liked to believe every person she brought to The Old Dairy deserved another chance in life, just like Drew. And just like her. On her first visit all those years ago she'd been dishonest with the honesty box at the bottom of the driveway and caught by one of the owners. Rather than reporting her, Marjory and Ted had given Joy a roof over her head and the best chance to make something of herself after everything she'd been through. She'd gone from a skinny, mousy-haired young woman with an office job in her twenties to an almost-seventy-year-old grey-haired surrogate mother to more than a dozen young adults over the years, lover of cows, keeper of chickens and land owner. Her life had turned out well, all things considered, but the less said about that the better. As far as everyone here knew, she'd simply run away from home, stumbled upon this place and the respected Ted and Marjory and everything else had worked out. Nobody ever need know what else had gone before, because the shame would swallow her up whole if she let it.

Cameron schlepped into the kitchen as they were clearing up the lunch dishes.

'The water's still warm, mate.' Drew indicated the sandwich toaster and the dirty iron plates that would need a good scrub.

'So?' Cameron, small round glasses with a smudge on them that didn't seem to bother him, obediently in place just below a fringe that he'd cut himself yesterday, and not well, immediately leaped on the defensive.

'So, you could use it to clear up your things,' Drew suggested firmly but not horribly.

'You're not the boss of me.'

'Just trying to help.' Drew backed away from the sink and Joy assumed Cameron would ignore the request, but as Drew and Joy got back to discussing the paddleboards Drew was adding to the shed to introduce another water activity, out of the corner of her eye she saw Cameron slide the iron plates out of the sandwich maker and put them in the water.

It wasn't long before he was complaining that the debris wouldn't come off. Drew opened his mouth and Joy knew he was going to say something along the lines of it being far easier if you cleaned them straight away, so she put a finger to her lips to shush him.

'Let's have a look, shall we?' She was too soft some of the time, she knew, but most of what these young adults or even adults had in common when they first came here was a lack of love, an absence of empathy and understanding, and she knew that if she could give them some of that, as Ted and Marjory had given her, then she was paving the way to change. It hadn't worked on Gill, but Joy had had more successes than failures, and that was what fuelled her determination.

Joy and Cameron and a plastic scrubbing brush between them got those iron plates free from muck and back to black, the way they should be, before Cameron headed back upstairs leaving a trail of crumbs from an oat biscuit Joy handed him. She'd leave him a while before she tackled requesting his help for anything else. She knew he loved the puppies, she'd seen him glance their way plenty of times, his body almost taking him over there to play with them before his head told him not to show emotions, no weakness, no feeling. And tonight Joy would be ready to go into battle again, encouraging him little by little, and she'd ask him to give the puppies their dinner. All he'd have to do was fill two big bowls with food, take it out to their pen, set them down and watch the pups go nuts in a feeding frenzy. These puppies had arrived just in time. They could be the magic ingredient to get Cameron to come out of his shell a bit and start to move forwards, she just knew it.

With Drew traipsing across the fields to find Freddie who'd be tending to one of his many veggie patches or in his greenhouse, Joy took herself back to the sitting room and her letter from Libby.

It was time to lose herself in correspondence from someone who hadn't turned their back. Joy liked to think of it that way when in reality, Libby probably kept in touch because she'd never been told the truth.

And that was fine by Joy. She hoped it would stay that way.

She settled down in her favourite spot in the armchair next to the open window at the front of the farmhouse again and opened up the letter, but rather than relax and lose herself in her niece's exciting new life on the other side of the world, her mouth went dry and a feeling of dread coursed through her body.

Libby was coming back to England, but not only that, she was coming here to see Joy. And rather than be excited, Joy couldn't summon anything other than a fear she was about to lose the life she'd so carefully rebuilt.

What if Libby wanted to dig into the past? After all, she knew the family had disowned Joy, she'd been writing to her auntie without anybody else knowing, and now she was older, perhaps at long last Libby would question the reasons why Joy hadn't been welcome in her life.

Joy's hands shook as she dropped the letter onto her lap and stared out of the window, out past the gate, across the road to the fields beyond, the landscape she'd become so used to.

The landscape that might be about to alter all over again.

Was she about to lose everything?

Chapter Two

Libby
Two weeks ago

'Taxi!'

The yellow cab came to a halt and Libby ran from the sidewalk, yanked open the door and leaped inside before reciting her address. She was soaking wet, the New York summer a mix between stifling heat and heavy rains, or at least that's the way it had been over the last week. She'd set out this morning to the city bathed in sunshine and hadn't brought a coat, or an umbrella, and right now her chestnut hair with its natural highlights was stuck fast to the sides of her face as she shivered in the back of the cab.

Home at her apartment on the Lower East Side Libby jumped straight into the shower to wash the day away and warm up. It had been a crappy day too. She'd once loved her job as an actuary for a reputable insurance firm, she loved being suited up and chairing meetings, using her specialised maths knowledge and skills to analyse the financial consequences of risk. Her expertise had seen her head-hunted by several major firms and years ago when she first arrived in the Big Apple she'd have eaten every opportunity up. She'd operated on fast forward for the last five years, but as the zingy shampoo she used on her hair in the shower awakened her senses she realised that she was still just as lost as she'd been when she first arrived on American soil.

Her body wrapped in a towel and another towel twisted turban-style around her hair, Libby sat on the edge of her bed and picked up the photograph of her and her parents. It had been taken the year before her mum died and they were all laughing their heads off outside a perfumery in London's Soho after her dad was accosted by an over-enthusiastic sales assistant who'd liberally sprayed him in something way too floral for a manager at a bank. He had meetings lined up all afternoon and both Libby and her mum had been in hysterics thinking of how he would have the entire room sneezing with the amount of fragrance on his shirt.

Libby ran a hand across the photograph in its frame before she put it back on the bedside table. It had been a happy day for the three of them, one of those simple days that didn't involve anything more than beaming sunshine, a regular lunch and time well-spent together. But if Libby had known she'd only have twelve more months with her mother she would've taken a ton of shots that day and every one since, she'd have photographed her mum sitting in St James's Park concentrating on the book on her lap, she'd have captured a picture of her with her eyes squeezed shut she was laughing so hard at the comedy show they'd been to in Brighton together the following month. Libby would've caught moments when her mum least expected her to be lurking with a camera, when she was baking for Christmas, flour in her hair and on the side of her face as she made the family favourite boozy Christmas sponge with a hidden mousse inside that Libby and her dad adored every year and wished she'd make more often.

All of those moments had disappeared in an instant, and the photographs she still had would freeze her mum, age sixty-five, forever.

Libby checked her watch. She had thirty minutes until she was supposed to meet friends on the corner of Canal Street. Looking out of the window, she noticed that at least the rain had stopped now. She'd planned to go out straight from work in her dark grey fitted and flared tailored dress, but instead she pulled on a more relaxed printed floral dress that finished just above her knee along with her favourite sequinned ballet flats and she transferred her purse and accessories to a more relaxed leather tote.

She couldn't wait to meet friends and have a sympathetic ear or two after the day she'd had.

'It's just the two of us?' she asked as she and Brandon, her boyfriend of eight months, headed to a restaurant she knew you needed reservations for.

'I'm sorry, I should've told you.' He pulled her to him and kissed her firmly on the lips. 'I wanted you all to myself tonight.'

'I suppose I can't argue with that.' She let him take her hand and lead her into the restaurant which was one of those lowly lit places, all hushed voices and candles in the centre of tables with wax dripping down the glass bottles they'd been pushed into.

Usually it was a group of six friends who met up and went out for dinner, and while she and Brandon had started off as friends, they'd become a couple somewhere along the way, moving faster than she would've liked. But he was a good guy, he was handsome and well-dressed, had a good job and seemed to put her first. Her friends thought she was crazy to have any doubts, so she stopped being frustrated that he'd changed tonight's casual meet-up with a crowd of them for a romantic dinner for two, and confided in him about her dreadful day at the office.

'It feels so good to get it all off my chest,' she said after she'd told him everything, her frustrations rising to the surface.

'Hey, any time, I'm here to listen.' He took her hands across the table, which worked to calm her down. 'What do you think of this place?'

'It's amazing, thank you for bringing me here.' She felt so ungrateful when he was trying really hard to impress. But really she'd have been content with grabbing a burger from the Shake Shack and strolling through the park. It was Brandon who favoured fine dining, not her. He'd chosen tonight's wine, the bottle of red he topped her glass up from now, a Merlot he extolled the virtues of even though she knew she'd have a hard job telling it apart from one she'd buy at the local liquor store on the corner for five bucks.

But she couldn't fault the food. It was another thing entirely, and ravenous after the adrenaline pumping around her body following her stressful day, she fully appreciated the mushroom pappardelle with truffle oil and tarragon that swiftly arrived at their table moments later. Talk turned to his plans for another skiing holiday and an invite to go with him.

'I'm not much of a skier,' she reminded him as she twirled pasta around her fork. They'd talked about this before. 'I could come and watch, drink hot chocolate from the chalet.'

'Let me teach you,' he said, cutting his steak and running it through pepper sauce, 'you'll enjoy it I bet.'

She shook her head. 'My next vacation really needs to be in England. It's a long time since I went back.' And yet, she still hadn't gone. It was as though she didn't know her place there either and she was worried that if she did return she might find she had nothing there at all and feel even more adrift than she already did. She'd tried to disguise it with a good job, a busy work life and hectic social life, but underneath all that, she was lost.

He began to talk about what they could see in England and how they might tie it in with travel around Europe. His eyes lit up at thoughts of the Eiffel Tower in Paris, seeing the canals in Venice, the mountains in Switzerland, they could immerse themselves in London's Oxford Street, see Westminster Abbey, Buckingham Palace, the Tower of London. Libby did her best to join in with the eagerness but really she needed to go back to the places that weren't for tourists, the parts of the country that weren't filled with people only after a slice of England to add to their memory box.

Lately Libby had been pining for her birthplace in a way that had taken her by surprise. It wasn't that she'd be heading back to a family home, that had long since gone with her dad starting over somewhere else entirely, and her friends here, who were all born in this very country, didn't understand. Brandon had never left America for more than a couple of months' vacation so while he said he got it, he understood her need to visit, he didn't really because he was still talking about places in Europe that would take forever to get to and defeat the entire purpose of going over there.

'I think I need to go on my own,' she admitted, taking him and herself by surprise. Maybe she'd stay in a hotel somewhere in the Lake District, try to see her dad but not at his place, let them both have some breathing room and try to work out how to be a family when part of it had gone.

'You don't want to go on holiday with me?' Brandon always had a way of sounding hurt, as though her actions were devised to cause him pain.

'It wouldn't be a holiday, it's a visit home.'

'I don't see the difference. I thought you and I were heading in the right direction, Libby.'

She shook her head, frustrated that he didn't get it. 'We were . . . I mean, we are. Let's drop it, vacation time is a long way off anyway with everything going on at work.'

He seemed happy to oblige and ordered another bottle of wine. It wasn't long before they were back to talking about her day and the moment a work colleague showed his true colours. And to be honest it was a relief to change the topic from England to something else when he wasn't beyond sulking if he didn't get his way.

'He's been bad-mouthing me,' she said, pausing to thank the waiter when he took their plates away, 'and telling my boss . . . my boss! that I'm stressed out again and they probably should lighten my workload as he was worried about me having another breakdown.'

'They won't listen, surely.' He closed his eyes appreciatively after a taste of the Merlot and gave the dessert menu a cursory glance.

'I worry that they will.' And she worried that they'd

see Nick was right, because she was beginning to feel the same way she had six months ago when she'd had what her doctor had termed a nervous breakdown. She'd been overworked, surviving on only a few hours' sleep most nights before coming back into the office to do it all over again. She never said no to anything that was asked of her – that was, after all, how she'd managed to be so success-ful, securing whopping bonuses year after year. Brandon had been attentive in that time, bringing her lunch at her apartment, visiting some evenings if he wasn't wining and dining clients. He'd been there for her and he'd helped get her through what was a terrible time, although she'd picked up on his frustration that they weren't going out as much as they usually did, they weren't hanging out with other people, as all Libby wanted to do was curl up be-neath her duvet and hide.

Her closest friend of the group, Abigail, had been there for her too, not minding that Libby didn't want to go out on the town. Libby and Abigail had spent many an evening at Libby's apartment watching movies, eating popcorn and talking the night away. Abigail had suggest-ed Libby's turmoil, aside from her breakdown, might be partly due to her age when Libby confided that she felt all over the place, didn't know where she fitted in or what she wanted any more. Around the same time Abigail had been planning her wedding – with the desire to conceive on her honeymoon soon after, which she'd managed, with a baby on the way before the end of the year – and cited part of Libby's stress as being the ticking of the biological clock that according to Abigail ticked as loudly as her parents' grandfather clock in their hallway at home. But for Libby, it ran so much deeper than any kind of clock. Libby's problem was that somewhere along the way, amidst the busyness of her life, she'd lost a part of herself. She barely knew who she was any more. What had seemed so clear when she hopped on that plane from London to New York five years ago following her mother's death, to get away from everything, was now a murky shade of grey and she couldn't wade her way through to find the other side.

'Go to your boss yourself,' Brandon advised now after they'd agreed to share a crème brûlée for dessert. This was where he was assured, confident, talking about office politics. 'It's always best to get in there early and tell your side of the story. Come on, Libby, this isn't the woman I know and love, you're strong, you've taken that company from strength to strength, you're an asset not a liability. And the episode you had was just a blip.'

Episode. Brandon knew she hated it being called a breakdown, the only person she admitted that to was herself. She hadn't told her dad about it on the rare times they spoke either, their conversations were rigid and revolved around the weather comparisons, her high life in a big city he'd never once visited and his hobbies now he lived in the Lake District. Anything resembling feelings was side-stepped and had been by both of them since the day they'd lost Libby's mum.

Despite Brandon's advice at the restaurant, come Monday morning something inside of Libby snapped. Or perhaps not quite snapped, but rather a switch flipped, like a switch on a circuit board when the electrics failed and suddenly you put it back on allowing you to see a bit more clearly.

She'd been standing by the floor-to-ceiling window in the office block that looked down onto Lexington Avenue. Human Resources had asked to see her and she could only imagine what they were about to say. But rather than being worried they'd have her carted off to the nearest mental asylum she felt strangely calm. And for good reason – they wanted to see her to offer her more responsibility and another pay rise which meant she'd be able to afford the rent on the apartment she'd turned down only last week because it was too steep. It meant she could afford a lengthy vacation in England and more of Europe if she really wanted to, but would she ever have the time to go? Because with the shift in responsibility and more money, there would be more demands, and she wasn't sure she had much more to give.

With one hand on the glass window Libby looked down at the pedestrians on the sidewalk, the cars cramming the streets all trying to get to where they needed to be in the quickest time possible, and it was then she realised that the only person who could stop herself from falling apart again and having another breakdown was her. Not Brandon, not her work colleagues or friends, her.

'You know it makes sense,' Nick's voice called out from his desk as she emerged from the meeting room leaving behind a stunned Human Resources manager. He wore a smug look on his face, the same one he'd had for days since he tried to get her bosses to think she was weak and about to fall apart.

Libby turned on her Jimmy Choo heels that had taken her years to perfect the art of walking in. And she went right up to Nick. 'You know what, they offered me promotion, more money, more responsibility, and given how good I am at my job it makes perfect sense.' That shut him up.

The waffle at his desk that looked as though it had already gone floppy in the sun blazing through his window went untouched. 'You got the VP position.'

'I did.' And she almost wished she'd taken it just to stick one to him. 'But I turned it down. And you know what that means, don't you?' The look on his face suggested he was waiting for her to congratulate him. He was almost panting with excitement. 'So if you'll excuse me, I need to tell Elsa Human Resources are waiting for her.' And she promptly made her way over to the twenty-five-year-old who'd started here a year ago and had been close on Libby's heels. But unlike Nick, she'd never trodden on them, she'd simply hovered in the wings, and now HR had every intention of letting her take the VP position. They'd told Libby, not directly, but the undercurrent was there to suggest they knew Nick wasn't a team player enough to hold the VP position. And, after Libby told them her decision they'd wanted recommendations for who should fill the spot. She'd recommended Elsa wholeheartedly because Elsa was the exact same hungry workaholic Libby had been when she first came here. Maybe that workaholic was still in there somewhere but right now it needed a rest.

It was company policy to leave as soon as you made the decision to move on and so Libby cleared her things, invited a select few to a bar down the street to celebrate what was a massive change coming her way. And for the first time, the not having firm plans didn't bother her at all. Maybe it was the adrenaline, she wasn't sure, but whatever it was she wished she could bottle this feeling.

She called Brandon the minute she kicked off her shoes in the hallway of the apartment that wouldn't be hers for much longer, with its hardwood floors, the cute window seat in her bedroom where she liked to curl up and watch the rain fall against the pane, and the miniscule kitchen with the oven that had no temperature control and the wonky shelves in the lounge that had never been fixed. She'd missed his call when she was at the bar and apologised.

'I would've come for a drink if you'd told me,' he said.

'It was very spur of the moment.'

He tried to convince her she should go back and take the job on offer. 'I think you may have overreacted, Libby.'

She took a deep breath. 'I'm not going back.'

'Why not insist on a vacation, then return.' And then he began harping on about going to Europe together, so much her head felt as though it could burst any second.

'Let's see what happens. I've got lots of contacts,' she replied with a confidence she was unsure of.

'That's my girl,' he said. 'Positive and strong.'

'Maybe I'll take a holiday. Go to San Francisco or Napa Valley, drink my way through being jobless.'

'Go for it,' he laughed. 'I'll miss you but if you need a vacation to get this all out of your system then I get it. Listen, why don't I take you out this weekend to celebrate pastures new.'

'Since when do you use phrases like "pastures new"?' she chuckled.

'I think I picked it up from you. And listen, when you get back, what do you say to moving in with me?' The request came like a thunderbolt and she didn't have time to react. 'Your apartment lease is up soon, you can keep your things here, come on, Libby. Move in with me.'

'We've not been together that long.'

'Long enough.' When she said nothing the enthusiasm dropped out of his voice. 'You're never going to want to take the next step are you?'

'Brandon, I—'

He made an excuse about being in the middle of watching the game, and she didn't even challenge him on it. It was enough to deal with her own emotions right now, she didn't have any room in her head for Brandon and their relationship that was going faster than she wanted. If her mum was still alive she would pick up the phone right now regardless of the time of day or night and she'd call her to yell, I quit! At the top of her voice. And then she'd tell her about Brandon, the man who was there for her, who had so many qualities she loved but who somehow wasn't the one for her. And it seemed, perhaps he was beginning to realise it too. Maybe one major change had been the instigator to face everything else that was wrong in her life.

Libby didn't even consider calling her dad because since her mum died it was like they'd forgotten how to talk to each other, as though their joint pain was worse than their individual loss. Instead, she lay on the sofa, cuddling the cushion against her stomach, one hand tugging at its tassles. She thought about the hurt in Brandon's voice. They'd moved from friends to lovers and she wished they'd stayed friends all along. She thought about the job she'd left behind, the possibilities she'd have if she put feelers out with other firms. She wondered whether she should send emails off now, make applications, then take some time out and go to the West Coast but have something to come back to.

She sat upright. Maybe that wasn't what she'd do after all, because it was something else Brandon had said that made her think on a different wavelength.

Pastures new.

It was a phrase she had probably used, but couldn't remember saying it. And it made her think of life in the countryside, the British countryside, and the one person in her family she hadn't seen many times since she was a little girl, but who was a constant in her life. Her mum's sister Auntie Joy lived in England's West Country, a part of the world Libby wasn't familiar with herself given she'd been brought up near Southampton. But she'd heard enough about The Old Dairy and the village of Bramleywood in her auntie's letters. And right now, the pull of England was greater than that of the West Coast of America, and perhaps the countryside where Joy lived was exactly where Libby needed to be to get her head sorted and work out her next move.

Libby went online and booked herself a flight. Everything was happening at once, but perhaps that was the order of the day after she'd left work without a backwards glance. And after she'd booked a flight she took out her writing paper and envelopes, something not many people demanded these days, to write to Auntie Joy.

Libby had always been curious about the auntie who, for some reason unbeknownst to Libby, was cast out by her family, never spoken about and who was never allowed to be a part of her life. As a little girl Libby could remember Joy visiting briefly. Joy and her mum, Maggie, had talked, although the conversations had always been hushed, and

Joy had never hung around except the time she stopped by and neither of Libby's parents were home. A childminder was there that day and when it was clear Libby knew this person, Joy had been allowed to play with her in the garden. She'd set out a tea set in her cubby house, served pretend tea and cake, she'd shown her auntie how high she could get on the swing and then shown her how long she could hold a handstand. Joy had shown she could still do a cartwheel and Libby had been in fits of laughter, the sunshine lighting up their faces, Libby's tummy hurting from giggling so hard. It was when she was holding another handstand as Joy checked her watch to time her and see if she could beat the original record that Libby remembered her parents coming home. Her mum had taken her by the arm and dragged her inside, her dad had spoken in that serious tone he used if Libby was in trouble, and must've asked Joy to leave because after a small protest and what looked like a few tears, her auntie had left.

Libby remembered Auntie Joy as fun, kind, interested, and a little bit sad. And after that day and her parents' refusal to answer any of her questions, she'd got even more curious. She'd begun to snoop and eventually found a collection of unopened letters to her mum, and she knew they were from Joy because her name and return address were on the back flap on a small sticker, the sort you had printed and used on all your correspondence. Libby had copied down the address without her mum knowing, taken a stamp from her mum's purse, and sent that first letter a few days after she'd met her auntie. And they'd been writing to one another ever since. It hadn't always been easy of course, but that was all a part of the adventure. Libby had had to grab the post before anyone else did, something fairly easy given it usually came after her dad went to work and before she went to school. Thinking about it now, Libby was surprised they'd never been caught out, she didn't always get to the post first, but sometimes her mum or her dad had put a pile of it on the hall table ready to wade through later and Libby had been able to search through it all before they did.

Over time Libby and Joy had slowly got to know one another through their letters, but you couldn't find out everything about a person until you met for real, and maybe now, it was time to do that. After all these years perhaps it was time to meet again. And the more Libby thought about it, the more she realised the timing couldn't be more perfect. The little village of Bramleywood would be a place away from it all, where Libby could finally catch her breath, before she had to think about going up to see her dad.

With the flight booked, Libby was operating on fast forward and she couldn't write the words quickly enough to explain to her auntie that she was coming to see her. She was going to visit her in the glorious Somerset country-side and hoped Joy had room for her at The Old Dairy. She put in her email address in case Auntie Joy really didn't want her to go, it would be an instant way to put a stop to the visit and Libby could find a bed and breakfast or hotel, but Libby suspected she wouldn't do that. Letters revealed enough about her auntie's personality to tell Libby this would be a very welcome surprise.

She was, at last, going home.

Libby put the letter on the little shelf in the apartment

hallway ready to post in the morning, tucked herself into bed and let her head sink into the pillow, exhausted.

And for the first time in a long time, she didn't even bother to set the alarm.

Chapter Three

Joy

The farmhouse stayed lovely and cool despite the long dry, English summer that was begging for rain. Built of stone, even the upstairs remained a pleasant temperature, and according to Drew who'd moved into a new build at the other end of Bramleywood Joy should be thankful her home didn't come with the same industrial insulation they'd installed at his place that had seen him coming over here three evenings in a row and even staying last night. Joy didn't mind a jot of course, she'd have him living here permanently if she could. Ever since she'd taken him under her wing she hadn't wanted to let him go.

Now, upstairs in the farmhouse it was time to get a room ready for Libby's arrival. Because he was the tallest, Freddie had the bedroom with the level ceiling, only one corner of it angled with the shape of the house. Cameron had the largest room and didn't mind having to duck in certain places. This room Joy had chosen for her niece had angles here and there, but it gave it a characterful quirkiness the way the ceiling sloped towards the window in one part, slanted up and over the old-fashioned armoire in battered pine that needed a key to keep the doors shut. One wall was painted a sunny yellow, the others white, and the lampshade, also in white, was made up of clusters of tiny flowers. One of seven bedrooms along the corridor, each with reclaimed pine doors, this room had a bathroom right next door that would be just hers, and the jewel of the room, as well as the free-standing claw-foot bathtub, was that like the others on this side of the farmhouse it had a terrific view across the Somerset countryside and the patchwork of fields that were part of The Old Dairy.

With the window open the breeze wafted the scent from the orange quilled-petal dahlias Joy had arranged in a glass vase. It clashed with the yellow-ness but that tickled Joy and she suspected it'd amuse Libby too. They hadn't seen one another for years, but somehow Joy felt she knew this girl who'd injected a positivity in their correspondence that at times had been the only thing that kept Joy going. She shook out the fresh sheet to feed the duvet into and undid the buttons at the end. Libby's letter had been like all her Christmases and birthdays bundled into one, her niece coming to stay, she still couldn't believe it. Libby had given her an email address too, in case Joy had a reason she couldn't have her here at the farmhouse. But Joy had no intention of turning her away and she still wanted to pinch herself to make sure this was real.

'Who is this Libby anyway?' It was Cameron, lurking in the doorway of the room as Joy unfolded a freshly laundered bed sheet. The bedding Joy had chosen was the set in yellow and white checks which weren't so bright it was too much with the yellow wall, and with a wicker chair in the corner, a small bedside table in the same wood as the wardrobe, and a modest chest of drawers, Libby should be quite comfortable.

'She's my niece,' Joy explained acting as normally as she could when it was early days with Cameron but one of the first times he'd hung around and tried to make everyday conversation.

'How old is she?' he shrugged.

'Now you're asking. Thirty-six, if my old brain is working well enough.' She attempted to get the duvet into the cover.

'Why's she coming?'

'She's taking some holiday – or vacation as she put it, too many New York phrases for my liking when she's English through and through.'

'How long's she staying?'

'I've no idea.' Libby had said she was coming for a couple of weeks, if that was OK, but Joy already hoped it would be longer even though she'd initially been worried Libby might want to dig around in her past and bring to light things Joy wanted to forget, for ever. She wrestled with the duvet cover some more. 'Now, do you have any more questions to fire my way, or could you help me with this blessed thing?' The bed in here was a double, the duvet refused to stop bunching up, and Joy had already sat down on the wicker chair in the corner for a breather.

'You're doing it all wrong you know.' He pushed his glasses up his nose and removed the part of the cover she'd wrangled on.

'Hey. You're undoing all my hard work.' But she didn't mind. This was positive progress in her eyes.

He turned the cover completely inside out, put his hands inside and shook it down his arms until his fists were in the opposite corners. Then he grabbed the corners of the duvet between his fingers, stood on the bed and shook the material with all his might so the cover fell down over the duck and feather duvet Libby might need at night if the weather chose to flip over to cooler temperatures any time soon. Which Joy hoped it would. There was supposed to be a storm tonight and she loved a good storm to clear the air, but right now, there wasn't a cloud in the sky.

'Magic,' she claimed, looking at Cameron's handiwork. The duvet was on already. But that was enough of an accolade for the boy and he scarpered.

Joy straightened up the bedding and pulled on the pillowcases. 'Baby steps,' she said out loud to encourage herself, pleased at some kind of thaw in the boy's attitude, no matter how minor. He'd been here at The Old Dairy for a little over a month and Joy felt she was making progress, albeit slow.

The day Joy had met Cameron she'd parked her car at the village station and it was a day much like any other. She hadn't been getting the train anywhere – everything she needed was right here in Bramleywood, but locals used the car park to bring them closer to the other end of the street that wound from one end of the village to the other. It meant she wouldn't have to carry the shopping all the way home which would be a struggle with tinned items, washing powder and all the other bits and pieces they couldn't grow on the land. The Old Dairy was at one end of the village, although not at the furthest point – that would be Bramleywood Cider Farm which was on one of the country roads that sprouted off the main road taking people through the village. Nearer to the station was the pub, a decent fruit and veg shop which also sold eggs – lots of produce courtesy of her and Freddie at the Old Dairy – and there was a good bakery which had improved a lot since new owners took over five years previously. Bramleywood had plenty of pretty houses, some with traditional thatched roofs, others behind the Indian takeaway squished together like a row of toy soldiers keeping watch over the rest of the village. There was a hairdresser's too and Joy made sure she went for a pampering every other month. That was what she'd been doing when she met Cameron, if *met* was the right word. The kid had looked terrified when she caught him attempting to break into her car and he'd run off quickly. It wasn't until Joy saw him later on mooching around near the big house behind the grand gates near the sign that welcomed people to Bramleywood that she spoke to him again.

'You'd better not let the owner catch you out here,' she warned him. 'Rick won't let you off as lightly as I just did if he catches you sniffing around, up to no good.' The owner of the house – which was, admittedly, very pretty – Rick Oxley was a local who appeared to have the power to upset anyone in his path. He'd even upset Freddie one day when she'd seen them having words. Freddie had said it was just a misunderstanding and had never elaborated, and Joy only hoped it had been nothing to do with her because ever since Ted and Marjory left her The Old Dairy Rick had been after the farmhouse and all the land. He wanted to develop it and build unsightly new houses, but never in her lifetime would Joy allow that to happen.

Cameron took one look at her and sensing she was telling the truth, went on his way. Good job because Rick came out of the house before Joy could get away herself and demanded to know what was going on. She'd shaken his query away as though he was imagining things, and thankful she'd got Cameron out of the way, muttered under her breath and walked off before he made any further effort to engage her in conversation. The last person she wanted to talk to was someone rich, entitled and who thought everyone should bend over backwards to do what he wanted. Perhaps that's what people did, and because Joy wouldn't, it really got his back up. Something about that tickled her even though she knew it shouldn't. People like him never did it for Joy. She preferred genuine, kind-hearted personalities and there were plenty of those at home and in the village. Zelda who ran the bakery was always up for a chat no matter whether she had no customers or was elbow-deep in pastries as she fought to restock her shelves at the busiest of times. Walter, whose family owned and ran the estate agents opposite the bakery, was a serious gentleman but always nodded a hello in passing as did the rest of his family; Cora who worked behind the counter at the post office never stopped smiling it seemed whenever Joy went in to post another letter to America; and Dahlia who worked in the village shop next to the post office and who had a smile for everyone who came her way, especially Cameron apparently. Alex, who worked in the library, a shy boy with angel-like wispy hair that looked baby soft rather than the hair of a grown man, was gently spoken and didn't like any form of confrontation. The most animated Joy had ever seen him was when Rick tried to buy up the library and close it down and Alex as well as pretty much every other resident of Bramleywood took to the streets with placards in protest. No amount of Rick throwing his weight around was going to take the library away from them and Joy knew more than most the importance of escapism, and what books meant to a lot of folks including her.

Joy was on her way back to her car when she saw the boy again and this time she saw him pluck a loaf of bread from some poor lady's wicker basket as she set it down on the pavement outside the hairdresser while she studied the sign in the window. The woman didn't notice, but Joy waited round the corner, grabbed Cameron when he tried to go down there and he took one look at her when she refused to let go of him and rather than fight her off, which he could've easily done, he burst into tears. Joy promptly told him to wait, took the loaf and miraculously deposited it back in the woman's basket without her even noticing. The woman, not someone Joy recognised, really should keep a better eye on her belongings Joy concluded, and with no harm done, nobody yelling Thief! at the top of their lungs, Joy expected the boy to have scarpered, that the tears were fake and a ploy to stop her taking him to the police.

'Why did you do that?' Joy asked when she found him still loitering. It had been raining and he was kicking a stone along the walkway that led from the main street to behind the station and the car park. When she looked at his feet, his shoes were sodden, one torn to reveal a bright red sock, and he wouldn't meet her eye.

'Dunno,' he said.

'Where do you live?'

'What's it to you?' he snapped, but the accompanying sniff didn't match his tone. It was as though he was trying to hide his vulnerability, but it wasn't fooling her. 'I've been sleeping over there,' he admitted.

She looked in the direction he was pointing but all

she could see were surrounding fields, their angles, their bumps, and if her eyesight was still as reliable as she hoped it was, a derelict building in the distance that she knew was in the process of being torn down. Her heart thumped, she had visions of him being asleep and the walls caving in around him.

'I live at The Old Dairy,' she told him on her next breath.

'That's nice for you.'

'No need to be rude,' she batted back. She didn't need to ask more about his living situation, she knew the signs only too well. 'I'm Joy,' she tried again, putting his hostility aside.

'Cameron,' he muttered.

At last, they were getting somewhere. 'I take it you stole the bread because you're hungry.' When he opened his mouth, most likely to say something sarcastic, she quickly added, 'There's a hot meal at my place on offer if you want to take it.'

'What's the catch?'

'No catch,' she said, walking over to her car. 'You coming or not?' she called behind her without turning round. Nonchalance sometimes worked if she'd read the situation correctly.

That day Cameron had come for his hot meal. He'd left right after, barely saying a word the whole time he was at the farmhouse, but Freddie, Drew who was there at the time, and Lauren who'd turned up with a cake of which Cameron had a generous slice and accepted another to take with him, knew the deal. They all did.

Cameron turned up again a week later and hovered at the end of the driveway for a good thirty minutes before

Joy decided it was time to go outside to talk to him. They'd started the summer dry spell that seemed everlasting and this time his feet weren't sodden, but he was grubby and the smell, oh my days, when Joy went up close. She told him she needed help constructing a pen as her dog Luna had given birth to a litter of six puppies who were wreaking havoc in her utility room and needed somewhere to play outside where they couldn't run off into the fields. Joy had shared with Cameron the story about taking Luna in as a stray – she'd had her checked over at the vet's and wanted to ensure she hadn't been microchipped. She wasn't and she had no collar and was therefore genuinely homeless. It was at that visit to the vet's that Joy had found out Luna was pregnant. Cameron had liked hearing the story when Joy told him and she'd hoped it let him know a bit about who she was, how much she cared and wanted to help, without having to say those exact words to the boy. She hoped too that even though Luna was a dog, the way she was so at home and a part of Joy and everyone else's lives already, would show Cameron that it didn't matter where you came from, you could always find your way.

Joy had told Cameron that day that if he could help with making the pen, then she'd let him take a shower, have a meal and even stay the night. He did the work, took the shower thank goodness, but he was gone soon after, head hung low not wanting to converse with anyone. It wasn't until Joy saw him again a couple of days after that, sitting in the fields beyond the station car park nursing a damaged wrist that she whisked him up properly and refused to take no for an answer. And with the building he'd been staying in finally demolished, he knew Joy was his best bet. Joy took him to A & E to sort out the wrist he'd badly sprained when he slipped running away from the owner of the building who'd discovered him on the property, and then took him home to The Old Dairy where he'd stay in exchange for helping out to earn his keep. He hadn't done much so far but she had every faith he would. Over time, and from her own personal experience, she'd found that making it a two-way street was the best way to encourage people in Cameron's situation. Many still had their pride, and handouts weren't the way to go, so suggesting working for their board and lodgings seemed the right choice. Not that she enforced many rules and made anyone work too hard. Most of the hard work, she knew, would be for them to find themselves again and start to believe they were worthy of this life, worthy of love and kindness.

Joy finished making up the bed now and when she heard laughter she looked out of the bedroom window. She had to get right up close to the glass to see down below, but when she did, there was Cameron sitting in the pen he'd helped to construct, the puppies leaping all over him and him loving every second. 'Well I never,' she smiled before moving away from the window in case he saw. Her eyes filled with tears. Another step closer for Cameron and another step towards her helping someone. It was what she lived for, breathed for, it was her anchor to do this for other people.

Thrilled Cameron was showing signs of beginning to want to settle, she wondered if it had anything to do with the young girl, Dahlia, who worked in the village shop. Although Cameron didn't do much to help at the farmhouse yet, he had gone with Freddie to deliver eggs and produce to the shop, and according to Freddie, whenever they went in there, Dahlia would blush. Freddie suspected she liked Cameron and he'd told Joy the feeling might be mutual because Dahlia and Cameron often talked while Freddie discussed the next order with the shop's owner.

Thinking about it reminded Joy very much of what first love could be like. When you gave your heart to one person and thought they'd never ever break it. She'd had that herself one day and as she watched Cameron she thought back to the boy who'd taken her heart all those years ago.

Gregory Taylor – or as his closest friends called him, Tay – was a breath of fresh air in Joy's life. He'd come into it on her twenty-seventh birthday, full of riotous colour in personality and with suntanned skin, having returned from a year-long trip around Australia.

Joy had been sitting in the pub with one of her friends dissecting their days spent temping as admin clerks, typists, data entry clerks, you name it, although they didn't mind what the given title was as long as they got paid.

'You ask anyone,' Joy's friend Sita announced over a pint of Stella, 'admin staff are the backbone of any successful office.'

'We're just the lackeys,' said Joy, staring into the depths of a pint of Guinness which had long since lost its cool appeal. 'Two more days of that job and I'm outta there.'

'Think of the money.' Sita, nose stud glinting beneath the pub lights, tilted her glass to her friend's and clinked it a little too hard, slopping some of hers into Joy's. 'I've been inputting so much data about plants and seeds in my latest position that my head is spinning, I feel like a gardening encyclopedia. Honestly, I'd rather be doing what you're doing.'

'No, you wouldn't. I work for a woman who calls me Julie, leans over my desk to talk to me, almost drowning me in her cleavage – which, by the way, is on display no matter the weather – and starts every sentence with, "Not to be difficult, but . . . ." '

'Which means she's about to be difficult,' said Sita before she excused herself to buy fresh pints for them both.

Joy tried to insist she didn't need another and she didn't care it was now made up of lager as well as Guinness, but Sita was off, and when she was adamant she rarely backed down.

Joy had been laughing at her friend and rolling her eyes when a guy of around her age came over to her table and sat right down. Just like that, slid in next to her on the red leather seat in one of only three booth areas of the pub.

And he was looking right at her with a smile that left Joy in no doubt as to what he wanted.

Stuck for what to say, she looked at him, he looked at her, and that's all they did for a good few minutes until Sita came back and wanted to know what was going on.

The guy stood up, held out a hand and shook Sita's. 'I'm Gregory, my friends call me Tay.'

'You can't even make "Tay" from the letters in your name,' Joy noted.

'Didn't say you could.'

He hadn't shaken Joy's hand, but his eyes were back on her and it wasn't long before Sita, recognising the signs of a possible hook-up, claimed her need to go have a game of pinball. It wasn't a lie, she'd been doing well to ignore the machine all night knowing Joy wasn't interested, but Joy knew she was doing it to give her friend a chance with this bubbly stranger.

Joy pushed her blonde hair over her shoulder. Her hands

were clammy and the fresh pint of Guinness was at least a way to cool down even without drinking it. She clutched it and looked up to see Sita glancing her way with an urge that said, 'Go for it, what are you waiting for?'

'Aren't you going to tell me your name?' Dressed in board shorts in the height of summer, Tay's floppy chestnut hair was highlighted from the sun. He had a pint of his own but showed little interest in it.

'Joy.'

'I like that. A happy name. And are you happy?'

'I guess so.' She began to laugh.

'What's funny?'

'You . . . you don't get embarrassed easily do you? You came over here and just sat down assuming I wanted to talk to you.'

'Would you like me to leave?'

She shook her head.

'People who don't go after what they want should be the ones who are embarrassed,' he claimed. 'And I always go after what I want.'

She couldn't help it, her heart leaped, he was the most excitement she'd had all week. She hadn't had a boyfriend for almost eighteen months, and he was the best-looking guy who'd ever shown her an interest, unless you counted last week when the boy – and that was the best word to describe him – who worked for the temping agency asked her out. He was gorgeous, but she wasn't even sure he'd legally be able to buy her a drink, and so she'd politely declined even though Sita had told her she was nuts.

'And what is it that you want?' She could do this, she could flirt.

'You,' he said bluntly. And this time he gently took her hand, his fingers across hers, his thumb rubbing across the *top of her skin. 'I'd ask if I can buy you a drink, but you have two already.'*

She had no idea how to reply to his direct comments and just like that he asked, 'Wanna get out of here?'

It was instant. She'd been bitten by the excitement, the audacity of the guy, his sexy body that didn't disappoint the moment he slung his T-shirt onto the floor at the hotel he was staying at, the way his strong torso took charge and made her feel things she hadn't felt in a long time.

Gregory Taylor was about to change her life in so many ways. Ways she never saw coming . . .

Joy pushed her memories to one side and tried to focus on the present. Libby was coming and she couldn't wait to see her.

She crept downstairs without alerting Cameron in case he scarpered. If she feigned indifference and didn't pass comment on his involvement with the puppies he might even stay there for a while and so she grabbed her sun hat and ventured outside, walking past the puppies' pen as though Cameron was stationed in there every day. She plonked her sun hat on her head and didn't allow herself to smile until she was well past the pen, as Cameron's laughter continued to lace the air. She crossed the fields towards the area Freddie had taken over and established a business which was helping to bring him back to the person he wanted to be. He'd been a broken man when he first moved in here, but he was getting it together more and more as time went on.

She stopped halfway over to Freddie. She often did this to soak up the feeling of freedom, the space around her, something she'd done without for years and the memories still haunted her at times when she least expected it. Coming outside, no matter the weather, was the way to restore her sanity every time. But she also stopped now because her legs were aching. She was getting older, and what had once been easy was beginning to take its toll. She wasn't yet seventy but sore knees plagued her more than she liked to admit. She closed her eyes and breathed in the West Country air. From the brow of the hill she could see the sheep that peppered the land, their tiny forms, heads bent as they nibbled at the grass to keep it as healthy as her heart was these days. As she turned round she could see back to the old cowshed at one side of which was the chicken coop and an attached run with an under-cover section should the chickens need it for shelter that gave the ginger-headed chickens enough space to imagine they were totally free. She hated to think of anything kept in an unnaturally small space and chickens got the same privileges as anyone else here on the farm as far as Joy was concerned.

Once upon a time, when Joy first came to The Old Dairy, the near fifty-acre property had been a thriving dairy farm with even more land and a herd of twenty-one cows, a mixture of Brown Swiss, Norwegian Red and Friesian. But over time Ted and Marjory had faced the harsh realities – it was getting harder and harder to compete price-wise and more difficult for them to run the business as they got older, and with enough money behind them to be comfortable and the sale of some twenty extra acres beyond what still remained today, they'd wound up the business and eased into retirement. Joy had assumed that they'd eventually sell the entire property, but with no family, they'd wanted it to become Joy's. They'd never been able to have children themselves and Ted had told Joy she'd saved them the day she turned up in Bramleywood. He openly admitted their marriage was a mess, they'd pushed themselves to breaking point over their sorrows, but through their shared devotion to helping a girl in trouble, they'd found their way back to one another.

Without Ted or Marjory around, Joy had found comfort in the familiarity of being here at The Old Dairy with the land, the Somerset skies that blanketed her each night, rain, hail or shine. She'd had company with the remaining two cows in the herd who lived out their days here on the farm, but that hadn't lasted, and for a while Joy had been lost when she found the last of the herd, Gerty, lying in a way Joy knew meant it was the end. It hadn't just been the end of Gerty's life but the end of life as Joy had known it since the day she'd arrived at the farm, lost and desperately in need of help. Somehow Joy had found a way to pick herself up and carry on after life threw so many changes her way. She funded herself, and everyone else who'd needed her help since, by renting out some of the land, twelve acres to a local who owned horses and wanted somewhere for them to roam freely when they weren't in their stables at night, another fifteen acres to a local sheep farmer. She'd also agreed the sale of a further four acres at the outer edge of her land for a buyer who intended to grow sunflowers. She couldn't wait to see the colour that came with it.

Over time Joy had also filled her home with people she cared about and who cared about her. And those relationships as well as the freedom of the land were things she'd never ever take for granted.

She was watching Freddie for a few minutes before he turned and noticed her. Not like him, he was usually as jolly as the sunshine, the man rarely stopped smiling especially recently since he said he'd been in touch with his ex-wife Ivanna. He said they were talking at long last and he was beginning to prove he had his life in order, he had a business and could support not only himself, but her and his son too. And given he'd waited years for her to even consider having him in their lives, Joy was surprised the development hadn't left him giddy. Then again, he'd been through a lot, maybe he was right not to get carried away and he was being cautious.

When he saw her approach Freddie was quick to put a grin on his face. 'Joy, you timed it well.' His eyes lit up from beneath a floppy dirty blond fringe. He had the rake in his hand, going over the earth in the new patch he'd dug over the last few days. The scent in the air suggested he'd already incorporated a good layer of compost with the soil.

'Oh dear, I'm not sure I like the sound of that.'

He had a garden tool belt around his waist, a couple of wooden-handled implements poking their way out, and he pulled a packet of seeds from one of the pockets. 'Want to help?'

She beamed. 'Of course, it was the heavy lifting or pushing a wheelbarrow I was going to run away from.'

'How are your knees, still sore?'

'They play me up all right.'

'It's never too late to think about yourself you know.'

'We've been through this Freddie.' She loved that he worried, as though the roles had been reversed, but giving up The Old Dairy wasn't going to happen, no matter how much her body groaned. 'Now, sowing cabbage seeds I can handle.' She liked getting involved and even though she couldn't deny she was no longer as quick on her feet, she felt she had plenty more life in her yet. Freddie shouldn't worry about her, he had a family out there who might one day see everything she saw, that he was a changed man, a strong character who put others before himself, and soon he could have everything he'd ever wanted.

He handed her a packet with a nod. 'Right, we want them half an inch deep, spaced an inch apart. You take one side, I'll take the other.'

Freddie had a passion for his business you couldn't conjure up unless it came naturally and as he had eased into his role, with him and Drew, Joy had found the company she'd been craving since the farmhouse went from being filled with voices and the busyness of two dairy farmers with cows on the land, to somewhere so quiet she wanted to weep. Drew had brought companionship Joy had never expected, and Freddie was such a force of nature that he'd injected life into the farm and her home in an instant. Her home was filling up and she'd found what she needed.

Joy watched Freddie start the sowing process. With his shaggy blond hair and nut-brown skin as well as his height he had a touch of the Nordic in him with a heart of gold to match the sun beating down from above. Ice-blue eyes glanced over at her. 'Come on, stop watching me and get sowing.'

Joy made her way all along one side, pushing the seeds in half an inch, ensuring she left even spaces between them. The first modest veggie patches she'd started had been resurrected after Freddie's initial arrival and they'd successfully grown carrots, garlic and onions. Those two patches had soon become four, then six, and had multiplied to sixteen with this latest one, and had gone from small sections to enormous spaces with narrow grassed walking paths separating each of them. These days Freddie not only helped to feed Joy and anyone else staying here or visiting with plenty of produce, he also supplied the local store, and customers loved to know fruit and vegetables had been grown on the land locally. He'd worked his magic with all sorts of things from beetroot, kale, broccoli, corn and potatoes to strawberries you could smell as you walked across the fields. He had a plentiful supply of blackberries, redcurrants and raspberries too and the apple trees Ted had planted years ago still stood by the fences than ran across one of the sections of land. Freddie had installed an enormous greenhouse for cucumber, chillies, a variety of lettuces and an abundant supply of the juiciest tomatoes Joy had ever tasted. The old cowsheds that Joy would never want to see demolished were used to house tools, empty planters, gardening materials, lengths of wood and pieces of cane, wheelbarrows and the tractor Freddie used to mow the acres surrounding them that weren't rented to anyone else. The farm and farmhouse were what she liked to call their own little haven.

Her knees groaned by the end of the seed planting but it was worth it and when Cameron came running her way hollering that a car had pulled up on the drive, she took a deep breath before turning to Freddie, her smile wide, her heart soaring. But she was nervous too. 'That'll be Libby.' Her feet were all of a sudden rooted to the spot.

'Go on then,' came Freddie's soft voice. 'What are you waiting for?'

She'd been wanting this moment to happen for years,

but at the same time had dreaded it too. Her emotions were all over the place, one minute excited, the next fearing what might happen if Libby were to probe into her past. Nobody here in the village knew her full history and she wanted nothing more than for it to stay that way.

Joy gathered herself and hurried across the fields, back towards the cowsheds where she washed her hands in the sink there. She couldn't very well meet the niece she hadn't laid eyes on since she was a child with mucky hands. It was bad enough she'd managed to get dirt all over her trousers and the cotton shirt she had on, but she'd have to do. And she hated to think what her hair was like beneath her hat, so she left it on.

Cameron had disappeared off already, most likely back to his room that Joy had kept its original pale blue, which went for the walls, the lampshade and the bedding. Visitors weren't something Cameron handled all that well just yet but at least he'd come outside to be with the puppies today and managing to take responsibility for announcing their latest visitor was a step in the right direction.

Joy made her way from the old cowshed, along the side of the farmhouse, now in the shade, and onto the drive. And there she was. Libby, beautiful Libby, the spitting image of her mother Maggie, Joy's sister, smiling a thank you at the man who'd climbed out of a smart black Jaguar and lifted her cases from the boot.

Her breath caught in her throat as she walked closer. The gravel crunched beneath her shoes and she smiled at the girl she knew mainly via the written word. Face-to-face contact was something else altogether.

'Auntie Joy.' With a flawless complexion, full lips with a

ruby red lipstick, brown flowing hair that caught the sunlight, her niece Libby was even more beautiful in the flesh than her photographs.

Joy held out her arms as the driver of the car waved and left them to it. She wasn't sure whether to or not given the last time she'd seen Libby was when she was a little girl, but the instant Libby relaxed, beamed a smile and walked towards her for a hug Joy knew it had been the right thing to do. 'It's wonderful to have you here at long last.' Joy took Libby's hand and squeezed it as they pulled apart. Libby's other hand was on her handbag looped over her shoulder and Joy sprung to attention to grab the wheelie suitcase waiting patiently on the driveway for one or the other of them to haul it inside.

'This place is huge,' Libby gushed. 'I'm used to poky New York apartments,' she explained as she picked a piece of gravel out from her neat white plimsol trainers with delicate sheer bows instead of laces. Joy hated to tell her they were the most inappropriate footwear for this property, even when the sun was blazing, and that the puppies would have an absolute field day if they got hold of them.

'The farmhouse comes with almost fifty acres, we'll go walkabout later if you like.'

'I'd love to. I've been cramped up on a flight for almost eight hours and then it was straight into the car service all the way here.'

'Some fancy car service, I saw the Jag. Whatever happened to a regular taxi?'

'It was easier to arrange for someone to meet me rather than wondering if I'd find anyone willing to take a fare all the way to the back of beyond.'

Joy was about to defend the village and say it was

perfectly adequate thank you, when she realised her niece was joking. She wanted to hug her again, her smile so much like Maggie's that it held an unexpected pain her niece wouldn't be at all aware of. The pain that spoke of years of separation from her own flesh and blood and all because they'd never been willing to let her prove herself, never given her another chance. Ever since Libby had announced she was visiting, just like that, Joy had wondered how much Libby really knew, how much Maggie had told her. Probably not a lot, or she wouldn't have come, would she?

'As long as you got here safely that's all that matters,' said Joy. 'Now, would you like to go for a sleep?' she asked, leading the way inside the farmhouse. 'The bed and the room are all ready for you, you have your own bathroom, fresh linen and towels on the bed. Or I could make you something to eat, a late lunch perhaps, or—'

'Auntie Joy.' Libby reached out and squeezed her arm. 'All in good time. You know what I'd really love? A good cup of tea. The States aren't big on tea like us Brits.'

'Then you've come to the right place. You drink the tea and we'll get rid of that American twang of yours,' she teased.

'Now if you told people over there I sounded American they'd laugh.'

'I've got some cake too, Lauren left a whole tin.' She beckoned Libby inside, bumping the suitcase up the three front steps where she left it in the hallway.

As Libby sat at the kitchen table Joy busied herself pulling out mugs, brewing a pot of tea, finding the milk and sugar. She made sure she used her favourite duck-egg-blue mugs and plates too, nothing but the best for the only member of her blood-related family who'd given her the time of day in years. She watched Libby as she looked around the place, drinking it all in. And if she wasn't mistaken, up close, despite the girl's skin that showed no real signs of ageing yet, something told Joy this was no ordinary holiday for her. Her letter had been so out of the blue, Joy wasn't daft, something was up and perhaps in time, The Old Dairy and Joy's halfway house would work its magic and Libby would share what it was. She was a whizz at solving other people's troubles, just not her own.

'Excuse me.' The sound of the phone ringing had Joy leaving Libby for a moment to go and answer it.

'The Old Dairy,' she announced as she always did when she picked up the call. No matter whether there were cows here or not, this place would always have its original name.

But the cheery edge to her voice didn't last when she heard Mr McKerrick on the other end of the line. His sheep had been grazing her land for almost nine years and his money regularly depositing into her account, and all of a sudden he'd found a more favourable arrangement. That was all he'd say, he wouldn't tell her whether it was cheaper or more convenient, all he wanted was to give his month's notice.

'Mr McKerrick, I do wish you'd reconsider.' But he ignored her final plea. His mind was made up.

Joy put the phone down aghast, and even knowing that her beloved niece was in the next room at long last didn't make her feel any better. Because in another month her finances would take a big hit unless she found someone else who wanted to use the land.

She couldn't lose this place. Not ever. Could she?

Chapter Four

Libby

'It's here!' came Auntie Joy's triumphant yell from down below in the farmhouse, along with a heavenly waft of the home-cooked lasagne for tonight's dinner.

Libby was upstairs in the beautifully yellow bedroom, unpacking her suitcase. She smiled at the orange flowers that clashed with the rest of the décor. She'd have done exactly the same in her apartment, injecting colour however she felt like it. The small room had everything she needed – a double bed with beautifully scented linen, a wardrobe, bedside table and chest of drawers, and a wicker chair with a white cushion. And best of all there was a prime view of countryside as far as the eye could see. Although right now, Libby noticed as the room darkened as though someone had turned down a dimmer switch, black clouds were beginning to roll in, and Auntie Joy's call from downstairs made sense. The storm they'd all been waiting for had apparently finally graced this part of England.

Libby finished hanging her clothes in the wardrobe. She'd only been here a matter of hours but after gabbling away in the kitchen to Auntie Joy it was hard to believe they'd not seen each other since Libby was a little girl. She couldn't explain it, but the letters over the years had brought them a closeness Libby hadn't felt with anyone since her mum died. The woman could talk, something they had in common, and she'd filled Libby in on the history of the farmhouse and The Old Dairy including reciting the names of the entire herd of cows they'd once had as well as their little characteristics. Libby had loved hearing it all. She'd learned that Bertha had been the bossiest of the herd, never waiting in line at milking time and always wanting to be first, Penelope was the friendliest of the bunch and always interested whenever you walked the land, Nettie was stubborn and took a lot of cajoling to get up and move, and Candie was inquisitive, always stationed as near as she could be to whatever else was going on whether it was mowing the next field or the vet coming to tend to one of the herd.

Auntie Joy was a great multitasker and as she pulled out ingredients for the evening meal she told Libby how hot an English summer it had been so far and they compared the brutal city smog and cloying temperatures of Manhattan to the equally unforgiving sun over the open acres of West Country land. Between them they'd chopped and measured ingredients for the dinner and put together the lasagne, the simplicity of cooking together something quite special. Libby was used to take-out, eating at restaurants, or at most whipping up something very quick and balancing a plate on her lap to eat it, and so plans to gather for dinner at the kitchen table set for six people had come as something of a surprise. She knew Auntie Joy took in waifs and strays and in her letters over the years she'd talked about each and every one of them, but Libby hadn't reckoned on meeting them all tonight. She'd left Joy downstairs fussing over the puppies who were six of the cutest little things Libby had ever seen and Libby had come up to get sorted and have a shower.

Libby headed downstairs following Joy's call to announce the storm. Her hand graced the wooden handrail that curved at the bottom, and ran over the smooth rounded end of the banister as she turned to go into the kitchen where it seemed everyone was already gathered, judging by the hum of chatter.

A low rumble of thunder had Joy excited when Libby went into the kitchen, then a big clap and a streak of lightning made Libby jump so suddenly the young boy Cameron who hadn't uttered a word since Libby got here couldn't hide a smirk.

Joy made the introductions. 'This is Freddie,' she said introducing the blond Viking who immediately stepped forward and shook her hand formally, 'and this is Lauren,' she went on introducing a girl with russet hair and almost symmetrical dimples as she smiled her hello. 'And of course you've already met Cameron. We're just waiting for Drew.'

Libby nodded her hellos to everyone. They'd all got mentions over the years but it was nice to finally put faces to the names. 'It's great to meet you all.'

Lauren was immediately curious about her accent and everyone was so friendly Libby was instantly at ease as she told Lauren all about her life in Manhattan. Lauren told her about the cake business she'd started and how well it was going. She'd even done a course on wedding cakes.

'I'm not quite ready to take on those commissions,' Lauren admitted, 'they're very fancy, but I practise a lot.'

'She does.' Freddie patted his tummy. 'And we are happy for her to do so.'

'They get all my attempts,' said Lauren, putting the last word in air quotes.

'She's very talented,' Joy announced as she washed salad greens over at the sink. Every now and then Joy would look around at everyone gathered much like a proud mother welcoming her kids home at the end of the day.

They all chatted between themselves, Freddie about the produce he grew here, Cameron even managed to join in with talk about the puppies and their antics, and when the noise of a vehicle coming up alongside the house had Joy looking out through the open back door and announcing Drew was here at last, they all began to take their places at the dinner table with melodramatics about just how hungry they all were and how they were weak, feeble and it was all Drew's fault for taking his time. Libby had never asked Joy why she didn't have a husband or children of her own, but she guessed she'd found her place in life, right here at The Old Dairy. Everyone seemed to just fit, like a big noisy family.

Libby could see from her position that the latest arrival had parked his jeep up outside near the cowsheds alongside what she assumed had to be Lauren's little sky-blue car. It couldn't be Freddie's, he'd be far too tall to fit in it for a start. And from there, he ran across the yard, the rain pelting him, much to everyone else's amusement. In board shorts and a dark patterned T-shirt with sun-kissed skin, Drew passed the puppy pen, empty now that the puppies were safely tucked in the utility room away from the storm, and shook off dark hair that Libby felt sure would curl if it got any longer, before he came into the kitchen to give Joy a big welcome hug.

'Took your time,' Freddie quipped.

'Freddie almost passed out,' teased Lauren. 'You know what he's like if we don't feed him on the hour every hour.'

Drew reached across to steal the edge of cheese that still clung on to the lasagne dish awaiting its turn in the dishwasher.

Joy laughed. 'Plenty already on the plates young man, there's no need to go for the scraps.'

He grinned as he helped by lifting the jug of traditional lemonade over to the table. His eyes fell on the newcomer. 'You must be Libby.' He held out a hand. 'It's good to meet you at long last.'

'Likewise,' she smiled back.

Joy set a plate down opposite Libby and indicated Drew should sit there. He shook his wet hair near Lauren making her squeal and Libby got the distinct impression it was a brother-sister relationship that had somehow come naturally to both of them. He sat down opposite and a wide smile that gave him creases in his cheeks along with dark eyes that took everything in, had her mesmerised for a second until she realised Cameron was prompting her to take the plate Joy was holding out her way. Cameron gave her a little smile that suggested he could tell she'd paid the latest arrival more attention so far than anyone else she'd met.

There was an enormous, colourful bowl of salad in the middle of the table with wooden utensils standing waiting for people to help themselves and Freddie told her, 'Everything here is home grown. Your auntie has high standards.'

Joy confirmed it. 'He's right of course. Now Libby, there's lemonade but you might prefer wine?'

'There's wine?' Lauren's eyes lit up.

Libby would welcome a glass to settle her nerves. She'd

been fine meeting everyone, talking away with them, but now as they began to eat she felt the anomaly of the group even though she was a member of Joy's family. Joy poured wine for whoever wanted it although not Drew because he was driving and not Cameron who despite being old enough to drink, wasn't interested.

'Joy,' Drew prompted when Joy stayed standing at the sink after handing out glasses of wine looking out across the fields, her own glass in hand. But Auntie Joy didn't turn round. She was mesmerised, watching the rain as it hammered down on the roof of the cowshed causing them all to have to raise their voices to be heard.

Drew went over to Joy. 'It's time to eat,' he said, one hand on her shoulder.

Joy smiled, still looking outside, way beyond the farm-house. 'We need this storm after such a long dry spell, good for the land.'

'The views here are something else, Auntie Joy,' Libby confirmed, Lauren laughing at how loud they were having to talk. 'The one from my room is incredible.' She wondered if Joy did that a lot – in the room one minute and the next her mind seemed elsewhere. Drew hadn't seemed all that surprised by her behaviour and Libby wondered how often it happened. It had happened earlier too when Joy left their conversation briefly to answer the phone. After the call Joy was aloof, the atmosphere had shifted. It had made Libby realise how little she knew this woman even though she was her auntie. She had no idea what had made her own family turn their backs on her either, and there was only so much you could get to know about a person through letters. Seeing and talking to them in person was another thing entirely.

'I'll never get tired of them,' Joy smiled, finally taking her seat at the head of the table. It was a spacious kitchen but with the huge battered pine table and enough chairs for everyone as well as two spare carvers, there wasn't room for much else.

With the rain and the smell of home cooking and Joy back to chatting away with everyone else, Libby put any reservations aside. She hadn't thought she was too hungry – it was only mid-afternoon New York time but her body was a little muddled, and that included her appetite, and as soon as she started eating she realised she'd been kidding herself. 'It's ages since I've had a home cooked meal like this,' she beamed across at Joy. She'd never felt so welcomed into the fold.

'Hey, I didn't work alone, you helped.'

'And I grew the onions to go inside,' Freddie interrupted, prompting Lauren to roll her eyes and berate him for telling them all the time. He gave as good as he got and Libby shared a smile with Drew at their banter back and forth entertaining everyone else at the table.

'So how long are you here for?' Drew asked Libby, scooping up a forkful of lasagne from the enormous serving Auntie Joy had given him.

'How long will you have me?' she directed Joy's way with a grin. She hadn't thought much about her return, only the getting away part. Her belongings were in storage in Manhattan and she had no fixed address, no job, so she'd thought she'd take a break and then try to sort things out for her return. She had plenty of contacts in the industry, friends who could help with an apartment hunt.

'You stay as long as you want,' Joy confirmed. 'The room is free, make yourself at home.'

'Yeah, some people come here and never leave,' said Lauren, 'and even if we do, we don't go far.' Lauren told Libby all about the new house she and her husband had bought. 'It's got a wonderful garden, Freddie came and helped us sort it, Jonathan didn't know a weed from a flower when we moved in, still doesn't, but it's our own and we're pretty settled.'

Libby had to wonder how all these people had met under such stressful circumstances and yet, their bonds appeared set in stone.

'Talking of those who come and never leave,' said Drew, his focus on Libby making her stomach turn all kinds of somersaults. 'Have you met Ronald?'

'I don't believe I have. Is he new?'

'You'll love Ronald,' Cameron piped up and if Libby wasn't mistaken, Joy looked about to burst with excitement that he'd come into the conversation. The others took it all in their stride and didn't make a fuss. 'Ronald is old and a bit . . . loud should we say?' Cameron grinned.

'Why isn't he here at dinner?' She pictured a little old man joining them shortly for his evening meal.

Neither Lauren nor Freddie could keep a straight face. Drew finally put Libby out of her misery. 'Ronald is the rooster.'

'Well now I see why he didn't get an invite to dinner.'

'He's up pretty early,' Drew added, 'one thing I didn't miss when I moved out.'

'Come to think of it, I have heard him already,' she answered. 'It's a nice sound, a sound of the country.'

Joy offered to top up glasses of wine. 'I'll remind you of that tomorrow, Libby.'

Talk turned to work and Libby gave a quick explanation

of what her job involved, dropping no hints that she was between gigs at the moment, and flipped the conversation around to someone else before she could get too specific. 'What do you do?' she asked Drew. 'It's something on the water isn't it? Joy told me in her letters.'

'They must be long letters if written correspondence is anything like her conversations,' Freddie quipped earning him a laugh from Joy who was trying to coax everyone into accepting the idea of dessert except they were all far too full.

'I own and run a kayaking business,' Drew explained. 'This is my work suit.'

He'd probably look good in a suit, but the shorts and T-shirt were a pretty good fit too, showing off strong fore-arms Libby could imagine hauling kayaks around or using oars to plough through the water.

'Do you enjoy it?' She shook her head again at Joy's suggestion of apple pie and ice cream.

'I love it, all that space on the water never gets old. I've got paddle boards too.'

'They look incredibly difficult to master,' said Lauren. 'My sense of balance is rubbish.'

'I'd spend more time in the water than out of it,' Freddie grinned.

'Do you live close by?' Libby asked Drew. 'I know Freddie lives here, and Cameron, how about you?'

'I finally bought my own place,' he told her. 'Now we've cut the apron strings, eh Joy.'

Joy seemed amused by the teasing when he explained he was Joy's prodigy, but something in her auntie's smile hinted at a tentativeness Libby was surprised to see, as though Joy loved the affection but was holding back

for some reason. It soon gave way to amusement however when Freddie insisted that no, it was he who was the
prodigy.

'I bring farm to table,' Freddie claimed victoriously.

'Anyone can grow a carrot,' Drew mocked.

'You couldn't.'

He looked about to argue back but grinned across at
Libby. 'He's right. And I tried lettuces but the slugs got
those, I attempted strawberries but planted seeds at totally the wrong time of year, and as for making compost
myself . . .' he shrugged.

'I'm with you on that,' Lauren put in. 'Cakes yes, stuff
with poop and mud, no thank you.'

'Gives a whole new meaning to chocolate mud cake
doesn't it?' Joy laughed.

Libby loved getting together with friends and that's exactly what tonight felt like, but in all this time she'd never
found such a closeness as this bunch of people had. She
wondered, if her mum was still alive, would she feel so
adrift as she had done for so many years?

The storm had at last passed. Everything outside was
sopping wet but the sun had come out as if to pretend
nothing had happened and the chickens had ventured out
from beneath the sheltered part of the run once again.
Freddie opened the door to the utility room to let the
puppies outside into the pen and Lauren went with him
– apparently whenever she was here she found it hard to
resist Luna's litter.

'You not going with them?' Libby asked Cameron who
looked about to follow the others but then changed his
mind at the last minute.

He shook his head and got up from the table. But he

stopped in the doorway on his way through to the hall and presumably upstairs. 'Thank you for dinner, Joy.'

'Anytime,' she trilled from the sink. 'I'll see you in the morning.'

The minute Cameron was out of earshot Joy conspiratorially spoke in hushed tones to Libby. 'This is the most he's been engaged with anyone else in a long time.' The excitement was plain to see and given the way Joy talked in her letters about anyone she took into the halfway house, Cameron would be another project she didn't want to fail on. There weren't many people with Joy's determination, and Libby liked to think that was something else they had in common. Libby stuck with things and didn't give up either and when she was in, she was all in.

'He'll be like all the others in the end,' Libby encouraged, smiling at the sight out of the window of Lauren, Freddie and Drew around the puppy pen. Freddie was fussing over the mum Luna the most. They all looked so happy, so grounded and sure of their place even though once upon a time they hadn't been.

Joy set down the cloth she'd used to wipe the table after everyone had shifted the plates to the surface next to the sink. 'Come on, the clearing up will wait. The rain has eased off so I want to show you around the place before it starts up again.' She looked at Libby's feet. 'I've got some wellies you can borrow. What size are you?'

Libby grinned. She'd wear a pair ten sizes too big if she had to. She was the most relaxed she'd been in a long while and real life could wait. She was ready to explore the outside now she'd seen inside the farmhouse with its teal front door, weathered in a way that didn't look scruffy but lived in, just like the wonky path that led up to it suggesting life here didn't always stay between the lines. The mullioned windows and the exposed brickwork in some rooms inside the farmhouse gave it character, as did the furniture in the bedrooms. All of it was wood, most of it mismatched, even the bedroom doors were different from one another but somehow just fit. The farmhouse felt lived in in a way her apartment never had, from the reclaimed wood mantel over the open fireplace in the lounge that Ted had apparently helped to install, to the bureau in the dining room that Libby now knew kept Joy's writing paper. Libby had seen the bureau in photographs but seeing it for real, she could imagine Joy sitting there writing her letters, putting them into envelopes and sealing them ready to go across the miles. Libby had put a few photographs of the farmhouse into frames, her way of bringing her home country to her American life, but seeing it all for real now was another thing entirely.

Joy found her a pair close to the correct size and they set off for a tour of the outside. They squelched their way across the fields, past a cowshed she could quite imagine having had cows in once upon a time, moos and the smell of cattle filling the air, loud voices of Ted, Marjory whose faces Libby had seen in pictures and Joy as well as any other farmhands, as the milking machines were put into operation. Ted and Marjory sounded wonderful and Libby knew Joy missed them, but she'd never asked why or how Joy had come to live with them here at the farm.

When she was younger Libby had occasionally mentioned Auntie Joy to her parents, but she'd soon learned that whenever she did her mum got a pinched look, her dad got agitated, and so she'd always let it lie. Then, when her mum died, she'd asked her dad whether Joy would come to the funeral and he'd got so distraught she'd never ever mentioned the name Joy again. She got the impression he was upset at the loss of her mum rather than because Libby had mentioned her auntie, but emotions were running so high she hadn't pushed the fact that her own sister wasn't coming to the final goodbye. Then again, if they hadn't had much to do with one another when Maggie was alive, why would they after her death? Libby had been the one to write to Joy and tell her and the return letter had taken far longer than usual. And when it had come all it said was that she was very sorry to hear that Maggie had passed and they'd left it at that. Libby had a feeling she might be left in the dark forever when it came to finding out what went on between them to cause such an almighty rift.

Joy showed Libby the area Freddie was using to grow vegetables and fruits as far as the eye could see, they trudged on to see sheep dotted in the distance, heads bent as they grazed. The land had beautiful views, slopes and curves, it was so very different to the fast pace of America, the unstoppable energy she'd had to have in her job. Being here was literally like taking a big breath of air and letting it filter through her body at long last.

They had no chance of covering nearly fifty acres but when they'd been outside for a while and Libby had got enough of an idea what this place was like, they looped back to the farmhouse via the chickens. Ronald had most of his hens in order and he was so docile given his age he didn't mind Joy and even Libby helping to jostle the last few stragglers into the coop for the night, which was a strange but amusing experience. Some of the hens knew the deal, others appeared to pretend not to and had Libby darting here and there after them.

'I'm not exactly a natural,' Libby puffed, out of breath as they got the last of the chickens into the coop.

They found Lauren outside saying her goodbyes to everyone.

'I was never any good with the chickens either,' Lauren smiled to Libby, 'and I'm sure Ronald despised me and told his hens to give me dirty looks for taking their eggs to use in my recipes.'

'Oh they did not,' Joy admonished with a giggle.

'I'll bring along a sticky date pudding next time I come,' Lauren smiled to Libby. 'You're going to get to try plenty of my baking while you're here,' she said before whispering to Libby, 'I've never seen Joy as happy as she is today with your visit.' She squeezed Libby's arm in encouragement.

Libby had been writing to Joy ever since she could remember and sometimes she'd wondered what it was that had kept them in touch all these years. Perhaps it was the excitement of writing to her in secret or maybe it was a curiosity and the need to solve the mystery of the woman who had nobody in the family on her side. But whatever the reasons Libby was glad they'd kept in contact and even more glad to be here now. Seeing Joy with so many genuine people in her life made Libby feel less like the whole family had turned their back on one of their own.

Drew was saying his goodbyes now and because he'd hugged Joy and then Lauren, and grabbed Viking-like Freddie in a bear hug, which was obviously done with the sole purpose of winding him up, he hesitated in front of Libby and then held out his arms. 'I don't like to leave anyone out.'

Her heart thudded and she was glad nobody was really watching. She let him pull her close and couldn't help but inhale the warm smell of him, his body close and sending dizzy feelings cascading through her own.

'Can I interest you in a nightcap?' Joy offered Freddie and Libby on their way back inside. Cameron had, without being asked, begun to get the puppies back inside the utility room where they would sleep.

'That's a good sign,' whispered Freddie to Joy as they went inside where he was able to speak louder. 'I'll help him, leave you two to your nightcap. Have a proper catch-up.'

Joy linked her arm through Libby's. 'Now that sounds like a wonderful idea.'

'You've got to be kidding me.' Libby sat up in bed, dazed, her hair across her face. The sun was warming the other side of the curtains and peeking out from the top near the rail. It seemed Ronald was awake and announcing it to the world with a deep, loud crow. Libby wished she'd thought to bring those ear plugs they'd supplied on the plane and she hadn't needed.

She tossed and turned, drifted off a couple of times, but finally emerged into the kitchen by seven o'clock where Cameron was getting the food ready for the puppies. One look from him suggested he knew exactly why she was up at this time and looked anything but refreshed.

'Good morning, Libby.' Auntie Joy, fresh-faced as though she'd had a luxurious sleep-in, came through the back door. She must've been up for hours, she had a wicker trug filled with strawberries and blackberries as well as leeks, their tops flopping over one side. 'You'll get used to Ronald,' she smiled.

'Doubt it.' Libby stumbled over to the coffee machine and poured herself a generous mugful to take over to the table.

'What can I get you for breakfast?' Joy set the trug full of produce down beside the sink to deal with later.

Libby adjusted her pyjama shorts that had twisted after a fitful sleep and pulled up the spaghetti strap of her top when it fell from her shoulder. 'I'm not much of a breakfast person. Honestly, coffee is enough for now. And you don't have to wait on me.'

'What a load of nonsense,' Joy admonished. 'I've never heard of not being a breakfast person, it's the most important meal of the day, especially out here. All this country air.' She smiled across at Libby. 'Indulge me. I won't do this every day, but you've only just arrived, let me spoil you.'

Libby grinned from behind her coffee cup. 'What have you got in mind?'

Joy reeled off a whole load of choices with everything from eggs done whatever way she liked to pancakes or cereal, toast, or fresh fruit and yogurt.

Libby settled on poached eggs on toast and had to admit her stomach was thankful when Joy set them down in front of her. She'd had a couple of glasses of wine last night, perhaps that was why she was so hungry, or maybe it was the treat of Ronald waking her so early.

Joy busied herself washing the produce before storing it away in the relevant places in the kitchen. Leeks went into one of the generous wire baskets of the three-tiered vegetable rack, heart-shaped strawberries were left in a bowl on the worktop, their aromatic fragrance hanging in the air and their bright red flesh adding a splash of colour to the cream country kitchen with its range cooker, large double-door fridge-freezer and hard-wearing timber worktops. The minute Libby had laid eyes on this kitchen she'd felt it emanated warmth and homeliness, with its décor, with Auntie Joy and with the comings and goings of people who had one thing in common. They all cared about one another. It was vastly different to the tiny place she prepared food in her apartment, with a window covered in a yellowing net curtain that didn't even hang straight and only enough space for one person to get in and out at a time.

Joy washed the strawberries and put those into a bowl too and Libby was told to help herself to fruit whenever she liked. At most she managed to buy a bunch of bananas or a punnet of grapes for her apartment back in New York, and even then the fruit often went off before she remembered it was there. She got the feeling that would never happen around here, Cameron had already grabbed a bowl of colourful fruit after he came in from feeding the puppies.

'I think you coming here has helped Cameron,' Joy confided when it was just the two of them again. Cameron had taken his bounty off upstairs and Freddie was out on the tractor today cutting the grass which Libby could only imagine took hours. 'He's no longer the new person and I think it's helping him to find a bit of confidence.'

'I'm glad I could help. He seems like a great kid.' He reminded her of herself at that age, lacking confidence, trying to make sense of the changes around her as she moved through her teenage years. 'And he loves those puppies.' Libby had heard his voice and his amusement, talking to them as he set the food bowls down. She scraped the last piece of toast through the rich golden yellow of the remaining egg on her plate. 'And why wouldn't you? They're gorgeous. I don't know why Luna's owner abandoned her.'

'Something I'll never understand,' Joy sighed. 'I wondered when the puppies were first born whether the owner had had Luna mated on purpose. I mean, they're proper Labradors, there's no cross-breeding there,' she shrugged. 'I guess we'll never know the truth. All we know is that Luna is safe and happy now with us.'

'She certainly is.'

'And I've decided we'll keep one of her puppies.'

'That's a lovely idea – which one?'

'I can't choose.' Joy took Libby's plate and landed it in the soapy suds already in the sink. 'I want to keep them all.'

'Now that would be interesting,' Libby filled a glass of water at the tap before sitting back down again. She urged Joy to sit too, she always seemed to be on to the next job and was already planning what would be for tonight's dinner. 'Do you ever relax, Auntie Joy?'

Joy pulled the thin strap of Libby's pyjama top up onto her shoulder after it fell down yet again. 'I like to be busy.' The strap didn't stay put.

'Me too usually. But if Ronald hadn't woken me this morning I suspect I'd still be in bed right now.' Last night they'd talked about her job, the day-to-day workload and sometimes the stress, but she hadn't let on that she'd had a breakdown previously and had now left the company permanently when the offer of more responsibility sent her running the other way for once. Not revealing every bit of detail about her troubles and her life was allowing Libby now to step back and have a proper break without worrying about the next step. She wanted to enjoy being here, have a much-needed holiday, something she hadn't done in a very long time, and she wanted to get to know Joy, which so far was easy. She didn't even feel like a guest which was crazy, she'd not even been here twenty-four hours.

'From what you told me last night you sound as though you worked crazy hours at your job, Libby. Is that something you can alter when you go back?'

Libby shrugged. 'I'm not sure, not if I want the same job. But it's certainly something I need to think about.'

'And do you enjoy it? You didn't really say last night. I mean, do the long hours, the weekend work, do those things make you happy?'

To avoid the hotspot Libby made another cup of coffee. She offered Joy one but she declined, she was waiting at the table for more information so Libby had no choice but to sit back down. 'I always enjoyed maths and problem solving, I loved being a part of a big corporation with a heap of responsibility. But . . . well there's a colleague there who made things a bit difficult,' she admitted.

'Let me at him, I'll have a few things to say.'

Libby laughed. 'Thanks for being in my corner. I think it's jealousy that his career wasn't moving quite as fast as he wanted it to. But it's honestly not worth wasting our time talking about him. I'm on holiday, away from it all. And it wasn't just him, it was the whole job, lifestyle, whatever. I needed a change, or at least to think about a change.'

'And how's your boyfriend, Brandon?'

'He's fine.' She took a mouthful of coffee and found, when she set down her cup, that Joy was watching her. 'What?'

'Just fine?'

Libby was glad of the distraction when Luna ambled through the back door, because she wasn't ready to talk about everything that had gone wrong in her life. 'Hey, Luna.' She fussed over the black Labrador. She wouldn't have been allowed a dog in her apartment, and she'd never had one as a kid, but already she could see what wonderful company they were. They were also a good way to avoid Auntie Joy's questions.

'I have to ask, Libby . . . Have you told your dad you're visiting?' Joy looked across the table at her niece.

'No, I haven't.'

'But you're going to, right?'

'Of course.' Being reminded of it wasn't easy though, she'd been blocking it out for as long as she could.

Joy looked doubtful. 'I assume you're not going to tell him about coming here to see me first. Because I don't think that would be a good idea. We haven't talked about it in our letters, but I'd say it's a safe bet he wouldn't appreciate it.'

'I won't mention it.'

'But you'll tell him you're here in England?'

'I will, in my own time.' She knew Joy was pushing for her to agree, waiting for more. 'I promise.'

Joy's scrutiny had her asking, 'Why *are* you here with me and not staying with him? I know from what you've said in your letters that you've struggled to connect with him since your mum passed, but he is your dad.'

'I know, and I love him . . . I just don't know what to say to him. And worse, I don't think he ever knows what to say to me.' Her voice caught. 'It makes me sad and if Mum was still here it would make her sad too.'

Luna moved over to Joy and was rewarded with a good fuss along the length of her coat from head to tail. She soon settled at Joy's feet. 'Is there something you're not telling me, Libby?'

'What do you mean?'

'You've come on a holiday with no end date, you're stressed at work, you change the subject when I ask you about your boyfriend.' She caught Libby's hesitation; it was no surprise this woman worked wonders with young adults or kids in trouble. 'What exactly is going on?'

And that was when the dam burst. Blame it on jet lag, Ronald's early wake-up call, or Joy's ability to see beneath the surface, or perhaps it was all of those things. But right now Libby couldn't hold her emotions back any longer and Cameron, about to come into the kitchen, quickly doubled back along the hallway when he saw the latest arrival in floods of tears.

'Everything is such a mess,' Libby sobbed. 'With Dad, my job, my boyfriend, my life.'

Joy got up and found a box of tissues lurking near the kettle. She handed one to Libby. 'Then it sounds as though you've come to the right place my girl.'

And just hearing her use the same name her mum had for so many years made the tears flow even more.

Chapter Five

Joy

Was it wrong for Joy to be pleased that Libby needed her? As well as turning lives around, Joy had always liked people depending on her, it gave her a sense of purpose and a lift she couldn't explain. It also served as a good distraction from her own troubles. After the phone call from Mr McKerrick, Joy had done her best to pretend everything was fine, especially in front of Libby. But sooner or later she wouldn't be able to ignore the financial woes that mounted by the day.

She shook away the worries as she stood at the kitchen sink and pulled the pan she'd used for Libby's eggs out of the soapy water and set it onto the drainer. She'd sent Libby up to bed again, the girl was exhausted, not only from Ronald's wake-up call but from everything else going on in her life. Add all those problems together and it seemed her niece didn't know whether she was coming or going. Joy knew the feeling, and more than once she'd gone into a separate room from anyone else, closed the door and leaned on it before taking calming breaths one after the other. Not that breathing was going to solve much. She had to get control of her finances if she wanted to keep this farm. Because if she didn't, she'd lose her sense of identity all over again, and what would happen to everyone else who depended on the place and on her?

Joy abandoned chores in the kitchen for now and went into the dining room to use the computer. She couldn't put it off any longer and sent out four or five emails to locals who might be interested in renting some of the land. There was Mr and Mrs White out past the new doctor's surgery and they kept goats, perhaps they needed a bigger area for them to graze, they might want to expand if it was their livelihood. There was someone else with a riding school – maybe they had too many horses for the current stabling and would like to take her up on an offer to utilise some land at The Old Dairy. The farthest fields had direct road access if you reconfigured some of the fencing, so that could be an option for others. There were enough farmers still operating in various capacities not too far from here that she felt sure she'd find a solution. She didn't have much choice. After all, the alternative didn't bear thinking about.

When Libby finally came downstairs Joy had squashed down her worries again so she could take care of Libby rather than raise suspicions and risk having anyone try to look after her. 'You must've slept well. You look as fresh as the patch of daisies at the side of the farmhouse.' Joy loved the way their pretty yellow centres smiled up at the sunshine.

'I slept full stop,' Libby sighed contentedly. In cut-offs and a simple blue T-shirt she looked half the age of the sophisticated, put-together woman Joy suspected she was at work. She didn't have on the same ruby red lipstick she'd been wearing when she arrived here yesterday either, clearly thinking she needed to make an effort. This Libby looked refreshed after a talk, a sleep and a total change of scene. This Libby seemed to be relaxing again. 'I may have to buy some ear plugs if Ronald insists on doing that every morning.'

'You can get them at the chemist in the village,' Joy grinned, using the dustpan to sweep up some crumbs from the floor beneath the table. Luna usually got most of them, but she'd missed these ones.

'I might take a wander later, explore a bit of Bramleywood.'

'That sounds a nice idea. It's a small village, shouldn't take you long.'

'Small is good,' Libby smiled.

'It sure is. Anyway, there are a few shops, a train station if you want to venture further in your time here.' Joy held a finger in the air to pause the conversation and plucked a written list from beneath a pineapple magnet fixed on the fridge. 'If you're heading out I do need a few things from the bakery if you wouldn't mind.'

'Of course, I'm happy to go.'

'No rush. It's open until five, although I'd get there by three so you've got plenty of choice and what's there is at its freshest.'

Freddie came inside then and grumbled at how long it had taken him to mow the land, muttered something about needing more cattle to do the job instead of him and then he headed off for a shower.

'What's eating him?' Libby asked when he was out of earshot.

'I've no idea.'

'Mind you, I'd be fed up if I'd had to mow all that land with a lawnmower.'

Joy burst out laughing. 'Now that would take a long time and he'd be right to be annoyed. He doesn't use a lawnmower, he has a tractor for the job.'

'That makes much more sense. See,' Libby grinned, 'I'm a city girl.'

'We'll get you used to the country in no time,' said Joy.

But now she had an extra worry on top of her finances because Freddie rarely lapsed into a bad mood, especially when it came to helping out. And he teased anyone who was grouchy, so much so that they soon came out of their melancholy. He was humbled, kind-hearted, he could handle himself and when he'd told Joy that his ex-wife Ivanna was finally beginning to let him have some involvement with her and their son Timothy who'd be eleven by now, she'd thought his path to happiness was well and truly paved. She had no idea what was going on with him, but come to think of it this wasn't the first time he'd been snappy. Last week she'd asked him to climb up on the roof and see if he could put a tile back which looked like it had become dislodged, but he'd griped about how busy he was; the roof had leaked, and she'd ended up having to get a roofer out to the farm. It hadn't been cheap either, not that she minded, upkeep was her responsibility, but Freddie had always been on hand to help and until recently had always been happy to do it.

Maybe Ivanna was playing games with him, although Joy hoped not, Freddie didn't deserve that. Freddie had once told Joy that he needed to prove himself to his ex-wife, but surely he was doing that now? He had a profitable business here – she could come see it for herself if that was what was required – he wasn't going anywhere. Or maybe Ivanna had been so hurt before that she was holding back in case Freddie fell apart again. Depression could take its toll not only on the person suffering from it but on the rest of the family and Ivanna was probably protecting her son in case Freddie's depression returned. Joy guessed it wasn't simply a matter of forgiving him and forgetting everything that had passed. And unfortunately Joy knew better than most that some people never moved on, they held a grudge, made a judgement and stuck with it for good.

'I might send out a few job feelers later today,' Libby announced.

'I thought you weren't in any rush.' Although Joy should've expected it, it was like a punch in the stomach to think of her going back to New York. The ridiculous notion that Libby would love it so much here in Somerset that she'd want to stay and take over when Joy was too old was something Joy may have to accept was too crazy to ever come true, especially now her finances were about to take a hit. But still, everyone needed to dream a bit didn't they? It stopped you thinking of the harsh realities and getting so overwhelmed with them that functioning became an uphill battle.

'I feel better after talking to you, but I can't not work,' said Libby. 'I need to take charge of my life, be responsible.'

Joy thought she should enjoy being young, not having much responsibility at all. Because too soon it could be over, sometimes when you least expected. 'You know what's best for you, Libby. You know I'll support you whatever you decide, just don't rush it and stress yourself out, promise?'

'I promise,' she smiled back. 'And you've got quite a collection of books up there in the spare bedroom, I've already taken one to start later on today. It feels like forever since I read an entire book. Usually it's catching up on the news on my laptop or phone, or picking up the odd newspaper.'

'Then you've been missing out.'

'You're a keen reader?'

'Always have been.' And it had got her through some tough times. 'There's a library down by the station too, you could check it out, take my library card. Now, there's some money in the money box in the hallway, take some out for the bakery, it'll cost over twenty pounds I expect. We get through a lot of bread and rolls here.'

'Nonsense, I've got money in my purse, got to use some of my British currency somehow, especially when you won't take any money for my keep.'

'I won't hear of it.'

'You can, and you will.' Libby came to her side, hugged her and planted a kiss on her cheek. 'I intend to pitch in while I'm here and that includes paying for some things.' She stopped her from protesting again.

'Libby . . .?'

'I'll get around to it,' her niece answered, reading her mind and knowing full well Joy was about to ask her whether she'd thought again about calling her dad. She'd only just arrived, but it made Joy uneasy to think how her dad would react if he found out his daughter was with a woman he'd never let her have much to do with. She wondered what he'd say if he knew how long they'd been writing to one another.

Joy took out a wicker basket from the tall cupboard in the utility room and brought it back through for Libby.

Libby hooked it over her arm. 'Now I feel like a country bumpkin.'

'Hey, less of the cheek, and pick up some Belgian buns for afternoon tea while you're at it, get six that should be enough. Enjoy looking around the village.'

'I will do.' With a smile and looking far happier than when she'd been in tears telling Joy everything, Libby set off from the farmhouse. Over time so many faces had come and gone from here and Libby, with her injection of love and laughter was no exception. Joy couldn't bear the thought of her leaving, but it was out of her control like so many other things.

Joy parked up at the doctor's surgery on the outskirts of the village. It had moved from a smaller surgery in a converted house part way down the main street to this purpose-built medical centre with plenty of space for cars and Joy didn't mind a jot. She preferred to keep her medical business away from prying eyes and the only people who came this far out of Bramleywood were here for their own medical needs.

She got to flip through magazines for almost forty minutes before she was called. She hated waiting, all that sitting still, it just reminded her of counting down the days before something significant would happen. She made her way to the doctor's room. She didn't think she could ever remember a time when the appointments hadn't been running late, but she guessed she'd got one, not an easy feat, particularly in the winter months. She'd come here with some awful cough last winter that took months to get rid of and caused a chest infection in the end. And when Freddie thought she had something worse following that illness, he'd persuaded her to come here, twice, but each time they'd found nothing other than old age and general tiredness. It came with living on a farm Joy thought, although perhaps she was healthier than those living in a bungalow and barely walking a hundred metres over an entire day. She liked to think that was the case anyway, and she didn't want to stop any time soon. Even if she had to slow down, getting out each day regardless of the weather kept her sanity.

'How are you, Joy?' Dr Hall had been her GP since she made an appointment after Ted passed away and had terrible trouble sleeping. He was about as old as she was so he knew he could never suggest she take it a bit easier as she'd only throw the same back at him.

'I'm fine apart from my knees giving me trouble again.'

'Then let's take a look at you.'

As he examined her knees he ran through a ream of questions with everything from when they hurt the most to her general health, and her favourite question, her family history when it came to disease. Every time she told him she didn't really know much, but she was pretty sure nobody had carked it from anything too sinister. Maggie had died in a car accident so that wasn't hereditary, only heartbreaking, and even when they hadn't had anything to do with one another for years, Joy had still read the news in Libby's letter and felt tremendous loss that had seen her crying on and off for days, doing her best to hide her grief from everyone.

'I don't think it's arthritis,' Dr Hall concluded after checking for tenderness or swelling. 'I think we can blame getting older, happens to the best of us.'

He listened to her heart and then took her blood

pressure and when he removed the cuff that squeezed her upper arm like it wanted to clamp on for ever, he told her her blood pressure was a little higher than he'd like. 'Any sudden changes in your life, your routine?'

You could say that. 'Not really.' She wasn't about to admit her troubles to anyone. She could solve them before it came to that.

'Well that's good to hear. And you're otherwise healthy from what I can see. You don't smoke . . .'

'Never have.' Her dad had smoked, the stench cloying their clothes, and he'd had a permanent hacking cough she hadn't missed when her parents cut her out of their lives. She supposed everything had an upside.

'I already know you exercise enough,' he went on, 'you've said your alcohol intake is moderate and your weight is good.'

'Not hard when you've got land to look after as well as chickens, puppies and a niece who arrived more stressed out than I'd ever have imagined.'

Talk turned to Libby and Joy proudly told Dr Hall all about Libby's successful career, her life in New York, and Joy's wish that her niece would fall in love with Bramleywood and stay for good. 'I know I'm dreaming,' she admitted.

'Nothing wrong with that. But why don't you send her along to the surgery if you think she needs to see me or one of the other doctors.'

'I don't think she's at that stage yet and I'm not sure how long she's here for, but I appreciate the concern.'

'You've helped a lot of people so I'm sure she's in the right place, coming here.'

Libby's dad would probably have a different opinion altogether.

They left it at that and as Joy passed through the waiting room to leave she was more than happy to bump into the surgery's latest arrival, local vet, Samuel.

'How are those puppies doing?' Samuel asked the minute he closed the door and stepped inside. His voice radiated confidence and despite working with animals he brought with him a pleasant aroma of fresh aftershave with the merest hint of spice.

Over time Samuel had become more than a local she exchanged the odd hello with. He was a couple of years older than her and had lived on his own since his wife passed away more than a decade ago. Their chats in passing had got progressively longer as they got to know one another and since Luna came into Joy's life they got to spend even more time together and it was a pleasure to see him out and about or when he visited the farmhouse. As he'd checked over Luna and then the puppies once they were born, they'd talked at length, his visits lasting longer and longer as time went on. She'd even begun to confide in him about the people who came and went from The Old Dairy. He already knew some of them because they hung around all the time but she'd also told him about the ones who hadn't. She'd confided in him about young mum, Sally, who'd stayed with Joy for a month until she'd gone back to her husband and child. Sally had turned up in Bramleywood with a bruise that matched army greens on her forehead but she'd eventually returned home. Sally had written just once to thank Joy for letting her in when she'd needed it the most, and she'd included a cheque for her keep. Joy had suspected the husband had wanted to do that to prove they didn't need charity, that he could give Sally everything she wanted. Shame, because Joy had always been sure what Sally really wanted was to leave him, and yet she kept going back. Samuel had been a good sounding board the day Joy talked about Sally and he'd made Joy realise that she'd done everything she possibly could and that the rest was up to Sally now.

In the waiting room they chatted away, an easy banter Joy found herself falling into whenever they bumped into one another.

'Pass on my thanks to Lauren for the birthday cupcakes again if you would,' he smiled, grey eyes twinkling as he swept aside the deep grey hair that was in need of a trim. 'They were the best I've had. Not great for the waistline but worth it.'

She could say something about him staying fit enough looking after all those animals, but she'd never been much good at flirting no matter how appealing the company. 'Did you want to collect some more eggs soon? We have plenty.'

'Those hens of yours are too efficient. I'm still working on the last lot, but I'll be sure to stop by when I need more. Nothing like fresh eggs.'

She beamed back at him. 'There certainly isn't.'

Samuel began to laugh when his name was called. 'There was I thinking I'd get a chance to read the newspaper and they're ready for me.' He touched her briefly on the arm. 'I'll see you soon.'

Joy left the surgery on a cloud of delight, but when she reached the car a voice stopped her in her tracks and dissolved her mood at the same time. She turned to see Rick, her least favourite person in the village.

'Nothing serious I hope,' his voice croaked.

'Oh bugger off,' she muttered and then chirruped, 'Not at all.'

'I see you have your niece staying with you, Libby isn't it?'

How the hell did he know? 'That's right.' Her smile was as tight as his wallet when it came to helping out anyone other than himself and she gave a cursory wave and climbed into the car before he could attempt to engage her further. She even locked the doors, not that she thought he'd try to leap in or anything, but you never could be too careful.

After a detour to the supermarket Joy headed back to the farmhouse. Libby had brought back the bread, put it all away into the two wooden-topped breadbins in the kitchen, the Belgian buns were under a mesh food cover waiting for the hungry to pluck them away one by one, and she was sitting at the table engrossed in something on her laptop. It was a sight that made Joy instantly let go of some of the tension she'd been holding on to.

'Where have you been?' Libby quizzed when Joy came in.

'I had to pick up some things for dinner.' Libby didn't need to know where else she'd been.

'That's a lot of chicken.' Libby, distracted from what she was doing, eyed the two trays of meat Joy took out of a carrier bag and stashed in the fridge.

'I'm used to cooking for lots of people remember.'

'Who's here tonight?'

'You, me, Freddie and Cameron, and Lauren.'

'No Drew?'

Joy didn't miss the flicker of interest when it came to

handsome Drew. She just wasn't sure about Libby getting involved with him given the link between herself and the boy. He didn't know, nobody did, and long may it stay that way. But if he and Libby were to get involved, the guilt about keeping him in the dark would be even harder to bear, the secret she held from him even worse. And who knew, if Libby's dad ever did talk to his daughter about why they'd cast Joy out of their lives, the truth might not be a secret much longer, and Drew might never want to speak to her again.

'Drew's working late this evening,' she told Libby. 'He's teaching a kayak lesson, or was it two lessons?' She shook her head. 'I can't remember. I'm old, let's blame it on that shall we?' Although she was glad the doctor didn't seem to think she had arthritis in her knees. She hated the thought of not being able to walk across the fields, embrace the landscape in the winter months, wander along the tree line that separated her from someone else's land in the autumn and kick through the leaves, crisp and a sign the world kept on turning. She was a little concerned at her raised blood pressure, but Dr Hall had assured her it wasn't time to leap into prescribing medication just yet. As long as she tried to find some time to relax then she might just be able to keep it under control herself, he'd said. Mind you, it wasn't often the word *relax* and the name *Joy* were put in the same sentence. Dr Hall probably knew that because he'd asked her to come back in a few weeks' time and they'd check it again, but she suspected there'd be little change given her current worries.

Joy put the empty carrier bag in the drawer they used for the purpose and went over to see what Libby was up to. 'Are you investigating jobs for when you go back?' She tried to sound upbeat when really she was thinking, please don't let it be too soon. Perhaps that was why her blood pressure was up, maybe it was Libby coming here and the thought of her going again that had done it.

'There's quite a lot of work around for me,' she said flippantly, 'I'm sending résumés and putting the feelers out, but I've enough saved to not rush it.'

Joy hugged her niece. 'You're a very together young woman. It's good to see.'

'Thanks Auntie Joy. And fingers crossed . . .' she made the action herself, her fingers crossed in the air, '. . . it won't take me long to find something and it'll be better than before.'

'Have you heard from Brandon?' she wondered.

Libby shook her head. 'No, we both knew it was over and that there isn't much more to say. We're looking for different things and I think he can see that now too.'

'I'm sorry.' Joy resisted asking her what those things were, hoping part of it involved a return to England and even better, a move to the countryside, preferably in this direction.

'I don't think it'll be long before he meets someone else,' said Libby.

'And how does that make you feel?' Joy popped ice cubes out of their rubber tray into two glasses and poured them both a glass of traditional lemonade.

'I want him to be happy, but it won't be with me. Does that sound heartless?'

'Not at all. It wouldn't be fair on him or you to be in a relationship you weren't committed to.'

Libby sent off another email before turning her attention to her drink and Joy. 'Bramleywood is a lovely village,

I went to the library and picked up another novel, I even read some sitting on a bench by the village hall.'

'Now you're really spoiling yourself.'

'Totally,' Libby grinned. 'And the bakery is a good find. I had a nice chat with the owner, Zelda, she was pushing tasters in my face most of the time though.'

'She does that,' Joy chuckled. 'I think she tries out new recipes and pounces on people to test them. Maybe she gauges their reactions to decide whether to put whatever it is out on sale.'

'I tried bread with olives, another with sun-dried tomato and one with chia seeds and pumpkin seeds. But I stuck to the list and brought back a white loaf as well as a couple of wholemeal.'

'And the Belgian buns,' said Joy approvingly. 'They do look good.' She pinched one from beneath the mesh food cover, but Libby claimed she was too full from the tasters at the bakery.

'Can I help you prepare the dinner?' Libby wondered, switching her laptop off and closing the top as Joy tucked in to the bun. 'What are we having?'

'It's a simple chicken dish tonight,' she said before taking another bite. Covering her mouth she told Libby, 'If you want a job, you could go out to those veggie patches and get me some peas, shallots and some parsley – you'll find that among the other herbs.'

'Is everything labelled?'

Joy began to laugh just as Freddie reappeared and she relayed Libby's question. It seemed to bring him out of whatever mood he'd been in as his amusement rumbled around the kitchen.

'Come with me, city girl,' Freddie teased, pushing his

feet into his boots at the door. 'I'll teach you a thing or two.'

Libby put her hand to the side of her forehead and did a salute. 'Yes, sir. I'll get my trainers on.'

'You're going to need some boots on again my girl,' said Joy. 'Your white footwear won't cut it out here and you're going to get grubby picking produce too. The pair you had on before are on the boot rack in the utility room. I hosed them down with mine earlier.'

When Libby went to get them Freddie lowered his voice and asked how it went with the doctor.

'It went well, my blood pressure is up a little, but nothing to worry about.' Freddie had heard her confirming the appointment time at the doctor's earlier that week when she called to check when it was. She'd usually make a note of such things but as she hadn't wanted anyone to worry, she'd tried to memorise the time instead, and failed miserably.

'Did he tell you to take it easy?'

'No, because you know exactly where I'd tell him to stick that advice.'

'I wish you would take better care of yourself. Don't kill yourself for this place. It's not worth it.'

She put a hand to his cheek. 'Oh I don't know about that.'

'You know I'm right,' he whispered as Libby leaned round the door jamb wearing the wellies.

'Off you go the both of you,' Joy told them, 'Get some beautiful produce and Libby, please learn one herb from another.'

'I'll do my best,' she chortled.

'We'll make a country girl of you yet,' Joy called after

her, reminded of when she'd first tried to introduce fruits and vegetables to the land herself. She'd always thought how easy it looked and Freddie said it was once you got a feel for what you were doing. But she'd never really had the inclination to try again once he came along and made such a success of it. He was a natural.

Joy spent some time with the puppies, aware it wouldn't be long before they were all gone. Joy hated to think of the goodbyes but as long as they were going to happy homes and she was able to donate money to the animal rescue centre, that would make her happy too. The puppies had already been weaned and had their vaccinations which hadn't been cheap, but keeping them until they were a bit older meant they were each slowly learning socialisation and developing personalities. It also meant she'd got to see more of them and as a bonus, more of Samuel, who was only too happy to visit the farm and check up on them all.

Cameron came outside, a purple baseball cap over his scruffy mousy hair. He was learning socialisation as well, getting used to people around him who cared, and he didn't react to Joy already being on the stool at one side of the puppy pen. He got right in there too and it wasn't long before one of the pups clambered onto his lap and settled in for a fuss. Another tugged his shoelace undone and made him laugh, another jumped up against his leg, wagging its tiny tail.

'They like you,' Joy smiled. He seemed as taken with them as she was and she hoped when all apart from one moved on they wouldn't take part of the boy's spirit with them.

'They're great, all of them. It'll be weird when they're not here.'

Joy knew she was going to keep one but it hadn't been discussed before now. 'Which one could you see staying here at the farmhouse with us?' she asked, hoping their conversation would show he had a home here as long as he needed. 'I thought maybe you'd like to choose. I'd keep them all if I could so you'll be taking the responsibility out of my hands.'

He didn't have to think about it. 'I'd keep Bisto. He's fun, a bit cheeky, I think he'd fit in well.'

'He does rather sound like some of the characters I've had staying at the house. That's settled then.' The pup who'd been wrestling one end of a chew toy from her eventually won and took his prize to the other corner of the pen, wagging his tail as he went.

'Really? We get to keep him?'

'You sure do.'

She left one happy boy to it, fussing over Bisto as she went into the dining room and back to the computer to check for responses to the emails she'd sent out that morning. Her prices were reasonable, she had a lot of land for the taking and it was well looked after thanks to Freddie.

But there wasn't a single answer to her queries.

And her heart sank that little bit more, especially when Cameron's laughter drifted in from outside and found her. It wrapped around her heart and tugged at it that little bit more when the stark reality was that all of this, this life she'd built, could crumble if she didn't find a solution.

Chapter Six

Libby

Libby had fun out in the fields with Freddie and whatever had caused his bad mood earlier had certainly disappeared as he talked freely and taught Libby plenty. They began by briefly walking along the thin paths between some of the patches and he gave her an overview of everything he grew.

'You've got a good thing going out here,' she said, admiring how anyone could produce so much to feed so many.

'Thanks to Joy,' he replied, taking her to the herb patch. It took her quite some time to pick out parsley and tell it apart from basil or chives or the mint and rosemary and a whole heap of other herbs, some of which she'd never heard of. Once she knew what each one was it seemed quite obvious. 'What's your story, Freddie?' she asked before cringing. 'Sorry, that's nosey of me. Tell me to mind my own business if you like.'

He laughed. 'I don't mind you asking. It's no big secret. I moved into the farmhouse eight years ago and I've been here ever since. I already knew Joy, but let's just say I fell on hard times.' He used his fingers to rake over some soil near one of the herbs, ensuring his produce was as it should be. 'Once upon a time I drove around in a posh car and wore a suit and polished shoes.'

She grinned. 'No way. You seem so at home out here.'

'I am, now. But back then this was as far from my normal life as I could get. I was once Ted and Marjory's solicitor.' He found Libby's surprise quite amusing. 'Honestly, I was. But then I was made redundant and depression took over.'

'I'm sorry.'

'Not as sorry as I was. Depression won and I lost everything. My marriage fell apart, I lost contact with my son.'

Her heart broke a little bit for this gentle man who looked as at home here as Joy was.

'Ted and Marjory weren't around to see it happen and Joy only found out when she bumped into me as I came out of my rented cottage at the other end of the village. I'd been talking with Ivanna, my ex, I was upset, Ivanna didn't want to know. She had my son Timothy in the car and drove away. Timothy had his hand pressed against the window as though he didn't want to go but I knew I was useless to him. I couldn't keep myself together let alone help him grow up with a stable home life.'

'It must've broken your heart.'

'It did. Anyway, Joy listened in that way that she does, she heard the whole story over coffees in a nearby café. I hadn't been working as a solicitor for a while by then, I was just about making ends meet stacking shelves in a supermarket.'

'Did your wife ask you to leave?'

He shook his head, dirt falling between his fingers after he plucked another herb from the ground. 'No, when I was at my worst I walked out and was incommunicado for six months. I didn't contact them; for all they knew I was dead. And then one day I came back expecting to pick up where I'd left off. I should've known what I'd put them through. Ivanna didn't trust me, she was frightened I'd do it again. She asked me to stay away because I was confusing our son. She said it wasn't fair. In the end she filed for divorce and by then I'd started to believe I didn't deserve either of them, Ivanna or Timothy, so I tried to build a new life.'

'You're doing well too.'

'I've found my calling you could say,' he smiled. 'But the thoughts of what I've lost have never been far away. I threw myself into building my fruit and vegetable business. Joy let me help on her land at first in exchange for my keep. She took me across these very fields to see her own disastrous attempts at starting a couple of vegetable patches.'

'Not good?'

'Terrible,' he laughed along with Libby. 'She didn't have a clue – she hadn't removed enough of the weeds before she started which meant they competed with the plants for moisture and nutrients, she hadn't used netting to cover young brassica – broccoli, cauliflower and Brussels sprouts, and she wasn't watering the patches nearly enough. I leaped at the chance to turn it all around and make it work. I was a gardener's lackey in my teenage years so that helped a bit. I'd often wished I'd stayed doing something on the land rather than an office and suddenly I had the chance. I installed a trio of water butts by the cowshed, I set up composting bins and I taught Joy the importance of nurturing the soil with organic matter so its structure improved over time.'

'There's more to it than a lot of people think, I suspect,' said Libby, enjoying the chatter with this man who meant so much to Joy.

Over at the onion patches, Freddie led her to where the shallots grew, plentiful in their clusters with their green tops sprouting out of the earth and beginning to brown at the edges and droop. It had felt odd pushing her hand into the soil: she grimaced when he recited what he'd used to make the magic compost – his name for it, not hers – but she pulled up enough copper-skinned onions for to-night's dinner before they headed over to the patch filled with all sorts of makeshift contraptions Freddie told her were needed to grow peas. He took her through a few of the varieties, one group growing up against single stakes, others growing in trellises made out of three pieces of wood joined together in a tripod.

'How do I know when they're ready to pick?' she asked Freddie, standing there with the big basket Joy had given her, anxious not to pick something that wasn't ready and ruin all his hard work.

He steered her in the right direction, over to the stakes. 'You know they're ready when the pods start to fill out.' He handled a pod and she peered closer to see the round-ed shapes of the vegetable bulging beneath the surface. 'I plant them at different times after the last frost of winter which means we get supplies for months and months. You like peas?'

'Love them.'

'I used to hate them,' he laughed. 'But I think everything tastes better when you grow it yourself.'

'I get that. And Joy seems to love having all this here.'

'She sure does. I think she may want you to take over

this place one day – the land, the farmhouse, taking people in who need your help.'

Libby began to laugh but it soon fell flat. He seemed as though he really was asking the question. 'Oh my goodness, you're serious.'

'You're the only family she has – as far as I know – and I know she's beginning to feel more tired, her blood pressure was up too.'

'She didn't say.'

'She wouldn't. Joy never makes a fuss. Don't let on I said anything.'

'I won't, don't worry. But do you really think she's contemplating me . . . and this place?' It seemed so ridiculous. Libby wouldn't have a clue where to start. She was all about numbers, calculations, getting lost in problem solving, looking after a huge farmhouse and all the land that came with it wasn't on her agenda at all. And taking in strangers to put them back on track with their lives? Impossible given she couldn't even do that for herself or her dad.

'I think it's gone through her mind. So . . . would you? Take it on I mean.'

When she told him no she got the feeling he wouldn't mind being asked to run this place himself. It sounded like he did a fair bit of it already and Libby almost suggested he talk to Joy about it but she didn't know him well enough, perhaps he'd do it of his own accord somewhere down the line.

'You have broccoli too,' she noticed as they walked away from the peas. She bent down to see what looked like a tiny floret among the leaves. 'Will this grow into a big broccoli like you get at the supermarket?'

'Of course it will. Here, this one isn't far off being ready.' He pulled back the leaves to reveal another, rather impressive vegetable. 'It's important to keep an eye on them as you don't want to miss picking time and have the vegetable ruined.'

'Broccoli is one of my favourite vegetables.' Libby set down her basket and tightened her ponytail, a summer essential out here with the unforgiving sun. 'My mum used to make roasted broccoli. She added garlic and lemons.' Her taste buds sprung into action. Amazing after all these years that she could still remember it. 'What are you doing?'

Head down, Freddie was peering all the way along the veggie patch, beneath leaves, until he sprung up with a smile and a couple of heads of broccoli in his hand. 'We'll have it tonight.'

'Oh no, I've no idea how to make it.'

'You remember the three ingredients, can't be that hard. Come on, let's get the garlic.'

And so with her basket filled with the fresh ingredients she headed back to the farmhouse where she found a good supply of lemons meaning there was no need to head out and buy more.

At the porcelain farmhouse sink she washed everything except the onions that would be peeled. She knocked the excess mud off those and left them ready to use. It wasn't long before Joy came inside to join her. She had a basket of eggs and she took her sun hat off, wiping her brow. 'It's hot out there. I should've put more sunscreen on, the sun is fierce without much shade.'

Libby had noticed her arms were a little red. 'Freddie's got an impressive business going hasn't he?'

Libby had noticed her arms were a little red. 'I should've put more sunscreen on, the sun is fierce without much shade.'

'Freddie's got an impressive business going hasn't he?'

'It's a huge area.' She rinsed the parsley and shook off the drips before laying it in a colander. She wondered whether Freddie was right with his suspicion Joy might want Libby to one day take over here. 'It must be nice to know you're eating food grown on the land you own.'

'It certainly is.'

If Joy was thinking of her future and Libby's she wasn't leaving any hints. And now it seemed to be her turn to be out of sorts. Libby wasn't overly worried about what Freddie had told her about Joy's blood pressure and visit to the doctor's, but at the same time, she wanted to help in any way she could. 'Is everything OK with you, Auntie Joy?'

'Everything's fine,' Joy dismissed, transferring eggs she'd just been collecting to the wire basket housed on the worktop in the kitchen. 'There, that should keep us going a while. Freddie can box up the rest and take them to the store for selling.' She spied the lemons, the garlic and the broccoli. 'I see you've added a few extras to what I needed.'

'It's hard to resist anything out there and when I saw the broccoli I remembered something Mum used to make. She used to roast it with some lemons and garlic and I honestly could eat an entire plate of it, didn't need anything else.'

'You remember the recipe?'

She pulled a face, dried her hands and headed over to the laptop. 'Unfortunately not, but I'm sure I can find something online. Would it be OK to serve it alongside the chicken dish? Unless you think it won't go of course.'

'Libby, anything goes in this house and I for one love trying new foods.'

She opened up her laptop, powered it on and got searching. It wasn't long before she found something that sounded remarkably similar to her mum's recipe and felt an enthusiasm to be in the kitchen that was something she never would've predicted when she came here. It must be all the country air getting to her.

'I wondered if you could do me another favour,' said Joy. 'Could you draw up a poster on that fancy laptop of yours? I need to advertise the puppies for sale. All proceeds are going to be donated to the local animal rescue centre. I meant to put something together sooner.'

When she met Libby's suspicious gaze she admitted. 'All right so I've been dragging my feet a bit. I don't like the idea of saying goodbye.' With a sigh, she added 'but I know I have to. So, would you do it for me?'

'Of course, I'd love to. I can't vouch for my artistic talents but I'm sure I can come up with something.'

'Perhaps we could put one in the church hall on the noticeboard and they have a board outside too.'

'It sounds like a very good idea,' Libby assured her. 'Any requirements for what you want on the poster?'

'Make sure you include a little bit about Luna, the puppies' age, vaccinations already given, and ensure people know we're looking for good homes and the money raised is going to a really worthy cause. I'll jot some things down for you.' She grabbed a notepad and scribbled out the relevant details.

'I think those particulars with a photograph of Luna and all six puppies will be perfect,' said Libby, 'and easy to do if you have a printer? I'll add your phone number and some tear-off tabs on the bottom.'

'Thanks, Libby. I have plenty of photographs, so I'll send one on my phone, and the printer is in the dining room.'

'The unused dining room?'

'Hey,' Joy laughed, 'we use it, just not for the purpose it's intended.'

'Mum never used ours either. I think once or twice at Christmas and that was it. She always preferred to be in the kitchen.' She didn't miss the way Joy's jaw tensed at the mention of Maggie, the sister she never got to see before she died, certainly not in recent years anyway.

'If you're OK to sort the poster, I'm going for a lie down for a bit,' Joy announced.

'That's not like you.' But maybe she shouldn't draw attention to it, it sounded as though she needed to take it easier and maybe Auntie Joy was listening to the doctor. She may have only just got here but Libby still knew it wasn't like Joy to stop until the very end of the day, then fall into bed and start all over again at the crack of dawn. She'd never seen it with her own eyes, but it was certainly what she'd learned over time from their letters.

'Must be the sunshine,' said Joy flippantly, 'and Lauren says she's coming over later with a sticky date pudding for dessert, so I want to be chatty rather than tired.'

She'd let it go, she wanted Joy to rest, she wanted her auntie to do exactly as she'd said and join in because she loved her company. She'd somehow always known she would.

'What's the story with Lauren?' she asked before Joy left her to it.

'Lauren?' Joy hung her hat on the coat hooks in the hallway and hovered in the doorway. 'She's doing well, married to a lovely chap. She's happy.'

'Why is she here so much if she's happily married?'

Joy hovered some more. 'You know, that's a good question. Her husband works shifts, I'd presumed that was why. Although come to think of it, he seems to work a lot of evenings these days. Maybe I'll ask her about it. It can't be good for their relationship, can it?'

'Don't ask me, I don't exactly do well in the relationship stakes.'

'Me neither.' And with a shrug Joy went off to take her nap.

Libby got the impression hiding her own problems was yet another thing she got from her auntie who seemed pretty good at doing it too.

When Joy emerged later on, Libby had things in the kitchen under control. 'What's all this?' she asked, watching Libby weigh out some sugar.

'You had so many lemons in the house that I got carried away,' Libby admitted, halving the remaining lemons and squeezing out the juice, 'so I thought I'd make a lemon drizzle cake.' It'd been years since she'd actually baked anything. She'd let work take over her life and although she wouldn't be away from it forever, there was something to be said for taking a decent break and doing things that were totally out of your comfort zone.

'I'm impressed.'

Libby paused. 'You don't think Lauren will be put out?'

She hadn't thought of that. 'I know she's bringing the sticky date pudding.'

'It's not like it won't get eaten. Lauren won't mind at all.'

Luckily they had two ovens which meant the vegetables could roast away and emit their delicious cooking smells without impacting on the cake. And when Joy peered in to investigate what was in the ovens, Libby explained, 'I'm roasting lemons and garlic. I'll mix those together and toss the broccoli with the dressing.'

'You've surprised me. You never mentioned a love of cooking in any of your letters.'

'That's because I never did it.' She grinned. 'Perhaps this is the new Libby.' She certainly felt as though the weight of the world had lifted from her shoulders and if this was what it took, she'd keep the apron on permanently. She almost couldn't wait to explore those veggie patches again and think of something to make with the ingredients.

'Then I like the new Libby. Although the old one was pretty good too,' Joy smiled.

Libby mixed the lemon juice with the sugar, all ready to drizzle over the warm cake which only had five minutes to go. 'Check out the poster I did for you,' she added when she remembered. She wiped her hands before bringing the laptop back to life to show her auntie. 'Will that do?'

'Perfect, a woman of many talents.'

'I do my best. And I can go to the church hall later to put it up if you like – I'll print two, one for inside, one for outside. I'll need a post-dinner walk if I'm going to have this dinner plus lemon drizzle and sticky date.'

Freddie brought in a good selection of mushrooms

and dumped them into the sink. Libby turned her attention to them after she'd taken the cake out of the oven, and wiped their skin with wet kitchen towel before setting them on a chopping board. She poured the drizzle over the cake so it could ooze into the sponge, Joy shelled the peas, Libby took charge of the shallots and between them they had the dinner on in no time, bubbling away in its casserole dish. The roasted lemon and garlic were ready to squish together and toss with the broccoli and the smell had everyone complimenting their efforts the minute they came in.

'It smells like a restaurant,' said Lauren when she turned up.

'My stomach hurts I'm so hungry,' moaned Freddie before heading to the bathroom to scrub his filthy hands.

Lauren and Libby soon got into talking catering when Lauren realised how much of a hand Libby had had in tonight's dinner preparations. 'I'm going to try the roast garlic recipe out for myself,' said Lauren.

'I'll email you the link.' Libby pulled the ring pull on a can of Diet Coke and Lauren did the same as they sat at the table waiting for the oven timer to ping. 'What business is your husband in? Auntie Joy said he works shifts.'

'He's a taxi driver, works a lot of evenings.'

'I suppose there's more demand than in the daytime.'

'Yeah.' But Lauren wasn't all that convincing. And she didn't seem to want to talk about it because she focused on Cameron when he came into the room, asking him how the puppies were behaving and whether Shiloh, one of the black female labs, was still the cuddliest, Bisto still full of mischief.

'They all are,' Cameron smiled, Libby noticing herself

how he was beginning to relax in the short space of time since she'd arrived.

'Check out what's in the Tupperware,' Lauren urged Cameron, indicating the tub she'd brought with her that sat at the end of the table as Joy mashed the potatoes and Libby set the table for five.

Cameron looked in heaven when he pulled back the lid and took a whiff of the butterscotch drizzle to go on top of the sticky date pudding. 'My stomach's growling louder than Freddie's now,' he claimed.

'And Libby made lemon drizzle,' Joy called over seemingly glad at how much Cameron was integrating with everyone else at long last.

Libby's face obviously gave away her reticence at making a dessert, her doubt it'd be any good, and Lauren jumped in to give her praise. 'It looks good, Libby, nice and moist, I'm first in line for a piece.' It seemed Cameron would be next judging by his sudden interest too.

'I didn't want to step on any toes but I'd started making the cake before I realised it might be rude if you'd said you'll bring dessert,' Libby explained.

'You'll soon learn Libby that if there's one thing that upsets people in this house,' said Joy, dishing up portions of chicken and mushroom casserole onto plates, 'it's not enough food.'

'No danger of that,' Freddie remarked, eyeing up both cakes and taking his place at the table. He was frowning at something on his phone and switched it to silent before putting it into his pocket.

A low rumble outside announcing another arrival had Joy leaping up to pluck another plate from the cupboard narrowly missing Cameron's head as he ducked to the sink for more water. 'It's a madhouse,' she announced in the busy space, clearly not minding one bit. 'Make room for Drew.'

Libby was secretly thrilled with the latest arrival although she wished she'd had a chance to check what she looked like. She'd spent so long dressing smart and keeping up appearances with her job and then going out on the town with friends that not having to do so was an unexpected release. She'd got lazy, but she was happy to be so for a while, apart from right now when she suspected she looked a total mess given how hot she'd got baking, cooking with garlic, preparing the rest of the meal.

'Did I hear my name?' Drew came through the door looking as good as he had the other day, dressed similarly in shorts and a T-shirt, his arms kissed with the suntan he wouldn't be able to help getting being out on the water so much. He kissed Joy on the cheek. 'Do you have room for another one?'

'Of course we do, shuffle up everyone, pull in that chair, Cameron, Drew sit yourself down.'

Everyone moved up and Drew nodded his hellos, smiling in Libby's direction. She'd been with Brandon for a while and before that she hadn't had time for a boyfriend, so the anticipation and prospect of someone new took her by surprise, especially when really she knew nothing about the guy.

When Joy had dished up another portion and was seated herself she asked him, 'To what do we owe this pleasure? I thought you were teaching kayaking tonight.'

It seemed out of the couple who were due to have a lesson, the guy had broken his leg and his other half had broken her arm.

'Don't even want to know what they were doing to

'instigate that.' Freddie's comment earned laughter from around the table.

'Nice apron by the way,' Drew nodded to Libby. She'd forgotten she still had the garment on with its frilly edges around the purple fabric. 'Did you cook?'

'She's been an absolute dream helping me,' said Joy.

'I had to teach her a little bit about how to recognise different herbs,' Freddie announced.

'I'm not much of a gardener,' Libby admitted. 'Or a grower for that matter.'

Drew grinned. 'Me neither, but I am an eater and the smell in this kitchen . . .' His words drifted off as Joy fetched a big bowl filled with the broccoli, another with roasted carrots, one more with the mashed potatoes.

Over dinner it was the same deal as any other meal Libby enjoyed here. The chatter didn't stop, neither did the eating, and it seemed whatever had been on Joy's mind earlier had abated as she was surrounded by familiar faces and laughter. The men all had two rounds of dessert, the cake and the pudding didn't stand a chance with their appetites. Lauren accused Freddie and Cameron of having hollow legs with the amount they ate, and Lauren and Libby exchanged a laugh as Lauren declared it was much like her childhood. 'I grew up with three brothers who always ate everything in sight. I'd experiment with a new recipe, set whatever it was in the tin or the fridge overnight and come down the next morning . . . gone,' she shrugged. 'They were always so skinny too, I never understood how that could be.'

'Are you still in touch with your brothers?' The question was out before she had a chance to wonder whether she really should've asked it.

'I wasn't for a while, after I left home I didn't get in touch until Joy took me in and it felt like the right time. Lucky for me they didn't hold a grudge and we get on well now. Two of them live in London, both project managers, both married, and the youngest is a writer and he recently moved up to Aberdeen.'

Libby wouldn't mind betting it was Joy who'd persuaded Lauren not to give up on her brothers. She was doing the same when it came to Libby's dad despite the way she'd been treated by him and Maggie with their refusal to include her in their family. Auntie Joy was a good person, Libby could see it, and she wondered whether her dad might eventually see it too.

When the washing-up was done and the kitchen cleared, Lauren made cups of tea for everyone. It seemed her husband was working a long shift this evening. That, or for some reason she was stalling going home. Cameron volunteered to take Luna for a good walk across the fields but neither Joy nor Freddie were interested in the exercise that might work off the dessert.

'Manual labour,' Freddie defended, 'I've earned my spot on the sofa tonight.'

'I think I'll stay here too,' said Joy. 'I'd like to spend a bit more time with Lauren, but you go for a walk, Libby, it's still light.'

'I have been out after dark,' Libby teased. 'I'm thirty-six, not six, Auntie Joy.' But she didn't mind the concern at all, it had been a while since she'd felt as though someone were looking out for her in a parent-like way. She went into the hallway and picked up the pile of puppy posters she'd printed out. 'I'll take these to the church hall unless you think it's too late and all locked up?'

'The yoga group is running at the moment,' said Drew, 'I saw them all filing in there on my way here, their mats tucked under their arms, ready to contort themselves into positions that are in no way relaxing.'

'Thanks for the tip.' Libby popped her sunglasses on top of her head.

'Want some company?'

'Sure.' If Libby wasn't mistaken Joy sent a concerned look her way. She wasn't sure what her auntie thought she did in New York but she was used to company of the male variety, she wasn't going to eat him alive. Or maybe it was Drew himself she had a problem with because she hadn't reacted that way when Libby and Freddie were in cahoots as they had been with the herbs earlier. Then, Auntie Joy encouraged it. She wondered, had Drew done something terrible before he came to Joy for help? Perhaps Joy was worried he'd do the same to Libby.

'Ready?' he asked, pulling her from her contemplation about her auntie's motives and whether Drew had a more sinister side.

Outside he looked up at the grey clouds hovering, some of them the slate grey that implied rain wasn't far away. 'I think we might get our second storm soon.'

'Joy loves a good bolt of lightning and the rumble of thunder.'

'That she does.'

'I love the seasons too, even the rain, it's cosy when you're inside.'

'It's nice out on the water too, even more serene kayaking down the river. Storms aren't so appealing though.' He smiled at her and then asked, 'Joy seems out of sorts this evening. Is there anything I should know about?'

They were following the pavement round the curved bend that led to the main street of the village. 'You noticed? I thought so myself, but given I've not been here long, reading her moods isn't something I'm used to. But maybe there's something in the air – Freddie was stomping about this morning as though he'd forgotten how to smile, and apparently that's very unusual.'

'It really is.' Drew pushed his hands into the pockets of his shorts. 'Freddie is usually the life and soul, guaranteed to make fun of you if you're in a bad mood and pretty much able to pull anyone out of a strop.'

'I guess none of us know what anyone else is going through. We can put on a smile to hide it so nobody asks questions, but beneath that façade there's usually more going on.'

'You sound like you're speaking from experience.' They waited for a car to pass and splash through a deep puddle before they scuttled past.

'Not really, but it's human nature isn't it? We don't always want everyone to know everything about us, sometimes we choose to let others see what we want and unveil it piece by piece. I guess that's what getting to know someone involves.'

'You're right. Question is, Libby, will you be here long enough for us all to get to know you?'

It sounded like flirting and her tummy fluttered at the unexpectedness of it even though she knew it couldn't go anywhere when she wasn't exactly a permanent fixture in Somerset. 'Who knows.' They crossed a lane that Libby knew after exploring Bramleywood led down to a group of four cute houses, not old but built sympathetically to fit in with the village.

Her attempt to brush off the question didn't work. 'Come to think of it you've been nothing but smiles since you arrived.' He'd noticed? 'But you're here all of a sudden, your visit is open-ended . . . that suggests to me that something might be up.'

'Very astute of you. I'm a bit stressed out with work, that's all.'

'That's it?'

She grinned. 'Ten out of ten for probing. There are other things bothering me.'

'Don't tell me, boyfriend trouble.'

'You make me sound as though I'm a hormonal teenager.'

'I don't mean to, I apologise.'

'And there's no boyfriend trouble.' She thought she felt another spot of rain. 'Not any more.'

They walked on further, past a couple of independent stores Libby might go into when she got a chance, past the bakery and the station and on towards the church hall.

'So we've covered work,' said Drew, 'and love life . . . that leaves family.'

'I'm here with Joy, I'm with family.'

'What about the rest of them? Joy told me you lost your mum a while ago.'

Her focus suddenly went down to the ground rather than his hair that was cut short at the back and sides but floppy enough in other areas that it gave him an apparent laid-back approach to the world. She looked instead at the cracks in the pavement.

'I get it,' he went on, 'I lost both my parents. Although maybe in a way it was easier for me, they both died before I was old enough to even know about it or remember them. I was three.'

'I'm sorry. That's really sad. And way worse than what I've been through. Not that it's a competition . . . I just mean it must really suck. It's unfair.' She was getting her words muddled but he made her nervous when his focus was solely on her.

'Very unfair, and for years I battled with the anger I held on to, I couldn't find happiness anywhere. I lived with my uncle for a while and then he died too. Then I felt *really* sorry for myself.' His tone had her smiling until he turned serious again. 'I guess I went through this whole phase where I questioned the point in getting close to anyone if they were going to leave me behind.'

'You seem to be in a good place now.' They'd reached the village hall with its pitched roof and stone exterior and the small green space in front.

'I am, and that's largely thanks to Joy. She's one in a million.'

Libby smiled as yogis began to file out, some rosy-cheeked with exertion, others looking all Zen and relaxed. 'I'll go inside, see if I can put a poster up,' she said. 'Do I need to ask permission?'

'Not in Bramleywood. As long as it's tasteful you should be fine.'

'What about outside? The board looks quite full.' She looked over to the village noticeboard that looked far too busy.

'I'll shuffle a few things around,' he whispered, sending a shiver down her spine when he got close. 'We'll make sure your ad doesn't go unnoticed.'

She went inside, dodged a couple of people still making their way out, found the board and pinned the notice up.

The yoga teacher's interest was piqued straight away and she tore off a number.

Outside, Drew had done exactly as he'd said he would and her advert was sitting there behind the glass screen with plenty of space around it so it would stand out. People wouldn't be able to tear off a number but they could note it down.

'Already had one person take the number from the bottom of the advert inside,' she told him.

'That's great, although The Old Dairy will feel weird without the puppies.'

'I hadn't thought of that.'

'If I didn't live in a two-up, two-down with virtually no garden I'd buy one for sure.'

'Oh come on, that's no excuse. Now I have a genuine reason not to – I can't take it in my carry-on back to New York.'

'Are you telling me you would if you could? You don't seem the type.'

'And what type might that be?'

He held up his hands. 'Steady on, I'm not criticising, but you're a corporate girl, I'll bet you live in an apartment, eat at fancy restaurants and the most you ever get your hands dirty is by handling the post.'

She began to laugh. 'You're pretty much spot on. Should've seen my face when Freddie told me to shove my hands into the soil to retrieve vegetables. I don't take after Joy in that respect, she's right at home on the land.'

'She sure is. But you're fitting in too. I mean, I know Joy has a knack for including everyone and making them feel welcome, but it isn't just that, you're enjoying being around her and out at the farm, I can tell. And you're clearly at home in the kitchen. Tonight's lemon drizzle was amazing, but that broccoli, now that was better than amazing.'

The black clouds were still teasing them from above as they made their way back to the farmhouse, the shops, the library, the estate agent and bakery all closed for the night. 'I never was in New York. I got used to eating out, I didn't have anyone to cook for – my boyfriend liked to be out, to be seen, which I liked too for a while. And besides, I was always so busy I never had the time to shop let alone cook.'

'Must be nice to take a step back here and do things you wouldn't usually do.'

'Yeah, it is.' He was remarkably easy to talk to and she found herself saying, 'What I don't want is my being here to stress Joy out in any way.'

'And why would you be doing that?'

'I can tell she's got something on her mind and all I can think of is that it might be me.'

'Does she have a reason to be worried?'

'I got upset and fell apart on her,' she admitted.

'Well if you're falling apart you've come to the right place.'

Libby grinned and turned to face him. 'Funnily enough Joy said something similar.'

'Perhaps she's getting restless because she knows you'll be off soon. She takes people in and gives them a home, is attentive when she needs to be, backs off when the situation warrants it. And then she lets us all make our own way in the world. But . . . she hates goodbyes, always has. She's not one for change. I've seen her be down for days when somebody moves on, even if they're happy and in a good place. I guess in a way she's become a parent to all of us and I can't imagine it's easy to say goodbye to your kids when it's time, especially when she knows there are no biological ties, some of us won't stay in touch. She always perks up in the end, but it's as though her head goes someplace else for a while.'

'She's never going to manage a farewell with the puppies then.'

His laughter caught an admiring glance from a couple of teenage girls walking past The Old Dairy, one of them blushing when Drew said hello. Amazing the effect he had on women without even realising. The fact that he was good looking, cool, level-headed, made it hard to believe he'd ever had such a rough time he'd needed Joy's help. And Libby was starting to really like him for his kindness and understanding, qualities he never seemed to mind sharing with others. She wondered what had happened to him along the way and found herself wanting to be there for him even though she didn't know any of the details. He was so different from Brandon who she'd never felt the need to coddle or even comfort. Brandon had always carried with him an air of high achievement, not that there was anything wrong with that, but Drew on the other hand seemed selfless without even trying.

'Are you definitely going back to New York?' he asked, just like that as they hovered at the end of the gravelled drive. They'd come to a stop by unspoken agreement but she didn't mind one bit.

'I do live there.'

'Not right now you don't. Technically, you're of no fixed abode.'

'You have done your homework.' She dug her shoe into the gravel but scraped it back over again not wanting to ruin it. 'It's not that I haven't thought about it – coming home to England.' She'd done a lot of thinking on the flight over here wondering whether she'd land at Heathrow and wish she could get straight back on the plane again and go back, but in the short time she'd been at Joy's those feelings hadn't hit her yet and she'd been enjoying herself far too much to think about long-term.

'You could look for work in London, plenty of big firms there for you. Or there's Bristol, even closer.' Her hesitation had him asking, 'What's stopping you from coming back? I mean, you don't sound like you've got too much tying you to being out there. No boyfriend, no job . . .'

'Way to make me feel special.'

'I apologise,' he grinned. 'But you headed back because you wanted to make a change in your life, am I right? Perhaps you need to weigh up what you have in each country and where you see yourself long-term.'

'I've been so busy with work up until now that I've never thought beyond a couple of years ahead.' That, and she'd blocked out any tugs of pain at losing her mum, any niggles that packing up her life here and getting away from it all in another country hadn't necessarily been the healthiest solution.

'What's stopping you from thinking a bit further into the future now?'

'I suppose not having a fixed abode here either,' she said, using his terminology. 'I mean I know there's Joy, but that's it, my dad and I don't exactly see eye to eye. There's no family home any more, he upped and left to live in the Lake District near Lake Windemere.'

'You fell out with him?'

'No nothing like that. But since Mum died it's as

though we've both picked ourselves up and pulled apart as far as we can. He doesn't even know I'm here yet. Joy keeps nagging me to call him. I will, soon.' She hated to think that her reluctance to do so was adding to Joy's worries. 'Did you know my parents never wanted us to have anything to do with Joy? They never let me near her as I was growing up. I was too young to question it then. But I started writing to her in secret after I found her address.'

'Wow. That's some admission, she never let on that was the case.' He'd been leaning up against the metal gate but stood straight now. 'We all knew she'd been writing to you, but we didn't know it was all a big secret. I assumed you were the only one of her family around. I feel selfish now for never asking her more. Do you have any idea why they didn't want her in your lives?'

'I don't, and something tells me I could ask but I might not like what I hear. I'd rather live in ignorant bliss.'

'Sometimes it is best,' he winked and they went round the back of the farmhouse. They both headed straight over to the puppies. 'Right, if you could put one of these in your carry-on, which one would you take?'

She laughed at the game. 'Buttercup,' she said without a doubt. Buttercup was the golden Labrador pup who had a habit of picking the food bowl up in her mouth when its contents were gone, and walking around like it was a begging bowl. Maybe she was hoping someone would throw in a treat or two. 'She's a big softie, aren't you Buttercup?' She'd lifted the pup up onto her lap and cuddled her against her body. 'And getting bigger by the day. How about you?' She watched Drew sitting on the ground in the pen after checking it was clear of anything he didn't want to sit in.

'Maybe Bisto,' he said, back pressed up against the edge of the pen, tanned limbs extended as he fussed over the chocolate lab leaping all over him.

'No way,' came a voice. Cameron. 'Joy said I could choose a puppy and we were going to keep Bisto!' He didn't hang around for an explanation, he turned and ran and the way Drew reacted suggested it hadn't been the first time Cameron's emotions sent him away from the farmhouse.

Drew shook his head at himself. 'I wish Joy had told us. I had no idea he was keeping Bisto. I'll go after him.'

Joy had already heard the commotion or perhaps she'd seen Cameron run, and she'd come outside with Lauren. Libby reiterated the misunderstanding.

'I should've told you all,' said Joy, 'it slipped my mind completely.'

'We'll find him,' Lauren said firmly as she and Freddie by mutual agreement went after him. Drew said he'd join them and Libby stayed at Joy's side.

'He'll be Ok,' Libby assured her auntie as they went into the kitchen. But it was as though Joy was trying to act as though nothing had happened. She'd got a cloth, the spray cleaner and was giving the table a good going over. Perhaps her way of coping was to throw herself into being busy. Libby was no stranger to that coping tactic.

'It's still light,' Libby plugged away at trying to convince Joy everything would be all right and that they needn't panic. She wasn't going to ask about the other times Cameron had done this but she got the impression this was an informal routine they all fell into when it happened. 'Lauren and Freddie will find him.'

'He'll come back,' Joy said, not really to anyone other

than herself. 'This is his home as long as he needs it, I won't fail him.'

Maybe distraction was the order of the evening. 'I put the posters up, someone already took a tab so you might get a call about the puppies.'

'That's nice.' Joy rinsed the cloth again and squeezed it out. She wiped the front of the fridge concentrating on a stubborn mark.

'I thought I might smuggle a puppy into my carry-on.'

'Go for it,' Joy replied without a hint of humour.

'Maybe Buttercup.'

'Of course,' Joy said in the same jovial tone.

'See now I know you're not listening.'

Joy stopped what she was doing, the cloth beneath her hand. 'My mind is all over the place, always is when someone I have a responsibility to takes off.'

'You do what you can.'

'But is it ever enough?'

'Sit down, Auntie Joy. Please.' It took a bit of persuasion but eventually Joy sank into the chair. Libby made her a cup of camomile tea and hoped it might calm her nerves.

With the hot drink in front of her Joy recapped Libby on some of Cameron's history. 'He's done this before, more than once. And I always think this is it, he won't come back. Common sense tells me he will.'

'How long does he go off for?'

'Sometimes less than twenty-four hours, other times it's days.'

Libby noticed in her sadness Joy looked closer to her age of nearly seventy than she did when she was happy and laughing and everything was running like clockwork.

'He really has to learn not to flip out every time something doesn't go his way,' Joy worried. 'The problem is, the boy has never been encouraged to do anything in his life.'

'You know his story?' She added a sweet biscuit to the saucer in front of Joy.

'Most of it. His failures as a kid were given focus, never anything he did right, and I suppose he's waiting for that to happen again. It's as though if any bad words are exchanged or something looks like it's going down a path he doesn't want, he'll run before he has to face the consequences. Perhaps it's his way of protecting himself, so rather than have Bisto taken from him he's choosing to leave first.'

'I'm sorry, it was my fault, and Drew's. We made him think he might lose Bisto. We were messing around and he overheard us.'

'I won't hear of it. It's nobody's fault apart from mine.' She appeared to disappear into herself and put on a stronger front than she'd let herself show moments ago. 'It's my job as the person who runs this house and takes people in, to make them feel safe, to not give them a reason to run.'

Libby covered her hand with her own. 'Now that may be partly true, but at the end of the day, you can't control people's emotions and if Cameron has such a troubled past, it's going to take a while for him to learn to battle his way through those emotions and deal with situations differently.'

'When he comes back I need to make it clear I haven't gone back on my promise about Bisto.' Joy finished her biscuit. Libby might not be the only one stressing Joy out but she knew she played a part and there was only one thing she could do about that right now. 'I think I'll go and call my dad.'

Relief spread across Joy's face, but only for a moment before it was replaced with trepidation. 'I won't disturb you, go into the lounge and close the door. Then when Cameron and the others come back,' she said confidently, 'they won't disturb you either.'

'Doesn't matter if they do. I had some noisy neighbours in my apartment and more than once Dad would ask who was there with me when it was voices drifting in through the open window,' she grinned. 'It'll be more suspicious if it's too quiet, might need to put the television on.'

Libby shut herself in the lounge and dialled her dad's number. It was about time. She told herself she was doing it to ease Joy's worry, but it was to ease her own too because she'd been dreading this moment.

They did the usual, small talk covering the weather, with Libby talking as though she was dealing with a scorching Manhattan summer as usual, they discussed the fence he'd replaced on his property that had concrete posts now ready to withstand what the winter threw at them, she talked about her job and admitted she'd left the firm and wasn't sure what her next move would be. That much, at least, was true.

And then when conversation dried up it had been on the tip of her tongue to say she was here in England, but she just couldn't do it.

She wanted this bubble she'd created to last a while longer.

Next time. Next time she'd do it.

Chapter Seven

Joy

Joy was sitting in front of the computer in the dining room. She'd been up early this morning thanks to Ronald's wake-up call. She usually came to just after he did, but more often than not got up in her own time. This morning however, her determination had kicked in again and she was getting on with more investigations. Without a single positive response to her email blast she needed to put out the feelers and advertise her land for use. Without Mr McKerrick's sheep grazing and therefore no rent money, she'd be finding it hard to make ends meet sooner than she'd like. The farmhouse and the land might belong to her but she still had bills to pay, repair costs to cover whenever they arrived – usually more so in the winter – and food to put on the table. Freddie paid for his keep, Drew and Lauren both contributed to shopping expenses – even though she'd tried not to let them they still pushed notes and coins into the money box in the hallway.

Things had settled down a little over the last week since Lauren found Cameron huddled up in a bus stop out on the road after he ran off. She had a knack for diffusing a situation and Joy suspected that came from refereeing between her siblings growing up. Lauren had told her enough about it, pushing away the bad days with their parents, instead remembering the happier times that had finally made her get in touch with the three boys she'd all but excluded from her life out of guilt for leaving them in the first place. It was Lauren who'd found Cameron on other occasions too – the time he ran off into the fields so hadn't left the property at all, another time she'd found him in a shop doorway on the main street in the village. He always took some persuasion to come back but Joy was only thankful he came in the end. And now he had Bisto for company. Joy was trying not to smother him with affection and worry, doing her best to let him settle in once more. She'd never let him know she peeked in on him at night to make sure he was in his bed and hadn't done a midnight flit. He wouldn't appreciate being babied, it was a fine line with Cameron. She wanted him to know how welcome he was here, how much he was already a part of the family at The Old Dairy, but a tiny part of her always gnawed at her conscience every time he ran because she berated herself for not being good enough.

She'd been so preoccupied with Cameron over the last week that Joy hadn't asked Libby much about the conversation with her dad. She knew they'd spoken and Joy hadn't asked whether her name came up, she suspected it hadn't or Libby would've told her. That or her dad would've come to rescue his daughter from the enemy. And she wasn't really asking for details now because she knew how she'd feel if her niece announced she'd be spending the rest of her time in the country up in the Lakes rather than Bramleywood and then before they knew it, she'd be back in New York. Which, in Joy's mind, was the last thing she wanted. She could see for herself that Libby wasn't one hundred per cent committed to returning either.

One lesson Joy had learned over time was that she shouldn't stress about the things she couldn't control, and so she got back to finalising the advert on the website she'd originally used to advertise land for rent and kept her fingers crossed it wouldn't be long before someone responded. She hoped this would work and at least she still had the purchaser buying four acres lined up. They wanted to plant sunflowers, which Joy had to admit she was thrilled with and couldn't wait to see, and the paperwork wasn't far off being completed which meant the money transfer to her account wasn't far away either. She still had the Whittakers' rent coming in too for the four horses they kept grazing here at The Old Dairy and they seemed happy enough. Joy had never had any complaints from them. Then again, she'd thought that about the McKerricks and look how that had turned out.

Joy went through to the kitchen, but rather than grab a quick bowl of cereal for breakfast she knew what she could do to feel calm, safe, remember the people she'd brought to the farm and who were still in her life. She'd cook a good old-fashioned country breakfast for them all.

Buoyed with her idea she moved the pile of placemats from the centre of the table, found out the red-and-white gingham tablecloth from the end drawer of the Welsh dresser and flicked it out across the table. The colour brightened the kitchen instantly with the cloudy sky making the kitchen darker than usual. She got out the special silverware too. Most of the time anyone staying here helped themselves to breakfast as and when they got up. The kitchen was usually a constant flow of action, almost a tag-team event with one person leaving, another taking over. But today, she wanted a settling, special time for herself, for Cameron, for Libby, for Freddie who was still not quite himself. She wanted to make everyone around her feel as safe and secure as Ted and Marjory had made her feel.

Joy found the rest of the bacon in the fridge, she had plenty of bread, eggs, some mushrooms in the vegetable rack and spinach in the fridge. Catering for the masses was something she'd taken to easily. It was hard to imagine ever being here all alone the way she was after Ted and Marjory both passed away. Joy had plummeted into the sort of misery grief could easily cause and some days it had been an ordeal to get out of bed and function. But that's exactly what she'd done, she'd looked after the chickens they had, she'd got on the tractor to look after the land because there was nobody else to do it, her company had been Gerty the last cow to live out her days at the farm. Somehow she'd gone from there to here and it was a content place to be in at last.

By the time Cameron and Freddie showed their faces the table had four place settings each with the heavy, polished cutlery usually reserved for Christmas, birthdays or special occasions, a straw placemat, and a plate as well as a bowl. A glass sat on a coaster at each setting waiting for whoever wanted some of the juice in the tall glass jug in the centre of the table. She'd used the juicing machine from the utility room to push through umpteen apples to fill it, and added ice, each cube clinking and splashing as it fell from its mould.

'What's all this?' Freddie smiled at the sight before taking the empty ice-cube tray and refilling it for Joy. 'I was all set to have my usual cereal and two rounds of toast before I rushed outside.'

'No rushing today,' Joy told him and Freddie acquiesced without hesitation.

Cameron came to Joy's side. 'I was going to feed the puppies. But I can help if you need me to.'

Joy didn't look at Freddie. She knew his bushy eyebrows would be raised at this development. This was the first time the boy had asked her in a full sentence whether she needed him. And she suspected he was doing it to make up for last week's drama.

'Give us a minute?' Joy didn't have to glance Freddie's way for him to understand she meant him, and he disappeared off down the hallway. She ushered Cameron into a chair.

'Am I in trouble?' His fingers toyed with the fork at the place setting, pushing its prongs down so the tail spun around and chinked against the plate. 'I'm sorry about last week, running off I mean. I was angry, I didn't want Bisto to go with anyone else.'

'The main thing is you're safe,' she said, voice calm and not giving away her fears. 'That's the first thought that goes through my head when you bolt out of here. Nothing else. I don't get angry and think of ways to punish you, I only wish you would talk to me instead of running. Do you understand that?' When he shrugged she said, 'You can't take off every time something goes wrong or takes you by surprise.' Facing up to the consequences of your actions was the right thing to do. She always had, but others in her life hadn't and she'd paid the price.

He was biting down on his lip so he wouldn't cry. 'I don't know what else to say. Do you want me to leave?'

'Of course not.'

'You don't have any obligation to give me anywhere to live, to do all of this.'

'To care?' She said it because she knew he wouldn't, that would be skating way too close to talking about feelings. 'Well I'm afraid I do, and the caring makes me do everything else. This place has seen a lot of people come and go and that's the way I like it. You're welcome here any time and apart from almost giving me a heart attack by running off, you're good to have around. Your help with the puppies has been a godsend when I have so much else to do.' She hadn't needed his help as such but because he'd given it, it had given Joy something for herself – contentment at seeing him blossom in moments he didn't realise she'd witnessed, his smiles, his laughter, everything that had been missing in him for so long.

'And we're definitely keeping Bisto?'

'I told you, yes. But, if you've chosen the puppy, then he's your responsibility. I think that's fair.'

He perked up. 'I'll feed him, walk him, do everything he needs.'

Joy nodded, suspecting he would. And perhaps having a puppy dependent on him might make him think twice about running off again. 'Right then.' She put her palms firmly on the table top to end the conversation as it was. 'Let's get this breakfast made shall we?'

She pointed Cameron in the direction of the toast racks in the cupboard that would need to go on the table as she found out a big mixing bowl and brought over the wire basket of eggs. If Cameron would settle down a bit it might just do her nerves and her slightly raised blood pressure a favour. She'd never been a mum before. She'd been a mess for a long time and the prospect hadn't even been something lurking on the horizon, she'd taken it as a given that it would never happen. But over time Joy had come to learn that she could find the same bonds, the same long-lasting relationships and strength with others in different ways. And she liked to think she was doing a decent job of being a substitute mother for Cameron because even though he'd run, he *had* come back, every single time.

When Freddie came through, sensing Joy and Cameron had done their talking, Joy asked him to go and fetch Libby, wake her if he had to.

'I think I heard her running a bath,' said Cameron.

'I'll go in that case.' Joy didn't want Freddie interrupting her niece if she was having a long soak or in the middle of getting changed.

She took the stairs and made her way along the corridor. A lovely scent of summer dew came from the open door of the bathroom and Joy imagined her niece had found some beautiful expensive bath products to treat herself with now she was in the countryside but when she pushed open the door after Libby didn't answer, she heard the gurgle of the water as it disappeared down the plug hole, she saw suds clinging to the outer edges of the tub, and a row of three scented candles still lit lining the windowsill.

'Libby!' She called her niece as she frantically blew out each candle in turn. 'Libby!'

Libby appeared still wrapped in a towel, her face flushed from the heat of the bath. 'I'm here, what's the panic?'

'You left the candles burning!' She wafted away any smoke from the wick, double checking they were definitely out.

'I was only next door finding some underwear.'

'That's not the point. You never leave candles unattended.'

'OK.' She was grinning but she soon stopped when she realised how serious Joy was.

'Why do you have them on in the morning anyway?'

'They smell nice,' Libby shrugged. 'I'm sorry I left them burning and unattended, it won't happen again.'

'See that it doesn't,' Joy grumbled. 'There's a breakfast waiting for you downstairs, don't be long, it'll get cold.' And without looking at her niece because she knew she'd snapped at her unnecessarily, she bustled her way back to the kitchen.

It wasn't long before Libby joined them and the sheepish way she came into the room had Joy feeling terrible.

'I didn't know the chickens roamed freely in the fields,' said Libby when she passed by the window.

Joy, perplexed, took one look out of the window and ran, shrieking for the others to help. It seemed the run was damaged and the little blighters had got out at one corner.

Joy blocked the gap as Cameron went one way heading off the chicken that had gone the furthest; Libby did her best, but Joy could see she wasn't having much luck, and Freddie scooped up a couple of the others as Ronald signalled his alarm with a crowing that might have helped if he'd done it sooner.

Joy frantically counted the hens once they were back in the run. At least they'd got them before too many escaped. 'We're lucky, if they'd gone over the fields I might not have found them and I know there are foxes around.'

'Little bast—'Cameron stopped himself finishing that sentence.

'That'll need fixing.' Joy looked at the damage to the run wondering how the wire could've come out of the wood, it had always seemed so sturdy, but sure enough some of the nails were out and the chickens must've pushed the wire enough to escape, the gap getting bigger with every one of them that got through.

Cameron offered before Freddie which was unusual, Freddie was usually on to any repairs straight away but he was out of sorts. 'I'll get a hammer and some nails, I can fix it.'

'Thank you Cameron. Everything you need should be in the shed. I'll stand guard a while.' She also took the opportunity to re-count the chickens, paranoid they weren't all there, but they were all safe.

Once Cameron had made the repair, ensuring other nails around the run were in place and none of the wood looked likely to give up any time soon, they headed inside and resumed the country breakfast Joy wanted to give everyone today. But despite the drama with the chickens and the worry about foxes getting any chicken she'd missed, the events of the morning had already brought Cameron into the fold that little bit more, she knew.

Joy put Cameron in charge of the rounds of toast now the drama was over. 'The butter dish is in the larder,' she called over before turning her attention to her niece. 'How did you sleep?' She began to take each egg from the wire basket in turn and crack them over a bowl.

'Good for a change. I think I might just be getting used to Ronald's wake-up call. And all this country air is working wonders, I think I sleep better than I ever did in New York.'

'Well isn't that something.' Perhaps all wasn't lost, maybe Libby could be coming round to the idea of being in England on a more permanent basis. 'This all looks very posh, Auntie Joy.'

'Thank you, and don't even think about telling me you're skipping breakfast.'

'Not a chance, I'm starving.'

Over scrambled eggs made with a dash of single cream, bacon, spinach and mushrooms on the side, toast, juice and sides of mixed berries, the country breakfast was everything Joy had wanted it to be. She'd slowly learned ways to cope when she felt overwrought. And bringing people together for food was certainly one of them. As was taking in people who needed her and gathering those people when she feared she was sinking beneath some of the negative thoughts she held inside and never shared with anyone.

'Would you like me to do some cleaning today?' Libby offered.

'You're on holiday.' Joy said, finishing her praise of Freddie for the mushrooms, grown here and full of flavour. He seemed glum again and she wondered where his head was at, where it had been when the problem with the run was discovered, it was so unlike him to hesitate about helping, but his wife and child must be filling every thought right now.

'I am, but it almost feels like I live here, I think it's because it's so relaxed.'

It hadn't been when she'd been yelled at earlier about the candles. 'I'm sorry I snapped at you earlier.'

'Not a problem. It was silly of me to leave the candles burning, not very responsible at all.'

'Even so, I apologise.'

'Apology accepted,' Libby smiled kindly. 'And I meant it when I said I felt relaxed here.'

'I'm glad you feel that way.' Although she suspected relaxed wasn't the right word. It was chaotic, full of unpredictability, but it was a change nonetheless for her niece.

'It's no bother, honestly. In fact you'd stop me going stir crazy and stop me baking another cake. I ate far too much last night and if I do that every day I'll have to buy two seats on the plane back to New York.'

Her comment extinguished Joy's hope that she might stay but she did her best not to let it show.

'What's your place like?' Cameron asked, hoovering those scrambled eggs like he hadn't just polished off a couple of slices of toast first. Joy sometimes forgot how young he was and that to him, Libby's life must seem like one big adventure when he'd never been encouraged to spread his wings.

'My apartment was what you might call compact, or bijou. Which means it was tiny. I had just the one bedroom, a very small kitchen, a lounge which had a small round table in it and a bathroom that also had the washer dryer in it. It was loud too, they're right that the city never sleeps, but I got used to that, I think you adapt to your surroundings after a while.'

'Like you're adapting to Ronald.'

Libby grinned. 'Exactly.'

Cameron still didn't look up from his plate of food. 'If you decide to stay in England, are you going to move in here with us?'

'I don't know. Are you going to run off again?'

'Wasn't planning on it.' He finished his mouthful of spinach and eggs.

Only Libby, or perhaps Lauren, could get away with saying something like that. The pair had begun to get on well ever since Lauren brought Cameron back. Libby seemed to be making a real effort with him and from the cupboards of the old bureau Libby had pulled out a few board games that rarely got used. Libby and Cameron had played a few of them and one evening Joy had hovered in the hallway watching them in the kitchen playing Boggle at the table. For the limited words he used out loud with everyone here he had a remarkable vocabulary and she heard Libby bemoaning the fact he'd beaten her three times in a row. She'd declared it was time to find a numbers game where she'd beat him hands down. And he hadn't taken exception to that remark, which was a sure step in the right direction. Cameron seemed to get on better with the females of the house than the other males, not that he had a problem with Drew or Freddie when they were around. Perhaps it was easier for him to not compare himself to the girls, or maybe they were gentler and that was what he needed for now.

'Good,' Libby told him. 'We still need to play a numbers game for me to claim my Winner title.'

'You can stay as long as you like,' Joy assured Libby and when Freddie went out to work and Cameron went to feed the puppies – although Joy suspected it was a lot to do with bonding with Bisto and staking his claim again – she knew it was time to ask Libby about her dad.

'How much does your dad know?' She came right out with it as Libby scraped the remains of Cameron's spinach he clearly wasn't all that keen on into the bin.

Libby set the plate down by the sink. 'He doesn't know I'm here.'

'Here as in England or here as in at the farm with your evil auntie?'

A smile broke out. 'You're hardly that. I didn't tell him anything.' With a sigh she admitted, 'The whole conversation was awkward when I phoned last week and I just couldn't do it. I'm having such a good time, Auntie Joy.' Her claim had Joy stopping to look at her niece.

'It'd be lovely if you stayed.'

'I know. It has crossed my mind to look for a job in England rather than back in America, but I still feel all over the place, like I need to take a bit of time to think. I need a bit more time before I have to face reality, does that make sense?'

'Perfect sense my girl.'

'You know Mum always called me that.'

'My girl?'

Libby nodded. 'My dad didn't, but it was Mum's thing. She'd tell him she was off to the movies with "my girl", taking "my girl" to the supermarket, helping "my girl" with her schoolwork.'

'You must miss her.' Regardless of her ostracism from the family, that wasn't what was important here.

'Every single day.' She brushed away the tears that pooled in the corner of her eyes. 'Oh my goodness, look at me. It's been a long time, you'd think I'd be over it by now.'

'You'll never get over it, you'll just learn to cope.' Part of what Ted and Marjory had done for Joy was to make her realise that accepting what had happened in her life was part of the solution to moving forwards. And it was the same with grief. She wanted to encourage Libby not to block it all out, but rather to find a way to process it.

'I do manage to hold myself together most of the time.' She leaned against the kitchen sink, her back facing the window.

Joy left the plates where they were. The egg remnants could set hard for all she cared. 'When did the problems between you and your dad start?'

'After Mum died. It's as though neither of us could cope with the other's pain. Dad tried, he said he was there for me; I tried to talk to him but turned to friends mostly. And then after I moved to America it got harder. It's my fault, maybe if I'd hung around we could've worked through it.'

'When did he move up to the Lake District?'

'Not long after I left England. I was angry at first. I mean, I didn't even have a family home to come back to if I wanted and I resented that. All those memories with my mum were just gone. I felt cheated.'

'Does he know you felt that way?'

She shook her head. 'I never told him. I let him get on with his life, I got on with mine. We tiptoe around each other and that's the way it's been ever since Mum died.'

'The house and the memories aren't a package deal, Libby.'

'What do you mean?'

'You don't need to have the house to keep the memories, not at all. Being there would rush everything back into your mind at once but not after a while, then you'd be where you are now, relying on what you recall. I'll bet the times you remember with your mum aren't necessarily all under the roof of the family home.'

Libby sniffed but laughed. 'Actually no, they're not.'

'What are some of your favourite memories that don't involve the house?'

Libby thought for a moment and her face broke into a smile. 'One time we were driving on the motorway, I'd just passed my test, and this car cut us up. I then had to overtake it a while later and Mum made a very rude gesture at them as we went past. I couldn't believe it,' she laughed, 'I'd never heard her swear let alone do anything like that. I was so shocked I almost laughed so hard I was crying and then she was laughing and had tears pouring down her cheeks and by the time we pulled off the motorway and into the car park of the shopping centre we'd laughed so hard my tummy hurt.'

'What else?'

'You're testing my memory now . . .' She thought some more. 'I remember she had this thing about daily walks. She took them rain, hail, shine, snow, ice, thunder, she'd be out there and she'd make me and Dad go too. One winter it was so bad in the snow that we were only out ten minutes before our faces hurt so badly we turned back, but she said the same as she always did – "at least we got outside". When we got home she warmed soup for us all and Dad took one look at me and told me to fake having the flu if she made us go out again in the week because he'd rather stay in bed than get frostbite. I can't remember if we went the next day or not.'

'Perhaps your dad's way of coping with losing his wife and his daughter to some extent was to move away, and that's why he sold up.'

Libby gulped. 'He didn't lose me.'

'I'll bet you and your dad stopped those walks after Maggie died.' The last word caught in her throat. This conversation was for her niece, it didn't help her own grief apart from giving her solace in Libby's happiness.

'I don't think I ever walked with him again.' Libby was frowning. 'You're too kind, you know. They refused to have you in their lives for whatever reason, and I'm not asking what that was, but why are you sticking up for Dad?'

Joy hadn't meant to bring up emotions like this but Libby needed to deal with them and tell her dad she was in the country at least. She'd regret it if she didn't, if something happened to him before they reached an equilibrium. She knew that from bitter experience. 'Because he isn't a bad person, neither was your mum. And he hasn't deliberately set out to hurt you. Sometimes good people do bad things, make poor decisions, none of us are perfect.'

'I need to tell him I'm here, don't I,' said Libby as they returned to clearing the table.

Joy loaded the dishwasher racks with as much as she could, dropping the posh cutlery into fresh soapy water in the sink. 'Tell him you're in the country, yes.' She probably didn't need to let him know she was with Joy because that wouldn't help in the slightest, given how he'd been since Libby was little and Joy tried to mend what was broken in her life.

'I will,' Libby smiled. 'But back to farmhouse business for now. How about I clean the two bathrooms upstairs for you?' She dried each piece of silverware as Joy passed it to her, freshly washed. 'I could do it next before I'm distracted by those puppies,' she said looking out to see Cameron having all the fun. 'And I should probably let you know that I'm heading out to the pub with Lauren this evening. Is that OK?'

'It's more than OK. I like how easily you're settling in.'

Joy's heart soared to hear Libby was making friends and with Lauren, a girl whose heart was in the right place and who still played her cards rather close to her chest. She'd talked to Joy over the last few weeks but she still hadn't really said what was troubling her. Perhaps Libby, a girl of similar age, would have more luck getting her to open up.

When Libby went to do the cleaning it was on the tip of Joy's tongue to ask her to stay on longer, make this her home too, be the person who took all of this on one day. But that wasn't real life was it? She couldn't fit Libby into a life she'd carved out for herself just because she couldn't stand the idea of The Old Dairy not continuing on as the place she'd built it up to be.

Joy took Luna for a wander across the fields. She used the ball launcher to get a ball as far as possible for Luna to chase and with the weather cooler Luna was happy enough to run about a bit more. When the puppies were first born Joy hadn't wanted Luna to feel neglected. She'd kept her distance when needed – Luna was a mum after all, and Luna's job had been to give the puppies their first experience of touch sensation. She'd licked their skin clean, encouraged their eyes to open, fed them, and when the time was right, Joy had begun to get involved some more with Luna and her litter without encroaching too much on mum's domain. Luna now seemed as placid as she'd been pre-arrival of her litter. She'd had the odd moment being protective of the pups but on the whole she knew the place she'd found in Joy's life and heart. Joy hoped that everyone else who came her way did too.

They passed Freddie who was in the greenhouse sorting out tomato plants, the ruby red of the plump skins visible among the greenery even from outside. She loved it when they were picked fresh and their flesh still warm. The first bite was a reminder of why home-grown was so good. She waved over at him three times before he looked up, a deep frown on his face. What was going on with him? Perhaps she'd been neglecting his problems with all her focus on Cameron and Lauren, and now Libby. Maybe she'd talk with him later, see if his wife was making life more difficult than it needed to be. It seemed to Joy that ever since he'd got in touch with her, rather than his life getting easier, it had got that much harder and he'd clammed up, refusing to discuss anything.

After their walk Luna lapped up the water from her bowl outside the farmhouse and Joy refilled it as well as the puppies'. She answered a call from a lady who was interested in the puppies and went over to Cameron who was in the puppy pen playing tug of war with Taz and Ace, their little teeth tugging at the opposite end of the rope with all their might. 'We have someone coming to see the pups in ten minutes. Would you be able to talk to them for me?'

'I don't know,' he hesitated. 'Wouldn't it be better if you did it?'

Part of staying at the farmhouse was to help get him back to the big wide world out there, and that meant facing strangers. 'I'll be here the whole time. But if you could take the lead, tell them a bit about each puppy – not Bisto, tell them he's yours – and I'll leap in if there's anything you can't answer.'

He hesitated, but eventually shrugged and agreed to do it.

Joy did her best not to fuss over Cameron too much before the lady came over, she tried to act nonchalant as though she thought he'd find it easy, but really she was nervous he'd feel overwhelmed and panic. He didn't like company that wasn't familiar.

When the lady pulled up alongside the farmhouse, he went out to greet her and to Joy's absolute surprise, shook her hand. Round at the puppy pen the woman took an instant shine to Taz, the golden Labrador who was first to run to her when she arrived. Joy had thought she might end up buying two puppies when black Lab Shiloh caught her eye too and she was visibly torn, but she was certain she could only manage one pup at a time.

Not only did Cameron answer every single one of this woman's questions, he asked a few of his own. He wanted to know whether she'd had a dog before – she had, when she was little – he asked if she'd be at home with it during the day – she explained she ran yoga classes so wouldn't be out for more than a few hours at a time and that was only four times a week. He questioned whether she had outside space, other pets, children who would make the puppy a part of the family. He couldn't offer her much advice on training their new addition, but Joy jumped in to that part of the conversation even though she hadn't had Luna all that long. On the whole he did really well and she couldn't be more proud. Of course she'd had to tone down her enthusiasm, she didn't want to smother the kid when his shoulders looked an inch taller as he brimmed with confidence.

This was a good sign. A good indication he was settling in and perhaps he wouldn't run off again, especially now he had Bisto to look after.

*

'What time are you meeting Lauren?' Joy asked Libby after dinner. What she really wanted to ask was whether Libby had called her dad yet but she wasn't going to nag. Libby, relaxed in jeans and a T-shirt, her beautiful thick hair let loose and freshly washed, had come outside to fuss Taz knowing that in a couple of weeks she'd be going to her new home. But it was Shiloh who wanted the attention right now and Joy assured the little black Lab with the white paw, that it would be her turn to be chosen soon enough. And then she would have to say goodbye which wasn't something she relished. But life had to move on.

'In half an hour,' Libby replied, giggling when Shiloh and Taz tussled in the pen. 'You're sure you don't mind?'

'Don't be daft, someone your age should be out and about, not stuck at home with an old battle-axe like me.'

'Come on Auntie Joy,' laughed Libby, 'you're hardly that. You could come with us.'

She shook her head as she turned down the generous offer. She was quite happy here, always would be.

Drew turned up next and when he saw Cameron looking so content the look he shared with Joy suggested he'd also been wondering ever since last week, whether the boy would do another flit. Drew had a good heart, worried about anyone he saw going the same way he'd unfortunately gone once upon a time. And Joy didn't miss his interest in Libby, taking in her slender figure, the way her hair fell back off her face as she laughed. There was a strong attraction there and Joy didn't know quite how to handle it.

Lauren's sky-blue car pulled up at the back of the farmhouse a few minutes later and after a quick hello all round, Libby went off to grab her purse so they could go to the pub. Drew and Freddie, not to be outdone by the girls, asked if Joy minded them hogging the lounge and opening the whisky. She'd smiled and assured them it was fine. The whisky had been her gift to Freddie at Christmas, an expensive one and one to be savoured.

When Freddie went inside for a shower she grabbed Drew's attention, a hand on his arm. 'See if you can find out what's going on with him.' They were standing outside, the fresh breeze cooler now summer was preparing to come to a close. 'I don't know whether it's Ivanna bothering him or something else.'

'You're worried?'

'I am.' Everyone got in a bad mood now and then, but this had been going on a while. He wasn't as willing to help around the farm – last night he'd pretended not to hear her request to help get the chickens into their coop from the run, but she knew he'd heard. She didn't mind, he worked hard, but usually he enjoyed a bit of a talk at the end of the day and it seemed they hadn't done that in quite some time. A few days ago she'd had a mystery leak in the utility room next to the radiator and whereas usually he'd be getting out tools and doing what he could to find out what it was and maybe fix it, he'd hurried out to his vegetable patches saying he had a lot on and he'd sort it later. She'd ended up calling a plumber because she got the impression Freddie would never get around to it.

Drew rested a hand on her shoulder before he went inside. 'I'll see what I can do.'

She put her hand up to meet his and gave it a pat. It was ironic, for a woman who'd never been a mum she sure had plenty to contend with – teenage emotions, runaways, marital problems that she all took onto her own shoulders as though they belonged as much to her as the one really suffering. It seemed remarkably similar to parenthood from what she could tell.

The phone rang again inside and Cameron's face lit up. 'Might be another call about the puppies. Do you want me to get it?'

'I'll do it,' Joy smiled, 'but be ready in case I need the sales pitch again.'

She went inside to answer, expecting Cameron's prediction to be correct, but the warm feeling of having him settling in some more soon disappeared when she took the call. She took the phone outside and scuttled down the side of the farmhouse for privacy.

'What do you mean you no longer want the land?' she asked, her voice quiet but the disbelief evident. It was Mr Whittaker announcing that after eight years of a reliable two-way arrangement he was giving his month's notice to stop renting her land. First Mr McKerrick, now him. What on earth was going on? Was the rumour mill spreading that her land was unsuitable? Was it spreading something worse?

Deflated she agreed, 'Of course I'll accept this call as your giving notice, if you could back it up with an email please.' She closed her eyes and leaned against the cool stone of the place she called home. 'But if you change your mind, do let me know,' were her desperate parting words at the end of the call. But she'd tried that with Mr McKerrick.

And it hadn't worked then either.

Chapter Eight

Libby

Libby sat opposite Lauren in the cosy pub near the station in Bramleywood. It had the same bright purple blooms spilling from baskets either side of the porched front entrance that sat in big square flower beds dotted at intervals on the edges of the pavements of the main street. At the front was a low white chained fence and a patch of lawn, and set back from the road the pub had a beer garden that circled all the way around the outside. But tonight the girls had opted to sit inside away from the wasps that seemed intent on badgering anyone who opted for a summer's evening in the open air.

'Hello Samuel.' Lauren smiled at an older gentleman standing by the bar, a pint in hand, eyes dancing at something his friend had been telling him.

'Hello, young Lauren.' Libby supposed they were young in comparison to many people in here. She'd not been to an English country pub in a while but it was clear to see that the one in Bramleywood was a meeting place for locals who didn't have to come here in a group, but who could turn up and always find a friendly face and conversation. 'How are you keeping?'

'I'm very well thank you, staying busy.'

'The cupcakes you made were sensational,' he announced, 'best I've ever tasted.' He smiled to Libby and held out a hand. 'I don't think we've met, you're new here, but I have a suspicion you might be Libby. Joy has told me all about you.'

Lauren excused herself to go get a couple of drinks and Libby smiled. 'You're right, I'm Joy's niece. And I'm sure I've heard Joy mention you before . . . you're the local vet?'

'I most certainly am.' He nodded his head in acknowledgement. 'And how are you finding our beautiful village, Libby?' A lot of men, particularly his age, would have short back and sides or shorter if baldness was a problem, but Samuel still had grey hair that flopped on top in a way that suited him. He wore a smart checked shirt with jeans and had a smile that spoke of kindness.

'It's very quiet here compared to New York, except for Ronald.'

He laughed, setting his pint down on the bar in case it spilled. 'Yes, Ronald definitely has a voice. Luckily my little house is on past the station so I'm safe from his wake-up call. You'll get used to him.'

'I'm sure I will.' She saw Lauren had the drinks and was indicating with a nod the last remaining inside table they'd have to nab quickly. 'It was lovely to meet you.'

'How's Joy?' His voice stopped her and Lauren got to the table first.

Libby smiled. It wasn't her imagination was it, the quick grabbing of her to ask the question before she could get away and leave him wondering. 'She's good, busy as always, I'll tell her you asked after her.'

'Please do.' He gave a slight tilt of the head and Libby

felt sure his interest in Joy didn't have anything to do with Luna or the puppies.

Libby and Lauren talked about Cameron and the puppies and Bisto who was going to be staying at the farm for good. 'Joy told me Cameron has run off more than once,' said Libby. 'But she also told me you'd got him to come back more than once. He seems to listen to you.'

'And you, you seem to get on well with him.'

'I never had brothers, or sisters for that matter, but I like to think I treat him the way I would a little brother. He's lost, confused I think, but when he forgets to worry about the bigger picture he relaxes. We've had a few rounds of board games back at the farmhouse, it's been fun, especially in the evenings and I think it takes the strain from Joy because if he's occupied with me she can see him, hear him laugh and chat, rather than watching him head to his bedroom or worrying he might try to run again. She thinks nobody notices she's on guard the whole time.'

'She's good like that, she doesn't like to make us feel overwhelmed or claustrophobic, it's a tough balancing act.' She sipped from her glass of lemonade with extra lemon slices. 'I think maybe he's afraid of men. Or perhaps wary is more the word. I know his father in particular wasn't pleasant, although he hasn't shared much of that with any of us. He's fine with Joy, you, and me, and usually Freddie and Drew get on well with him, but when the chips are down, he runs from most of the male species.'

'I hope that doesn't mean he had to deal with being physically bullied before he came here. It doesn't bear thinking about.' Her home life had been a struggle but she'd always felt out of harm's way, she'd never felt threatened, kids never should. Even the times either of her parents got angry, with her, with each other, with a situation, it was all part of life and it had never gone so far as to make her want to run away from home the way Cameron had.

'Nobody really knows,' shrugged Lauren, 'and Joy doesn't really share our stories with anyone else. Usually we end up doing that between us, but only when we're ready. Maybe in time Cameron will realise that he can too. We're all a work in progress.'

'Hey, even I know that,' Libby smiled. It was warm inside the pub so Libby opened up the cream-painted window to try to get some air. 'We'll only open it a bit, shut it if wasps find us.' She sipped her beer, relief in the ice-cold amber liquid.

'Joy is an amazing woman you know.'

'I agree,' said Libby, smiling at Samuel when he lifted a hand to wave his goodbye to them. 'Someone else thinks so too.'

Lauren giggled. 'I had noticed. Did he ask after her?'

'Yes!'

'He did that when I saw him yesterday outside the post office. He's around her age,' she mused.

'Has she ever been out with anyone since you've known her?'

'No and it's a shame, she has so much love to give, I'd love nothing more than to see her get something for herself. But you know Joy, she insists we and the farmhouse are all she needs.' She rolled her eyes and Libby knew they all heard the protest regularly, she'd heard it a few times since she arrived, Joy's certainty that she wanted for nothing.

'She hasn't shared your story much either,' Lauren smiled in a way that suggested she wanted to know more.

'I mean we all knew she had this niece who lived in New York but she never told us anything else. Is she your mum's sister or your dad's?'

'My mum's. Or at least she was. Mum died a while ago.'

'I'm sorry.'

'What about your parents?'

'They're still alive, I think. But not in my life . . . thank god.' She said it matter-of-factly, she'd clearly put that part of her life behind her. 'My brothers are and that's all that matters.'

Libby looked up when the door opened. She had wondered whether Drew and Freddie might make their way down here. She'd heard them talking about sharing a whisky but maybe they meant at home. It wasn't Drew, it wasn't Freddie, it was the lady who'd served her at the bakery and she nodded a hello. She hadn't had a regular drinking or eating spot in Manhattan, there was so much to choose from you could've gone somewhere different every night, but with no restaurant in Bramleywood this was it. And Libby didn't think that was a bad thing at all.

'Anyway, this isn't about me,' said Lauren, flipping the conversation back again, 'I want to know more about Joy's life.'

Libby shrugged. 'I'm afraid you can probably cast more of a light on that than I can. I'd only ever met her twice – at least I think it was twice – I was very young. And then I kept in touch by letter.'

'Why did you never see her?'

'My parents banned her from the house.'

'No way!'

'Yes way.' Libby had missed having another girl to gossip with. 'Please don't mention anything to her, I don't want her upset. I'm only telling you because I can see how much you – all of you – care about her.'

'I won't say a thing, I promise.'

'The letter-writing was done in secret after I found her address.'

Lauren's eyes widened and she tore open the bag of peanuts so they could share them. 'Why would anyone ever ban Joy from their home?' She popped a peanut into her mouth. 'She's one of the most generous, giving people I've ever met.'

'I'm beginning to see that. I mean, I kind of got to know it through our letters, but there's still plenty of questions I have and that I don't feel I can ask. She hasn't mentioned anything about her time before she came to Bramleywood?' Libby took a handful of peanuts.

'No, not a word. Can't you ask your dad more about her, if they banned her from your house then he knows something.'

Libby smiled. She'd got away without many questions about her family from friends in New York. Over there she'd kind of been one step removed and when it came up she quickly extinguished the questioning by moving on to something else. But here it was different. Being around Joy and all these people who'd had troubles ten times worse, she assumed, than she'd ever faced, it made her more open. Or perhaps it was being back in England that did it, she was closer to her past now. 'My dad and I speak regularly, but we're not close. Since Mum died, things changed between us, we became unsure of each other.'

'Perhaps he didn't know how to deal with his grief and yours at the same time.'

It sounded simple that way. But as a parent, wasn't he supposed to find a way? 'He doesn't even know I'm here in England. And he would totally freak if he knew I was at Auntie Joy's. I'll tell him, eventually, but right now I'm having too much of a good time.'

'Don't feel guilty.' Lauren picked up on the vibe quickly and she was spot on. Libby was having a good time. She loved Joy, they were growing closer, the farmhouse was a warming place to be.

Libby felt relaxed and open enough to ask more about Lauren's home life and her husband. And Lauren let her guard down enough to tell her how she'd met Jonathan. She'd been drunk and fallen into a taxi one evening after an early departure from a nightclub, muttered her address to the driver who ferried her home.

'He waited until I was inside the farmhouse, he didn't pull off the driveway until Joy waved over her thanks,' Lauren explained. 'I was too drunk to even notice I hadn't paid him. Apparently I'd told him I'd spent all my money, had no cash left, and he should come round in the morning for the fare.'

'That's embarrassing, but amusing.'

'I paid up when he stopped by, Joy was laughing at me, and she says now that she could tell he wouldn't have done the same for anyone else. She says she'd seen it in his eyes the night before, that he was falling for me almost as hard as I'd fallen in the front door.' She smiled at the memory. 'Jonathan asked me out before I'd even handed over any money, and he wouldn't take the fare either, what he wanted was a date instead. I said yes of course but I didn't expect to fall in love so quickly. He took me to his own local pub about ten miles from here, we saw each other the next night and the one after that too, and I don't think we've had much more than the odd night apart since.'

'Now that's a love story,' Libby smiled. 'Must be hard with him doing so much shift work.'

'It's a bit of a challenge.'

Libby could tell there was more to it than that, especially when, to avoid the question, Lauren went to the bar to get more drinks and some crisps. She'd not eaten many of the peanuts as it was and she still had a lot of lemonade left.

'You can talk to me you know,' she told Lauren when she sat down again.

'About what?' Her attempted composure failed miserably. 'We're trying for a baby.'

'You and your husband?'

'No, me and the post man,' she grinned.

'Sorry, stupid thing to say. What I mean is, that's a good thing, surely?'

Lauren shrugged. 'I suppose, but I have a business, I'm not sure I have time to start a family.'

'Plenty of people do it. I admire them, I'm not sure how sometimes. My friend Abigail is due before the end of the year and she's giving up work for a minimum of five years she says. But she's only putting her career on hold, once she's had her family, she'll get back to it. I admire her grit let me tell you.'

'You see, I'm not sure I have it, the strength to do it, the exhaustion for years on end, the worry. I've been avoiding home,' she admitted sheepishly. 'Jonathan doesn't deserve me.'

'Hey, don't be too hard on yourself.'

'I worry I'll lose the business I've worked so hard for. Crazy isn't it?'

'Fears aren't crazy,' said Libby.

'It's already a lot to manage myself. I don't cope well with paperwork. I'm in a total muddle with it – receipts, order forms, even labelling. I have boxes of papers and couldn't tell you what's in each, business is doing well and I've managed with word of mouth, but I need to advertise and I don't have a clue how to do it other than Jonathan keeping a set of business cards in the taxi and handing them out to anyone he can,' she bumbled on. 'I don't have a website, my Facebook page and Instagram accounts take up a lot of time. And then there's the cleaning – oh the cleaning, Libby.' She put her head in her hands. 'It's not just home cleaning, I have standards I have to adhere to, running the business from my home, imagine what would happen if I had a baby, or babies, I could never keep on top of it.'

Libby put her hand on Lauren's and pulled them away from her face. 'First of all, breathe.' She could see Lauren fighting back tears and having never looked after children herself or been privy to kids' demands, Libby could fully understand why Lauren was freaking out at the responsibility of it all.

Lauren took a deep breath in and then let it out. 'I don't know what to do any more.'

'Does Jonathan know how you feel? You say you're avoiding home, but have you talked to him about why?'

She shook her head. 'I've been making excuses, that I've been helping with Cameron or cooking for Joy because she's strung out. And all along I've been taking the pill and pretending us trying for a baby isn't happening.

What kind of person does that?' Tears pooled in her eyes.

'A person who isn't sure of what to do. And you're not a bad person, just someone who's confused right now.'

'We both always wanted to have children. I really saw it happening at the start, but then when we talked about actually trying, it became real. I'm afraid that if I stop working I'll never start again. I never want to be in that position. It's how I ended up in so much trouble I needed Joy.'

'Tell me how you and Joy met.'

Lauren pulled a tissue from the pocket of her denim skirt and dried her eyes, dabbing the corners so it didn't upset her mascara. 'I had a job at a supermarket out of town but it was only temporary and when the work dried up, Joy found me sitting on the wall outside, sobbing. I'm a crier,' she laughed making Libby grin too. 'She asked what was wrong, I said I'd lost my job, she took me for a cup of tea at a café and she offered me some work at the farmhouse. She said she needed a cleaner because her last one had left.'

'I never knew she had a cleaner, I thought she did it all herself which is why I offered. It's a big place, too big for her to do all on her own.'

'She's never had a cleaner. It was a fib to get me there, but it worked. I mean the farmhouse is huge. She didn't know then that I was living in a dodgy bedsit and only just making the rent. She gave me plenty of hours' work, paid me generously and I worked hard. She was nice to be around and despite not loving cleaning as such, I enjoyed the company. We'd end up talking for an hour or more at a time after my shift, she'd ply me with biscuits and tea, I think she enjoyed the company as much as I did.

And then one day when we were enjoying some chocolate cake from the bakery, I let on that I loved to bake but my kitchenette at the bedsit only consisted of a mini oven with two hotplates on top. She offered for me to bake at the farmhouse, then the baking invite became an invite to stay for dinner, which led to the offer of a room. And the rest is history.'

'From what I know about Joy and how people have come to her over the years, that sounds about right. And she thrives on company.'

'That she does . . . it's an open house, and a busy dinner table is her idea of heaven.'

'I can't imagine her ever having the farmhouse or the land to herself. Even from her letters I could always tell how much she loved to be around people.' Although Libby had a sneaking suspicion there was a bit more to it than that. Because Joy seemed almost uncomfortable when she didn't have much to do, or the place was a little quieter. More than once Libby had seen her with a far-off look in her eyes as though she had something weighing her down. She seemed somehow afraid of being on her own. 'You must've loved your time with Joy,' she said. 'But can I ask why you left home in the first place? Is that way too nosey?'

'I don't mind you asking. My home life wasn't a happy one. My parents fought all the time, always in front of us kids. My dad was actually my stepdad, he was with Mum since I turned twelve. I never really liked him, didn't get on with him, and the teenage years were miserable. He was handy with his fists too, drank a lot, and one day he turned on me. I think I'd left the gas cooker on and he went ballistic. Mum wasn't much help, she told me I had done something stupid so what did I expect.' Libby's jaw dropped in disbelief. 'It was then I realised she thought more of that arsehole than she did her own kids. I stayed, I put up with it, I couldn't bear the thought of leaving my brothers to put up with it all, but one night he hit me so hard I was petrified I'd end up in the hospital if he kept going the way he was. I seemed to set him off with every little thing I did.' At Libby's shocked expression she added, 'He said it was a mistake. He didn't try anything again so perhaps it was, but night after night I was petrified he'd come in, I'd barricade my door, and then in the end I couldn't take it any more. My friends were all getting jobs or going to college, I was lost. All I really knew was that I had to leave. And so I did.'

'Makes my problems seem trivial,' Libby admitted.

'No it doesn't, and it's all in the past now anyway, although part of my parenting doubts stem from those days, knowing what can and does go wrong.' Her eyes filled with tears again. 'How can I bring a child into a world that lets crap like that happen?'

'Crap like that doesn't just happen, sometimes people make it happen.' Libby wasn't sure her reassurance was working. 'Accidents happen, terrible things sometimes, and all you can do is your best.'

'I know,' Lauren sniffed. 'Logic tells me you're right.'

'What about your real dad? Is he around?'

'I've no idea what happened to him. He upped and left one day, who knows why, but given my mum's apparent disregard for shitty parenting, you never know whether she drove him away. I've put that all behind me.'

'Sorry, and here I am bringing it all up again.'

'No, don't apologise, it's good to talk about it now and then. Joy tries to get me to as well, I think she worries that bottling it all up is worse. I've not told her about trying for a baby though.'

'I won't say a word.'

'Thanks, I'm not sure I can handle any questions or going over it when I'm not prepared. You're new, a fresh face, easier to tell my problems to I'm afraid.'

'I don't mind at all.'

'Enough for tonight though, yeah?'

'Of course,' Libby smiled. 'Let's get back to your paper-work troubles.'

Lauren managed a laugh. 'That's a much better topic. Any advice you can give me in that regard would be welcome right now. I don't know where to start. Every time I think about it I end up baking instead.'

'I love figures, spreadsheets.' Lauren was pulling a face. 'Hey, each to their own.'

'I suppose so. But no need to gloat,' she batted back. 'It's so not my thing.'

'Then let me help you.'

'Really? You'd do that? I had thought about getting an assistant, but my finances wouldn't stretch to it I'm afraid.'

'I don't need paying.'

'I couldn't ask you to work unpaid.'

'You could. And you'd be doing me a favour. I'm helping out around the farmhouse but that only takes up so much time. I'll bet once I get my hands on the paperwork it won't be long before I get it into some kind of order. Do you have an accountant?' Lauren's look told her she didn't. 'Who files your tax returns at the end of the financial year?'

'Me usually . . . at the last minute, and just hope I get it all right.'

'I'll get everything in order for you, I'm already looking forward to it.'

Lauren began to chuckle. 'We have very different ideas of what constitutes fun, it seems.'

Libby could see why Joy was so addicted to helping people, immersing herself in their stories, feeling the pleasure of taking the pressure off someone just a little bit but enough that they could make changes. She'd been too busy to do it before aside from the odd time she'd had friends confide in her about problems that were, now she thought about it, easy enough to solve with time and patience. Lauren on the other hand seemed to have got herself in a bit of a tangle and Libby hoped helping her with her business paperwork would help her sort the muddle in her mind some way. Even if it didn't, it could help her to feel a bit better and know it was time to talk to her husband properly, share her fears. That was what relationships were about after all, and it was another reminder that she and Brandon weren't quite right for one another, because while he'd always helped her get her head around work problems, she'd never quite found the right time to tell him how she felt about the loss of her mother and the way she and her dad had drifted apart. He knew the basics, but he didn't know how much it still weighed on her.

'What do you say?' Libby asked now, eager to help. 'I'm not bad with a computer. I think I can find my way around and set up a basic website if you like – although nothing fancy you understand.'

'I'd have to pay you for that surely.'

'I'll tell you what . . . you cover the costs of the domain name and the package I end up using, and I'll donate my time.' She lifted her beer bottle and clinked it against Lauren's glass. 'Helping a friend is fine by me.'

'A friend,' Lauren replied. 'I'm glad you came to Bramleywood.'

'That makes two of us.'

And when they left arm in arm to stroll back to the farmhouse, chattering away, the only thing Libby didn't like about the village was the way the man Lauren had already explained was Rick, looked at her across the bar. His beady eyes surfed the top of his pint glass in a way that left her really uncomfortable.

Samuel might be the sort of man she'd stop and talk to in the street, some people were like that from the word go, but this man Rick was someone Libby suspected it was best to avoid.

The next morning, still fuzzy-headed from the pub, Libby came downstairs. She picked up the envelope that had come through the door. 'There's a letter for you, Joy,' she called out as she straightened the sunflower painting on the wall in the hallway that didn't want to hang straight, and went through to the kitchen, where the back door was open and held that way with the hedgehog door stop Libby had sent Joy last Christmas. She looked out of the window but couldn't see her auntie, and so left the letter on the table. It was hand-delivered, way too early for the post. She wondered whether it was from Samuel, perhaps a love letter, and chuckled at herself for her imagination running riot in this country setting.

Libby made a much-needed coffee and set it on the

table along with a bowl of mixed fruit. She was getting used to having breakfast after so many years of relying on caffeine to get her through the commute and office arrival. More often or not she'd grabbed a muffin at morning coffee time she was so hungry. Now, she kind of liked the habit, and her stomach certainly appreciated it.

Joy came in moments later and asked whether Libby had managed at last to sleep through Ronald's morning ritual.

'I stirred when I heard him,' she answered, popping a firm but juicy raspberry into her mouth, but I think finally I'm getting used to the sound. I might go tell him later, really annoy him.'

Joy laughed as she emptied the wicker basket of produce, loading up the vegetable rack with a couple of varieties of potatoes, a whole heap of carrots and some beetroot she was talking about roasting or pickling, she wasn't sure.

'Samuel was in the pub last night.' Libby tested Joy's reaction while she popped a blackberry into her mouth. 'He said to say hello.'

'He's my vet . . . or at least he's Luna's,' she said, as if that was the only explanation that was needed. 'Why are you looking at me like that?'

'No reason, just wondering whether he asks about all his clients.'

Joy laughed and dismissed the notion of anything untoward with a wave of her hand. 'He's being kind, that's all.'

Libby suspected it was more than that. She put her bowl into the sink. 'There's a letter on the table for you,' she prompted.

'Bit early for the post.' Joy washed her hands and briefly glanced at the awaiting envelope.

'I think it's hand-delivered.'

'I don't recognise the writing.' She dried her hands and picked up the letter.

'If you don't need me, I'm going up for a shower and then I'll head over to Lauren's place.'

'You two really did hit it off last night. I'm pleased.'

'Me too. But today, it's not social, it's business. She admitted she's in a complete mess with her paperwork.' She wiggled her fingers in the air as though itching to get her hands on it and organise her friend. 'I'll have her sorted in no time.'

Joy put an arm around Libby and kissed her forehead. 'You're a fine woman, Libby, having you here is a blessing. And I've been worried something was bothering Lauren, I'm just glad it's only paperwork.' She tore open her letter.

Libby, surprised at the gesture and the compliment could only smile. Her mum had always told her how proud she was of her daughter, her dad still did in their somewhat stilted conversations, but hearing it from Auntie Joy made her feel like she was still a part of a family even though some of the relationships had splintered apart. Knowing Lauren's problems went a lot deeper than Joy knew she said, 'I'm only too happy to help her and we had a lovely time last night. I liked the pub, very quaint,' she prompted when a peculiar look passed over her auntie's face. 'I said I loved the pub, Auntie Joy.' She gave her a nudge and wondered what was in the letter.

'Sorry . . . yes, it's lovely isn't it? Did you sit outside?'

'Too many wasps,' Libby laughed. 'We sat inside which was nice, we had a corner to ourselves. It was good to meet Samuel but there was another man called Rick there who I didn't like very much at all. Lauren says he lives in the really big house behind the gates,' she rambled on. But Joy didn't appear to be listening again and so she gave up for now. 'I'll see you later.'

At least whatever had distracted Joy had stopped her from asking Libby, yet again, whether she'd told her dad she was here yet.

Libby knew she had to do it soon though. She couldn't run from her problems forever and maybe they had to stop here, at the home that had given plenty of people a second chance. Perhaps she wasn't any different from anyone else who came through these doors.

Chapter Nine

Joy

I t was still summer, but with the weather cooler today you couldn't deny autumn was just round the corner. Soon the nights would be cooler, the mornings dark until a little later, and they would no longer need to have the windows open round the clock. Things at the farmhouse were carrying on as usual, but Joy knew there was more of a change to come than the mere flip of a season.

She didn't need to read the wretched letter again that had arrived hand-delivered to her home to know what it said, because she could pretty much recite it verbatim, every word and every syllable a needle of pain she couldn't get away from. 'I know your guilty secret,' it said at the start before it went on to talk about the 'price of silence', 'what happened in Dorset', and that 'secrets had a way of getting out'. Whoever the author was knew what The Old Dairy meant to her too because they talked about the life she'd built, the home she now had, and how it could crumble around her if she let it. The writer of the letter had placed the onus on her to do the right thing so her secrets weren't exposed to hurt anyone else. That was the most horrific part of all of this – Joy's pain was one thing but causing it to anyone she cared for was unimaginable.

Standing at the kitchen window she watched Luna's litter, their compact forms growing by the day, tumbling across one another, their mum doing her best to keep order. Libby's advert had worked a treat – Joy finally had a home for each puppy and it was almost time to say goodbye. Dogs had such a carefree life, or at least Luna and the puppies did because they were all loved and treated well and Joy hoped they'd found owners who would continue to do the same. Each of the new owners had been pleased their money would go to a good cause and a couple of them had even added a bit more to the total in the hope that it would help the animal rescue centre. But she supposed there were no guarantees in life for anyone, canine or human. There certainly hadn't been for her, and with the arrival of that letter that was now hidden away in the back of an already-read Agatha Christie book on the shelf in her bedroom, her world had once again become a raging mess. The day she opened it, it had sent her off into the nearly fifty acres of land well away from the farmhouse and Libby, far from the perimeter of the land where she could be spotted, away from Freddie working hard as always, and she'd screamed at the top of her voice. She'd wailed a sound she'd heard often between the walls of a place she never wanted to go near again. She sank down onto her knees and sobbed. It was as though she was that same girl, twenty-five years ago, only a small box of things to her name and no place to go, nobody to help her, her life whittled down to nothing. The same girl who had once thought, almost four decades ago, that she'd met the love of her life. Until everything changed forever.

'Joy,' came a voice again and she realised Cameron must have been trying to get her attention for a while as she disappeared into her memories. He was at the back door, his purple cap pulled firmly down to protect him from the summer sun and he was asking her something.

'I'm sorry, I was in a world of my own,' she smiled.

'I was asking if I could take Bisto for a walk in the village.'

She pulled herself together. She had people who needed her. Without them she'd probably still be crouched in one of the fields beyond, balling her eyes out. 'That sounds like a terrific idea. He'll need to get used to having a lead on as well as the sight and sounds of traffic.'

'I feel a bit bad not taking the others, it doesn't seem fair.'

'They'll all get their turn soon enough with their new owners. Or we could rotate them. Start with Bisto and then give each a turn after that. Doesn't have to all be today.' He was hesitating and she knew why but she didn't want to seem as though she was babying him. 'Would you like me to come with you? I've done a bit of reading up about puppies and Samuel shared some stories. He told me when he first had a puppy it had hated the road and it had taken forever to make him move, as though the poor puppy's feet were stuck in cement on the pavement.'

'I think Bisto is confident. He'll have the opposite problem like he's got a rocket up his—'

Joy gave him a stern look. 'He's a live wire, but let's see how they go. Now, let me get a lead – actually I have a few so I'll get two and we'll take Baxter. The company might make it easier for each of them, a bit of familiarity down at their level if you like. You get the bags in case we need to pick up after them.'

Once they had the two puppies on their leads and

everything they needed, they set off from the farmhouse, Joy more than happy to do this if only to get away from the thoughts that came to her when she had too much time and space to think. Luna didn't seem put out that she wasn't going either. She'd had a good roam around first thing and was happily snoozing near the patch of daisies at the opposite side of the farmhouse, her favourite spot.

Baxter was the more confident of the two puppies and Joy had to stop him pulling her all the way into the village, he didn't seem at all wary of traffic, even when a tractor rumbled on past, and as for any sitting or coming to heal, both puppies were a long way off that command having an effect. Cameron spent a lot of the time laughing, especially when Bisto was so hesitant to cross the road like his brother that he ended up scooping him into his arms and carrying him across.

'Maybe try the next road, Bisto,' Cameron encouraged with a sigh.

They got plenty of admiring looks from people in the village, milling and going about their everyday business, Bisto and Baxter both a novelty. It meant the walk was a slow one with the puppies enjoying every second. They were asked the names, age of the pups, whether there were any left for sale. And it brightened Joy's day no end to be out in the sunshine, at least it did until she saw Rick coming towards them. She wasn't in the mood for him making disparaging remarks or in fact talking to her at all. But again, Cameron had trouble getting Bisto to move and brave crossing the road. And now the pup didn't want to extricate himself from the two young girls who'd come up to make a fuss of him, one of whom was Dahlia from the village shop who clearly liked Cameron judging by the way she was hanging off his every word and twiddling her long hair around her fingers as he spoke solely to her while her friend crouched to give Bisto all the attention.

Joy wasn't about to hang around. She crossed the road, she'd wait for Cameron outside the estate agent's instead. She pretended to be engrossed in looking at the listings in the window and hoped Rick wouldn't come and bother her.

Eventually Cameron joined her with Bisto in his arms. 'I don't like the look of that one,' he quipped, looking at the advert of one particular property she was standing in front of. He set Bisto down on the pavement. 'I don't think you'd fit us all in your kitchen if you lived there.'

Joy had been staring at the listing for a two-bedroomed cottage to avoid Rick, but she'd actually begun to study the details because in reality, she might have to start looking for somewhere else to live, and soon. 'Dahlia likes you.'

He shrugged. 'She's nice to me, when we go into the store.'

'She's your age too.'

'No matchmaking,' he warned, but Joy picked up on the note of happiness in his voice.

'OK, I promise.' She guessed it was one thing to help him get back on the right track, but she shouldn't interfere with his love life.

It seemed Cameron was still thinking about the unpleasant experience of having anything to do with Rick. 'It was nice to see Dahlia but I really don't like that man,' he told her, on his haunches, tickling behind Bisto's ear.

'He didn't bother you did he?'

'No, but he was being nice in that smarmy kind of way, you know the way people are when they want something. I thought maybe he was after a puppy he was asking so many questions.'

'What sort of questions?'

'You know, the usual. How many puppies there were, how many we'd sold – he even wanted to know how much they were going for. He lost interest when I said the money was going to charity.'

'Cheeky beggar.' She didn't want any of her puppies going to Rick, she wasn't sure he had the heart to treat them right at all. She shot a look across the road but he'd already gone. It seemed she wasn't the only one who didn't like him – Cameron clearly didn't, Libby hadn't appreciated him gawping at her in the pub the other night. He'd never approved of the halfway house, always said it gave Bramleywood a bad name having layabouts hanging around. Joy had taken particular exception to his description of people who'd come to mean a lot to her.

When Joy had first taken in Drew, they'd bumped into Rick outside the station. He'd just come in from London, briefcase in hand, dressed to the nines in a suit and when he saw Drew at her side he did that thing where the eyes travel from head to toe and back up again, sizing up a newcomer to the village. Ever since Joy let him know that the farm was going to be hers, he'd had his nose put out of joint not being able to get his hands on the land to develop it for housing. Plenty of villagers had thanked her for not selling up and they'd all stuck together in the same way when he'd tried to get rid of the library. Folk around here liked Bramleywood just how it was, she didn't know how he could be so blinkered he couldn't see it, although there was a rumour his son who hadn't been seen in years had gone off the rails and despite Rick's attempts to get him back in line to find a reputable job and live up to the family name, his son hadn't wanted to know. Nobody really knew many of the details and Joy certainly wasn't ever going to ask him.

Cameron did his best to try issuing the sit command for Bisto, simultaneously tapping Bisto's bottom to encourage him. Joy burst out laughing. 'He'll get there, don't worry.'

'It's good to see these little guys out and about.' A man's voice came from behind and Joy didn't mind one bit that it was Samuel.

She watched Samuel making a fuss over the puppies, each of them wagging their tails, snuffling against his shirt sleeves and Baxter doing his best to knock the carton of milk out of his hands.

'Watch out, they'll have it out of your hands and spill it if you're not careful,' Joy laughed when Bisto put a paw onto the carton and almost did just that.

Samuel stood up and adjusted his wire-framed glasses as Cameron told him they were keeping Bisto. 'You'll enjoy every minute – busy time with a puppy but a lot of fun. Watch out for your shoes and slippers and never leave food uncovered on the table or you'll never see it again.'

'You sound as though you're talking from experience,' said Joy, a hand shielding her eyes from the sun, a firm hand holding Baxter's lead as he jumped up against the vet's legs and Cameron did his best to get him to stop by issuing the command 'down'.

'My dog Buddy might be old now but there was a time he'd chew my slippers or jump up to get my food from my plate. He's been good company over the years.' He held up his carton of milk. 'I'd better head back to the surgery, this is my quick lunch break and a necessary trip to get an essential ingredient for my tea. Good to see you.'

'You too.' Joy smiled after him and then said to Cameron, 'I think these pups have had enough for a first walk, don't you?' She encouraged Baxter with a gentle pull on the lead as they started walking home to the farmhouse.

When she heard a snigger as they walked away she turned to her companion. 'What's so funny?'

'Nothing,' Cameron replied. 'I just didn't know old people flirted, that's all.'

She looked back in Samuel's direction. 'Don't be ridiculous, he's being kind because we're clients of his.'

Cameron's raised eyebrows were accompanied by another laugh and he got a good nudge from Joy. 'And we're not *old people* thank you. Just people will do fine for a description if you need one.' It was ridiculous too to think that someone like Samuel was at all interested in her. What a crazy thing to say, although part of her lit up at the thought, at the feeling she was thirty or forty years younger until she thought about the contents of that letter and wondered if her world was about to fall apart.

'Fine by me,' he grinned, crouching down to fuss Bisto, his hand stroking the floppy ears, the pup's eyes gazing up at him like he was the only person that mattered any more. 'Let's see if you can make it across at least one road on your own.'

Cameron wasn't yet done with puppy walks, and took Shiloh out next, but only across the fields to get her used to having a lead on. He took Buttercup after that and passed Freddie coming Joy's way as Joy made herself a strong cup of tea.

'Tea?' she asked Freddie, having to repeat herself three times. The frown etched into his forehead was so deep it would leave a permanent mark if he wasn't careful. 'What is going on with you?' Drew had apparently got nowhere the other night when he quizzed him, and according to Freddie everything with Ivanna was going as well as could be expected. She pulled out a chair and pointed to it after he refused the offer of tea. 'I think it's time you and I talked.'

'About what?' He was jittery, most unlike him, and looked frightened, almost reminding her of the shell of a man he'd been when she first took him in. She hated to think of how he was going to react when she told him, or anyone else for that matter, that her days at the farmhouse might well be coming to an end sooner rather than later.

'Talk to me, Freddie. You might find it helps.' Not that she was telling anyone about her problems.

He slumped into the chair and she thought he was going to refuse before he blurted out, 'Everything is such a mess.'

'What is? The business? Your head?'

He wouldn't look at her. Instead, his still mud-stained fingers were raking through that beautiful blond hair of his. Perhaps getting to specifics would help. When Drew had first come here this was all new to her. She'd had to learn how to talk to someone who needed her, not pushing too much, asking just enough to encourage and then being able to read the signs to back off as necessary. She'd done it by reading up on helping kids with mental illness, by reading parenting books occasionally, and by casting her mind back to how Ted and Marjory had helped her, what they'd said and done, how she'd reacted, when she'd flipped out.

It was time to try to do the same with Freddie and ask for but not demand answers. 'Have you heard from Ivanna again?'

'We've been talking regularly.'

Maybe she wasn't the problem then. 'That's good. It's a start.'

'She says she's spoken to Timothy about me as well. He'd like to see me.'

Joy threw her arms around him. Sod reading the signs, this was amazing news. And although he tensed for a moment, he soon relented and let himself enjoy the feeling of reassurance that no matter how bad things got, he could find a way back up again. 'How do you feel?'

'Thrilled, scared, ecstatic, terrified,' he said but managed a broad smile. 'I'm a bit all over the place to tell you the truth.'

Freddie hadn't had the tenacity to battle for custody when Ivanna asked for a divorce. He'd given up by that point and let the misery seep in, he truly had believed that Timothy was better off without him. Joy had high hopes now Ivanna was back in touch that somehow he could get back to being the dad he deserved to be. 'Believe in yourself, he'll love you I bet.' And for all the crap being thrown in her face right now, this was a positive she couldn't ignore. 'It's what you've wanted for a long while, I knew it would happen. So smile, please, Freddie. No more mooching around the place.'

That had him laughing, but there was still trepidation in his eyes. And when Drew's car pulled up outside,

Freddie shut down once more, heading out again, claiming he needed to plant baby carrots in the greenhouse to get a late harvest.

'What's eating him?' Drew had called to Freddie but got a wave and no banter in return. 'He didn't say much the other night but I at least thought he was cheering up.'

'Ivanna and Timothy are weighing heavy on his mind, that's all.'

Drew accepted the offer of a cup of tea but insisted he made it himself. 'He mentioned them when we were talking over whisky, I'm glad he's going to get a chance to be in their lives again.'

At least Drew brought a positive attitude with him, something he'd fought to find for a long time. It was a good reminder that sometimes Joy's time and investment in anyone who came here could be measured in their happiness when they left and were independent once again. It was an easy thing to forget if she let herself. When he smiled, he was so handsome, his mouth bracketed by creases rather like dimples but not quite. The poisonous letter she'd received at the forefront of her mind, she knew if Drew found out the truth about her, he wouldn't be sitting here like this ever again. And to avoid hurting him and herself all over again, she had to do what the letter asked. She had to save herself from losing everyone in her life who mattered to her. But quite how she was going to share the news with Drew, with Freddie, Cameron, Lauren, Libby, she had no idea.

'It sounds as though what Ivanna wanted was to know Freddie wasn't going to run again,' Drew went on as he stirred milk into his tea and put the carton back in the fridge. 'I get she's worried, especially when there's a kid involved, but he's surely proved himself by now with the thriving fruit and vegetable business, the fact he has orders left, right and centre. He's well and truly stable I'd say. Maybe he's worrying in case she does a U-turn and changes her mind.'

'I wonder if part of the trouble is that he might want Ivanna back as well as Timothy.' Joy frowned. 'Perhaps he doesn't know where he stands.'

'He wants them both in his life, but that's different to wanting her back and to be in a relationship again,' said Drew. 'No wonder he's confused.'

More than eight years apart changed people, no matter how together Freddie was now, it surely wouldn't simply be a matter of him slotting in again. It might work some way with Timothy, but with Ivanna?

Drew leaned back in the chair opposite Joy. 'I've never been married, but it's a commitment perhaps both of them think they didn't honour. Or, on the other hand, it may have been too long and given they're divorced, perhaps there's no going back on that score.' He shook his head. 'Since when did life get so complicated?'

Joy knew exactly what he meant and when he rambled on more about Freddie and how hard he'd worked to prove himself, realisation that selling up to find the sort of money the author of that letter wanted to keep their mouth shut about Joy and her personal history, wasn't going to affect only her. Freddie was going to lose his business. And that meant no matter the protests to Ivanna, she might see it as his failure rather than something brought about by circumstances beyond his control.

Her mouth went dry, her palms sweaty, and all her limbs seemed to stiffen at once.

Drew didn't miss the change in the atmosphere and reached out to touch her arm. 'You look strung out.'

'I'm fine.'

'No, you're not. Why don't you have a lie down, everything else can wait.'

She was going to protest, but her head and her body said differently, because sitting here, trying to pretend to be upbeat, that nothing was going on, was suddenly getting too much. She could feel her pulse quickening, her blood pressure rising, and she only had so much strength to hold it together. The past was resurfacing, memories spiralling out of control, and only she could put a stop to the damage that letter threatened to do.

Drew encouraged her up from the table, out of the room. 'I'll take over getting the dinner ready and you lie down.'

'Don't be daft.'

'I've seen the lamb on the side,' he said as they took the stairs, 'it's seasoned and ready to go in. I think I can take charge of some vegetables and potatoes.'

It had been a long while since she'd let herself be fussed over or relied on other people to take the strain. She hated feeling weak and useless. She was only glad Cameron was too engrossed in whatever was on his headphones to notice them walk past his bedroom or she might have him worried too.

'I'll be down soon,' she assured Drew as she sat on the edge of the bed and reluctantly lay back.

'No rush.' He pulled the curtains for her, blocking out some of the daylight. 'Dinner in a couple of hours gives me plenty of time.'

She sat up. 'There's plenty of vegetables in—'

But he cut her off, indicated for her to lie down, and shut the door with a gentle click behind him.

She waited until she could no longer hear his retreating footsteps. And then she got up and opened the curtains. She never closed them, it made her feel too trapped, a part of her past she didn't want to relive. She had the window open most months of the year unless the weather really prevented it with high winds that might take it off its hinges, and even then she'd lock the latch so there was a small gap to filter in the outside and the sense of freedom that came with it.

Back in bed it wasn't long before her gaze across the fields began to fade, her eyelids fluttered shut, and she succumbed to sleep. A sleep that would remind her of everything she'd once thought would make her happy.

Joy and Tay, Tay and Joy, whatever way you said it it sounded pretty good to Joy.

Gregory Taylor was addictive, a bit like having something you knew you shouldn't touch but you couldn't help it. Tay became like an itch you shouldn't scratch but you couldn't stop yourself, you knew it was wrong but that made it so right. And he adored her from the very beginning. She'd never had that from a man and from the moment they met he was the only person in Joy's world and she was the only person in his. Their togetherness gave her a feeling like no other.

Joy hadn't told many people about Tay. He was hers to enjoy, her secret to keep. Tay lived life to the full, to hell with the rules half the time, it was an existence Joy had never experienced in a home where their parents had strict expectations when it came to behaviour, tidiness, what was acceptable and what wasn't. Joy knew that was what parenting was, but they'd taken it to the extreme and she and Maggie had always felt they missed out on the fun their friends seemed to have. Maggie had been more accepting of their ways than Joy, but then again Maggie had escaped and got married already and given them what they wanted to present to the outside world – a daughter who'd got a degree, a good job, and settled down. Joy had joked once that she was joining a circus to work with the animals and it hadn't gone down well. The way they'd looked at her wasn't with the belief and approval of a parent who thought they could take on the world, it was a disapproval she never wanted anyone else to have to feel. It had made her feel worthless, not good enough. But then again, they'd always made her feel that way without even trying.

Joy's days with Tay were filled with fun, happiness, a blessing to her self-worth. She wasn't so young she had to account for her every move with her parents, and so they went on day trips together, he took her on the back of a friend's motorbike, they went skinny dipping in a lake, they hitch-hiked to get to the beach. Maggie had a feeling Tay would do whatever she asked and it felt good to have someone like that on her side, someone who didn't pigeonhole her into being this person she was supposed to be. Tay, having travelled around Australia, floated from cheap hotels to caravan parks, to a tent in a mate's garden on occasion until the mate's girlfriend put a stop to it. Their days were as varied as they wanted them to be and the freedom that came with that like nothing Joy had had before.

Maggie asked after Tay often after one day Joy let it slip that she was seeing someone, but Joy shrugged it off as casual when it was anything but. She was falling head over heels in love. She just didn't want anyone else to know, anyone to *disapprove and put an end to it. She wanted to get a better job, save up, get away from her parents' home and be with the man she loved. But if they found out what a free spirit he was, she knew they'd put a stop to it or have her pack her bags, something she couldn't afford to do just yet. But soon.*

And the sex with Tay? Well that was unlike anything Joy had ever experienced. He knew all the right things to do, where to touch her, where to go lightly, where to go a little bit further. They'd been daring too, they'd had sex outside, at a festival, on a rowing boat. Tay was wild, next to impossible to tame, with the hair that he spent most of the time pushing away from his face, those eyes that sparkled with misadventure, glorious intent.

Joy would confide in Tay how desperate she was to save up and move out of home and he'd take her soft hand in his much rougher one with the leather bracelets on his wrist and he'd say, 'One day it'll be you and me, Joy . . . you and me against the world'.

And she'd believed every single word.

Joy's eyes flew open. It took her a moment to orientate herself and realise she was at the farmhouse stirring after a lie down rather than in a room with Tay, decades ago, back when she thought her future would always have him in it.

A voice called her name again and she realised it was Libby at her bedroom door.

'I'll be down in a minute or two,' Joy called back as brightly as she could and it seemed to pacify her niece's concern because she didn't come in, merely told her she'd see her downstairs.

The old-fashioned farmhouse had basins in a few of the

bedrooms, Joy's included. At the taps in the small basin by the window, Joy splashed cold water on her face and used the soft towel to bury her face in before she looked in the mirror. Staring back at her was a different girl from the one who'd come here to this beautiful farm in Somerset, that one had been youthful, uncertain, but with a spirit buried deep inside somewhere. Now, age spots peppered her hands, lines ran deep around her eyes, her skin lacklustre on most days. She wasn't one for wearing make-up very often, usually a new hairdo was as far as she went to pampering herself, but she got why people wore it. Makeup masked what was beneath, could hide a person's true age, their true self. But she already did a good job of that without the help of anything in a tube or a jar.

Joy came out of her bedroom to meet the enticing aroma of roasting lamb that had found its way upstairs. As she made her way down the staircase she could hear voices which meant the kitchen was full of her favourite people. And she took comfort from the familiarity, especially now when things were so uncertain.

'Now don't fuss, I've only been asleep,' Joy admonished when Libby came straight to her side in the kitchen.

'Drew said you weren't feeling well. Should I call the doctor?'

'If I need a doctor I'm perfectly capable of making an appointment,' she sighed.

Back in her domain Joy almost wanted to take over as Drew prodded the juicy lamb to check how close it was to being ready. Cameron was piling up the scraps of potato peelings to take to the compost along with other vegetable detritus, picking some up from the floor as he went. Drew checked on the roast potatoes next and jostled them around to ensure they were crisping up nicely and the minute he removed his oven glove he was opening cupboards to find the gravy powder. Libby had turned her attention to setting the table and Cameron, on his way back from the compost bin, informed everyone Freddie was on his way.

It was business as usual in the farmhouse kitchen and Joy welcomed it. Although when Freddie joined them it was almost too much when again she reminded herself that selling the farmhouse and the land would mean the end of his business, and watching him now she knew he'd be hit the hardest by her decision. He'd found his feet, he was about to get his son back in his life and maybe even his ex-wife, and she was going to have to ruin it all.

Could she negotiate with a buyer to let her keep part of the land. Was that even practical? When Freddie started the business, it hadn't been done thinking he'd ever have to change its location. He'd chosen an area that got good sunlight, didn't have too many issues with drainage in the wet months, his greenhouse had been built with the same considerations. But the water butts and the compost bins he'd installed and maintained were done with the entire property in mind, the old cowshed was a storage facility he'd filled with his things. And Joy very much doubted a buyer would want part of the land used by someone else unless it was in the way she'd rented out land, right at the very edge. Her head began to fill with thoughts of how they could move Freddie's business to the perimeter perhaps, dig new patches, build another greenhouse. But then they'd need water butts and compost and storage that way too, and was it even practical?

Libby was watching her, scrutinising the way everything

carried on around her and she wasn't joining in like she usually did. To discourage her from asking yet again whether she was OK, Joy asked, 'Where's the mint sauce?'

Libby sprung to attention. 'I didn't think of that. We can't have lamb without it. I'll go get the mint.'

'Don't for goodness sake pick the wrong herb,' Freddie called after her but in the next moment, headed out too. 'I'll make sure she doesn't,' he called back with a wave over his shoulder. He seemed a lot cheerier than earlier, which was a blessing, unless he was putting it on. Joy was the queen of doing that, it was far too easy a lot of the time.

Perhaps this was what family did. They had their challenges, their downright terrible moments, but they had the power to lift one another from the depths of despair.

She had to believe that would be the case for her too when she told everyone the farmhouse and land wouldn't be hers for much longer. She had no choice but to sell up and she'd send the estate agent an email tonight, she couldn't wait any longer. Because if the horrible truth about her life before Bramleywood came out, as the letter threatened to make happen, she'd lose the trust and love of everyone in this room.

And that might just destroy her.

Chapter Ten

Libby

Libby had plenty to think about. Not only had two companies in New York got back to her regarding the résumés she sent them, but one had links with London and other sites around the UK and they'd made contact to ask her to go for an interview there tomorrow. Ever since Drew had floated the idea of working in one of England's cities, the thought hadn't entirely gone from her mind and she'd sent out a few résumés on the off-chance that a position might come up. Tomorrow she hoped her trip to London might well be what clinched it and helped to make up her mind about England versus a return to America.

'You're looking lovely today, Libby.' Sonia behind the counter at the bakery smiled at Libby's floaty summer frock, cream with tiny flowers in all colours of the rainbow. She'd bought it at the charity shop two doors down, in need of more clothes. She hadn't realised how much she'd relied on business and formal wear until she'd left the workforce and had to make do with everything else she had. It wasn't as though there was much left in America either, her wardrobe was strangely bereft of clothes that didn't warrant a trip to the office.

'Thank you, that's kind. Two loaves of the chia whole-meal please, and I'll take six soft white rolls.'

'Coming right up.' Sonia got to it, filling paper bags with everything Libby asked for, ushering the box of tasters her way as usual. This time it was lemon and almond slice Zelda was trying out on customers and the citrus zing had Libby taking a second piece and then buying an entire tray. 'You got me,' she called over her shoulder as she left Sonia to serve her next customer. Although when she turned and bumped right into Rick she wished she hadn't lingered so long choosing what she wanted. Ever since that night in the pub, the way he'd looked at her had given her the creeps and his presence wasn't doing much else this time.

'Libby isn't it?' The cool green of his eyes were that of someone who couldn't be trusted, so Lauren had told her on the way home from the pub. She'd cited his behaviour over the local library mainly, something that had upset plenty of people. According to Lauren he was the sort of man to watch out for, someone who was plotting what trouble he could cause next.

'That's right,' she said flatly.

'How are you settling in to the farm?' He looked her up and down, one side of his mouth hooked up as though he were a trout on the end of a line. 'Bit different to living in New York I'll bet.'

She didn't appreciate that he knew that little fact about her – or anything about her for that matter. 'It's very different, but a good different.'

'You're going to run the place are you?'

'The bakery?'

'The farm and the house for the homeless.' His mouth twitched on the final word.

'It's not a house for the homeless, Joy takes people in and helps them.' OK so most of them had nowhere to go, but the way he'd said it got her back up.

'And what about you? Will you be the next Good Samaritan?'

'Maybe I will.' She couldn't resist goading him. Joy had told her he wasn't too happy he couldn't purchase the land and farmhouse after Ted and Marjory passed away but he wasn't exactly being very subtle now was he? 'I'd better get going,' she complained, 'these bags are heavy.'

She could feel him watching as she walked away, but she held her head high and didn't turn back.

'That man is awful,' she said dumping the bags on the kitchen table when she got back to the farmhouse.

'What man?'

'Rick.'

'Steer clear, that's all I can say,' Joy advised. 'Be around people who make you happy, not those who drain you every time.'

Libby smiled. She couldn't claim Joy had been lifting her spirits lately. She'd erred on the side of draining with her moods, and the house had had a shocking atmosphere for the last week with her biting people's heads off and then apologising and when she wasn't doing that she was disappearing into a world of her own and forgetting to do the things she always did. They were simple things that others could do and did do – rustling up a group breakfast on a whim, bringing in bright fruits and vegetables and enjoying the challenge of working out what to make with them. But they were the little things Joy took pleasure doing, they were her routine, and she was lost without it yet couldn't seem to get on top of it. Libby had been staying out of the way as much as possible, throwing herself into organising Lauren's paperwork, because it wasn't only Joy whose mood had dipped, it was Freddie as well, and spending time around both of them had been as dark as the clouds that covered the Somerset countryside last week.

'Thank goodness the storms have passed,' said Joy, looking out of the window at the land graced with a bright August sunshine and light winds that gently rustled through the leaves of the mighty oak.

Libby helped herself to a shiny green apple from the fruit basket. 'I'm glad it won't be raining tomorrow.'

'What's happening tomorrow?'

'I have an interview, remember? I told you.'

'I'm sorry, it totally slipped my mind. Of course you did. Remind me, where is it?'

'London. So not as far as America,' she added hoping to inject a smile on her auntie's face, '. . . if I decide that's what I will do.' She wasn't going to tell her she was seriously considering other locations as well as London, she didn't know how she really felt about the change herself yet. Being in the bigger cities brought a certain vibe with it that so far had buoyed her along in her job, that city kick that had kept her going. But maybe it was time to leave that behind, make a sideways move if not a total change. When she'd got the email about the interview she hadn't expected to feel such little emotion about not returning to America. America was what she'd known for five years, she'd thought she would've felt torn, but she hadn't, and she could only put it down to being here with Joy and so many people she'd begun to get to know and value in her life. She'd even had fun doing Lauren's paperwork for the last few days, her company was a welcome escape from the farmhouse on days where she wanted to avoid Joy or Freddie, and when Lauren said she was in a mess, she hadn't been lying. Receipts, invoices, all of them were muddled together, dates were illegible on some, and she'd ended up starting a spreadsheet to record them all, then finding a file to stash them neatly. She had no idea how Lauren had managed so far not to get in trouble when doing her tax returns.

Joy hugged Libby. 'I've got used to having you here that's all.'

'I know. But let's see what happens, I'd better not get ahead of myself thinking it's all my decision. They haven't offered me a job yet.'

'Oh they will, they'd be crazy not to hire you. You know this means—'

'I have to call Dad.' She nodded but they said no more about it. She'd called him again yesterday but still clammed up before she told him she was in England. She wasn't even sure why now, perhaps it was the threat of reality looming.

Libby ate her apple as they talked about where the interview was exactly and Libby showed Joy a map of London to explain where the company's offices were, where she'd have to work, possible places she could rent.

After she'd eaten Libby took over the task of hanging out the washing on the line that ran from the back of the house by the patch of daisies, all the way out to the pole some ten metres away. She was pegging the final T-shirt of Joy's when Freddie came over from the fields.

'Sun's out,' she smiled at him.

But he had to force a smile in return, she could tell,

because no way did it reach his eyes. 'Finally . . . thought my veg were going to drown last week.' His attempt at a joke followed her into the utility room where she dumped the basket.

'Freddie,' she began as he washed his hands at the sink. She swore his skin was permanently stained from his job on the land, but every day he'd scrub at them before he went through to the main part of the farmhouse or anywhere near his room. 'I hope you don't think I'm speaking out of turn when I say this, but are you all right?'

He shook off his hands and reached for the tea towel. 'I appreciate you asking, but really, I'm fine. And Joy's already been asking me.'

'Do you know what's wrong with her?' Maybe she'd shift the focus to get answers.

'Why, what's she said?'

'Don't panic,' she said, not expecting such a strong reaction – he looked as though he was waiting for her to deliver terrible news. 'It's nothing in particular, she's just been cagey, irritable, not like herself.' Maybe she was like that now and then, Libby wouldn't know given they'd only really known one another through their letters.

'She seems the same to me,' he said.

Libby shot him a look that said she didn't believe him and he muttered something about getting back to work even though he'd literally only just come inside for something to eat.

What was going on around here? Had they put something in the Bramleywood water that drove everyone to breaking point?

*

Thanks to Ronald there was no chance of Libby over-sleeping and missing her interview and the next day, in her suit and with her heels once more – although she wore trainers for the commute – she was on the train from Bramleywood to London. She had a couple of changes along the way, but settled in to the journey with a good book and watched the countryside whizz by.

It gave her a buzz when the train pulled in to Paddington Station. She was with commuters, jostling one another, all seemingly knowing exactly where they were going, and for a moment she basked in the crazi-ness of it all. She'd missed it! The feeling continued as she got the Tube to Marble Arch and a good half an hour ahead of time she took some photographs of Hyde Park to show Joy and the others later. She couldn't believe Freddie had never been to London, Lauren had once on a school trip, and Drew had plenty of times with no intention of ever returning. That hadn't surprised her, he was a coun-try boy, she couldn't imagine him being trapped in an office all day. His second home clearly appeared to be on the water.

Libby put the farmhouse and everyone there out of her mind once she headed inside the offices in a converted period building with spectacular views of Hyde Park. It was time to wind back to her work days in Manhattan, talk up her experience, her responsibilities, her vision. And she did it well, because mid-way through the inter-view they'd called in another of the bosses to see her.

'It sounds promising,' Auntie Joy beamed that evening when Libby got back to Bramleywood and told them all about it.

'I think so.' Libby cut a piece of salmon and speared

it with her fork. 'And they were all so nice. All so very British.'

'I suppose you're used to American accents,' Lauren smiled.

'And West Country accents,' Libby batted back which prompted Drew and Cameron doing their best 'Oo . . . aar' farmer impressions which even had Freddie laughing tonight.

'When will you know if you've got the job?' Drew asked.

Libby always felt slightly skittish when he focused his attention on her but she never ever let it show. 'They said they'll be in touch soon, whatever that means.' They'd also talked about other locations she could work from, but she wanted to get her head around it all first. She also knew she had to get in touch with her dad before she made any major decisions.

'I need a day out in London,' said Lauren. 'I've a whole list of cake shops I want to go to so it'll be the perfect excuse – The Hummingbird Bakery in Soho, Konditor & Cook, Cutter & Squidge.'

'I'm on board with that,' Libby readily agreed. 'I walked past a fancy bakery after my interview and I would've run in to get something if I didn't want to make my train on time. We should do it, go for the day.'

'I'd really like that.'

'If you get a swanky flat in the centre of London,' Cameron began, 'can I come and visit?'

'That could be arranged. Although I doubt it'll be anything too posh, rents are staggering in the capital – or any capital for that matter – but I'll ensure I have a sofa bed.'

'Talking of homes,' Joy began, although she wasn't

looking anywhere but her flat palms on the table on either side of her plate, as though she'd been building up to saying whatever she was about to come out with. 'I have some news.' All eyes were on her, Libby's included, because she didn't miss the wobble in Joy's voice. This wasn't going to be good news. 'It's about this place.'

'The farmhouse?' Drew put his cutlery together, but still plucked a buttery boiled potato from the bowl in the centre of the table and ate it with his fingers. He didn't seem to have picked up that this wasn't a particularly good announcement.

'The farmhouse and all the land that comes with it.' Joy looked up from her focus on the table, her nail picking off something stuck to its surface. She looked first to Libby, then Drew, Cameron, Freddie, but then down again, as though it would make it less painful to share this if she could pretend they weren't there.

And what she said next had the entire table stunned into silence.

'I'm selling up.'

Drew was first to speak. 'You can't sell up, I mean, whatever for?'

'It's time. I can't manage this place at my age,' said Joy. 'And I got a quick reply from Walter, manager of the estate agency. They were hungry to get the place on their books and I have an agent as well as a photographer lined up to come in the morning.'

'It's all so sudden,' said Lauren, shell-shocked.

'You seem to be doing a perfectly good job of managing this place from where I'm standing,' Drew assured her. 'And you have help from all of us.'

'I do and I am grateful. But you all have your own lives, I don't want anyone having to stay here out of obligation.'

'Auntie Joy.' Libby couldn't believe it. 'What's brought this on. You seemed so adamant it would never happen. In all your letters, you've always believed you'd live out the rest of your days here.'

'Yes, well.' She pushed back her chair and began to collect the plates. 'Maybe that was all a pipe dream. Perhaps I was crazy to think it could be so simple. Money's tight, the renters have both pulled the plug . . .'

'Wait, both renters?' Drew asked. 'What happened?'

'No idea, all I know is that without the rent money I really need to act before it's too late.'

'Aren't you selling up part of the land?' Libby suddenly remembered. Had Joy forgotten? 'That should help surely, and we can find others to rent some more of it. Don't just give up. Freddie, say something. You've got the most to lose. Your business runs from the land.'

He shrugged, he was probably in shock. 'I'll have to transport it elsewhere. Or hope the new owner will rent me a field or two.'

'But the fields you're using aren't exactly at the edge, you'll be in their way, nobody is going to buy this place and let you do that.' She was getting wound up, indignant on her auntie's behalf, because this couldn't all be coming from Joy, could it? There had to be another reason for this.

Joy still wouldn't look properly at any of them. She was multitasking, talking and clearing up until Drew stopped her and made her sit down again. She cleared her throat. 'I haven't heard much more about the partial sale of the land, something tells me I won't and that it'll all fall through.'

'Then something's up,' Libby concluded. 'Bit of a co-incidence that both renters pull out of the arrangement after years of being very happy here. And then the buyer of the extra land goes quiet too? There's something amiss, Auntie Joy, this isn't right.'

Joy went over to the sink and angrily turned on the taps causing water to spurt all down her front. And then she swore; Joy never swore, and it left an eerie silence from everyone else in the room.

The only person who hadn't uttered a single word since Joy told them she wanted to sell up was Cameron, and without looking at any of them he flew out of the back door. One look from Joy told them all she suspected he was off, but her shoulders slumped when her gaze went out the window, the worry leaving and defeat kicking in.

When Libby looked out she was relieved to see Cameron had only gone as far as the puppies' pen. 'Auntie Joy,' she said softly. 'Talk to us. We're all adults.'

'Please,' Joy's voice shook. 'Leave it, Libby. Leave it alone.'

With nobody knowing quite what to do, practical-ities took over. Drew took charge of the washing-up, Libby picked up a tea towel, Lauren covered the cake again now that dinner seemed to be over and set it into a plastic container. 'It'll keep till tomorrow,' she told Joy, who had nothing to say as she began to pull out mugs for tea.

'You staying?' Joy asked Lauren as though she hadn't just made one hell of an announcement.

'Can't, I'm exhausted today. Another time though.' She hugged Joy and kissed her cheek. 'We're all here for you, remember that.' She made a good-luck face to Libby and

Drew and made a sharp exit. Libby got the impression Joy got everyone to open up somewhere along the way, but rarely did that herself.

Freddie said a tentative goodbye to Lauren before heading out himself, miserable as anything again, which was no surprise given the sudden threat to his business. Presumably he was going over to tend to his veggie patches, something he might not have for much longer. Cameron stayed firmly in the puppy pen fussing over Bisto more than any of the others. At least he hadn't run away, or they'd be scouring the streets for him and that was the last thing Joy needed.

When Libby looked over at Joy again she'd flicked off the kettle, left the empty mugs where they were and announced she had a headache and was going to bed.

'Auntie Joy . . .' But Libby's voice fell on deaf ears and she stood looking at the empty hallway as Joy reached the end and took the stairs, away from them all.

'This is bad,' was all Drew said, his hands plunged into murky water that needed changing.

Libby dried the lid of the saucepan, Drew drained the sink of its filth and he turned, leaned against the sink, a wet mark across the tummy section of his T-shirt from leaning against the porcelain. His soft West Country accent portrayed his worry over Joy when he asked, 'How long has this been going on? How long since she decided to sell up do you think?'

'I've no idea.' She set the pan lid onto the saucepan and put it away in the right cupboard.

'She looked exhausted, worried.'

'The decision is out of the blue don't you think? I mean, she's never even hinted that's what she might do.'

'There was I thinking she wanted you to take over.'

'I was beginning to think it too.' She hung up the damp tea towel and leaned against the sink as he dried his hands. 'I mean, I don't think it's really me, but I assumed she would've asked me outright before she made such a huge decision. Or I thought she'd offer it to one of you, Freddie maybe.'

'Me too.' He got a cute line in the middle of his forehead when he frowned. It didn't look ugly like it might do on anyone else like Rick for example, a man who wore his deceitfulness on his expression for all to see, it looked a part of him, and she almost wanted to rub it away.

'She seems to have made up her mind,' said Libby dejectedly.

'From experience, it's pretty hard to convince Joy to do anything she doesn't want to do. So if her mind's made up . . .'

'You'll let her sell up, just like that?'

'It's not a case of *letting* her. It's her farmhouse.'

She rubbed her neck to relieve the tension building, and then knocked on the window and asked Cameron if he wanted any ice cream and apple pie, a sure way to keep him hanging around. He said yes but he wanted to eat it out there, sitting on the stool while the puppies attempted to jump up onto his lap. And Libby wasn't going to argue. She took a bowl outside and willed him not to run off. So far it looked like he was suppressing the urge, unless he was waiting for everyone's backs to be turned.

Her worry must've been showing when she headed back inside because Drew pulled out a chair and motioned for her to sit down. 'I don't know what we should do, but you look like you need a break.'

She dismissed the concern. 'I've been having a break for weeks.'

'I mean you need time away from here, not for an interview, for relaxation.'

'Oh yes, and what do you suggest?'

'You need time on water,' he grinned mischievously.

'Don't tell me, you want me to get in a kayak.'

'Is that so wrong?'

'It's very kind of you.' She swallowed hard because the way he was looking at her now made her insides dance. 'But I'm no water baby. I've never tried a water sport.'

He pretended to be horrified. 'Then it's time you learned. And I know someone who happens to be very familiar with the water, and not only that, can teach too.'

Their chairs at the table were so close her legs were almost touching his bare limbs, in shorts as always. 'What time do I need to be up?'

A broad smile on his face he told her, 'Early. And pack an overnight bag.'

Her jaw almost dropped, he was a bit forward, but she was embarrassed when he picked up on the confusion.

'It's not on the river near here, I'm going farther afield, I've got a couple of brand new kayaks to pick up, but we'll make a couple of days of it, there's a lovely boathouse I've got rented out for two nights.'

It sounded romantic, was that what this was? Her heart pounded at the possibilities.

'It has two bedrooms,' he assured her and she felt crazy for even thinking otherwise.

'Where is it?'

He didn't answer straight away. 'The Lake District, Lake Windemere to be exact.'

She closed her eyes, and sighed. 'Why do I get the impression you have an ulterior motive?'

'You haven't told your dad you're here yet have you?'

'How do you know?'

'I asked Joy.'

So he'd asked about her? But that wasn't her focus now, it was whether to take him up on his offer. 'I don't know, it's all a bit sudden.'

'Yeah, what a rush, you must still be terribly jet-lagged.' When she laughed and pushed his arm with her hand he caught her fingers. 'Go call him right now, rip off the Band-Aid.'

And with a deep breath she found her feet taking her through to the lounge to make the call in peace.

She got straight to the point and before they could talk about anything else she announced she was in England and was scheduled to come up to the Lake District tomorrow. He was so gobsmacked he didn't ask much else and she'd wrapped the call up quickly as though she was at the helm of a particularly difficult meeting.

'You did it?' Drew asked, putting his phone down on the table when she went back to the kitchen.

She nodded, head in her hands thinking how she was going to get through this when they headed up there tomorrow. 'Why didn't you mention before that you were planning on going to the Lakes. You must've known before today.'

He shrugged. 'I did, but I didn't want to give you a chance to back out.'

'So what's the plan?'

'I drop you at your dad's, should be there just after lunch. What time did you tell him?'

'I didn't, I said I'd be in touch.'

'You can text him then, tell him the details. And then tomorrow, after you've seen your dad we'll get you on the water. The weather is supposed to be dry, still, perfect conditions for your first kayak lesson. Unless you want to try a paddle board, I can take one there if you like.'

'I think kayaking will be quite enough for a non-watersports person,' she smiled wryly.

'There's nothing like it, I'm telling you, you'll be hooked.'

She might get hooked on him instead, and perhaps that thought would be enough to let her sleep tonight and not think about her dad and how awkward tomorrow was going to be.

'I'll pick you up at seven.'

'Where are you both off to?' Joy asked, floating in so quietly they hadn't heard her come down the corridor. She filled a glass of water at the tap. Perhaps she'd decided she'd left the room for long enough to let the dust settle on her announcement.

'I'm going with Drew to collect some new kayaks. From Lake Windemere,' she added.

She leaned against the sink, glass of water in hand. 'You called your dad.'

'Drew didn't give me much choice.'

Joy sent a look of appreciation his way, but there was something else in that gaze, a look of anxiety Libby had picked up before whenever she and Drew were getting on well, becoming closer. Libby was sure she hadn't imagined it.

'I'll leave you to it.' Drew picked up his keys and phone and kissed Joy on the cheek. 'Please change your mind about selling up,' he said.

'I told you, it's time.' And with that she went off to bed and Libby suspected she'd stay there this time.

'I'll see you tomorrow,' Drew smiled at Libby, his enthusiasm of earlier no longer there.

'See you in the morning.'

And when Libby climbed into bed she wasn't sure what she was dreading the most – seeing her dad, getting into a kayak for the very first time given the last time she'd been in anything similar it was a dingy and it had capsized in the seas taking her with it, or spending a few days with Drew.

Chapter Eleven

Joy

'I've got to go back to Dorset.' Tay, duffle bag packed with every single one of his belongings, was standing outside the caravan he'd been staying in. He'd been working at the holiday camp not far from Joy's house, bartending, and as an exchange, had had a caravan for seven weeks. It was the closest he'd come to having a fixed address in a long time. And both he and Joy had loved every second of it. She'd cooked on the tiny two-ringed hob — only baked beans on toast with extra grated cheese, but a comforting meal nevertheless, and it was romantic, just the two of them, not house guests, but alone to do whatever they liked.

'Why?' Joy had turned up to find him packing and she couldn't help the wobbly voice. He picked up on it straight away and put down his bag.

'Come here.' He pulled her to him. It was the least animated she'd ever seen him, all the brightness had gone, but the love was still there, she knew it. The way he held her tight, he might be wild and a lot of fun, but she could tell he felt strongly about her not just by the words he said, by him telling her he loved her, but in moments like this when his whole body let her know how important she was to him. 'I'll come back. But it's my mum.'

'Your mum?'

He sat down on the step of the caravan and pulled her onto his lap. As he talked she felt the breath in her hair. 'Mum had a boyfriend I never got on with, that's why I left home and bummed around.'

'You never told me.' As far as Joy knew, he'd just decided life in a neat house with a modest backyard, a car to get him from A to B, and a job for life simply wasn't for him. He was a free spirit and now it was hard to believe that deep down he had some kind of real life, he had roots, an existence she'd not even thought about. 'Are you sure you're coming back?'

He squeezed her closer and nuzzled her neck, making her laugh in the way he must've known she would. 'Yes I'm coming back. But Mum is really sick, she needs help. She doesn't have anybody. Th e boyfriend left her in her hour of need, put it that way.'

And now he was stepping up.

She turned to face him then, straddled his lap and took his cheeks with her hands. 'You're a kind person, Gregory Taylor. A good man.' And she kissed him, hoping he'd remember the feeling so much that he wouldn't be able to stay away for long.

Those lips, his face, the eyes she'd trusted . . . it was hard to believe they could be the source of so much happiness and yet so much devastation . . .

Joy's mind was all over the place. She was either thinking about the past, or thinking about Libby and Drew who'd left this morning for the Lake District, or she was thinking of Libby's dad and how the visit was going to go and whether he'd tell Libby anything. Her thoughts were also preoccupied with the photographer and the estate agent who'd been crawling all over the property since first thing this morning. They'd praised the farmhouse itself with its features, the land that was well kept and she'd felt protective, possessive, wanting to wipe their grubby little hands off her beautiful old dairy farm. Not that she minded Walter at all, it was more his occupation that was the problem than his approachable demeanour, friendliness and unwavering support of what she'd done here over the years. But she wasn't quite sure how she'd managed not to yell at them to leave as they took shots of the rooms, trespassing inside, others of the old cowshed and even the chicken coop, to give buyers a real feel for the place they'd said.

Joy had always had a feel for the place. And that was what made it so damn hard to contemplate letting it go.

After Walter and his photographer left and Cameron bypassed her to take Bisto for a walk – on his own, he insisted, and she knew why, he was angry with her announcement – she tried to get Freddie talking again, but he was having none of it. He'd hidden out in his greenhouse to avoid bumping into either Walter or his sidekick, probably laughing at their inappropriate suits and shiny shoes and hoping they stood in mud that sprayed all up the material.

'Freddie, please, talk to me,' she pleaded.

But he shrugged and claimed there was nothing to talk about before he headed back outside with a dry slice of bread for a snack. Not a chance of him having a cuppa with her then.

She slumped down at the kitchen table thinking about the way Drew and Libby had looked at one another earlier. There wasn't just an attraction there, they were starting to care for one another, it seemed the hole she'd dug for herself was getting bigger by the day and she wasn't sure she'd ever climb out of it.

Sometimes she wished she'd never gone to that pub, never met Tay, and certainly never held him in such high esteem she let all the responsibility for what happened land on her shoulders.

Tay's mum was ill for some time. Joy got to see him when she could, she went to him at weekends and any fool could see he wasn't coping financially or mentally. He was strung out from being his mother's full-time carer as well as trying to bring in enough money for them both to survive.

'She won't leave the house,' he told Joy one evening as they took a couple of beers down to the end of the garden. It wasn't a nice house where she lived, it was an old, shabby bungalow that smelled of damp and probably needed as much spent on it as the asking price for sale would be, but it was her house and nothing Tay had been able to say to her could convince her to move somewhere else, to get help from the government if she could. 'Since my dad died, she had a couple of boy-friends, none of them stuck. One of them took money from her, cleaned her out of her savings, another one turned out to be married himself, and now she's refusing to let anyone push her around.'

'But that's not what you're doing.'

He picked at the label on his beer bottle. 'Try telling her that.'

'I can help you. I can't give you money, I'm only temping and I have to pay board and lodgings at my parents' but I can give you my time.'

And reluctantly he took her up on it. Joy came whenever she could, cleaned, went shopping for them and cooked some of the meals. She noticed Tay looked like the load had light-ened somewhat when she did it, but his mum sniped at him all the time, nothing he could do was right, and the next minute she'd be apologising, telling him she loved him and in tears. Half the time she didn't seem to have any idea what was happening around her.

When Joy went up there one gloriously sunny day in April after spring really had sprung for most of England, Tay greet-ed her with the biggest smile she'd seen on him in months.

'You look happy.'

'I am,' he declared. 'Got myself a job, a real, well-paid job.'

Joy threw her arms around him. 'That's brilliant! I'm so pleased.'

'I'm working for a car dealership, get to drive some of them when I want to.'

'Fancy,' she grinned.

He'd held her in his arms, told her how much he loved her. Gregory Taylor was proving he was a good man. Not many would move home to take care of a family member no questions asked, fall into a nine-to-five job they'd vowed was never for them.

But Tay had.

And Joy thought in that moment he was surely the man she'd been looking for her whole life.

Ever since she'd received the letter that threatened to expose her past, it seemed Joy couldn't get the memories out of her mind. She'd learned along the way that mem-ories could assault you from any direction, mostly when you least expected – the scent of a new washing powder that reminded her of the one her parents had used for her sheets the last time she stayed at their house all those years ago; the smell of rain that brought back fond times camping with Tay, both huddled in the tent naked but warm even in the depths of winter; the stench of smoke on her father's clothes that at times felt suffocating; the roar of a slightly too-deep engine travelling up the main street of Bramleywood had the effect of throwing ice-cold water over her head.

'I don't understand why you don't have the money,' she said, exasperated at having to pay for Tay's shopping yet again when she went to see him one weekend. It wasn't that she wanted him to be accountable for every penny, it was just that she didn't have a lot herself, and buying food for two people for an entire week had clean wiped her out of cash. 'What happened to your wages?'

'They're coming, I promise.' He had his hands on her waist, his body pressed against hers at the end of the driveway.

It was dusk but she could just about see his mum sitting in the lounge and knew he'd have to get back to her soon. He had to leave her in the day even though he hated doing it, but when it was dark, that was out of the question. And right now Joy hated being the bitch who demanded things from him when he was doing his very best in trying circumstances.

Just then a deep throaty groan from a car coming up the road had them both turning round. She was about to make a joke about whoever it was lowering the tone of the neighbourhood when Tay raised a hand to wave. 'You know them?' she asked.

'He's from work, this is one of our cars.'

'You sell those?'

'Wait here,' he said, kissing her on her forehead. 'Let me

know if mum calls out, I've left the window open so we'll hear her, I'll just have a word.' He indicated the guy in the car now idling at the end of the driveway, its tinted windows rolled down.

His mum seemed fine and Joy hovered, trying not to give dirty looks over at the driver who'd clearly been checking her out when Tay went round and got something from the boot. The driver's eyes had lingered on her chest and his eyebrows had gone up and down in a way that suggested he wanted to be better acquainted.

Joy was happy when the guy left. He gave her the creeps sitting there in a car all souped up with a light tower on top that looked like it was straight out of a funfair and a front spoiler almost the size of a small snow plough.

Tay had hold of an envelope and took out some cash. 'For the shopping.' He leaned in and kissed Joy on the lips, warm and tender the way he'd always been. 'Thank you for doing it.' He looked inside and waved at his mum. 'I appreciate all the help.'

But Joy was still thinking about the boy racer whose noisy car had only just faded into the distance. 'They pay you cash in hand?'

He shrugged. 'Sometimes.' He turned again. 'Mum's getting anxious.' They both heard her call for Tay. 'I'd better go inside.'

Joy hugged him tight. 'I'll go back to the hotel.' She hated saying goodbye to him but they couldn't be with each other here, they didn't want to confuse his mum more than she already was. Today she'd looked at Joy almost as though she was a stranger even though they'd met plenty of times before. 'I'll try to come again next week.'

'It won't be like this forever, I promise.' He held her like *he was trying to persuade himself more than her. But it was positive. Last week he'd been at his wit's end wondering how much more he could take when his mum had a go at him after he'd taken her to the doctor's. Tay had come into Joy's life bubbly, full of personality, but slowly it was draining out of him with this existence, and she hated it as much as he clearly did.*

But Joy had no idea of the steps he was taking to move on from this.

Because if she did, she might just get far away from Gregory Taylor now. Before it was too late.

A knock at the door put a stop to Joy doing anymore reminiscing. She answered it to a family of four who'd come to collect Buttercup. She led them around the outside and to the back of the farmhouse where Cameron had just finished feeding them all. The new owners were early and the disappointment was plain to see on his face. But he handled it well. He scooped up Buttercup, gave her a big hug and then encouraged one of the girls who looked about seven or eight to sit on the stool he'd placed next to the pen so he could settle Buttercup on her lap.

Buttercup was usually one of the more placid of the puppies, her personality gradually developing over the weeks to what it was now, playful when she wanted, but a pup who would be hugged, fussed over and be happy enough to sit at your feet when it was a tiny bit older. Today Buttercup was jumpy, perhaps she knew a change was coming, but Cameron caught hold of her, she sat at his feet while he kept a loose hold and the girls stroked her head. Joy was proud of him, he told them not to hug her too tight, that she'd hate it if they tried to dress her in silly clothes – that had made both girls, the parents and Joy all laugh – and he reiterated the importance of daily exercise for their new puppy.

'Another one gone,' she sighed, when she and Cameron waved the family off in their 4×4, happy as anything, not a care in the world and all the attention ready to lavish on the fifth member of their family. They'd done an immediate bank transfer to Joy's account via the App on their phone and she'd be transferring it to the local animal rescue centre which gave her such a feeling of accomplishment to be helping. Earlier they'd said goodbye to Taz and Shiloh, but Joy supposed getting it over with quickly was better than the pain lingering day after day.

'Goodbyes are horrible. I don't like them.' Cameron led the way back down the side of the farmhouse. At least he'd uttered a few words to her since her shock announcement.

When she caught him up before he went in through the utility room she told him, 'I hate goodbyes too, so how about we make a deal? We don't say goodbye – you and I.'

He eventually looked up from beneath his cap which he pulled further down if he didn't want to talk to anyone. 'We'll have to if you sell this place.'

She bent down to fuss Bisto wondering if he too felt the separation from another of his sisters, the loss and the realisation he'd never see her again. 'You can come where I go.'

'But I like it here.' He had the sulky tone down pat as though he hadn't quite left the teenage years behind.

'And I like it here too. But I'm getting old, money is tight.'

'I'll help, I promise. I'll pull my weight some more. I can get up earlier, go to bed later.'

She let Bisto run to him and didn't mind one bit that he was Bisto's favourite. 'I appreciate you saying so. I'm proud of you, Cameron. These puppies have loved having you here and you've really taken to them all, you've been mature when you've said goodbye, and Bisto here is coming along with training.'

'Now I know you're just trying to think of something nice to say. He's not at all. He still prances around when I say sit and I think he only ends up on his bum when he doesn't know what else to do.'

'He'll get there.'

'Stop changing the subject. I'm not dumb.'

'I know you're not.' But she also knew she was avoiding answering him. And she had no choice but to sell up, it was the only way to avoid everyone finding out what she'd done, hating her, no longer seeing her as the woman who did so much good.

But she still meant what she'd said. Cameron could go with her, she'd buy somewhere big enough, she just wouldn't have the stunning farmhouse with the great outdoors on her doorstep. Her world was about to change. Cameron's was too. Freddie would lose his business, moving it was difficult, and that's if he found somewhere suitable or could afford the extra rent.

She was letting people down and that was something she'd vowed never ever to do to anyone she cared about.

'Why is she called Luna?' Cameron asked, Bisto's mum settling beside him, her tail the only part of her in the sun.

'Now who's changing the subject,' Joy grinned. When the stray had come unexpectedly into her life, Joy had known right away what she wanted to call her. 'Luna was a very good friend of mine.'

'Was?'

'We lost touch in the end.' And Joy would give anything to be able to talk to her right now because she'd worked out who the author of that nasty letter was and she knew her friend Luna would've been able to sort him and his morality out in a flash.

'That sucks, if she was a good friend that is.'

'She was, and yeah, it does suck.' She'd always thought she might try to find Luna, but never had. Perhaps it had been for the best. They'd met at a terrible time in both of their lives, perhaps a time both of them wanted to put behind them.

Joy was glad Cameron was staying put despite her announcement about the farm. She turned to look out at the land but it was too painful now, she was close to tears, this morning she'd woken in a sweat and for a minute had forgotten what was happening in her life. But the second she'd remembered, she'd felt sick to the stomach with fear, sadness and most of all regret.

Regret she was going to let everyone down. Because she knew exactly how it felt to be let down by the one person in your life you looked to for assurance, reliance and to help you find your own sense of happiness.

Joy didn't usually visit Tay mid-week, but tonight she wanted to surprise him for his birthday and so she made the hour-long drive, her overnight bag packed for the hotel, glad the weather was fine and mild for October so they'd be able to take a blanket outside in his garden when his mum was asleep and enjoy the picnic she'd made for both of them. She had red wine, Scotch eggs – Tay's favourite – sausage rolls, crisps, basically a lot of junk snacks they could scoff all evening as they caught up. And she had a cake too, far too big for just the two of them, but decorated with red-piped Happy Birthday on the top.

Joy was almost at Tay's when she got a phone call and she could see from the display that it was Maggie. She pulled into a side road to answer it, knowing Maggie was having a hard time with their parents. She wasn't the one who lived under their roof any more, she'd got out, but it seemed they were still interfering, and this time it was to try and tell her the renovations she and her husband planned for their new home weren't going to work. Joy didn't know why Maggie couldn't just ignore them, but then Maggie had always been like that. Where Joy could switch off and distance herself, Maggie let their stupid opinions and need to control influence her life when it no longer needed to. Joy had often wondered why their parents had even bothered to have kids, but maybe it had been the social norm, the acceptable and right thing to do. Because they always had liked to fit in. Joy and Maggie's friends growing up had mainly been the children of their friends, pre-approved if you like, they'd got no say in the matter. It was no wonder Joy didn't get on with them, she was too outspoken, wanted to lead her own life and not conform. She suspected they only let her stay in their home because they wouldn't want local gossip churning if they threw her out. In their own way they did seem to love their daughters, but it was the having to strive to be the ideal that Joy couldn't take. It was wearing, not being allowed to be yourself.

Maggie sounded better as they talked. Joy suspected she just needed to offload and she'd sure done that, ranting about their mum and their dad. Joy wished she'd put on her big girl pants and tell them to their faces to stay out of her business. But Joy knew Maggie was never going to do that. She was timid when it came to their parents, she seemed to need their blessing and approval to do anything.

Joy hung up the call, but looking round, the side road was too narrow to execute a safe three-point turn so she had to drive on quite a way to find a suitable place. She pulled up in front of an old wooden gate that even in the dark she could see was on its last legs, and it was as she was turning round that her headlights caught the face of someone bending down pulling off a car's number plate. Joy froze because she'd know that face anywhere. It was the same driver who'd been leering at her from the car outside Tay's house in the summer and she didn't want to be anywhere near him, especially in the dark in the middle of nowhere.

She quickly drove away before he could see her and luck-ily it was dark enough he wouldn't have a hope with her headlamps blinding him as she reversed. Heart thumping, she didn't get far before curiosity got the better of her. It was late October by now and a few things Tay had said or done lately hadn't added up, and seeing that face raised Joy's suspi-cions some more.

Tay always had cash at the ready even when Joy was sure he wouldn't have had a chance to go to a cashpoint given his mum barely let him out of her sight now as she gradually got worse; he'd been unreachable late at night when Joy usually called him but had always claimed an early night when she'd asked him why he hadn't answered.

She got out of her car, hoping she'd left it close enough to the edge of the road that it wouldn't be hit by another one, and using her phone torch to see the brambles at the side and walk back towards the wooden gate, she sneaked her way along. Sure enough, through a bush that hid her but not them, she could see that horrible man, and she covered her mouth when she gasped at the sight of Tay with him.

Joy drove on to Tay's house and parked up a few doors away where she could find a space. She walked towards the house, unsure of what to say to Tay when he came back. She'd come at this time knowing his mum would probably be in bed, but she hadn't expected Tay to have abandoned her. She toyed with the idea of ringing the doorbell to see if she was all right, but as there were no lights on his mum had to be asleep, and the last thing she wanted to do was frighten her.

Tay came walking down the street not long after she arrived and he didn't spot her sitting on the low wall next to the bush as he headed down the driveway. He was about to put his key in the door when she moved and called out a hushed, 'Surprise.'

He dropped his keys. 'Jesus, Joy! You scared the living crap out of me!' But his fright soon turned to adoration and he hugged her to him.

He smelt of booze and he was kissing her neck but it didn't give her the same fuzzy feeling it usually did. 'I thought I'd surprise you for your birthday.' She indicated the picnic basket she'd left beside the wall.

'This is why I love you.' He kissed her again. 'Is there cake?'

'Of course. Chocolate cake, your favourite.'

He put his hands on his heart. 'You're the best.'

A perfectly formed half crescent of the moon hung idly above them as she asked, 'Where were you?' She made sure she didn't sound accusing, just interested.

'I went for a walk to clear my head. Just around the block.'

She didn't pull him up on the lie just yet. 'Is your mum on her own?'

'She's fine, she's asleep.' He sighed, shook his head as though she'd really pissed him off. 'I barely get five minutes to myself, I'm allowed out you know.'

She felt terrible then, she put down the basket and gave him a proper hug. 'I know you're having a tough time but you'll always have me.' She hoped he'd remember that and whatever else was going on, whatever reason he'd had for lying to her earlier, he'd leave it alone.

There was something in the way he looked at her – hurt, lost, scared of what was to come.

'You and me against the world remember?' she reminded him, kissing him gently.

At that moment she was young enough to believe that their love could conquer whatever came their way and they would always be together . . . but she was also naïve enough to not know what was about to come round the corner and flip their lives into a whole new stratosphere.

Chapter Twelve

Libby

'I know you're worried,' said Drew as they pulled onto the motorway at long last, 'but you might find talking helps.'

'I'm sorry.' Libby had done her best to pretend she was absolutely fine. And right now Drew was assuming her lack of conversation was all down to seeing her dad today, but it wasn't just that, it was so much more. She leaned back in her seat and turned her head to look out of the window, but it wasn't exactly picturesque right now and when it didn't hold her interest she looked across at Drew. 'It's not just my dad.'

'You're worried about shacking up with me at a boathouse?'

She began to laugh. 'Actually no, I'm really not.' She was even looking forward to giving kayaking a go and her spirits had lifted when she'd seen Drew's jeep with the empty roof rack ready to carry the new kayaks he was buying. It had made her think of the fun they might have if she didn't fall in the water, a step out of her comfort zone after facing her dad which was in a zone all of its own.

Drew indicated to pull left, perhaps he knew something

big was coming and to be able to talk he needed to be comfortably in the slow lane for a while. 'What's up? There's something else bothering you. Last night you seemed nervous but almost relieved you'd finally let your dad know you were here. Are you regretting calling him, is that it?'

'No, that's not it.'

'Come on, Libby. I'll keep asking you if you don't tell me, and there are a whole lot of miles to cover yet.'

'I found something,' she confessed.

This morning Joy had insisted on feeding them both bacon and eggs before the long drive. She'd heaped on mushrooms, tomatoes and spinach as well as though she thought they might not eat for the next few days. And if she was worried about them spending time together for whatever reason, she didn't show it. She didn't seem too rattled by Libby going to see her dad either when there was a good chance he'd tell her why Auntie Joy was never permitted to be in their lives. They'd eaten, they'd talked, they'd laughed, and when Libby asked whether she could borrow the book Joy had just finished reading, Joy had told her it was on the shelf in her bedroom so she should help herself.

Libby went upstairs and into Joy's room where the curtains were billowing because of the open window bringing the outside in, the way Joy always liked it. She found the book on the shelf that had the natural curve of wood as though it hadn't been altered at all from its natural state except for the varnish to make it smooth. Before she left she pulled the window closed – it was way too windy and she hoped the weather forecast was right and it wouldn't be this blowy in the Lakes. But she didn't shut it in time and the curtain blew hard enough to take the trinket box and the coaster from Joy's bedside table along with two books from the end of the bookshelf.

She picked everything up. Thankfully the trinket box was a sturdy silver, the kind that didn't even dent, and the coaster was fine. One book had fallen open and the pages were bent. Libby straightened them out and closed it but there was a stubborn page that must've come away from its binding. She opened up the hardback cover to sort it out but it wasn't pages, it was an envelope and a letter that hadn't been tucked back inside.

She closed the book, she shouldn't be nosey. But her feet didn't quite make it to the bedroom door because she'd recognised the envelope and could well remember the day the letter had come. It suddenly hit her. That was when things had changed. Ever since the letter's arrival, Joy had been different. She'd tried to hide her feelings, but there was something going on. At first Libby had put it down to her and her auntie not really knowing one another all that well, but she had a feeling there was more to it than that.

Libby was in two minds whether to respect Joy's privacy or delve and try to get to the bottom of it and help her auntie with whatever was going on. And when Joy called her to see where she'd got to she yelled down that she was coming.

And she made a snap decision.

She read the letter before she slotted it back inside the book.

When Joy had waved Libby and Drew off with a smile an hour ago, Libby's heart had broken at the pretence she'd put on her face. Because she knew how hard it would be for Joy to do, how difficult it would be to keep a part of yourself a secret from everyone who cared about you, a secret that was big enough for someone to be able to hold it over her.

'What did you find?' Drew asked now, some of his attention on her, the rest on the road. He wouldn't be able to pull over to talk properly even if she wanted him to, because he was picking up those boards at a certain time. She'd wondered whether she should be mentioning what she'd seen to anyone else at all, but she didn't know what to do with the new and appalling information she had at her disposal.

'A letter.' She met his gaze when he turned to look at her for just a moment before his eyes went back to the road. 'I know why Joy's selling up. Someone knows something about her past and they're threatening to reveal everything unless she gives them money.'

'What?' He chuckled. Maybe he thought it was a joke. It took a couple more glances in her direction before he realised it wasn't. 'How much money?'

When she told him he swore. 'So that's why she's selling the farm. What the hell has someone got over her that she can't tell everyone in order to save her home? It'll break her giving that place up when she doesn't want to.'

That was exactly what Libby thought too. 'I've got no idea. The letter was a bit cryptic, designed to get to Joy obviously but not revealing anything to anyone else who might see it. Oh it was horrible, Drew.'

'I'm sure it was.'

'It'll break her heart to sell The Old Dairy.'

'I know.'

'I've been trying to think of ways I could help her raise

extra money so she can stay – she could diversify even, perhaps have glamping, or let people hire the fields as a wedding venue with a backdrop of the farmhouse. There are so many possibilities.'

He sneaked another glance at her. 'You have thought this through.'

'It's what being unemployed does to you, it makes you need a sense of purpose,' she laughed despite the underlying misery of the situation for Joy.

'I think you've found a natural sense of purpose,' he said as he indicated to pass another car. 'You're just like Joy is, helping people. You've brought Cameron out of his shell by treating him like anyone else and playing countless board games with him.'

'Hey, I've got time on my hands remember.'

'And what about helping Lauren? She told me all about how you're rescuing her from beneath a mountain of messy paperwork. She joked about it but I could tell how grateful she was for having you in her corner.'

'I like helping out.'

'Exactly. So why don't you diversify too?'

'How do you mean?'

'You're obviously good with numbers and business, what about a consultancy role? You could help other companies sort themselves out.'

She beamed a smile across at him. 'You know, that's not a bad idea. It's something I could look at once I get my foot in the door somewhere. I could start earning a bit of money and then think about my next move.'

'Stategise,' he said and laughed at how serious he sounded.

'Strategise,' she repeated. 'Which is something I'd love

to do with Joy but I can't exactly broach the subject of her finances and selling up, can I?'

'You could, but I'd tread lightly if I were you now you know about that nasty letter. And be there ready to help when she needs you. We all need to do that.'

Libby sighed. The situation felt so hopeless. 'I hate that someone is doing this to her. And I tried searching online using the clues in the letter but found nothing at all.'

'Who do you think is behind it?'

She shrugged, but her non-committal response had him trying to look at her as well as the road. 'I don't know,' she told him.

'But you have suspicions?'

'I didn't say that.'

'Come on, Libby, out with it.'

He wasn't wrong, and she had to admit it to see if there was some way she could be right. 'I wondered whether Freddie might be behind it.'

'What? Are you serious?'

'I wish I wasn't. But think about it, he's been very odd lately, even Joy thinks so. He's snappy, away in his own world half the time.'

'Not a chance,' Drew said firmly. 'I know Freddie well enough and you're barking up the wrong tree there. Surely.'

It was the word 'surely' on the end that had her worrying she might have picked up on something neither of them wanted to believe were true.

'Whoever it is, I'm furious they'd do it to Joy,' she said hoping her theory was completely off course. 'I wish I knew what hold they had over her. Perhaps I could ask

Dad about it all today, find out what went on, but I don't think it's really the right time.'

'No, don't do that. Today should be about you and him. He may well volunteer information about your family including Joy, but I wouldn't push it.' He turned and gave her a grin she expected he didn't realise was quite so sexy in its concern and determination to make her feel better. 'Not that I'm an expert in these matters given I'm an orphan.'

She gave his arm a little tap. 'Don't say that.'

'It's true.'

'It must be hard for you, never having known either of your parents.'

He negotiated overtaking a driver who was pootling along at about thirty on the motorway in a car that looked like even that speed was a bit of a stretch. 'It is sometimes. I'm lucky, I had my uncle for a long while and then when Joy took me in, I had her. And she's always been easy to talk to, confide problems in, help you work out what to do.'

'Shame she doesn't have someone to do the same for her,' Libby said sadly.

'I guess she has the local vet.' His eyebrows went up and down.

Libby began to laugh, enjoying Drew's company more and more by the minute. 'You've noticed it too.'

'Of course I have. He asks after her whenever I see him, I saw them talking in the street the other day and Joy was laughing like she was fifty years younger, he was lapping it up.'

'I wonder what she's hiding from everyone.'

'No idea,' he said as he pulled out yet again to overtake. 'But whatever it is it must be bad to sell the farm.'

They pulled up at the end of her dad's street a few hours later, on a steep hill like most of the adjoining roads.

'What time should I come and fetch you?' Drew had waited for her to have a moment, sitting here, looking towards the house at the end of a group of four. She knew it was her dad's place, she'd seen a picture of it a long time ago and it still had the same light blue door and window frames that must take a battering in the colder months.

'Not sure.' She had no idea whether she'd be here half an hour or for the rest of the day and having Drew so concerned was unexpected. It was something she wished she could savour, but how could she when she had no idea what her next steps should be, where she'd find a job, where she'd settle.

'Why don't you text me when you're ready. Lake Windemere is only three miles away so I'll collect the kayaks and store them at the boathouse, then I'll amuse myself. We can go out on the water tomorrow.'

'Are you sure?'

'Of course I'm sure. You don't get out of it that easily.' His hand had been resting near the gear stick but it dropped now, close to hers as she almost clung to the edge of her seat unsure how she was going to get from here to her dad's front door. He put his hand on top of hers and the warmth made her relax. 'You're going to be fine. I'm a phone call away if it's a disaster.'

Libby pulled on her zip-up top and picked up the small bag she'd brought with her and with a smile she hoped would give her some confidence to see her dad again she climbed out of the car. She didn't look back as she made her way all the way up the rest of the hill to Cedar Cottage at the very end.

She knocked on the door eventually. There was no bell, no knocker, her knuckles would have to do. She'd given her dad an approximate time and then texted to say they were an hour away but still he didn't come to the door the minute she knocked. Maybe he was collecting himself the same way she was.

When he opened the door a look of hesitation flashed for a moment before he pulled her into a hug. 'Libby, you're here.'

'Hi Dad.'

'Come inside, you must be hungry, I've got chicken hotpot in the oven.'

He was rambling and Libby remembered he'd done that when he'd been nervous. He'd done it once when it was her mum's birthday and he'd booked a flight in a balloon but then panicked she'd hate every minute of it, he'd done it before he had an interview for a new job and her mum had straightened his tie, put her hands on her shoulders and told him he'd be fine, if he could stop talking at a rate of knots. He never rambled in their phone conversations, they were stilted and uncomfortable, but face-to-face it seemed a different matter entirely.

The juxtaposition of this domesticated father in his own cottage with the one Libby had last seen, lost and all over the place without his Maggie, took Libby by surprise, but she snapped out of it and closed the door behind her.

'Come through,' he beckoned as though she was only here last week.

He led her through what must be the lounge with its dark, low, oak ceiling beams and a coffee table that was so big it took up most of the floor space. Or was it that the room was so small it didn't allow for much furniture? And they went into the kitchen.

'I need to peel some potatoes. We've got broccoli – I remember you like that – carrots too. Or what about runner beans? I think I have those somewhere.' He pushed his glasses up his nose but they steamed up when he lifted a lid from a pan to see whether the water was boiling yet and turned off the gas.

Libby had last seen her dad three and a half years ago on a flying visit to a friend's wedding, before he'd moved up here. The visit had been short and she'd been relieved to get away again and part of her had wondered whether that was what it would be like today. But so far so good, perhaps the task of preparing lunch was a distraction that stopped both of them thinking about the last time they'd seen one another or the time before that when Libby said her goodbyes and flew away to America.

'Why don't I look after the potatoes?' she offered when he knocked two spuds off the worktop in the small cottagey kitchen with his elbow. 'And no need for runner beans, carrots and broccoli are perfect.'

When she looked around for a peeler he pulled open a drawer to show her where it was. 'Thank you for coming all the way up here, it's a long way from London, even further from New York.'

It was a long way from Somerset too but she wasn't going to mention that. Best to let him assume she was in the city for now, that she'd literally just come in from Heathrow.

'How did you get here?'

'I told you, a friend gave me a lift.'

'Where is this friend?' He looked around her as though the person could've sneaked in with her and was hiding. He looked much the same as he always had. He wore cords and a burgundy sweatshirt with a white collared polo shirt beneath, like someone about to go on the golf course, despite never having given the sport a second look. Unless he'd changed his hobbies as well as so much else. His bald spot on top of his head had got slightly bigger and the sides of hair that only had a mere hint of the same chestnut as her own needed a cut, the skin below his sea-green eyes sagged now, signs of old age creeping up faster when it was so long between visits.

'He's gone to Lake Windemere to pick up some kayaks, it's for his business.' If her dad was wondering whether this *he* was her boyfriend, he didn't ask. 'This cottage is lovely, and the surroundings stunning,' she said. Best to settle for regular conversation before they got too personal.

As she peeled the potatoes and her dad did anything but stand still, taking out cutlery, offering her a drink, fussing with placemats and crockery, she looked out of the rear window. It was a dreary day – fine, but no sign of the sun, even though it was officially still summer – and low hanging cloud obscured part of the view up here. She wondered what the lake was like for Drew, whether he was picking up the kayaks, or hanging around a boat shed waiting. Her gaze drifted over to an annexe type part of the house jutting out with the same blue-coloured door as the front except this was a stable door style. 'What's in the outbuilding?'

'Junk,' he laughed. 'Been that way since I moved in. It's actually self-contained, has an en suite and a kitchenette, but there seemed little point having it, I don't have many guests.'

'I'm sorry it's taken me so long to come.'

'I wasn't having a dig at you, I promise.' He put a hand on her shoulder and she froze for a moment. 'No need to apologise, you have a life of your own.' When she smiled tentatively he got back to business. 'Let's get those potatoes on. You know me and the kitchen, if we don't get sorted we'll be eating every item at intervals, I never could get my timings right.'

She appreciated the relaxed chit-chat and he was right, he'd never been very good in the kitchen. Libby guessed he'd had to learn that when her mum died and it couldn't have been easy. Libby wondered whether subconsciously her dad had timed preparing lunch for her arrival so they would have something else to focus on, easing in to one another's company before they dealt with anything heavier. Perhaps they wouldn't even get that far, maybe it would just be a pleasant afternoon, a father and daughter meeting up after a long time apart.

Drew and Libby hadn't stopped for any lunch and Joy's breakfast had kept her going until now, but the minute she had a plate full of aromatic chicken hotpot in front of her, she got stuck straight in. 'You've learned how to cook in my absence.' She sliced another piece of meat.

'I had to,' he laughed for the first time since Libby had arrived. 'I'd waste away, nobody else is going to feed me.' It wasn't a big laugh, but it was enough to show he was beginning to relax, which helped her do the same.

They talked more about the Lake District, how he'd joined a walking group and covered miles each week. He loved the rain up here when it came, heavy downpours that silenced the rest of the world, but he was with Libby on the water sports.

'I'm supposed to be trying out kayaking,' she admitted.

'Rather you than me, don't those things trap you inside and if you capsize you're stuck?'

'I'm still scarred from the time I capsized in a dingy and swallowed all that sea water.'

When lunch was over Libby's dad made them both a cup of tea while she stayed sitting at the small pine table pushed all the way into the corner of the kitchen. Here in the cottage was a complete contrast to the noisy farmhouse with comings and goings throughout the day, voices filling the walls. This place was like a scaled-down, muted version of the home in Somerset.

'Drew said we'll take out a tandem so at least I won't get lost,' said Libby, putting a positive spin on things.

'If you're on Lake Windemere I doubt that'll happen anyway. But watch out for the bigger boats.' At her abject horror he laughed for a second time. 'I'm winding you up. It's all fairly sedate, organised, and your friend will know the way it works if he's used to this sort of thing. What's he like, anyway?'

'Drew? He's nice, offered to bring me up here and still refusing to take petrol money.'

'How do you know him?'

She stumbled a bit over her words, holding her mug ready to sip her still steaming tea. 'Friend of a friend.'

She willed him not to probe for more details and he didn't when she asked more about the countryside walks he took with the group. He told her some of the hilliest, longest, and most picturesque.

'It's your mum's fault,' he went on cautiously. 'The

walking,' he added by way of explanation, conversation punctuated as he tried to choose the right things to say, Libby's mum not mentioned often and certainly not in recent times. 'She was always one for walks wasn't she?'

'No matter the weather,' Libby smiled.

'Sometimes I could've throttled her, the conditions she took us out in.'

It was Libby's turn to laugh, probably more out of relief that they could mention her mum without either of them leaping in to suddenly change the subject because they weren't comfortable. 'Do you remember our neighbours always used to wave at us?'

'From the comfort of their warm, dry living room, I remember. Lucky beggars.'

'Not beggars . . . buggers,' Libby said. 'They had a leaf blower and every autumn they'd clear their leaves and blow them all in our direction.'

'So they did, that's right. Took me forever to get rid of them too or they'd turn to mush and have us slipping all over the place.'

'Their dog used to poo on our lawn as well.'

'And your mum stood in it one day.' He pulled a face. 'I saw her from the window and went out to see what happened, I thought she'd hurt her foot the way she was standing, but she wasn't moving because she'd squelched in it and couldn't bear to prise her shoe off. I ended up getting the hose and cleaning off the shoe before I removed it.' He shook his head. 'You're right, they were buggers.'

Libby declined the offer of a biscuit but said yes to showing her around the cottage she'd never been to. The downstairs she'd pretty much seen – kitchen at the end with a view of a small lawn and the annexe on the side, and beyond, green banks of grass stretching up without any sign of habitation. Upstairs was a main bedroom with sloped ceilings and at floor height varnished dark wood cupboards with the same stable-style doors as the outside annexe. There was a box room too with a futon sofa she knew opened out to a bed because her friends had slept on that same bed for sleepovers.

'You still have the red sofa,' she said when they went back downstairs. She hadn't spotted it before because it was largely hidden beneath a charcoal grey throw, rucked up at one corner exposing its original colour.

'It still works,' he said, stacking the dishwasher, a slim-line version for one or two people, never an entire family.

'I guess so.' Her mum had chosen that sofa, she loved it for the colour it added to the room. He'd hated it at first, said it was too soft and squishy to sit on, but he'd eventually come round and Libby had memories of them both sitting together on it, watching television, laughing at something or other, Mum stretched out with her legs across his knees.

'How long are you here for?' he asked as Libby took charge of emptying the leftovers of chicken hotpot into the awaiting two plastic containers.

'Just the afternoon.'

'I don't mean *here* here, I mean England.'

She put the lids onto both containers. 'I haven't decided yet.'

'Can't be cheap, staying in a hotel.' He popped a dishwasher tablet into the appliance and selected the programme.

'I'm staying with a friend.'

He looked at her over the top of his glasses. 'The same friend who brought you up here?'

She smiled, ignored his question. And when she spotted a walking guide on top of a pile of books near the fridge, she opened it up. 'I missed our walks,' she said without really realising she was about to admit it until she did. She turned to face him and leaned against the worktop. 'When Mum died, I missed her making us go out. I mean, I hated it at the time, some days I'd have given anything to be left behind in front of the television, but after she passed away . . .' She shrugged as though she didn't know how to finish the sentence.

'You and I never carried on the tradition,' he said for her. 'And that's down to me.'

'It was down to both of us, Dad.'

He wiped around the sink and then stopped, the cloth still beneath his hand. 'I let you down, Libby. I was the parent, it was up to me to be there for you and I wasn't.'

'You were grieving too.'

'I felt terribly guilty when you went to America.'

'Why?' She put both plastic containers in the freezer for him, noting how everything was on the small scale – tiny portions of frozen leftovers, small packets of frozen vegetables, even the milk they'd used for tea was the smallest carton you could buy in case it went off before he could use it all.

'If I'd handled your mum's death better you might never have gone.'

'You could be right.' She motioned for him to sit down at the table and she sat next to him. 'You might have been able to get me to stay, but I'm glad I went. I had to do something for myself, break away, go somewhere nobody knew me, where I didn't have any more memories. And it was a brilliant step work wise which I think was what buoyed me along for a while.'

'You were rather angry when I called you to say I was selling the house.'

She took a deep breath. 'I was.'

'I almost pulled the plug. You sounded so down when I told you, you would have no family home to return to if you needed to, your childhood bedroom wouldn't be yours any more. I thought, this kid has lost so much, she doesn't deserve this.'

But neither did he. Libby realised how difficult it must've been for him to pick himself up and carry on. 'I was angry, upset, gutted, and in complete denial.'

'Denial?'

'It's reality . . . moving. I don't know of many people whose parents still live in the same house they grew up in. Things change, kids move out, parents move to a different stage of their lives.'

'Your mum never got to do that.' His words fell flat, both of them knowing exactly why it had never happened. Suddenly, just like that, her life taken too young, their very existence thrown into disarray. 'Part of the reason I moved up here was because it was what she always dreamed of. We'd never even been here. Money was tight when you were little, we spent most of it on the everyday things rather than holidays. I think we camped in the Isle of Wight a handful of times, Wales once or twice, but the Lake District was a place your mum had in her heart and I knew when you left the country I had to find something for myself. This was the first place I came.'

In all this time they had both avoided talking about

their loss, they didn't let her name come into conversation and if they did the subject was soon moved along. Libby wished now that they'd taken time to talk about her mum because doing so here didn't feel as painful as she feared it would. She wondered whether her dad felt the same and perhaps whether talking about her in a cottage she'd never set foot in, that didn't hold memories within its walls, was somehow less confronting.

'I came for a holiday first,' he went on. 'I stayed in Kendal, in the town. Hated it, too busy, but close by I found walks your mum would've loved. I stayed two weeks then after returning home came back for a month. After that I knew this was where I wanted to be. It sounds daft but when I'm out walking I feel like a part of your mum is always with me.' Libby bit down on her lip when his eyes misted. 'It's a walker's paradise, she would've loved it, and she would've leaped at the chance to join a walking group.'

'She would've bossed everyone around.'

He beamed a smile her way. 'That she would.'

'Have you made some friends up here?'

'I have, and I have your mum's voice in my head approving of characters, disapproving of others. There are some people in the group I avoid spending too much time with, but mostly they're all really good company.'

'I'm glad.'

'Enough about me, what about you? Are you taken with America so much you'll never return to your roots?' The question was one he hadn't tackled before, perhaps not wanting to know the answer. 'Because it's fine, honestly, I'm not going to make you feel guilty about finding your own way.'

'Like I did when you sold up.'

'I didn't say that and I certainly didn't mean it. I get that I was taking away your memories when I sold the house, you didn't even get to say goodbye.'

'It's just a house, Dad.' She hadn't got to say goodbye to her mum either and that's what had her choked up now. 'My memories are more than bricks and mortar, I have plenty to keep me going.'

'And so do I,' he said, taking the cups and rinsing the dregs of tea from the bottom. 'Do you have to rush away?'

'Today?'

'Today,' he smiled. 'I was wondering whether you'd like to come for a walk with me, see more of the place where I live?'

She looked down at her feet. She'd had the forethought to wear trainers in preparation for some time near the lake. 'I'd love to.'

Libby had texted Drew before she and her dad left Cedar Cottage, surprised she had any sort of signal, to let him know she wasn't ready to be collected yet. He hadn't replied, but she got the impression he was flexible as far as any of their arrangements went and she suspected he was right to think that if he'd suggested she accompany him on this trip any earlier than he had, she would've found a reason not to come.

Where Libby's dad lived literally had one shop for milk, newspapers, tea bags and a handful of other things including a dodgy selection of DVDs of films she'd never even heard of. That was the first thing he showed her and then it was right into the green, green grass of this place he'd taken himself away to. They walked, they talked about

New York, somewhere her dad had never visited, Libby telling him about locations he would've seen on the television, her trips out of the big city to see what else America had on offer. They talked about her job and what her next step was.

'I haven't really decided exactly what I'll do yet, but I do have several companies showing an interest,' she floated as she watched her footing on a particularly muddy path heading back in the direction of the cottage. They'd already covered three miles before they'd looped around. 'I had an interview in London recently for a company which has offices dotted around the UK – Liverpool, Bristol, Manchester.'

'Well any of those locations would be nice. You'd be closer, maybe we'd see more of one another. Maybe I could even make a start on that annexe.'

'That sounds like a wonderful idea, Dad.'

As they walked Libby wondered was this why her mum had chosen to walk so often and make them do it too? Within the walls of the house it was far too easy for conversations to fall flat when you didn't know what to say next, too simple to not linger in the same space for long and therefore never talk in the way you should do. Out here, the air vented their heads and gave them a freedom that enabled them to speak more truthfully. It was only outside, all the way up here in the Lake District, that Libby realised how stifled she'd feel doing this anywhere else, even back in the town they used to live in. Cutting those ties was something she'd thought terrible for such a long time, but now she saw how liberating it was.

Her dad opened a wooden gate with a bit of a shove as the grass was overgrown on one side and managed to shut it with a push. 'When do you need to decide about the job?'

She'd got the acceptance email this morning with an offer for the salary and package that came with it, but she'd told nobody after she'd quickly replied to say she'd review the offer and get back to them as soon as she could. 'Soon,' she smiled.

'Plenty to think about then.'

Her dad, a statistician for more than forty years before retirement, shared her love of numbers. He'd been the one to help her with her maths homework, her mum laughing at her own inability to do the simplest of sums, but excelling in other areas. She'd been a home economics teacher for years and meal planning and nutritional cooking came as naturally to her as mathematics did to Libby and her dad. Libby had forgotten about that closeness until now, the way they'd happily sat at the dining room table scrutinising problems and losing themselves in the textbooks and calculations, her mum bringing them snacks to keep them going, especially when Libby got to A levels and the work became a lot more in-depth.

As they walked, Libby's dad showed her the countryside that reminded her a lot of Somerset with its rolling hills, although some were so steep in parts it was a wonder she hadn't had to go up on her hands and knees. They stopped by a fence almost completely covered with ivy apart from the section with the gate they'd passed through, and rested on a huge rock. Libby had no idea whether it had been put there or was a natural part of the landscape, but it did the job, and with a drink of water each they took in the scenery.

'The views are something else,' she admitted.

'You're impressed, I can tell.'

'I wish Mum could've seen it.'

'Me too,' he nodded.

Closing herself off in her anger at losing her mum, at him selling the family home, had been easier than facing up to reality. And she felt selfish she hadn't even begun to think about what it must feel like for him, losing his wife and mother of his child. He'd lost a part of his identity almost, given they'd been together for decades, and while she was young and got to move forwards with her life, he must've been lost without the woman he'd fallen in love with, the woman he'd thought he'd have in his life for many years to come.

'I'm seriously considering taking the UK job,' she admitted. She went into the details of her life in America, how the excitement and change had been perfect at the time, but how the fast pace and stress wasn't quite the same as she got older. It was as though you grew out of it. 'What do you think I should do?' It felt like forever since she'd asked for his advice, but it felt right.

'Only you can know the answer, Libby. I know you'll make the right decision, you always do.'

They sat sipping their waters, the rock gradually getting warmer in the sunshine that appeared at that moment and had her dad moving further round to where she was sitting, his back to the sun. They laughed at how much mud she had on her trainers already.

'We shouldn't have stopped walking when your mum died,' he said. 'And we shouldn't have stopped talking either.'

'It was so unfair what happened to her.' Her voice broke. 'Why did it have to happen to her, to us?'

He put an arm around her shoulders the same way he had at her mum's funeral, except this time he was really there, he wasn't lost and a ghost of the father he should've been, trying to piece himself back together again, he was a man who was managing to do that, but now knew he had to be there for his daughter. And all this time later, she finally let him.

Libby hadn't cried much when her mum died. She'd cried a bit when it first happened, then again at the funeral, but mostly she'd been numb. And she'd never, ever cried in front of her dad, if he'd tried to comfort her she'd hidden her feelings, afraid that her misery would drag him down. He'd never cried in front of her either, perhaps afraid too that his torment would make his daughter's life harder than it needed to be.

They stayed like that for a while, not moving even when a couple of walkers with those funny poles some people used for balance came past and gave them a peculiar look, not even when a couple of women out on a hilly run asked whether they were OK. They just both nodded and Libby even laughed.

'What are we like?' She found a tissue from her bag. 'Mum would roll her eyes at our dramatics if she could see us both.'

'She most certainly would. And your grandparents would have me hung, drawn and quartered, they were always ones to keep up appearances. Put a smile on your face and get on with it, I'm sure that's what they'd have wanted to say to me if they'd seen me at your mum's funeral. Luckily they were no longer around.'

'You never got on with them?'

'I tolerated them,' he acknowledged. Another walker

passed them by. It was a popular trail, but past this point they seemed to be able to pick different directions. She wondered if you came often enough whether you'd learn the tracks by heart and pick your favourite. 'They were cold, your mum was well aware of that, but they were her parents. She didn't have the easiest of upbringings.'

'That's sad, she never told me.'

'She didn't like to think about it.' He nudged her gently. 'We made sure we never did the same with you though and I hope it worked, I hope you felt wanted, not constantly disapproved of.'

'Of course I felt wanted.' How could any parent make a child feel differently?

'Your mum was never brutal enough to cut ties, they still had a certain hold over her for years and years. We went through the motions half the time and then it whittled down to Sunday lunches every month like clockwork. Always at our house, we never went there.'

'Why not?'

'I think it was your mum's way of finally asserting her control over something. She'd had precious little of it until you were born. She did every little thing they wanted. We planned renovations and because they didn't think our plans were a good idea your mother changed them, when we got married your mum wanted silver bridesmaids' dresses, but her dad said it wasn't what he'd envisaged. Next thing I knew, we had the bridesmaids dressed in deep pink. When we fitted out our kitchen we were set to get an electric wall oven – your mum always wanted one so she could see what was cooking at eye level – but at the last minute she changed to a traditional range cooker. Your grandparents had one. And those were the little things. I knew when she was still living at home, Maggie was told who she could be friends with, the rules were strict in that regard, and it didn't stop after we married. We argued about it sometimes, I couldn't understand why Maggie let them get away with it. I didn't want her to disown them, but I wanted her to stand up for herself.'

'I never knew any of that. I mean, my grandparents weren't particularly warm, but I figured it was old age.' She'd never thought about it too deeply, in truth they hadn't had that much time together that didn't involve a formal sit-down dinner. They'd never been the sort to sit on the floor and play, her grandma in particular always dressed in smart suits on a Sunday as though she didn't have any idea how to wear anything else.

'When you were tiny your mum hoped they'd relax a bit with a grandchild but they didn't. And one day when we were at their house you dropped your ice cream on their kitchen floor and your gran yelled at you, went completely over the top.'

'I don't remember.'

'I wasn't there, but your mum told me about it. It was the first time I heard her berate her parents' actions in a long time.' He paused a while. 'The way she described it, she'd been like a mother lion protecting her cub, she wasn't going to let them do to you what they'd done to her, I assume, made her afraid to be her own person.' He cleared his throat. 'Not that being your own person involves throwing your ice cream everywhere, but you know what I mean. Now, your Auntie Joy was different . . .' Libby tried not to flinch at the mention of her name. 'She didn't conform, she always was going to be her own person. She always liked you, played when she came over, until we told her she could no longer come.' He looked down at his fingers clutching his water bottle, guilt coming over him. 'I'm afraid your grandparents got to your mum and she let them, she believed them when they said it was better for us as a family to never see Joy again. And your mum was so determined to do everything right for you and give you the happy childhood she'd never had. Your grandparents put the horrors into her let me tell you.'

'The horrors?'

He shook his head. 'I won't go into detail, it's not my story to tell. But I did try to persuade your mum to think differently, to talk to Joy and try to see her side.'

'Her side, I don't understand.'

'I assume hasn't Joy talked to you about it yet.' His expression had relaxed with the apparent confession he knew Libby and Joy were in touch.

'How did you know?'

'That you and Joy are in contact? I saw a letter come through the post one day, I recognised the writing. I put it back on the mat as though I hadn't found it, I waited to see if you'd tell me.'

'Did you ever read the letters?'

'Guilty. Only to make sure it was all normal things she was talking about, because a little part of me did doubt her, there was always the nagging feeling, what if she is this bad person everyone has made her out to be? But the letters were fine, they were chatty, I could tell she was a good influence rather than bad. I checked the letters when I could, I never let on, and I never told your mum because I didn't want it to stop.'

'Why not?'

'Because I had a hope that someday Maggie would stop listening to her bloody parents and listen to her sister instead. You get to know a person a lot through the written word and I felt I was getting to know Joy too. I wondered whether you'd ever tell us, but you never did.'

'I felt guilty, but it was an adventure too, my secret. Or not such a secret it seems. Are you angry?'

'I could never be angry with you my girl.'

She leaned her head against his shoulder. If he had meant to use her mum's name for her he didn't acknowledge it, it just came out, and it gave her a sense of home she didn't need the family house for. That sense was all around her, her dad, their memories that bound them together for good.

She sat up again. 'You know this is the most you've talked in a long while.'

He puffed out his cheeks. 'I shall need a lie down after this.'

After another walker passed by, the exertion of the slope causing them to pull out a handkerchief and mop their forehead, Libby told her dad, 'I never stopped writing to her.'

She could feel him nod as if he'd expected it. 'Where is she living?'

'Somerset, on an old dairy farm, she runs a sort of half-way house.'

'Is that right?' He waited a beat.

'I've been staying with her.'

He only looked surprised for a moment. 'I guess it took some bravery to come up here, to the unknown.'

'I'm glad I did.'

'Me too.' He nodded, accepting the fresh start for both

of them. 'How is Joy? Does she know you're here?'

'She kept telling me to get in touch. She didn't want me to tell you I was with her though as she said you'd be annoyed.'

'Not at all. Joy never got a chance with us and for that I'm sorry. Please tell her that would you?'

'Of course.' She took a deep breath. 'What happened, Dad? What happened that was so terrible Joy's own sister wanted nothing to do with her, and I'm assuming now after what you've said, that her parents didn't either.'

'Not my story to tell,' he said. 'You'll need to ask Joy. Come on, let's go home. I've got something called red velvet cake. Looks sickly but you'll probably like it.'

She was about to ask more, but he was right, whatever it was Joy hadn't told Libby or anyone else was so huge she deserved to be able to tell it in her own words. She hooked her arm through her dad's and they gingerly made their way down the muddy slope back to the road that led to his cottage.

She only hoped Joy would see sense and tell them all what was going on before she sold up and kept it quiet for good.

The Old Dairy was her home and seeing it go would break not only Joy's heart, but everyone else's, Libby's included.

Chapter Thirteen

Drew

When Drew got the text to go and meet Libby he wondered what he was going to get – a crying woman whose afternoon had been a slice of hell, the happy daughter of a man able to talk to her in the way she really needed about their joint loss, or someone who didn't say a word all the way back to the boathouse they were staying in.

He definitely hadn't expected to be beckoned inside Cedar Cottage by Libby's dad to find Libby in the kitchen cutting up cake before delivering a plate with an enormous wedge of something red with a thick slick of creamy icing and ordering him to sit down.

'Red velvet,' her dad told him as though they already knew one another. 'Watch these beams,' he said, his fork in the air gesturing to the dark wood on the ceilings. 'Not a problem for me, but you're tall.'

'I've already ducked,' Drew grinned, 'but thanks for the reminder.'

Libby was smiling at him and when he raised his eyebrows in a way that confirmed he realised it had gone well, the happy look only disappeared off her face for her to take another mouthful of cake. Her dad told him all about the walk they'd been on, asked about his kayak business, where they were staying tonight. When they were in the jeep ready to leave, her dad stood at the door of his cottage, his form taking up most of the doorway even though his height wasn't near enough to hit the beams inside, and waved at them until they disappeared out of sight.

The whole experience had been much like meeting a girlfriend's father for the first time, and Drew hadn't minded one bit. He now knew how Joy must feel, wanting Libby to stay, not wanting her to get a job in America and disappear once again, because he felt it too.

'It went really well,' she said when she stopped waving and sat facing the right way in the jeep.

'I could see that.'

She tutted, looking down at her shoes. 'I've brought mud into your jeep.'

'Don't worry about it, probably be plenty more by the time we head back to Somerset. The weather forecast has changed, with rain on the cards tomorrow.'

They were taking it slow down country lanes, most wide enough only for one car, dipping into lay-bys when required, coming out when someone the other way was generous enough to stop. 'Shame, I was almost looking forward to kayaking.'

He picked up on her sarcasm right away and her misunderstanding that a little bit of rain ever stopped him. 'We'll still be going, don't you worry. Now, thunder and lightning might be different, but there are no storms predicted.'

It wasn't far to the boathouse. He'd already gone there and dumped the bags and it was as impressive as he'd been told. The guy he'd bought the kayaks from was someone who'd supplied him before and this place was his bolthole, rented out at intervals throughout the year to eager holidaymakers. With a few days free between bookings, he'd offered it to Drew and that was when Drew had decided to suggest he bring Libby up here. And he was glad he had, not just because she seemed to have made progress with her dad.

'Wow,' she said, and then repeated it three more times in a row when he pulled up outside the stone structure with unbroken views of the water, a scene so picturesque it was like something out of a magazine spread.

'You approve?' It gave him a thrill she liked where they were staying. It hadn't been planned as a romantic getaway for two but that was definitely where his head was at now, which took him by surprise. And he liked Libby, he didn't want her to think he'd planned it this way. Because he hadn't. He'd only wanted to help.

She headed up the path outlined by small wooden posts with tiny chains looped between and the mishmash of sizes and shaped coloured pavers that took them up to the front door. 'I approve, I approve a lot.'

'I've put you in the top bedroom,' he said after they'd taken their shoes off and left them on the rack outside the covered entrance. 'I'll stay down here in the second room.' At the foot of the narrow iron spiral staircase he could tell she was itching to explore. 'Go on.' He was in no doubt she'd love the king size bed with luxurious white linen and a chocolate brown furry blanket laying across the foot of it.

Perhaps she wouldn't think he'd manipulated the situation, not if her mind was on taking a job in America and leaving for good. His mind went into overdrive – what if the US companies who had shown an interest made her an offer she couldn't refuse? She was clearly very good at what she did.

She came downstairs all smiles. 'That almost makes up for the fact I'll have to go out on a kayak tomorrow.'

He led the way to the kitchen, bypassing the other bedroom where he'd sleep, comfortable enough but not the proportions of the upstairs or the luxury. 'I bought in a few supplies. Nothing huge, just the basics.'

She perched on one of the wooden stools in the kitchen at the onyx Caesar stone bench that went so well with the walnut cupboards and the small island the designer had managed to fashion in here. The bench jutted out just enough round its corner that four people could easily sit on the stools for a meal. 'To be honest I ate so much at dad's and then there was the cake.'

'Toast it is then, if and when you're hungry. I ate at lunchtime too so perhaps it'll be a liquid dinner.' He indicated a couple of bottles of red he'd got in too.

'Sounds good to me.' She didn't stay facing him long, she spun round and took in the view and the small grass area outside the sliding doors sloping down to the lake.

There was private access and a jetty to launch the kayak from tomorrow, and on the grass was a fire pit they could use after dark. 'I'm going to take a shower,' he told her, 'I'm grubby after being out on the water. But make yourself at home.'

'Mind if I use the bathroom after you?'

'You didn't see the en suite upstairs then?'

'There's an en suite?' she raced up to check it out, back moments later grinning from ear to ear. 'That's me sorted for an hour or so, there's a slipper bath.'

He smiled. 'I've no idea what a slipper bath is, but if you tell me that's what it is, who am I to argue?' All he knew was that there was a white, roll top bath with one end higher than the other and behind the same door she'd obviously assumed was a cupboard earlier, there was a floor-to-ceiling view of the lake from the tub.

'No peeking,' she told him.

He smiled, knowing she was referring to the window that gave a stunning view, the window that if you stood at the end of the jetty, you'd be able to see right into. He assumed that as so few crafts came up close, there'd never been a need to install blinds or curtains. 'I promise I won't look, relax.'

And he wouldn't. He'd also do his best not to think about her going upstairs, getting undressed and stepping into the bath water when he was right here all alone.

Libby emerged almost an hour later, her cheeks flushed from the bath water, wearing a fresh pair of jeans and a loose linen shirt. Her chestnut hair was pinned up, only a few wisps escaping, the back of it damp as she brushed past him to grab one of the wine glasses he'd set out.

He went ahead and poured. 'Good bath?'

'The best. There were even candles, not that it's quite dark enough yet.' Although the light was fading fast. Amazing how those heady, long summer nights disappeared pretty quickly as August approached its second half and geared up to change over to September.

'Did you blow the candles out?'

She rolled her eyes. 'Of course I did. And you sound just like Joy. I left a candle flickering in the bathroom once, she was not happy.'

'Hey, in our defence, candle labels do tend to say not to leave them unattended.'

'You're right.'

'Of course I'm right,' he winked, clinking his glass against hers as she spotted the flames outside. 'I got the fire pit going, thought we could head out there.'

'That sounds perfect.' She looked away shyly as though she might be thinking this was bordering on the romantic side and only just realising it now.

She took a seat on one of the pair of wooden Adirondack chairs as he took off the mesh lid of the fire pit that prevented sparks, embers and debris escaping. He added a few more pieces of wood and prodded them into the flames with a poker.

'I didn't tell you everything about my visit with Dad earlier,' she admitted, watching him as he put the lid back on. 'He mentioned Joy.'

Drew faced her. 'He told you what happened between them?'

In the firelight her skin looked even softer, the glow highlighting her hair as it licked around the sides of her face. 'Turns out he's known for years that I was writing to her.'

'Blimey, wasn't expecting that.'

A small smile appeared. It wasn't the beaming smile he'd seen a few times, the one that showed off full lips and beautifully straight teeth, it was more uncertain than that, but no less mesmerising. 'He also knows I'm staying with her now.'

He tugged a hand through his hair, much smoother now it was rid of the water that got in it earlier, not that he'd fallen in, it just seemed to happen when you kayaked, or went out on the lake for any length of time. 'How did he react to that, did he freak out?'

'Quite the opposite, it seems he thinks Mum should've handled the entire situation with Joy differently.'

'He didn't hint at what the "situation" might be?'

'Unfortunately not.' She twiddled the stem of her glass between her fingers, head turning in the direction of the lake and the reflection of the sunset. 'He said it's for Joy to tell me.'

'Right.'

'You don't think she will?' She put her attention back on him.

'If she's going so far as to sell the farm to avoid it, then I doubt it.' He shrugged. 'It's a shame, like you say, that she's always let all of us talk to her but it's never been the same for her.'

'I hate to think of people crawling all over the farm looking to buy it, and I've only been there five minutes.'

'I haven't lived there in a long while but it's crushing me too, to think it won't be hers much longer.' He found a mostly even part of ground and set down his wine glass so he could sit back and look up at the sky, the changing colours of the sunset giving over to the deepest of inky blue as the night began to draw in.

'I wonder how the viewing went,' said Libby reminding him how real this was.

'Not too well I hope.'

'What was it like, living with Joy all those years ago?' Her question took him by surprise with its frankness. 'Was she like she is now, or different?'

'She's consistent.' He sat upright again, too restless to lean back. 'I didn't think about it much at the time because I was such a wreck myself, but I believe helping people was something she was hesitant about until she became more practised. It breaks her heart if she can't help people – and there have been some to come and go from the farmhouse without sorting themselves out – and she takes it as personal failure.'

'But you're a success story.'

He put a foot out to gently kick her for teasing and nearly knocked his wine glass over, forgetting it was there. He scooped it up to rescue it. 'I like to think so. I was the first, I wonder sometimes had I been trouble and not managed to get to the other side, whether she'd have ever tried to help anyone again.'

'I got the feeling from Dad that he would've given Joy a chance, with us, our family, but it was Mum who put the brakes on.'

'How does that make you feel?'

'Sad more than anything else. I don't have siblings, but if I did, I can't imagine them ever doing anything so bad I never spoke to them again.' He did his best not to watch her lips too closely when she took a sip of wine and wiped a drop of it from her bottom lip with the tip of her finger. 'You ever wonder what it would've been like to have a brother or sister?'

He laughed. 'People who've come to the farmhouse have given me some idea. Freddie and I rile each other good and proper, Lauren's good company – bit secretive sometimes, but nice to be around, she's like a sister I feel I could trust. And Cameron's still new but I like him. I like to think he can look up to me and Freddie.'

'It's good you're around. It's great Joy takes people in, but I think peers make it easier to find your place in the world. You have examples of how to behave and fit in. Does that make sense?'

'It does.'

'She's a good parent without even being one,' said Libby before she asked, 'Do you have any photographs of your parents?' Her question wasn't completely unexpected given the day she'd had.

He went inside to pick up his wallet and brought the wine out too, sliding the door shut behind him. The stars were beginning to peek out, but there was enough light from the flames to see.

'This is my favourite picture of them.' He handed it to her and she leaned closer to the glow to get a better look. 'It was taken on their honeymoon and it's exactly how I'd like to remember them. I have others, but this one never fails to make me smile if I'm feeling low.' The picture, taken on their honeymoon in Spain, was of both of them, bodies sandwiched together in an inflatable rubber ring being pulled around by a speedboat. He had no clue who would've taken it, that person would have no idea of the happiness they'd captured and the memory they'd created for him even though he would never know his parents' voices, their expressions, nothing.

'They look happy.' He didn't miss the emotion in her voice. He guessed she'd been going through it today with her own family.

He took the photograph and slotted it back safely into his wallet. 'I always wondered what they'd be like as grandparents. Well, not always, I wasn't thinking that when I was little or as a teenager obviously.'

'They'd probably have been a lot better than my

grandparents.' She was still watching him as he topped up both wine glasses.

'It's one thing that makes me really sad – that they'll never know my kids if and when I have them.'

'That's what makes me sad with Mum too. She'd have loved to have grandchildren, she'd've spoiled them rotten I bet.'

'I like to think mine would've had fun with grandkids, the kind of fun I see in that photograph. But mostly I'd like to have a role model, to see how to parent. I see it with Joy, but other than that . . .'

'Is that why you were in a bad place when she took you in? Because you'd lost your parents?'

'I was lost. I'd stopped caring much about myself, was hanging out with people who thought pretty much the same, it was a stroke of luck when she advertised for some-one to help her at the farm.'

'What were you doing with the people you hung out with?'

He shrugged. 'Not anything good.'

'I went to America to deal with my pain,' Libby admitted, making him feel less of an odd-ball. 'It worked, I threw myself into my job, earned a lot of money, got pro-motions, garnered respect. But beneath it all . . .'

'The hurt never goes away.'

'The hurt never goes away,' she repeated. He did his best not to watch the way her finger ran around the rim of her glass as she sat thinking, contemplating all the emo-tions that had come to the surface today.

'Hungry?' he asked after a while.

'Not at all, you?' She stifled a yawn.

He shook his head. The fire had dwindled and he'd let

it slowly go right out. He didn't add any more wood or prod it any more 'That cake finished me off.'

She laughed. 'Dad did well with the entertaining, not exactly his thing.'

'Will you visit again?'

'I'd like to.'

He turned and looked to the beautiful boathouse. 'If you time it right I might be able to sort this place for you, my friend does mates' rates.'

'I might take you up on that.'

Should he dare to hope? 'Does this mean you're not rushing back to America?'

She didn't answer right away. 'Before we came up here I was on the fence with the UK job, the possibility of London or one of their other locations, but seeing Dad . . . it makes me realise life is short. Mum's was.' She covered her eyes with her hands. 'I'm sorry.'

'Don't be, it happened, please don't tiptoe around me. My parents died way too young, and it sucks. Your mum died too soon, that sucks too.' He wanted her to realise she could say what she wanted to him, she could be open and honest, but he'd seen her hesitation when he batted away her question of what he'd done with the lowlifes he'd once hung out with. Not that he had much to hide, but he didn't want to talk about their crimes or the drugs some of them took. He wanted to leave those days well and truly behind him and that included talking about the loss of his parents. He didn't want to rehash anything and start getting emotional, not in front of a girl he was trying to impress. 'Come on, we need to get ourselves a good night's sleep if we're going to be champion kayakers tomorrow.'

She began to laugh. 'I'm not sure what you're expecting, but you should probably set the bar as low as it can go.'

He found the filled watering can he'd left nearby ready to extinguish the last of the flames in the fire pit and poured the water onto the fire before picking up the wine bottle and glasses. Heading inside he told her, 'I'm glad you're thinking of hanging around, Libby.'

'Me too.'

Their bodies were close as he shut the door behind them and it was almost the perfect moment with the faint smell of woodsmoke lingering in the air, the prickling of stars in the sky, the way they'd both been lulled into a more relaxed state with the wine and the conversation, but when he didn't move, she stepped away from him first, as though wary of getting involved.

'London won't be Somerset,' he continued, as she finished up her wine and set the glass in the sink, 'but it's England and it'll make Joy and your dad pretty happy.'

She nodded. 'Goodnight, Drew.'

'Goodnight, Libby.'

Was it too much to hope the smile she gave him before she went on up to bed might suggest she knew it would make him pretty happy too, and perhaps even her, if she were to stay in the country long-term.

'It's cold!'

Drew watched Libby as she dipped her fingers in the water from the jetty. 'I know you're new to this, but you don't need to put your hand in the water, it's feet first onto the kayak while I steady it and I'll hand you the oars.'

He'd helped her on with her personal flotation device, close enough he could smell her hair, see the curl of her eyelashes when she blinked. They'd carried the kayak out from the boathouse to here, her at the front, him at the rear, and he could tell she wasn't particularly looking forward to it, but the wind was light, no sign of rain yet, and a lick of sun had him hopeful it would be a good experience.

'Just checking in case I fall in.' The wind lifted her hair around her face. She had the beach shoes on that she'd asked him to pick up for her yesterday, khaki shorts and a dark T-shirt which showed a different Libby to the one who'd looked all stressed when they first met at the farmhouse. Back then she was the Libby he could tell had been plucked from the city and dropped into the countryside. Now she was a Libby who could easily flip between versions and he hoped she found it as welcome a change as he did.

'You won't fall in.' He held the kayak steady and gestured for her to climb on top. 'And sit-on-top kayaks are notoriously stable.'

She looked doubtful, but gingerly stepped off the jetty and with only a slight wobble sat down in the front seat. He'd sit in the back towards the middle so he had better control. He handed her the oar and had her hold the jetty so they didn't drift away while he climbed in himself. She giggled when he pushed them off, the kayak wobbling at first and her taking a few moments to work out how to paddle so they went in the right direction.

'I'll follow you so we put the oars in at the same time,' he said, watching her from behind. He'd have to make sure that didn't distract him too much on the lake or he'd be heading in the path of water crafts that would eat them for breakfast.

He didn't mind the spray from her oars as she got to grips with it, the personal flotation device large and bulky and unfamiliar at first, getting in the way of her arms moving, but she didn't take long to get used to it. He took a few wobbles, a couple of huge water sprays as she misjudged the water and flicked a torrent in his direction – she'd turned round a couple of times to see him drenched and apologised profusely – but on the whole it was more successful than even he'd thought it would be.

'It's an arm workout,' she told him as they let themselves drift near an island they'd paddle around and back the other way. She had a sip of water and he did the same.

'Sure is, but fun though, right?'

She turned again. Her grip on the oars had become less white-knuckled at least. He'd noticed her holding a lot of tension when they'd first set off from the jetty, but now she looked more relaxed. 'I'm enjoying myself.'

'Don't sound so surprised. So you'll come out onto the river with me back in Somerset?' He stowed his water again, ready for the off. They had a small picnic in a waterproof bag and planned to climb out somewhere convenient to enjoy it, but he wasn't sure now as the forecast for rain looked to be right with the dark clouds looming above.

'As long as we can do tandem again,' she said.

'You wait, a few more goes and you'll want your own kayak.' Something told him she'd be racing him before too long, at least that's what he hoped.

They set off again, arms propelling the oars into the water in time on one side, then the other, laughing when they almost collided with protruding branches of a tree, and by the time they'd circled the island the weather really was rolling in, and Drew detected an energy spurt from Libby as they hurried back to the boathouse.

'I've spent all that time in water keeping dry,' she laughed, shouting over the sound of the rain teeming down so much by the time they reached the jetty that it drowned out all else, 'and now I'm getting wet. The irony!'

He climbed out first and held the kayak steady while she did the same before they lifted it from the water. 'Watch your footing,' he called out as he felt the walkway slipping beneath his feet, but they were soon up at the boathouse, the kayak beneath a covered area, and both of them falling in through the back door.

'I'm heading for a shower.' She took her shoes off and threw hers and his outside the door.

Drew grabbed a towel from the linen cupboard so they could dry their feet and not walk the wet everywhere. And by the time she came downstairs in jeans, a cashmere jumper you only needed on weird English summer days where the weather changed in an instant, and with a towel around her neck as she dried the ends of her hair, he'd laid the picnic out onto plates.

Libby sat on the sofa, legs curled beneath her, the rain pelting against the boathouse. They ate in quiet contemplation, both spent from the kayaking, soothed by the rain. When she'd asked to see a photograph of his parents it had knocked him sideways. He'd not shown many people at all, the photograph something he carried with him all the time, almost a part of him, yet undiscovered to most. But Libby had been so open about her own dad, she'd got somewhere and he was glad for her, but it brought it home to him how he'd never have that chance. And the pain hit again at night when he woke from a dream about them both, they'd all been in the water, in a kayak together, all laughing the same way his parents had been in the photograph.

'That was good.' said Libby now, finishing the last piece of crust.

He dusted off his fingers too and set his empty plate on top of hers on the coffee table. 'It was just a sandwich, but I can't deny it was good.'

'I noticed you bought some hot chocolate supplies,' she said picking up the plates. 'Want me to make us a couple?'

'Sure. Mugs are in the cupboard.'

Soon after, they both had a mug of hot chocolate made with milk and proper flakes, the sort of hot chocolate he could get on board with. He never drank the stuff, but this was the real thing. 'Great idea.' He lifted his mug to indicate what he was talking about. He was a bit lost for words with her sitting down that bit closer to him now she'd finished in the kitchen.

'I love watching the rain,' she told him as it hit the glass as though it wasn't in droplets but a great wash from a giant bucket. 'Remember how excited Joy was when the storm came?'

'She loves a good storm. Me too, although not out on the lake.'

'Ever been stuck in a storm?'

He told her about the time he hadn't checked the weather forecast and had been out so long the person he'd set off with and who'd returned to the shed hours before had been about to start a search party. 'I soon learned to check the weather right before I set out. But it's still unpredictable. The rain didn't spoil today though, you're a natural.'

When her phone pinged she picked it up and checked the screen. But she soon put it down again. 'It's Joy,' she explained.

'You're ignoring her?'

'Not so much ignoring her as being wary.'

'Because she'll ask too much about your dad?'

'Because she'll quiz me about you.'

He pulled a face. 'Why would she do that?'

Libby put her hot chocolate mug on the coffee table and fiddled with the sleeves of her jumper as though she'd said something she shouldn't have. 'She watches me when I'm with you.'

'She watches all of us,' he shrugged. 'She cares, you know Joy.'

She took her time to find her words. 'She looks at me in a strange way when you and I are together, not in the same way she watches me with Freddie. When I'm with him she doesn't seem to mind, but when I'm in your company she gets edgy.' She hesitated, but then admitted what was bothering her. 'I wondered whether you've got something so dodgy in your past that she doesn't want me getting closer to you because it's so awful. You don't really talk about what happened before you came to the farmhouse, just that you were in a bad place.'

'I'm sorry if you think I've been evasive.' He wished he could tell her how he really felt about her, but with so much worry on her shoulders at the moment he didn't want to make her feel awkward. He needed her to know he was offering friendship with no strings attached if that was what she wanted. 'I haven't meant to be. I just don't like talking about myself that's all, I'd rather look to the future than remember the darker days. And I promise you my past isn't all that sordid. In a nutshell . . .' he cleared his throat, suddenly nervous and unsure of himself, '. . . my parents died, then my uncle died, I was lost, hung out with inappropriate characters – who, by the way, never did anything worse than petty thefts, smoking pot and the occasional usage of hard drugs, something I never tried.'

She nodded, he hoped in a way that meant she trusted what he was saying.

'I was pretty miserable,' he confided. 'I didn't care much about myself either.' And then he looked into her eyes. 'But I swear to you, I've never hurt another soul. And I never would.'

The look she gave him told him all he needed to know even before she said, 'I know you wouldn't. I trust you.'

He decided to ask the question he wasn't sure he wanted to know the answer to, in case she wasn't beginning to feel the same way about him as he was about her. 'So is Joy right?'

'Right about what?'

'About you and I getting closer.'

She said nothing, but when he moved towards her she leaned in, put a hand against his cheeks and pressed her lips softly against his. 'I'm sorry, was that—'

But he clasped her hand. 'Don't apologise.' He wondered what it would be like to kiss her again, properly, but when her phone went it broke the moment. 'Joy might be worried, you should get that, let her check up on you.'

Reluctantly she looked at the phone. And her face fell.

'What is it?' He really hoped Joy didn't have a problem

with him and Libby getting involved. It had been a long time since he'd liked anyone as much as he liked this girl he was sitting with, and to think it couldn't go further was like a punch in the stomach.

'It's Joy . . . she's got a buyer.'

'No way . . . that was quick.'

'Too quick.'

And now the moment between them really was over. 'We can't let her sell it.' He'd thought that at the start, but with reality fast sinking in he knew they had to do something. 'You need to tell her you saw the letter, tell her your dad thinks she deserves another chance. You don't know, it could be what gets through to her that she shouldn't give in to whoever's blackmail this is.'

'Can we go home?' Libby begged. 'Today rather than tomorrow?'

He picked up the hot chocolate cups. 'I'll clear the kitchen, put everything away, you start packing.'

The weather was kind to them on the way back to Somerset. The clouds parted, the sun came out for a while as they made their way down the motorway in a silence that hung heavy. They'd packed up in record time as though they were used to doing it, the kayaks were soon strapped to the roof, the rubbish deposited in the appropriate bins, they'd done their final checks to ensure they'd left nothing behind.

When they pulled round the back of the farmhouse there was nobody to be seen, but the back door was open, Luna waddled out to greet them as she did with most guests who came here. 'Where is she, eh, Luna?' Libby fussed over her while Drew took her bag and the book she'd taken with her but hadn't read much of at all, to leave at the bottom of the stairs ready to go up.

When he went back in to the kitchen Libby was still hugging Luna. He knew she was hoping the same as he was – that Joy hadn't signed anything away yet, not before Libby had a chance to talk to her.

Libby stood up, one hand on Luna's head and the dog loving every minute. 'Thank you, Drew. For a lovely time.'

'Shame to cut it short.' He gave Luna a fuss too. 'Where do you think Joy might be?'

'No idea, but I'll wait inside,' she said as a light drizzle began. It seemed it was almost Somerset's turn for the heavens to open. 'I'm sure she won't be long.'

He put a hand to her shoulder. 'It'll be difficult, but telling her you know about the letter is the only thing I can think of. Maybe she'll tell you everything and then she won't have to sell up at all.'

'I really hope you're right.' She leaned her cheek against his hand for the briefest of moments.

He wanted to kiss her. He longed to put his hands on either side of her face, draw her lips towards his and tell her it would all be fine. But he couldn't do that because neither of them had any idea whether it would be.

Their lives could be about to alter forever.

Chapter Fourteen

Joy

The rain had started off as drizzle when Joy was out in the fields with Freddie. She'd been about to tell him she'd found a buyer when it started, and as he hurried to finish what he was doing before it got too heavy a downpour, she lost her nerve and hurried back to the farmhouse. Drew's jeep was parked up already but there was no sign of either him or Libby.

When she went in to the kitchen she heard Libby's voice call out from the lounge. She went through to find her looking at the photograph of her standing with Ted and Marjory, Joy's favourite photo taken a long time ago, but which captured how she'd felt at finally finding peace with everything that had happened to her and beginning to move forwards.

'That was taken a year after I got here,' she said, hugging Libby hello. The photo in the mosaic-style frame had Ted on one side of her, Marjory on the other and two cows in the background. It was a picture she loved, yet right now found painful to look at knowing that her time here would soon come to an end. But she had to sell, she had to protect herself and those around her from hurt, from the shame she'd feel if any of them knew.

'How was the Lake District?' What Joy really meant was how did it go with her dad? She'd tried texting, but Libby had gone quiet on her, probably processing family troubles. She wondered had her dad told her the guilty secret Joy had been hiding? But nothing in Libby's demeanour suggested it.

'It's a beautiful place. And, it turns out I'm not bad at kayaking.'

Joy put on a smile at the indirect reference to Drew. She didn't want Libby hurt and she didn't want Drew hurt either, but together, she felt as though it was a disaster waiting to happen. The What Ifs raced around in her head constantly – what if they both knew the truth and Libby took her side but Drew quite rightly didn't? Neither of them deserved to fall in love and have it pulled out from under them. It wasn't a nice feeling, she wouldn't recommend it, it had almost broken her after all.

'Where is Drew?' Joy asked. 'Not like him to race off without a hello.'

'He's gone to pick up a pizza. We didn't have much for lunch.'

'You're back early, I wasn't expecting you until tomorrow.'

Libby's voice was soft when she told Joy they'd come back because of the text about the buyer for the farm. Joy had been cowardly delivering the news that way, but it had been fast, the only way she knew how.

But she didn't want to talk about the buyer or the farm. 'How was the visit with your dad?'

'It went well. Very well.' She told her all about the lunch they had together, the walk, the talking. 'He's known all

261

this time, Joy. All along he's known that you and I write to one another.'

Joy sat down slowly on her favourite chair by the window, open to let the air filter in. 'Is he angry?'

'No.'

She found that hard to believe. 'Did your mum know?'

'Never. And he'd wanted us to keep doing it as he hoped one day he'd change her mind about you.'

Joy's face crumpled and she felt the weight of losing Maggie consume her again, a loss before she'd had the chance to make peace with her sister. 'He never managed it. Did he tell you what happened?'

'He wouldn't. He said it could only come from you.' Perhaps, Joy thought, it would've been easier if he had told Libby everything. 'For what it's worth, he always thought you deserved to tell your side of the story.'

'I see.'

Libby said nothing for a while, but eventually she came and sat on the ottoman opposite Joy. 'I found the letter, Auntie Joy.'

Joy was about to ask what letter, but Libby's face said it all and she slumped further back in the chair, the wind knocked out of her.

'You can talk to me. Whatever is going on? What happened in your past that has someone with this kind of hold over you?'

'I can't talk to anyone about it.' She wouldn't, she couldn't. 'Someone obviously found out and is using it against me.' The bitterness in her voice wasn't something she could hide.

'You can, and you should. It's eating you up. I can see it, Drew can see it.'

At the mention of Drew's name, Joy breathed in as much of the outside air and the smell of rain, of damp, as she could. 'It's a terrible, terrible secret, Libby. You'll hate me for it.'

'Why don't you let me be the judge of that. And if you sell up and pay this person, what's to stop them doing something else down the line? They could ruin your entire life, the life you've built not just for yourself but for everyone else.'

Joy sat pulling the skin on the side of her right palm, she did it when she got stressed sometimes. She'd done it so much when she first came here that the skin had ended up bloodied and damaged and Ted had taken her to the doctor to get a prescription for a special lotion to clear it up.

Libby was waiting patiently. Joy wanted to run through the fields, scream at the top of her voice like she'd done before, maybe even turn back time. But nothing was ever going to make this better.

'Auntie Joy, start from the beginning.' She took both of her hands and squeezed them.

It took her a while to start, but when she did, she said simply, 'I fell in love.' Her voice shook. 'With the wrong man.'

Joy told Libby how she'd met Tay, how she'd been wide-eyed and trusting. She told Libby all his good qualities – his sense of fun, the way he made her feel like the only girl in the world, how he made her laugh, how he looked out for her, how he cared for his own mother when she needed him.

Libby's expression didn't alter when the conversation darkened and Joy told her how Tay began to change, how the sense of fun became dangerous as Tay tried to make quick money through the only ways he could see how. She told Libby about her surprise visit to him and finding out he was going to do something so completely crazy all she wanted to do was stop him.

And then Joy fell back into her own plague of memories and told Libby the rest.

'Please, Tay, I'm begging you, don't go,' Joy wailed. Her eyes stung as she implored him to see sense. They were sore and red from crying, but no amount of talking to him could make him back down.

Over the last couple of weeks Tay's mum had gone from bad to worse and he knew it was time to get her proper help. She needed someone with her 24/7 and while he could do out of hours and at night, they needed someone in the day. Selling the house not only wasn't what she wanted, it would take time, and they still needed a roof over their heads. Tay was putting in as many hours at work while he could, but now it was the winter months and it got dark earlier it was tougher to do with his mum frightened in the dark home alone. She had dementia and it was getting progressively worse. There were signs she didn't even recognise him on occasion, something Joy could see was tearing Tay apart. He didn't know what to do, he'd reached an impasse, and so when someone had dangled a huge carrot, so orange and bright, so attractive to his fiery personality, in front of him, he'd seen a way out.

'Don't do this, Joy.' He was adamant.

'Shouldn't I be saying that to you?' she screamed.

Two hours ago Joy had found out about Tay's job. It was all legit, he did work for a car sales garage, and he was doing well there. But what he'd never told her was that one of the lads – the horrible driver of the car that night and the same guy who she'd seen ripping off a number plate – had a side business that was about as far from legal as you could get. So far Tay hadn't done anything more than pick up some part from another dealer after hours, something the guy had paid for cash-in-hand the night she'd seen him outside the house. But this was something far bigger than that. And his evening walks like the one she'd caught him returning from last time suddenly all made sense, he'd been staking out a place.

'Tay, you don't have to do this, we'll find another way.'

It was then he began to cry himself and the sight of it shocked her. Tay didn't cry. He smiled, he laughed, he looked at her with adoration, he joked, he was the life and soul of a party and even when times were hard he rarely lurked in the down moments for long before he was up again. But now, he'd reached a depth she hadn't known he was heading for.

'I could move up here, move into the house, help out,' she pleaded.

There was a smile amidst the tears. 'Can you imagine my mother, my strict no-sex-before-marriage mother, ever letting us live under the same roof? With everything she can't remember or hasn't got a clue about, I bet she wouldn't forget her morals.'

Joy thought she had him, thought he was about to change his mind.

But all of a sudden it was as though he was on autopilot. He grabbed his coat, she followed him down the hallway where he checked his mum was sleeping, and then he headed for the front door. He froze there. 'Will you stay with my mum?'

She couldn't even open her mouth to respond. And he clearly assumed it was a yes.

Joy did stay, but Tay had only been gone five minutes when she knew she couldn't let the man she loved go through with this. She checked on his mum. She was asleep. If she was quick they'd be back here in no time, and she loved Tay too much to let him mess up his life.

Tay's job tonight was to go to the big house that sat in picturesque – at least by day – surrounds on the outskirts of a village. It was only a mile from where he lived which made it easy for him to go there on foot, undetected. But what he hadn't banked on was his concerned girlfriend following him all the way out there.

'What the fuck are you doing here?' he hissed when she showed up behind him, lurking in the bushes like some kind of predator.

He'd never spoken to her with such venom. 'I'm trying to talk some sense into you.'

'You've left Mum on her own.'

'You did that yourself.'

'I . . .' He didn't bother trying to argue, he just told her to shut up. And the look he gave her this time was something she'd never seen before. It was empty like something in him had snapped, and when a car went past, up the sweeping driveway and out through the gates, he pulled her closer behind the bushes.

'Go back to the house, Joy. I mean it.' He squeezed her shoulder, his turn to beg now. And then he was off. He scurried past a copse of trees, gone, just like that, to do what he'd come here to do.

Tay had admitted earlier that he'd been watching this house for some time, which sounded even more sordid to Joy. She hadn't wanted to hear it, but he'd said it all anyway. The owners had two cars, and every Thursday without fail they'd get into the Range Rover 4x4 and off they went out of the gates. Nobody cared where they were going, but like clockwork they'd return after two hours. Every Thursday he'd said, as though reassuring her that anything about this was right.

Joy would rather be anywhere than here. But she couldn't move, she couldn't leave him here. She could see him through the bushes, going up to the front door, the windows, peering in. And he must have seen what he was looking for because he disappeared round the back of the house.

Joy found her legs taking her there too. It wasn't too late. If he was correct, the owners would be a couple of hours and he didn't have to honour the request of stealing the BMW she could see from here, the moonlight bouncing off its glossy paintwork. Even without being up close she could tell it was expensive, highly prized, and this was what her boyfriend was going to take. He was going to get that car, drive it away like it was his, take it to that horrible man, get his money and run. And this would haunt him forever.

Part of her thought, let him do it and this will be over. Let Tay do this, get the money, get himself out of the rut he and his mum were in. Change their lives. She found herself repeating in her head the things he'd said out loud – they're rich, they'll claim on insurance, they're not there so I won't be scaring them.

But she couldn't see it as anything other than wrong. She couldn't sit back and do nothing.

She got to the house to find he'd smashed the glass in the back door and with no alarm, he was inside, holding a set of car keys she assumed was the coveted prize.

He glared at her. 'Get out, Joy.'

'No.' The house, as impressive inside as it was outside, had luxurious soft furnishings, a scent of vanilla in the air. But there was nothing sweet about this moment. Nothing at all. 'Put the keys down. Let's both go,' she urged. 'Back to your mum, come on.' She sounded like she was talking to a five-year-old and she couldn't honestly believe she'd followed him in here.

She saw her moment and snatched the keys from him. 'I won't let you do this.'

'Give them to me.'

'No.' She pushed them into her pocket.

'Give them to me now, Joy.' He was angry, detached. He lurched towards her to try to get the keys from her, but a light pinged on upstairs illuminating the stairway and they froze, their breath coming hard and fast with the adrenaline.

A voice called down. 'Who's there?'

It was then that Tay told her to run, at the same time as they realised that when he'd tried to grab the keys back from her, he'd knocked something. She'd heard a clunk, but not thought much about it, but now, she realised why the house smelled so sweet. It was a vanilla candle, left unattended, still lit, and in the scuffle one or both of them had knocked something else that must've caused the candle to topple over. The flickering flame of the glass jar knocked on its side had quickly ignited first the roll of kitchen towel on its shiny silver pole, then the underside of a wall cupboard, the wall planner, the pinboard . . . it was all going up so fast.

Tay grabbed Joy's hand. 'Come on . . .' He pulled her as the smoke filled the room.

She followed him out of the door. But as he ran, she couldn't.

She turned back. There was someone in the house, she had to get help. She needed to find a phone, call the fire brigade, tell whoever was in the house to get out. But she couldn't see a phone anywhere downstairs.

She began to run up the stairs, calling out to say there was a fire, but the smoke was overwhelming, her voice silenced. Her mind was already thinking of reasons to give for being in here – she could say she'd been passing, had seen the fire, come here to help. It would all work out fine, it would have to. If she could just get to whoever was upstairs. And now there'd be no car theft either, Tay would learn not to do anything like this ever again, and they could carry on living their lives.

The voice was calling out to her, louder and louder, she was crawling up the stairs on her hands and knees unable to see a thing.

She needed a fire brigade, and the relief when she heard those sirens was the best feeling. Tay must've done it, he must've gone for help. The sirens were getting louder and louder as she tried to work out where exactly the voice in the house had come from. Or was it two voices? She didn't know. Her head was confused, her sight impaired.

She pulled her top up over her mouth as she tried to get up to whoever was still in there, but she lost her footing and fell on the stairs, and as the smoke billowed around her, this time she couldn't get up.

The police and fire brigade had been called that night, but not by Tay. A neighbour had made the call, reporting a girl lurking in the bushes outside the country house, a girl they'd seen creep around the back of the house once the owner had left. Except it hadn't been the owner, it had been the brother of the owner leaving with their son. The owners had been home all along.

The police had found the keys to the BMW in her pocket

269

and along with the smashed glass of the back door, the evidence was damning. She'd tried to say someone else had been in there first, not her, but they hadn't believed a word. She'd taken the accusations from her hospital bed where she'd been treated for smoke inhalation and shock, shock that she'd almost died, and shock that the owners who'd been home at the time, both lost their lives. She'd been saved, they hadn't, and the knowledge overwhelmed her so much she couldn't make sense of anything. Tay came, he wanted to confess everything and put her in the clear, but when he broke down in desperation that his mum would die alone, Joy hadn't been able to do it. She was convinced the police would, in the end, believe she'd stumbled in to try to help anyone stuck in the fire. She was stupid, she'd believed it would all work out. They'd see she was of good character, she'd never been in trouble before, her family would be able to lend her money to fight this in court.

But Joy had been naïve on all counts. Her parents disowned her overnight for what she'd done and the shock from that had her curled into a foetal ball, disbelief washing over her. Her sister Maggie had hung in there for a couple of months, believing Joy's story that she'd tried to help, but even she knew there was more to it than that. Joy should've trusted Maggie with the whole story but she hadn't. She got a prison sentence with the courts showing no leniency, she tried in vain to get in touch with Tay and have him tell them the truth.

But Tay didn't answer his phone, he didn't come. He never went to see her in prison and knowing she had no proof, no names to give the police apart from the name of a man who was of no fixed address and whose own mother didn't always recognise him, her fate was sealed.

Joy spent her days dressed in dull grey tracksuit pants and

scruffy T-shirts. She had a single bed in a cold room bereft of any personality and when the door clunked shut, heavy, foreboding and marking the start of her first night alone, she wished that she'd died too in that fire.

Libby let her tell the entire story without interruption. And she kept hold of her hands too. Otherwise Joy wasn't sure she would've got through it.

'It makes sense now,' said Libby.

'What does?'

'You, changing your name. You haven't always been Joy Browne. I didn't think anything of it, assumed you'd done it because of your relationship with Ted and Marjory, but you did it to cover your tracks didn't you? So that nobody would find the truth because you were no longer Joyce Walsh.' No wonder her online searches hadn't resulted in anything that might help her. She hadn't been looking for the right name for a start.

'You make it sound so sordid. But yes, you're right, I wanted to be a different person. Part of it was the belonging to a family who wanted me, but at the same time, it kept my past more private in case anyone went digging. I obviously didn't cover my tracks well enough because someone found out.'

'I honestly don't know how you survived everything you went through,' said Libby, shaking her head in disbelief still, her face pale at the revelations, the sparkle in her eyes gone for today.

'You learn ways to cope.'

'But prison, Auntie Joy. It must've been a living nightmare.'

'On some days.' Sometimes she shut her eyes and she'd

be right back there. 'But I got used to a window that had slats so small I could barely see anything, I got used to the yells and calls from women I wanted to avoid. I got used to the way things worked in there.'

'Did you tell anyone in there about Tay?'

'Everyone on the inside says they're innocent. Well, nearly everyone. There's no point protesting, not if you want to make it easier on yourself. And Tay had done a runner well and truly. I'd be sending people on a wild goose chase if I claimed he was involved. Then of course I'd be asked why I hadn't mentioned it sooner and I'd have to say because I'm a naïve, silly girl, who was so desperate to love and be loved that she let her common sense and good nature be taken advantage of.' She felt so stupid, always had done, for what that bastard did to her life. And she wished she'd had parents who had made her feel loved so that she'd never needed to search for an emotion that should always be present in families.

'You're loyal,' said Libby.

'I am. One thing you should know about me is that if I'm in your corner, I'm there for good. I'd do anything for you.'

'Was Mum ever in your corner?'

Joy sighed. 'Your mother was a confused woman. I blame our parents, they weren't easy.'

'Dad said similar.'

'He did? Well I never.'

'He said they went through the motions. Mum, for some reason, never really stood up to them.'

'Well, given their refusal to help me out when I went to prison or even entertain the fact I might have a different story to the one everyone thought true, I'm not surprised.

Your mum always wanted to do everything right, I can't blame her for that. It was her personality. But I was never bothered. I lived with them because I couldn't afford to move out. Then I went to jail and you know, as strange as it may sound, on the odd night I'd lie there looking at the ceiling, the smell of the toilet in the room and the air putrid, but I'd think, you know what, I got away.'

'From what Dad says I think Mum was beginning to stand up to them, but it was a long road she never . . .'

Joy squeezed her niece's hands, an acknowledgement of the pain they both felt at the loss of Maggie who had never been able to find a life that didn't involve their parents. Perhaps if she had, they could've been sisters again before it was too late.

'Did Mum write to you in prison?'

'Only a couple of times at the start. I think our parents got to her by then. My friend Sita, she visited me a few times and brought with her a smile and a very pregnant belly. She'd finally moved to Liverpool after getting together with a drummer of a heavy metal band, much to her parents' distaste.' Her and Sita always had bonded over parental relationships, neither of them having the easiest of upbringings, and Sita had a sense of humour that shed light on the darkest of situations. She'd even had Joy in hysterics at prison visits when it was supposed to be melancholy, miserable, something never to be smiled at.

'Where did you go when you got out? Was that when you came here to Somerset?'

Joy shook her head. 'Not at first. Sita offered me a place to stay and I went there for a fortnight. But I couldn't outstay my welcome.'

'I don't understand how any parent can turn their back on a child.'

'Me neither, but I've seen it done enough with people who've come here. It happens more often than you think.'

'I was lucky to have Mum and Dad.'

'And you still have your dad.'

'I do, it was good to see him.'

'I'm glad,' Joy smiled. 'When Maggie fell in love with your dad, I felt even more alone. Until Tay. He brought me an ounce of happiness, laughter, I finally felt the centre of someone's world and I'd never had that before, not when I was little, never. My parents never did that for either me or your mum. I imagine that's why Maggie made such a great mum herself.' Libby smiled back at her. 'I always envisaged Tay would one day come for me, he'd admit his mistake, we'd get through it, start a family of our own. I had all these crazy notions and I know I was clinging on to whatever I could, wishing for the impossible. Stupid isn't it?'

'He was selfish.'

'You're such a together young lady, I bet you'd never have fallen for his charms.'

'You can't blame yourself.'

How could she not? 'I went to London after Sita's and tried my luck there with work but I didn't last long, I hated the big city. I hitched a lift to Somerset and bummed around wherever I could, sleeping rough. I got by.

'One day I stole some food from an honesty box at the end of the driveway of a farm. The Old Dairy,' she smiled.

'That's how you met Ted and Marjory,' Libby realised, unmoving on the ottoman, glued to the history of her auntie that had always been kept from her. They'd dropped hands now, but the warmth was still there between them.

'They caught me stealing, I was so ashamed I broke down, sobbing my pathetic heart out. I didn't do it for pity, but I'd been strong for such a long time, it was the final thing that broke me, taking advantage of someone else the same way Tay had tried to do that dreadful night. My actions may have been about survival, but it was the same thing.

'They gave me a chance, Libby. Without them I might not be here today.' Her voice caught. 'I don't think I had it in me to survive much longer. Ted and Marjory helped me get myself together and that was when they encouraged me to reach out to my family. I went to see Maggie. You must've been around four years old the first time. You were almost seven the second time, then it was when you turned eight I last saw you.'

'I remember. You'd always make me laugh with those puppets I had. You'd put on funny voices, a gruff one for the man puppet, a light squeaky voice for the girl and you'd make them dance together. That was the last thing I remember,' Libby said sadly, 'the day I heard my mum tell you you couldn't come back.'

'That's right.' Joy gulped.

'I got upset that day, I didn't understand. I felt as though our family wasn't real without all the extensions everyone else had, aunties and uncles, cousins.'

'Was that when you wrote to me?'

'I knew mum had a load of your letters,' Libby confirmed, 'I was a bit of a snooper as a kid, and I found where she'd hidden them. I got your address and wrote to you here at the farm. It always sounded such an adventure, a dairy farm, and I'd make up stories in my head about you owning a herd of cows, me coming to milk them.' She laughed. 'It was nice to have the dream.'

'I'm glad you had the dream.' She'd always liked to think she'd brought happiness Libby's way with their top secret – or at least so they'd thought – letter-writing.

'Did Ted and Marjory know what happened to you?'

'They did. I wanted to be honest, start afresh. I thought they'd ask me to leave when they knew everything, but you know what Ted did? He wrapped me in the biggest bear hug I'd ever had and told me it was lucky I'd come to the home of second chances.' When Libby smiled she confessed, 'Ted also wanted to find Tay and make him pay for what he'd done. He was almost like a father, in my corner, like nothing I'd ever seen before, but they soon found out Tay had died around the time his contact with me stopped. He'd been killed in a high-speed car chase, the car was stolen. I was devastated. You don't fall in love and wipe that person out of your life even if they did a terrible thing, and knowing he'd died explained the sudden loss of contact, and part of me clung to the idea that he'd certainly had his problems but deep down I always liked to believe he really did love me and would've come to me eventually.'

'Maybe he would've,' Libby encouraged. She'd crossed her legs on top of the ottoman now, yoga pose style, or perhaps youngster's pose. 'What was it really like in prison?'

'I lost a sense of who I was for a while. I spent those first few days and weeks in a daze, going through the motions. I think my mind tried to block out the claustrophobic feeling of not seeing the outside world for a long time, my senses tried to switch off to the stench, the yells, I drowned in the shame of what had happened.

'It wasn't too long before routine kicked in, and it became an unexpected way to cope. I liked it. Set times for getting up, exercise time, meal times, bed times. Routine gave me a feeling of control, even though it wasn't me who dictated the schedule. The strangers I was going to spend my days with were a mixed bunch. I learned not to seek out confrontation because if I wanted to, I'd find it. And I didn't want that. I just wanted to survive.

'Prison was the darkest of days, but it gave me some bright ones too.' At Libby's confusion she told a different side, the side that went with the routine. 'We were given jobs to do, responsibilities, and I worked in the prison library. It wasn't the biggest, but it felt like a slice of the real world, and it was almost as though ordering and tidying those books did the same thing for my head. I stopped panicking when I didn't hear from Tay, my nightmares of the night of the fire weren't as frequent, and one day a new prisoner called Luna was assigned to clean the prison library.'

'Luna?' Libby pondered, suddenly understanding.

'Yes, like Luna,' Joy smiled. 'Luna – human Luna,' she chuckled, clutching at a humorous moment amidst the whole pitiful tale, 'she came along and my life in prison changed. I was one of the supposedly lucky ones to get my own cell, but I didn't realise that actually, it wasn't quite so lucky. We'd be locked in those cells for such long stretches of time I'd often go hours without talking to anyone. And that day when Luna came along, at first I wanted to strangle her. I've honestly never known someone to talk so much. She rambled on about anything and everything. At one point it was about what she'd give to have her mother's roast potatoes one more time – we'd been fed a dreadful effort of a roast dinner the day before – then it was on to the three cats she'd left behind, next it was about her lack of love life as though that was even an option when you were locked up, she prattled on about star gazing when she came across a book about astrology, she told me she liked to do palm readings to which I rolled my eyes. She moved on to holiday destinations, telling me she'd always wanted to go to Egypt. "I want to see the pyramids," she said, before she turned to me and said "you don't talk much do you?" That was when I replied, "you talk enough for both of us" and she laughed, full on belly laughed. And because she was laughing, I did too. I think it was the first time I'd done so since I'd gone to prison, apart from on Sita's visits, and it was a release. We got told to pipe down of course, which made it even funnier, but after that we were as close as anything. Luna was liked by everyone and although she wasn't at all frightening to look at, being liked commanded a certain respect which made me feel safe around her. She read people's palms too – I've no idea whether it was all claptrap, but she did it anyway. Maybe she tailored their readings to be positive, gave them all a bit of hope, but whatever it was, she had a spirit that kept me and others going. Luna wasn't in for as long as I was, and she admitted her guilt right at the start, she couldn't shut up about it. She'd stolen drugs from a pharmacy and sold them, she knew it was wrong and she was paying for it here. It was that simple.

'When I realised Luna couldn't read, apart from the basics and of course the cards to tell fortunes, I taught her. I like to think that wherever she is now, she's enjoying books as much as I still do, that books can transport her to a better place if she's having a bad time.'

'What happened to Luna?'

'She went to her brother's place first, then she got a job, she wrote and told me all about the manager of the factory where she worked, and how he used to clip his toenails at his desk. Oh her letters always brought a smile to my face, it was some light in the dark. She sent me a postcard the month before I got out. It was of Egypt. She got to see those pyramids, and not only that, she'd got married over there to some businessman and they were moving to New Zealand. She told me when I got out I was to go over there, she'd set me up. I wrote a letter back but when I left prison at long last, it was returned to me. For some reason it had never been mailed. I sent it once I was out but I had no forwarding address so I doubt it ever reached her.'

'You lost contact?'

'Unfortunately, yes.'

'And you never wanted to find her?'

'I thought about it over the years, but once I was settled in here in Bramleywood, I thought it best to bury the past and leave it that way. Sad really. You'd have liked her. And she'd have read your fortune, told you what to do about America, about being here, your love life,' she teased, unsure of what Libby was going to make of the entire truth. Because she hadn't quite revealed everything yet. There was one more enormous secret to dump on her niece and she had the feeling this one would hit the hardest.

'Did you start to help people because of what had happened to you?'

Joy nodded. 'When Ted and Marjory passed away and left me with this place I felt guilty. I didn't think I deserved such an enormous handout. I hadn't done much apart from help out around the place. And then, after a time of feeling so low I could barely breathe, something in me changed. I wanted some good to come out of the house. I wanted it to mean something. I harboured a dreadful guilt I will never get over.'

'But the fire was an accident. And if you'd got the occupants out, you would've been hailed a hero.'

'Except I didn't get them out, did I? The candle got knocked over, the house caught alight, they both died, Libby. I will never stop blaming myself.'

Libby came to her side. 'You did everything you could to help after the fire started. That's all anyone could've asked.'

'They were parents, Libby. They had a son, I took them away from their son,' she wailed, the emotions threatening to overcome her.

Libby comforted her. She didn't deserve it.

'Is that why you started the halfway house and took in people who needed help?' Libby asked. When Joy nodded, her niece smiled at her in a way that showed she still believed in the goodness of her heart. 'Drew's lucky to have found you.'

She was about to say he wasn't lucky she'd ever come into his life, certainly not at the point she was thinking of, but before she could smile and pretend everything was OK, she looked up.

And she felt bile rise in her throat, the colour drain from her skin. If she'd been standing, her legs would've given way beneath her. Because in the doorway, stood Drew. Large as life, pizza box in his hand, and the look on his face suggested he'd heard enough.

'Sound travels,' he said in a tone that shocked even

Libby. 'I shouldn't have eavesdropped, but boy . . .' he harrumphed sardonically, 'am I glad I did.'

There was no hiding now, the truth was out without her having to even say it out loud. Because Drew had finished the story for her all on his own, and she couldn't tell him he was wrong. She couldn't claim it wasn't her at his family home that night, that she wasn't there the night his parents died.

All Joy could see was the candle falling, the fierce flames, the smoke that had enveloped her on the stairs of the finest house in the area. She could hear the voices of that night, the screams of one as they realised there was a fire, the yell of another indecipherable.

Drew knew her secret, and that was the worst thing of all.

Chapter Fifteen

Drew

'Libby, give us a moment.' He'd fallen for her and now he knew Joy's secret, he understood Joy's hesitation at the two of them getting involved. After all, how could he ever love anyone related to the woman who'd played a big part in causing the fire that killed both of his parents? The woman who'd never owned up, at least not to him.

Libby said nothing and left the room. Drew watched Joy, she wouldn't look at him. It was as though she was bracing herself for him to yell, scream, even lash out at her. This grim secret between them was out in the open and never before had he felt so raw, so exposed. Losing his parents had been something he couldn't remember happening. He'd only been three years old, staying over at his uncle's place, but it was the years that followed that almost finished him off.

'When were you going to tell me?' He wanted answers from Joy, but he knew the response to this one already. 'You weren't. Should've known. You were going to sell up, pay this person off, and never admit your part in derailing my entire life.'

'I didn't want to ruin you all over again.'

He laughed, an empty sound that came out of nowhere.

'And you don't think this will? To know I trusted the woman who took my parents from me, to know I've sat around the dinner table with her, laughing and joking, comforting, confiding, and all this time . . .' His legs suddenly couldn't hold him any longer and he slumped down on the ottoman that faced her favourite armchair. It was still warm from when Libby had been in the very same place moments ago. He'd sat in this spot often enough – in the summer with the cooling breeze as they talked, on winter nights turned round to face the fireplace, times when he'd talked through problems with the latest stray to come to the home of second chances.

He wasn't sure what to call it now. The house of doom felt a more appropriate description.

'Are you even interested in my side of the story?' Her voice came out timid, but he couldn't feel sorry for her.

'I think I heard enough.' Libby had taken the pizza box with her, but he still had hold of his car keys.

He had to get out of here. Far away from Joy, from the lies she'd told for so long, the truth he'd only just discovered. He felt sick to his stomach, but he stopped in the doorway. 'It was no coincidence we met that day at the café, was it?' He'd been in dire straits, in trouble with the police after a protest turned violent and he was arrested. He had no job, nowhere to live, and then all of a sudden there was a job advert on the board in the café he came into when he had the spare cash for a hot meal.

Joy shook her head. She'd engineered the entire meeting, manipulated him. Did he even know her at all? He wanted to dig his keys into the wood of the door jamb and rip it apart all the way down its grain.

*

'Please sit down, Drew. Let me talk to you.'

He stayed where he was, neither in the room nor out of it.

'I did find you in the café that day. I'd always wondered about you. I knew the couple who died—'

'My parents,' he barked.

'Your parents,' she corrected, hoping he'd listen. Even if he walked away after this at least he would know everything, he'd hear it from her and nobody else. Maybe he'd even see how sorry she was and how much she cared for him. 'I knew they had a son, I found out your name, and I discovered you'd gone to live with your uncle. It was in the news enough, it wasn't hard to find out. I found a certain type of peace thinking of you as settled.'

'You didn't deserve any peace,' he snapped. He was so angry, that seeing another side to this had to be impossible.

She tried to block out his reaction in order to get through this, to keep no more secrets from him. She needed it all to pour out before he walked away. 'One day, once I was settled myself and here at the farm, when I was no longer falling apart, because believe me that's what I was doing for a long while, I was flicking through the newspaper and found an article about an environmental protest turned nasty. A hero had come to the rescue of a little girl who'd been caught up in it and there was your name, the parents officially saying thank you for saving their daughter.'

Drew must be remembering it because he turned and looked her way.

'It didn't take me long to find you because in the photograph in the newspaper you'd been wearing a top with a distinctive logo I managed to find out was for a small restaurant in Devon. I went to Devon, I wasn't going to talk to you, I just wanted to see that you were all right. And when I got there somehow the waitress had me sitting down before I knew it and ordering a salad for lunch. When I failed to see you I ended up asking if you were working that day. I thought if she asks who I am I'll say I'm an old friend, if I was in the wrong place then I'd leave it alone. It was then she told me you no longer worked there.'

'It was only over summer, but they didn't need me for long before tourism dried up again and I was jobless.' His feelings hovered between the hopelessness back then and the wretchedness now.

'The girl must've thought I was a good friend and she told me where you were staying. I didn't go there straight away, it was a good couple of weeks and I only planned to hover outside, see that you were safe and be on my way.'

'So what changed?' He was pushing the end of his car keys into his palm, hard enough to leave a mark if he wasn't careful.

'You came back drunk one night, yelling obscenities at someone who'd dropped you off and roared off in their car. You had this look about you, a look that said you were angry, you were done with the world.' It was a look she'd seen before, from Tay. 'It was a look that told me a whole lot of trouble was coming if you didn't act fast.'

'You're making out you were a guardian angel.'

'I'm not trying to, I'm trying to tell you everything. I know what you must think of me, I've thought worse of me over the years believe me, and once I've told you everything you can yell at me, scream, wreck the place. Whatever. As is your right.

'I came back the next day, the one after that and the one after, and each time I sat in the café across the road from the broken-down house you lived in with those other men, and I watched you. I had no idea what I was ever going to say, but one day you came into that café and the owner didn't speak to you, she sat you down and took you over a bowl of soup, a huge mug of tea and didn't ask for money. I got the impression both of you were used to the routine.'

She wondered if he'd say something about that time, but he didn't. 'After you went on your way the owner came over to wipe down my table. I asked her who the strange man was who'd just come in. She told me she didn't know your name but you were the saddest person she'd ever seen in her life. She said she'd never seen someone look like they were so down on their luck that they no longer wanted to be a part of this world. Her comment stayed with me, it became part of my nightmares. I went back to the café a week later, three days in a row until you came in again and the second you did, I put up the job advert on the pinboard right near where you were sitting.'

Joy had devised a job advert offering work at her farm. She wanted someone to build a chicken run and a coop, look after some of the land, help out around the place. And in exchange it was free board and lodgings. 'No experience needed', the advert had said, requesting someone hard-working and trustworthy. 'The pay isn't much,' she told him when he ambled over to where she was sitting with a camomile tea, doing her best not to will him to head her way.

'I wanted to wrap you up in cotton wool,' she admitted, 'but I didn't dare. I was desperate to help you find yourself again. I had no idea how, but I figured it would start with a job and a decent place to live. And you accepting the position that evening in the café told me you wanted things to change so desperately you were willing to do anything.' Her smiled went unreturned. 'I thought you'd be with me for a few months and likely move on and I'd help you as much as I could. But then, you slowly started to smile again and began to enjoy life in the village. You'd found the kayak club not far away, you used to go by train remember?' He said nothing, not even a flicker of expression either. 'I was beginning to see a man blossom before my eyes, move on from the one I'd seen in the café, the one the owner described to me.'

'You kept your silence for years,' he sniffed. 'You lied to me. You did something so unforgiveable. I can't get past it.' His eyes, suddenly filled with anger, fixed on her. 'How could you do it, break in and start the fire that killed my parents? How could you? I thought you were genuine, loyal, someone with a good heart.'

Her bottom lip wobbled as his voice and emotions rose like a dragon emerging from the flames. 'Drew, I . . .'

But he was standing up. 'I can't be near you—'

'Drew, wait . . .'

And he headed out of the door without turning back.

Libby found Drew sitting on the bench outside the station, a pile of pebbles in his hand, slinging them one after another into a bush. She sat down beside him and handed him a takeaway coffee which he took without comment. She handed him a sugar-coated jam doughnut from the bag on her lap, but he still said nothing.

'Please eat it or I'll feel really greedy scoffing mine,' she said, 'and my mouth is watering. I left the pizza, cold, floppy, unappetising, but probably OK if we warm it up later.'

Her company made him feel good, and right now she was the only thing that did. He shoved the doughnut in his mouth in one go making her burst into laughter, a sound that was music to his ears. He tried to laugh too but could barely breathe with a mouthful of doughnut and his eyes began to water. He finally was able to chew, and bit by bit the food diminished, the sugar rush found him and his taste buds settled.

'You got some on your T-shirt,' she grinned.

He wiped it off with his finger and licked it, making her smile at him all the more, and then they sat there, in the grey afternoon, the smell of rain lingering along with puddles, the sound of a train coming in to the station and passengers disembarking, its arrival being announced over the tannoy to urge anyone waiting to get on board.

A low sound had them both turning to one another. 'Now that wasn't a train,' said Libby.

'Nope, not a train,' he said as they saw a flash of lightning.

'I thought I heard a rumble of thunder earlier, but I was too focused on where you'd got to.'

'You were more focused on those doughnuts.'

A boom of thunder made her jump. Drew put his arm around her as they ran, the gentle rain a pitter-patter of droplets that seemed harmless enough, soon changing to a downpour with a ferocity that took them both by surprise as they ran towards the library and its generous shelter without another soul in sight now it was closed for the day. Soaked through to the skin already they huddled together close to the doorway set back from the street.

Drew hugged her to him to keep them both warm and small talk about the storm and jokes about doing water sports in weather like this soon gave way to the real reason they were out in this, away from the farmhouse.

'Cameron's probably demolished most of the pizza you know,' Libby smiled up at him. 'I told him to leave some for us, but he's a growing lad.' Her smiled faded. 'Talk to me, Drew. I know you overheard what Joy told me, what I don't get is why you don't see how terrible she feels.'

Incredulous he stepped away from her. 'She's a liar.' And when he glanced at her, her confusion only had him turn away again.

It was a moment before she said, 'Oh my God, you only heard part of it.'

'I heard enough.'

'What did you hear?'

He'd stepped away from the shelter and hadn't cared he was getting wetter. But the rain began to come harder and it was too much even for him and he relented and joined Libby by the door to the library again. 'I heard her talking about the fire, that's the word that really got me, it's haunted me for a long time. Then every word after that was like a bullet in my chest.' He could feel the tension building up across his face, over his head, like it was being squashed in a vice.

'She told me a lot, you obviously heard enough to make you upset she never told any of you. But I see why she didn't want to. She's ashamed, she'll never get over her part in what happened.'

'Her *part?*' He harrumphed. '*She'll* never get over it?' He couldn't believe Libby wasn't seeing why he was so mad, devastated at the truth.

And then it dawned on him.

'It seems you only know part of the story too.' He leaned against the wall, one foot bent up behind him on the brickwork. 'I told you my parents died when I was only three years old. What I didn't tell you was how.' He looked right at her, the pain clear, the loss evident. 'They died in a house fire.'

She grabbed his hand, sticky from the doughnut residue, but the gesture didn't last long and she put her hand over her mouth, realising the terrible truth.

'Yep, so you see, Joy might be sorry she lied to everyone, but lying to me means a whole lot more. I've been duped, well and truly.'

Another clap of thunder and a bolt of lightning reminded them they were some way from the farmhouse in weather neither of them should really be out in.

'How did you and Joy ever get to where you are now?' she asked as they stood close for warmth, the summer feeling a million days ago now with the storm.

Drew told her everything Joy had divulged moments ago, the way she'd hunted him down, given him work and a roof over his head. 'She played me,' he said.

Neither of them spoke for a while, reality sinking in, and he did his best to sniff away tears.

He tried to turn and wipe his eyes before Libby saw, but she was too quick and reached up a hand to his cheek. 'I don't think any of this was a game for Joy.' He bit back more tears, more pain he didn't want to let come. 'She looked out for you and did what she could.'

'I never asked her to and I never needed her to!' He yelled the words and then shrieked his anger at the thunderstorm, hands clasped behind his head, out from beneath the porch and standing in the rain again.

Her soft voice eventually said, 'Except that you did. You did need help and nobody else was giving it to you. But she did. She could've walked away and got on with her life, put you and your family right out of her mind, it would've made it a whole lot easier for her. But she didn't. She kept her dreadful secret as well as a determination you'd get a good life.'

He shook his head. 'You know in all the years I've never bothered to delve deeper about what happened to my mum and dad. I wasn't interested, it would hurt all the more. Not finding out details was my way to protect myself so I only got the basics. I knew there'd been a robbery, my uncle told me that much, he said a fire started from a candle and it hadn't been deliberate, he said it'd all been a terrible accident. I knew someone was charged, but I didn't look into it any further. It was as though if I did I'd have those names, those events, haunting me more than they already did. Jeez, one search and I might have found all of this out a long time ago. I would never have let Joy get me into this mess in the first place.'

'You're right,' said Libby. 'You could've found out everything about that night, the fire, the woman who went to prison. But it wouldn't have told you everything, only Joy knows that.'

'What do you mean?'

'I didn't get the entire story because you came back so she never got to the part about you. But judging by what you're telling me now, you didn't hear the whole conversation between us, and Joy probably thinks you did, so wouldn't have said anything.'

'You're talking in riddles now.'

'Joy wasn't on her own at your family home that night,' said Libby. And as she told him the rest he leaned against the brick wall of the library, their bodies protected from the rain that at one point looked as big as hailstones. Libby talked, he listened, all about Joy's first and only love, her trust, her belief in the good of humankind, how she'd taken the wrap for something she should never have been involved with before.

'Say something,' Libby urged when she'd finished telling him everything.

'I'm not sure I can.' Although he didn't want this to come between him and Libby. 'She still lied to me, she still kept this and it's huge, I can't forget that.'

'It is huge, but I don't think a day has gone by where she hasn't questioned whether she was doing the right thing keeping it from you. Somehow she managed to channel all her guilt and doubts into helping other people, others like you who either didn't have parents any more or who did and still weren't any better off. She's lived a solitary existence – I don't mean the farmhouse is empty, she's filled it, but it's never been personal, has it? There's something in it for everyone who comes through the doors of The Old Dairy but she never fell in love again, never had children of her own. I think the reason why is because she's been punishing herself, never allowing herself to be fully happy, but making others find what they wanted and needed instead. She devoted every fibre of her being to you, Freddie, Lauren, Cameron, and every other person who at some time or another has lived at The Old Dairy.'

They stood in silence for a while, watching the rain, the rhythmic way it hit the windowsills of the library, how it landed on the leaves of the bushes beside the path, pooling, and then having no choice but to give in and fall off.

'I'm going to head back to the farm,' said Libby eventually. 'I care about you,' she smiled up at him. 'But I need to be there for Auntie Joy too. She's never asked for much and she won't ask now, but I want to do it anyway.'

'Do you think this is why she didn't want you and I to get together?'

'Because I'd have to choose sides? Probably.'

He didn't want her to go. 'I don't know what to say to her. I'm upset, I'm sad, but most of all I'm angry with myself.'

'Whatever for?'

'Because I got as close to Joy as anyone. She's been like family to me for years and now, to know she's had this secret for so long, I . . . well I don't know how to feel. Cheated? Betrayed? Or just plain stupid to never have asked more questions, to never have looked into what happened to my parents and realised who Joy was. And now you tell me she was the one trying to put a stop to the events of the night, she was almost the hero. I don't know what to do with that information. My head's all over the place.'

The wind picked up and started to blow the rain their way and another flash of lightning made him jump this time. All the bravado of being out here in the storm had gone right out of him at the next rumble of thunder that put fear on Libby's face. 'We might have to stay put for it to pass.'

'Not a chance,' she said. 'And I know this is unbelievably

hard for you, but I can't bear thinking of Joy tearing herself apart with worry over you, as I know she'll be doing. Come on, we'll make a run for it. Your jeep's back there anyway, you'll need to fetch it even if you don't face Joy yet.'

Without hesitation he took her hand but stood firm. 'Wait for more lightning, then thunder, then we'll start to run.'

By the time they made it back to The Old Dairy they were drenched head to toe. He hesitated by the jeep, ready to get away, but a tug from Libby's hand pulled him round the back of the farmhouse and into the utility room where they soon soaked the floor. Standing in puddles Drew squeezed out his shorts at the legs and the bottom of his T-shirt, Libby wrung out her hair and reached for a towel from the linen basket to get off the worst before passing it to Drew to do the same.

'I should go,' said Drew, looking at Libby, beautiful no matter the weather.

A voice stopped them and Freddie poked his head around the door. 'I thought you were Joy.'

'Surely she hasn't gone out in this,' said Libby.

'She went after Cameron.'

Libby's face fell. 'He ran off again?'

Freddie nodded. 'He overheard Joy and Drew, said their voices were heated, and the next thing I knew he'd gone.'

Drew swore.

'What's going on?' Freddie asked him.

'Long story I'm afraid, and not a pleasant one.' The hurt on Libby's face had him lose the edge in his voice. 'We need to find Cameron, that's the most important thing right now.'

Libby looked back out of the farmhouse and down the side. 'Joy's car is still parked beside the cowshed. She's gone on foot.'

Freddie looked up from scrolling on his phone. 'They're warning people not to go out in the storm, say it's the worst we've had in years.'

Drew reached for Libby's hand and squeezed it reassuringly, hoping she didn't hurl blame his way now for Joy being God knows where. And if Freddie noticed them closer than before, he didn't mention it.

Drew's heart sank. He didn't know what he was more angry about – losing his parents in the first place, Joy lying to him for all these years, or himself for getting close to her and right now not being able to switch off the feeling of worry in his head, concern that she'd do something stupid tonight, that she was out in this weather when she should be here, safe. He might be confused, but she had to be too, she had to have been all over the place for years. And she meant something to him, he couldn't help it.

When Drew was in the process of pulling himself together and first came to live at The Old Dairy, he'd almost fallen apart again. He'd sulked, he'd given up smiling, he was an ogre to live with, and he knew now why Joy hadn't told him to leave. She'd stuck by him when he was rude, obnoxious, lazy even. He'd hurled abuse her way and she'd let it wash over her. On some days he remembered trying to push it as far as he could, almost wanting bad things to come his way as though it was all he was fit for. Maybe she'd thought his temper and unpleasant attitude were no less than she deserved, perhaps she'd welcomed them like an extension of her prison sentence. In real terms she'd been given a life sentence, never letting go of what happened, and it was true what Libby said, she always did everything for anyone else and never herself. Libby was right too that Joy could've walked away from him and left it alone, never had to think about him, started over and been incredibly happy without ever helping a soul. And now, because of how she'd tried to give something back, she had to give up the one place she'd found peace in, the farmhouse.

He watched Libby grab a towel to squeeze more drops of rain from her hair when it dripped on the kitchen floor. Whatever was between him and Joy he had to put it aside for now and find her and Cameron, but before any of them could come up with a plan of action, the utility room door flew open.

'You're back!' Libby hugged Cameron who looked bewildered at the welcome.

Bisto tried to shoot through to the hallway, but Drew scooped him up. 'Oh no you don't, you're soaked through.' He handed him to Cameron so he could dry the puppy with a towel.

'You had us worried,' said Freddie, a firm hand on Cameron's shoulder to make his point.

Cameron looked at the kitchen floor. 'I'm sorry, I didn't think anyone would mind me taking Bisto. I went to get some bread rolls from the bakery before it closed – I was supposed to do it this morning and I forgot.' He noticed the strange looks passing. 'And I met up with Dahlia.'

'You didn't run off?' Libby asked.

'No.' He seemed relieved nobody mentioned him and the girl at the village shop who clearly liked each other.

Freddie went through the utility room and outside, returning pretty quickly. 'She's not here.'

Cameron picked Bisto up this time and hugged him tight. He wouldn't be able to do so for much longer, the puppy was growing every day it seemed. 'Did Joy think I'd run off?'

'Don't worry,' said Libby picking up on exactly what Cameron feared, that Joy had gone out in this because of him. 'I'm sure she'll be back any minute.'

But the minutes ticked on by. They tried calling her phone. It rang out. Libby got out of her wet clothes, Cameron did the same, Freddie lent Drew a T-shirt when he shivered from the sopping clothes he was in, and each of them waited despondently for Joy's return.

Drew wondered whether the guilt had got so much she'd done something stupid like put an end to it all, and when his mind went there, he realised how much the woman meant to him.

He stared out of the window, the rain pelting down. Another bolt of lightning silenced the four of them and the rumble of thunder told them they had no choice but to try to find her.

'Take the jeep!' Libby yelled when Drew opened the back door. 'Freddie stay here . . .' She went after Drew. 'Cameron come with us,' she shouted, on their way over to the car, the rain making it difficult to see, slippery underfoot. 'Show us where you run off to sometimes, do you have a favourite place?' she asked when they shut the doors and Drew slowly negotiated his turn so he could drive out to the front of the farmhouse and through the gate.

'There's the bus stop, the shops, the fields.'

It didn't sound any better than what they'd already thought of. They scoured the streets, the jeep crawling along as they attempted to check every crevice of Bramleywood, but they found nothing.

'I went to the station once,' said Cameron before Drew turned into a country lane that led to more farmland. 'I thought I'd hop on a train somewhere but Lauren found me before I got a chance. We could try there.' He was leaning forward between the passenger seats and Drew told him to get his seatbelt on.

They headed there next. But nothing. Cameron told them sometimes he'd sit down the lane near the bakery where nobody would bother him, but they parked up alongside and couldn't see any sign.

And when they headed home to the farmhouse heavy-hearted Drew knew exactly what Joy meant to him. She was family. No matter the past, the now was all that mattered. And with one look at Libby, worried sick in the passenger seat, he knew how desperately both of them wanted to find her.

Chapter Sixteen

Joy

Joy shivered. She'd had the forethought to bring a waterproof with her, but the hood had blown off as she ran up and down the main street of Bramleywood, past the bakery, to the station, back and down the lane Cameron sometimes lurked in, the same lane she'd first found him. She'd gone round to the car park at the back and looked around parked cars, peered in through the windows to make sure he hadn't broken in for refuge from the storm that was as fierce as she felt for letting this situation come to a head. She should've told people the truth, told Drew the minute his life was on track. She was selfish, she'd ruined it all.

She'd been about to give up and go back to the farmhouse when she thought she saw Cameron, the same purple baseball cap, walking into the station. She ran after him, through to the platform where he'd got on a train to goodness knows where. She didn't have time to check, she just got on, and when she'd realised the boy she'd seen wasn't Cameron it was too late. And so she'd had to plead her case with the ticket inspector who cautioned her for travelling without a ticket and let her off at the next stop. And now, here she was, not a decent phone reception to be had, in a Somerset village way more remote than Bramleywood. Still, at least the storm had been and gone here judging by the detritus across the street, the puddles dotted here and there, and so she walked out of the station until finally enough bars showed on her phone display for her to make a call.

It was Drew who picked up the phone at the farmhouse and Joy burst into tears.

'Joy, is that you?'

She couldn't stop blubbing. His soft voice, the hint of worry, it was more than she deserved after everything she'd done.

'Where are you?'

She managed to get out the name of the station and the next thing she knew she was sitting on the bench out front waiting for someone to come and get her. Drew had told her Cameron was at the farmhouse, that there'd been a misunderstanding and he hadn't run off. He'd only nipped to the bakery. She would've laughed if the situation between her and everyone else who'd trusted her for years wasn't so dire.

Twenty minutes later, handsome, dark-haired Drew strode over to her. She looked at her hands, her fingers entwined in her lap, she didn't want to read his expression in case she didn't like what she saw.

Drew sat down and neither of them seemed to notice the bench was soaking wet, there was a puddle at their feet and every time the wind blew it picked up some of the droplets ganging up on the nearby bin and wet them with a fine spray.

'We were worried about you,' Drew began. 'Where were you going?'

'I thought I saw Cameron get on the train, I had to go after him.'

'That kind of worry is what makes you, you,' he sighed.

She looked at him trying to detect a hidden meaning, but there didn't appear to be one, at least she hoped there wasn't. 'I'm so dreadfully sorry, Drew, for everything.' Her voice shook, she wasn't sure whether it was out of fear or because she was cold.

'Why don't we talk in the car? I'll put the heater on.'

'I'm not sure I'm ready to go back to the farmhouse just yet. Does everybody know?'

'Cameron may have overheard something but he hasn't mentioned it, and Freddie hasn't said a word.' He cocked his head for her to follow him to the car.

When she was sitting in the passenger seat and used the towel he'd thought to bring for her, he said, 'I didn't hear the entire story earlier. I only heard as much as I needed to assume it was all your fault.'

'And do you know everything now?'

'More or less, Libby filled me in.' The noise of the heater took away the awkward silence. 'You should've told me sooner.'

'Don't you think I know that now?' She was picking at the skin on her hand, her nails scraping it over and over. 'Do you think you would've listened to me?'

He put a hand onto hers to stop her from making her hand bleed. 'Probably not.'

'At the café when we first met, you weren't in the right frame of mind to cope with the truth . . . To hear about the fire, the dreadful accident, all because one person wanted to steal a car. You would've yelled at me, and that's if you'd actually heard me out, you probably would've gone off and drowned your sorrows at the nearest pub and then your life could've continued the way it was going. And it wasn't going well, I could see it wasn't. If it had been I would never have got you to come here and work, I would've let you be.'

'Guilt free you mean.'

She deserved that. She deserved worse. 'Yes, I suppose it would've appeased my guilt somewhat. But the guilt was, and always will be there. I was the only person who could've stopped Tay that night, and boy did I try . . .' Her voice caught, but Drew didn't need an emotional wreck, he needed her strong, giving him everything he needed to know.

'Libby says you tried to rescue my parents from upstairs.'

'I failed.'

He turned the heater down when it got a bit much.

'Tay ran off, I like to think he thought I was behind him but I'll never really know for sure. I couldn't go, not when the fire started. I tried to get to your parents but the smoke, it was too thick, I couldn't see, I couldn't get to them and I think the whole thing got out of hand so quickly they were trapped.' She dissolved into tears. 'I couldn't save them, I tried, I couldn't,' she said, gasping for breath, repeating herself over and over.

'You took the blame, your boyfriend got away with it.'

'I was loyal to Tay, I honestly thought I'd get a caution or do community service, even though I was told I might go to prison, I couldn't bear the thought of Tay's mother being all alone. Because she would've been. He was the only person she had. We talked, we agreed when the time was right . . .' her voice shook '. . . when his mum passed, he'd come forward.'

'But he never did.' He swore, a word she never heard him say, let alone in her presence. She almost wanted to yell it too, Lord knows she'd heard it enough on the inside.

They sat in the quiet, not even the heater for company any more. The rain began a delicate dance on the windscreen, gentle drops, nothing like the raging storms that had already swept through. 'Maybe he never got a chance, perhaps he died before that could ever happen,' she said knowing she'd never ever know the whole truth. 'I was so desperate to see the good in Tay, I held on to the belief he would in the end.'

'You seeing the good in people is another characteristic that makes you, you.' He put on his seatbelt and indicated for her to do the same. He looked across at her. 'Ready to go?'

'Back home?'

'Yes.'

'And then you'll be leaving?'

'Only if you want me to.'

She shook her head. This wouldn't be something they could move forward from overnight, but the fact he was here now gave her hope it wasn't the end for them, for a boy she'd brought into her life and didn't want to see disappear from it.

As he drove he told her Lauren was on her way too. 'It's time we all sat down and talked properly. No more secrets.'

'No more secrets,' she said as the windscreen wipers pushed aside the rain.

Back at the farmhouse, walking into the kitchen felt like the day she'd been sentenced. They were all gathered at the table, all waiting. But unlike the stark courtroom, the unsmiling and unfriendly faces, each of them in turn hugged her, relieved she was home. Even Cameron hugged her tight as though now he needed to worry she might run off.

'I'd like to get changed first if I may,' she said, mainly to Drew, but she wasn't looking at anyone in particular.

'Of course,' said Lauren. 'And then come and have a hot mug of tea and a slice of chocolate cake.'

She didn't deserve cake or kindness. And these kids all deserved more than deception and lies, they needed honesty, and once she was changed she was going to retell the entire story from the start, leaving nothing out.

It was the quietest she'd ever known the kitchen at the farmhouse to be when she went downstairs twenty minutes later. She'd dried her hair, washed her face and put on a chunky knit cardigan she didn't usually wear until the autumn, and when she walked along the hallway she ignored the crooked painting she usually took the time to sort out and headed for the hub of the house that was usually filled with warmth and laughter, but now had an air of trepidation hanging over it.

Libby had made tea for everyone and got up to fill a mug for Joy. Lauren shifted over, Freddie pulled out her chair. Under different circumstances she might have found their attention amusing, but not now.

'I don't know where to start,' she said when she had a steaming mug of tea in front of her. Lauren delivered a generous slice of chocolate cake she had no intention of touching.

Libby smiled kindly. 'Start from the beginning, how you met Tay, how you fell in love.'

Joy knew what Libby was doing. She was trying to make

her feel good first so that the later admissions wouldn't feel like every word was a razor blade making another cut, another piece of pain to endure.

Her tribe, as she'd come to think of them over the years, couldn't have been more patient. Cake was demolished, tea was refilled as much as it needed to be, Luna came to her side and settled, Bisto didn't take long to join her, and slowly Joy filled the walls of this farmhouse with the horrible truth, every last bit of it. Cameron, young as he was, seemed pleased she'd fallen in love until he found out how Tay left her to take the blame, Freddie stayed quiet throughout, thinking deeply she imagined and processing how she'd kept this all from him. Drew listened and even though at times his eyes filled with tears, there was no sign of the anger from earlier. He was probably exhausted by it. Libby stayed by her side and urged her on when she faltered, Lauren gasped at the knowledge Joy had been in prison, and by the end of the sorry tale the rain outside had completely stopped.

Libby opened the windows in the kitchen, the fresh air pouring in. 'I don't know about anyone else, but I could use a glass of wine right now, never mind a tea.'

'Crack open a bottle,' Drew smiled, the tension lessening. 'I wouldn't mind a glass.' He looked at Joy. 'Mind if I crash out upstairs so I don't have to drive home?'

Joy nodded, her hand over her mouth stifling the tears as Libby put an arm around her shoulders. It was his way of saying they would be OK. They might have a way to go, but they'd get there in the end.

'Where are you gonna crash?' Cameron quizzed.

'Spare room obviously,' said Drew confused at the question.

'Spare room or Libby's room?' Cameron grinned. 'Apparently you two were holding hands earlier.'

Libby's mouth fell open, Drew looked panicked and Joy began to laugh. 'You two need to work on making it less obvious there's something going on.'

'Do you mind?' Libby directed her question to Joy.

Joy shook her head. 'I want you to be happy . . . both of you.'

And it was all they needed to share a brief kiss that had everyone cheering.

'Talking of new love,' Libby grinned when she pulled away from Drew but stayed close to his side, 'How's Dahlia?' she batted Cameron's way, embarrassing him like only a sister could. Because Cameron had come into this big, crazy family of sorts and the smile he had on his face now hinted that things with him and the girl from the village shop were off to a good start.

Drew filled wine glasses for those who wanted it. 'Come on Lauren, have a drink. We all need it after the shock. And I think you know a taxi firm willing to come and get you.'

She grinned. 'I don't think Jonathan would be too happy if he found out I'd been drinking.'

'I don't know,' Drew smiled, 'Kind of romantic given how you met.'

When Lauren swiped him with the tea towel she'd been using to dry a glass, Joy appreciated the sense of normality that was beginning to return. They weren't family in the typical sense of the word, but in a different way they were.

'Come on Lauren,' said Libby, 'join us.'

'I can't.' And then she began to smile which had Libby

wondering, Drew studying her face for clues and Cameron being the first to call out.

'You're having a baby,' he said.

'I'm having a baby,' she beamed.

Drew wrapped her in a hug she claimed was so tight he'd squeeze the baby out too soon, Libby hugged her like a true friend, Freddie and Cameron offered congratulations and immediately started taking bets on the sex and the name, and Joy took Lauren's hand.

'I'm thrilled for you,' she said.

'I've been keeping it quiet, I've only just taken a test and I wanted to wait for the twelve week scan, but I don't know, tonight just feels like the right time.'

Joy touched a hand to her cheek. 'Now is the perfect time. Did you call your brothers and tell them?'

Lauren beamed. 'They're thrilled and can't wait to come visit.' Her voice cracked. 'They'll be wonderful uncles to this baby.'

'And you'll be a wonderful mother,' Joy reassured her.

'I'd never be this happy if not for you. And you should know, Libby is a lot like you are,' she said looking across at Libby. 'She's the one who made me see sense when I doubted I could ever do this parenthood thing. Jonathan and I have had a long talk – I think after Libby helped with the business side of things she got me organised and things in my head started to feel clearer. The business is running steadily now and I feel on top of things, all thanks to her.'

Joy looked proudly across at Libby, happy she'd been exactly what Lauren needed. But Libby was too busy with the others placing a bet on the date the baby would come and the sex it would be, to accept any thanks. She even urged Joy to do the same. It was as though they'd gathered here for a normal day at the farmhouse rather than why they were really all here right now.

When they settled down after the news, some with their wine, Lauren with another piece of chocolate cake, Libby announced, 'There's something else you all need to know.'

'You're not pregnant are you?' Cameron joked, earning him a dig in the ribs from Libby.

'No, I'm not pregnant. You've all heard Joy's story, but what you also need to know is her reasons for selling up here. Well, her reasons for *trying* to sell up here.'

In all the drama Joy hadn't even thought about the blackmail, the reason Libby had asked her what was going on in the first place, the reason the truth had come out in a way that had almost broken Drew.

Libby told everyone about the letter to reactions of shock and horror that anyone could be so nasty. But Libby hadn't finished. 'I had a bit of trouble at my job in America, someone was spreading rumours, or telling a story that wasn't theirs to tell, creating problems for me, you get the gist. But someone I knew told me to get in first, go to management and tell them. I think that's what we need to do here.'

Joy looked at her. 'What are you suggesting, Libby?'

'Whoever this is, they're threatening to expose the truth. I say we get in there first, go to the newspapers.'

Joy shook her head. 'Oh no, I'm not having my business plastered everywhere, I wouldn't be able to walk down the street without people knowing. No, not an option. It's bad enough you all know.'

'You're right,' said Drew. 'Everyone would know. They'd know you went to prison. But they'd also know you'd done everything you could to stop the crime happening in the first place, to save two people, and you'd taken the blame to help someone you believed in and trusted so that an old lady who had nobody apart from her misguided son wouldn't die alone.'

'He's right, Joy.' Lauren put her plate in the sink and came over to crouch down beside the woman they had all flocked to. 'The truth will come out, but isn't it better this way? It was unforgiveable for whoever sent those letters to threaten you, but this way, they have nothing over you. They won't ever be able to do it again. People around here love you. And if anyone has a problem with it, then they're not worth worrying about.'

'You make it sound simple.'

'It's the truth and it'll set you free,' said Lauren, earning an eye roll from Cameron who thought she sounded like something out of a psychology manual.

'If I ever got my hands on who sent those letters,' Libby began, but Joy didn't let her finish.

'I know exactly who sent them. Rick bloody Oxley.' She wasn't sure who was more shocked, Libby or Drew.

'How would he have known your history?' Drew asked.

'I doubt it would've been too difficult. His desperation would've egged him on to find out what he could. He's been living here long enough to know Ted and Marjory took me in, I'm sure it didn't take much to find out my name, maybe ask around with the odd question about where I'd once lived.' She frowned. 'You know what, the details don't matter to me now. All I can say is that it didn't take me long to work out it was him, he's not smart enough to fly under the radar if he thinks he has one up on you.

'The day after I got that letter he looked at me differently when I saw him in the street, you know, shifty, like he was planning something. Usually he frowns at me or avoids eye contact. I'd been in a daze that day and hadn't thought much of it at the time. But then he kept doing it, giving me a confident look like he'd found treasure. Which I suppose he thought he had. I mean he's wanted to get his hands on this place for years. The blackmail and demand for money would've been a smokescreen to frighten me, and once his job was done, he'd swoop on in and buy the place. I expect you can guess who the offer came from.'

'The swine!' Lauren yelled. 'I've a good mind to lace a cake with poison and deliver it right to him.'

'No need for that,' said Joy.

'I knew it was him too.' Freddie's admission came out of nowhere and he quickly added, 'I don't mean I knew about the letter, but I've known for a while that he was up to no good, and now I know exactly how low he'd stoop.' He'd gone across to the sink facing out to the farm he'd tended to for years, the land that had become his livelihood. It didn't make sense that he was involved. He'd stood the most to lose after Joy herself if she sold up.

He turned to face them all. 'Rick has been paying me off. He's been doing much the same to me as he's done to Joy. He blackmailed me.'

Joy couldn't quite believe what she was hearing.

'Bold as anything he approached me on the main street after I'd made a delivery of fruit and vegetables. He was talking, it sounded like praise at the beginning, about what I grew, its quality, how I'd built up a really good business with reliable clients. But then the conversation changed. He started talking about growing crops and how pests could devastate them. And before I could say I had it all in hand he started going on about weather hazards, vandalism, the unexpected, when my business was out there in the fields that could be reached by crossing the land from different directions.'

'The sneaky toad,' Lauren, ruffled, had always got on with Freddie. Joy had heard them more than once talking about his wife and son, her encouragement to hang in there so all would be right in the end.

'He left it there that day, but a week or so later, he was at it again, telling me about how some fruit and vegetable growers used harmful chemicals and they'd never get reliable customers that way. I took it to mean he could spread a rumour that I'd then have to deny. He might have thought my blond shaggy hair made me a dimwit, but I understood. What I didn't know was why he was doing it, I had no idea what he wanted in return for leaving me alone until the next time he came to me. He said he wanted to come to an arrangement. He wanted a few little favours – that's what he called them – and in return he'd talk up my business and pay me generously too. It wasn't long before I began to realise, when he told me what the favours were, that he was after The Old Dairy.'

'Rick knew I wanted my wife and child back and that I had to prove myself. So what he also did, apart from giving me money that I could pass on to Ivanna and Timothy for extras that at one time I never would've been able to provide, he also gave me the assurance he'd help me set up my business elsewhere before he made me leave this farm and everything I've built up. He came with the angle that sooner or later you'd be selling anyway, Joy, that as you got older you wouldn't want the responsibility any more. I told myself that over and over, especially on the days where you complained of sore knees, or when you told us the doctor had advised you to take it easy. I told myself it was right and I knew Rick would give you a good price for this place, possibly more than anyone else.'

Freddie shook his head at Drew's offer of wine. It must've been Joy's confession that had set the tone to-night because nobody was throwing accusations Freddie's way, demanding to know exactly what part he'd played, they were all waiting, all seeing the good in him the way they always had, no matter what he'd done.

'I never knew the truth about Joy,' Freddie told them all, 'I never knew there was anything to blackmail her about, that was all news to me until now, when we all found out about the letter and I realised it must've been him. But what it means is I played a part in this mess, bringing unbearable pain and anguish your way, Joy.' His voice broke and he pinched the skin at the top of his nose between his eyes.

'What did he have you do, Freddie?' Libby asked. She looked upset, as though it was her who'd been betrayed as well as her auntie.

'He got me to start talk around town that there was trouble at the farm with vandalism, animals being stolen. The horse that went missing a while back . . .' His face said it all. 'I looked the other way while Rick led it off the land, had everyone panicking and then hailed himself the hero when he found it at the side of the road as though it had wandered down the lane on its own.'

'Was it you who damaged the chicken run?' Libby wondered.

Freddie leaped straight in. 'No, I swear, that wasn't me. I'd never put animals at risk like that.'

Joy felt relief wash over her that it hadn't been him who damaged the coop and she waited for him to carry on and reveal what else he'd been caught up in.

'Rick was the one who convinced the Whittakers and the McKerricks to end their rental agreements on your fields. He scared them off, made them think their animals wouldn't be safe. He boasted about it too. And then he asked me to stop helping you out around the farm, Joy, to claim I was too busy, which meant I stopped offering straight away when you had a problem.' Guilt was written all over his face. 'It also meant you had to pay for the roof repair which wasn't cheap, the fence repairs, even the fields being mowed – which I know for a fact is a huge expense – when I was too busy to do them.'

'All designed to put a strain on my finances,' Joy concluded, crestfallen at the confession. The others remained silent, their faces darting from Joy to Freddie and back again as they took in what had been going on right in front of their noses.

'I was busy, I always am. You know me, I like it that way.'

'Why didn't Rick just wait until Joy decided to sell if he thought, as he'd convinced you, that it would happen sooner rather than later?' Lauren asked.

'It was greed and it was Libby,' said Freddie. 'Her arrival put the wind up him for sure. He didn't realise Joy had any family to speak of, because she never really talked about anyone and she only ever mentioned Libby to us, within these walls. When Libby came along it triggered more than one panicky angry phone call from him and I

313

thought maybe this is it, perhaps he'll back off and I can pretend I never tried to help him in the first place.

'Soon after that I told him I was done helping. I'd looked the other way with the horse, I'd stopped helping so much so that Joy had to pay people to come to the farm, I'd put enough stress on her for my own needs and I was done. It won't surprise you all to know he didn't take that very well. He told me if I stopped helping he'd tell Joy what I'd done, she'd throw me out and I'd lose my business because it's on her land. I'm sorry, Joy. Not because I'm frightened I'll lose my business, or Ivanna and Timothy if I'm not financially secure, but because you of all people did not deserve what I did.'

Joy put her hand on Freddie's arm when he stood up to go. 'Where are you going?'

'I think it's best if I pack up and leave.'

Joy wasn't the only one to say no. They all did.

'Listen Freddie,' Joy began, 'I don't like to be betrayed, part of me is angry, but given what Rick has been doing to me with the letter, the threats, I can see how he might have had your head all over the place. And from experience I also know that once you're in deep with something, getting out is a whole other matter.' Her gaze briefly met Drew's. 'To be honest, you were hardly very persuasive when you tried to convince me I was too old for all of this or should put myself first. You made the comments, sure you did, but you never carried on badgering me and it was only reiterating what I was thinking. And as for not helping me, that's easily rectified, I've plenty of jobs you can turn your hand to.'

He'd welled up and did his best to hold back the emotion by avoiding eye contact, biting down on his bottom lip. Joy put a hand on the side of his face, this gentle giant who looked like he'd never shed a tear in his life, and lifted it so he was looking at her. 'Do you think any differently of me knowing what I did?' She looked across at Drew whose gaze urged her to carry on. 'Because it was a terrible thing I was involved in, I've lied to you all, and it was for my own gain. I didn't want to lose the trust from any of you, because no matter how much I've saved each and every one of you, you have all saved me. By being in my life unconditionally, every single person in this room is here because they want to be. Not because they have to be or out of some sense of duty. I knew that if I told anyone, that might all change, people in the village would look at me differently, I'd lose the life I'd tried so hard to build up, my safety, my security. Don't you see it's the same?'

'It's not,' Freddie smiled, 'But thank you for trying to make me feel less of an arse for doing it.'

'It's Rick who's the arse.' Sniggers were shared around the room, Joy rarely swore or used bad language. 'Well he is.' Her assertion had wine glasses raised in the air to a chorus of Hear Hear.

'What are we going to do about him, Auntie Joy?' Libby came to Joy's side, one hand on her shoulder.

'I don't know. I think he'll go through with the threat if I don't give him the money, which I can only raise if I sell up.'

'But what do *you* want to happen? Long term I mean.'

Joy hesitated and looked at Libby, her eyes misting. 'I had this crazy notion that The Old Dairy might pass down through my family.'

Libby, shell-shocked, took the chair opposite as well

as a big glass of wine. 'I can't believe you thought of me, here, running the place.'

'Is it that bad an idea?'

'Goodness knows what she'd cook,' Freddie teased, pleasing Joy with the way he fell back into his role at the farmhouse as someone who was part of her new assembled family no matter what he'd done wrong. 'She'll be adding basil to cakes, mint to chicken dishes, the girl can't tell one herb from another.'

Libby reached for a tea towel and took a swipe at Freddie who sidestepped just in time. Joy was glad Libby didn't harbour ill feelings towards him for his part in Rick Oxley's blackmailing.

Libby turned her attention back to her auntie. 'I love it here, you know I do. But me running the place would be a huge step and not something to rush into if I even did want it. All I know for now is that you need to look after yourself for a change. You never do, it's always for everyone else. It's OK to put yourself first sometimes.'

Joy smiled at her niece. 'And so do you.'

'Me?'

'Yes, having you. You came here all stressed out and you're interviews in London, talking about going back to those ridiculous hours again, you need to put yourself first or you'll end up an old spinster, just like me.'

'And you think running a halfway house and looking after all this land when I haven't a clue would be less stressful?'

'At least you'd be in the fresh air,' she tried, seeing Libby's point with a smile. 'I want you to be happy.'

'Right back at you.' Joy saw her gaze drift over to Drew as she said, 'I turned down the London job.'

'You did?' Joy watched Drew's face fall as much as hers did when they both realised this must mean Libby was heading back to America, dashing both their hopes at having her stay. But he was soon grinning from ear to ear when Libby made her next announcement.

'I've accepted a position with slightly less responsibility, in their Bristol office instead.'

Joy threw her arms around her niece who was sharing a smile with Drew who looked as though all his Christmases had come at once. 'I'm beyond thrilled. Not quite as thrilled as I'd be if you were taking on the farm, but this is good, it really is.' Joy finally let go of her, smiling, tears pooling in her eyes.

'What are we going to do about Rick?' Cameron, mouth full of cake, had been as quiet as all the others through this, but now brought them back to reality. 'He can't get away with what he's done.'

Joy and Libby dried their eyes and Drew sneaked a wink in Libby's direction to let her know how elated he was with the latest development. Something good after so many bad things to come their way.

Each of the others took a seat at the table, congregated here, for her. Even Drew was still here when he could've – maybe should've – run a mile now he knew the truth.

'We are all here for you, including me,' said Drew. 'This is the home of second chances, and this is your time. It's time for you to give yourself that new beginning by taking control and not letting some egocentric local cheat you out of the life you've built. I agree with Libby's plan—'

'You would,' Lauren quipped, earning herself a brotherly nudge from Drew for her teasing.

'I think we have to get in there first, tell your side of

the story. And what's more,' he turned to Joy. 'I'll be telling mine too.'

'I can't ask you to do that.'

'You didn't ask, I offered. And look, if I don't tell everyone who I am, who do you think will be next on Rick's blackmail list?'

'He's right,' said Libby.

'But what if when the rest of the village knows I'm chased off the main street, out of the bakery and the library, and people don't want me near them?'

'Stop panicking,' said Lauren, a hand on her arm. 'If anyone has a problem with it they can answer to each and every one of us.'

'What are you doing?' she asked her niece who was looking at her phone and then put it to her ear.

'Calling the local newspaper.'

Chapter Seventeen

Joy

J oy left out a basket of eggs for Samuel to pick up from
the front step of the farmhouse and sent a text message
to him to say he could collect them at his convenience.
She couldn't face him yet, because soon she would be
famous around the town, and not in a good way. This
morning the article in the newspaper had appeared in
black and white and people would no longer look at her
in the same way. Her story would be devoured over the
breakfast table, covered in toast crumbs, there to mop up
spills of milk. Her guilty past was out for all to see today
and there wasn't a thing that could change it.

First thing this morning as the newspapers hit the
stands and therefore the local shop, she, Drew, Libby,
Lauren, Freddie, Cameron, Luna and Bisto had all been
waiting to snatch up their copies and they'd gone straight
to Rick's house where they waited outside the big gates
until his curiosity got the better of him and he came out
to demand why they were lurking.

'I'm doing free tasters,' said Lauren, beaming a smile
his way and opening a plastic container filled with cinnamon rolls she'd taken into the bakery last week and knew
full well he'd devoured.

'Free tasters and free delivery?' He wasn't buying it, but neither was he resisting the smell with the lid open and Lauren getting closer. Joy was pretty sure she saw his hand twitch, wanting to reach for one on the other side of the gate.

'They've been popular this morning,' Lauren urged, 'not sure how many I'll have left later on.'

'Very well.' He undid the gate so there was nothing separating them any more. He helped himself, his greed never far away, his chubby fingers squishing into the delicately baked roll. He was almost salivating and when he took his first bite he looked pleased they'd stopped by, but only for a split second before he began to cough hard with the eye-watering amount of cinnamon Joy had seen Lauren put in these – well, in just the one round of dough she'd made sure to give him, she hadn't wanted to waste them all.

'Are you trying to kill me?' he bellowed at Lauren.

'Someone should,' said Drew who stepped forward with the newspaper.

The spluttering continued, the taste too much for the man, but he didn't head inside for the relief of a drink, they had his sure attention with the headline on the front page: 'Local woman turns home into the Farmhouse of Second Chances'.

He had nothing to say, for once.

But he did read the article at the same time as a paperboy tossed his wrapped copy over the gate and cycled off. Joy knew he could read it later to his heart's content and realise he hadn't won, they had.

Joy and Drew had both been interviewed by an eager journalist who must've thought she'd discovered liquid gold with this scoop, but rather than be painful they'd both found it somewhat cathartic. The anger and grief Drew had been holding on to would always be there, the guilt Joy had would never go, but they'd reached a point where it wouldn't break either of them. The whole truth was out, in their words, the journalist had done a good job and now Rick could see there wasn't a thing he could do about it.

'So you see, Rick,' said Joy, right up in his face. She was glad the cinnamon stench was so strong, she didn't want any whiff of his actual breath. 'The farmhouse is not, and will not, ever be for sale. To you, or to anyone else. The entire village knows my history. They know who Drew is. And I'll deal with it if anyone has a problem. What I won't deal with is a blackmailer like you.'

'Get off my property,' was all he could offer in response.

'Rick, it would be my absolute pleasure,' replied Joy.

They left him all alone in that big house behind those gates that segregated him from everyone else while they all got to go home as a family.

At home now, Joy jumped when she heard a noise at the door and when the persistent knocker didn't go away she assumed it couldn't be Samuel.

But it was. And Joy had no idea what to say to him.

'Thanks for the eggs, these look like beauties,' he smiled.

She wasn't sure whether to be elated or completely distraught that he hadn't seen the article yet. If he had, he definitely wouldn't have knocked. 'Laid fresh this morning.' Perhaps he wasn't a morning news reader, maybe he preferred not to read about the doom and gloom in the world over his coffee and first meal of the day.

'How are things?' he asked when she wasn't her usual chatty self.

'Can't complain.' And for want of anything better to say she told him, 'I have a new job.'

'Good for you.'

He seemed to be waiting for more and she stumbled over her words in an attempt to save an already stilted conversation. 'I took a job at the library, three mornings a week as of Monday.'

The job in the library was something Joy hadn't considered until she'd sat down with Freddie, Lauren, Cameron, Drew and Libby and they'd all agreed she needed to take it a lot easier for her body and her mind. At first she'd thought it a crazy idea, especially now people would know the truth, but they'd all thought what better way to get over the next hurdle than by putting herself out there in public. And now Freddie didn't have Rick breathing down his neck he said he'd be free to do a lot more around the place and could show Cameron the ropes. Cameron was way more talkative these days and happy to take on more work around the farmhouse and on the land. It was as though everyone else having messy lives made him feel less unusual. He told Joy yesterday that he'd been thinking for a while how he wouldn't mind doing a qualification in farming. He'd even begun to talk about learning animal management, pondering whether The Old Dairy could ever go back to having cows. But that was a long way off and for now he was earning his keep helping Freddie with his vegetable patches and being in charge of looking after the fields to free up Freddie's time for his wife and child. They were due to meet soon and Joy, nervous for them, had high hopes it would be positive.

'I'm very pleased for you, Joy.' Samuel smiled kindly and patted the top of his basket of eggs. 'I will make a good quiche later today if you'd like to join me?'

'I . . .' How could she tell him the reason why he'd regret asking her that.

'Dinner will be ready at seven, I'll see you then.' He didn't let her get a word in edgeways. 'And it changes nothing you know.'

She looked at him, perplexed.

'I get the newspaper delivered every morning,' was all he needed to say.

Chapter Eighteen

Libby

'Are you ready for this?' Libby asked Joy on Monday lunchtime when they arrived at the farmhouse and she went to go inside the front door. Libby had been the one to go and meet Joy after her first shift at the library and walking her home to ensure she came in this way to the farmhouse rather than round the back.

'We never use the front door, Libby. What are you up to?'

Over the last few days since the revelations and the newspaper article, Libby and Drew along with everyone else's help had been working flat out. Joy turned seventy today and they'd already had a wonderful country breakfast with gifts, cards, and made her feel very happy to have everyone around her. But they had more in store. Libby was almost bursting to tell her because when they went inside there would be bright and shiny banners congratulating Joy on reaching her seventieth year. Libby had left the house battling her way through helium balloons standing to attention with the number seventy on them; an enormous square carrot cake Lauren had made was positioned in the centre of the kitchen table along with enough food to feed an entire army.

'You'll see,' said Libby and opened the door to let Joy in first.

There was an immediate yell of Happy Birthday from the guests huddled inside and Joy stopped, shocked.

'All these people,' said Joy in disbelief.

'All here for you,' Libby told her. She put an arm around her auntie and gently coaxed her along the hallway towards the gathering.

Joy stopped beside the rather straight picture of sunflowers. 'What happened to my painting?'

'Freddie fixed it for you, it should hang straight from now on,' smiled Libby. 'Now stop stalling, people are waiting.' When Joy gripped her arm she ushered her along closer to the eager gathering.

'You mischievous lot,' Joy laughed, standing at the door to the kitchen, tears welling, voice shaky. 'I didn't have any idea you'd planned any of this. The breakfast was enough. But a party . . .'

Drew was first to step forward and hug her and only pulled away for someone else to take their turn. And slowly Joy began to relax, she realised rather than accusations and abuse coming her way for what happened in the past, all anyone here cared about was the present and the future.

'Everyone I love is in the same place.' She took in the sea of faces. All her friends from the village were there.

The only ones not invited were Bisto and Luna who would create mayhem if they were to join in at the start with Joy's arrival. They'd be fussed over later, but for now they'd had a good roam in the fields, been fed treats and had to wait it out in the utility room with a run of the old puppy pen Cameron had taken apart, added more pieces to and made far bigger so that while Bisto wasn't quite up to wandering as Luna did often, they'd have a way of keeping the puppy from running off and them having to launch a search party.

'I can't believe you did all this.' Joy hugged Libby, then everyone she could get her hands on and just when Libby wondered whether this was all too much, Cameron restored normality by announcing he'd just seen Bisto out of the window, rolling in poo, and he was going to clean him up.

'I don't want anyone covered in poo at my party,' Joy quipped, spotting Samuel next. Drew enjoyed that part because Joy blushed, she actually blushed, something none of them had seen before. So confident and bossy and a lover of company it was odd to see her so coy.

'Happy Birthday, Joy.' The local vet kissed her – actually kissed her! – on the cheek, but dangerously close to her lips and left her tongue-tied as Libby and Drew watched on.

'Thank you, Samuel, I'm honoured so many people could make it.'

'We're all honoured to be here. I was thinking, with there being so many people here today, what would you say to dinner for two one evening next week?'

'You mean . . .'

'I guess we would have to call it a date, if that's all right by you.'

'It's more than all right,' she demurred and caught Libby and Drew eavesdropping.

Libby turned to Lauren and gave her the nod to go get their first mystery guest before Joy could tell her and Drew off for not respecting her and Samuel's privacy.

They'd had dinner with one another the night Joy's secret was unleashed in the village and all Libby knew was that Joy had had a smile on her face ever since.

The mystery guests were waiting in the lounge out of sight and it had been decided to welcome them one at a time because this was going to be a big shock for Joy.

Joy was about to bite into a chicken goujon dipped in sour cream and chive dip when Libby tapped her on the shoulder. 'There are a couple more surprises for you, Joy.'

The food dropped back onto Joy's plate and she let out a little squeal when she saw Sita standing behind Libby. They hugged, rocked side-to-side, their voices chattering at ten to the dozen after so many years apart, trying to catch up on decades in the space of seconds.

'You said a couple of surprises,' said Joy, drying her eyes, arm still around Sita. 'I'm not sure my nerves can take much more.'

'Hello, Joy.' A voice came from behind them. Drew had already welcomed the next guest in, and this time Joy burst into tears, she was shaking and it was Luna who stepped forward and held on to her. She held her up, both of them crying.

Sita stood beside Libby, arm linked into hers as Libby said, 'I knew this reunion would be the most emotional. Not that she doesn't love you, but . . . well you know.'

And Sita did know. As they watched Joy and Luna, women who'd met in the most hellish of circumstances, reunite on the outside, both Sita and Libby knew the entire story about this woman and how she'd been the one to get Joy through so many dark days. Everyone who loved Joy owed this woman their gratitude and she'd be sure to find it today as she mingled with guests, if Joy ever let go of her that was.

When they'd started planning this party, it was Lauren who'd suggested they find these friends who Joy had lost touch with. And it had been surprisingly easy. Sita and Luna were at least unique names, which was a start. Facebook had been very helpful as they'd found both of them on there – thank goodness for social media! Sita's profile had a photo of her with a man and three children, sitting in front of a drum kit, and her location was Liverpool. They'd suspected Luna might be traceable but wouldn't be able to come to the party if she was in New Zealand, but perhaps she could record a message if she was willing. There had been a few Lunas to scroll through on Facebook and a bit more investigating, but half of those they'd disregarded because they were too young. And then it hadn't taken much to find the woman they needed, because Joy's Luna had a website and when Libby had gone from Facebook to there, amidst all the information about Reiki and massage and wellness, was Luna's personal story. She obviously didn't want to hide, she wanted people to know her past, perhaps to cleanse and get rid of negativity, Libby had no idea, she was just thankful it was on there and not only that, she and her husband had relocated to Kent.

Halfway through the party, the chatter still at a volume that filled the farmhouse a little too much, Libby was looking for Joy and couldn't find her. Luna and Cameron were having a good chat, and after a quick look inside the house Libby headed out of the front door and round the back, where she found Joy sitting below her oak tree.

'Are you OK?'

'Fine, more than fine.' She patted the ground beside her and Libby sat. It was a dry, warm day, but pleasant with the breeze. 'It won't be too long before we can't do this any more. There'll be more heavy rain, then sleet and snow.'

'Christmas at the farmhouse will be wonderful.'

'You'll come?'

'Just try and stop me.' It was nice here beneath the tree Joy had told her she'd planted from an acorn. Hard to believe when it loomed above them, commanding respect with its size and place here at The Old Dairy. 'Did you hear, Rick's gone on an extended holiday to Spain?'

'I didn't hear that, but it's lovely news. A break from him would be good. There's no room in this village for anyone to be so vindictive.'

'I wonder if he'll change his ways after this.'

'I very much doubt it,' smiled Joy. 'I wonder now if he wanted to get to me because of his relationship with his own son. He went off the rails and whatever Rick tried to do, didn't work. He failed him, perhaps he didn't like that I was able to help people in a way he couldn't.'

'Maybe you're right,' said Libby. 'And in which case, I feel sorry for him. But not too sorry, my loyalties lie with you.'

'Thank you, that means a lot.'

'I saw the Whittakers and the McKerricks inside,' said Libby after they'd sat there a while longer, the sounds of clucking chickens filling the air, the odd crow from Ronald as he kept his hens in order, watching Bisto pester Luna in the pen when all Luna wanted to do was sleep. 'I hear they're renting your land again as of the end of the month.'

'They are. Rick played his games and he's been found

out, but we're all good. I've spoken to them both – I've spoken to everyone, including the buyer who wants to plant a sunflower farm, and the paperwork will be finalised at the end of the week. Rick never got to them, I was paranoid that he had so didn't chase them up, but it seems they were waiting for finance.' She blew out from between her lips.

'There are ways you could diversify too, you know,' Libby suggested.

'Now I don't need fancy words . . . what are you talking about?'

'If you need more cash, you could rent out fields for glamping, you could do up the barn for weddings, you have some amazing backdrops for photography. Or you could—'

'Stop there, young lady. All great ideas and I'm glad you've got your business head on, but for now I think I'll just enjoy the place as it is.' She nudged her niece. 'But I know exactly where to come if I ever need business advice.'

'Happy to help any time,' Libby beamed.

'I still can't believe all those people in my kitchen and hallway are here for a party.'

'All those people who are there for *you* Joy.'

'I'm blessed.'

'So when's the next date with Samuel?' Libby teased.

Coyly she told her niece, 'We're going to dinner at the weekend.'

'His place or yours?' But she held up her hands. 'You know what, I don't need to know.' And she planted a kiss on her auntie's cheek. 'All I need to know is that you're happy.'

'I think I am.' And it was a wonderful thing to be able to admit after all this time. To be properly happy, to have a weight shifted out into the open instead of resting on her shoulders.

Joy waved across at Dahlia who was heading up the driveway and round to the back of the farmhouse carrying a plate of cupcakes for the party. Cameron wasted no time coming over to greet her and take her inside. He really was finding his place here in Bramleywood and this might be Joy's party, but everyone seemed to understand that she needed time to digest all of this, time to process, and they carried on around her.

'Who's that?' Libby wondered when another two figures lingered at the end of the driveway. But she didn't have to wonder for long because Freddie came outside, passed them as though he hadn't seen either of them watching, and walked towards the pair.

'That's his family, his other family,' said Joy with a sniff.

Libby handed her a tissue, but her own emotions began to work overtime watching the scene unfolding just metres away. The young boy wasted no time running into his father's arms, Ivanna hesitated until Freddie held one arm out for her to join them. 'They look happy,' she gulped.

'About time, he deserves it. He's a good man,' said Joy.

'I know he is.' She was glad the horrible letter hadn't come from him. He may have played a part, but all of them understood his reasons, all of them knew they couldn't hold it against him.

They stayed outside long enough for Joy to tell Libby how she felt seeing Sita and Luna again, how the women had picked up as though they'd seen one another only a few days ago rather than years. And Libby told Joy she'd invited her dad along today.

'He didn't come because he thought it would be too much for you, you might not want him here.'

'I'd never turn him away. But maybe today it was right for him not to come.' She smiled across at Libby, their knees almost touching as they sat. 'Would you like to invite him down in a week or so? We have plenty of space. I'd like to see him.'

'If you're comfortable with it then I know he'd like a chance to apologise.' She patted Joy's hand and when Samuel spotted them and came outside Libby saw her cue to leave. 'Don't do anything I wouldn't do.'

'Cheeky mare,' she muttered before the vet got closer.

Libby could hear them laughing and turned to see him lowering himself to the ground, both of them talking about sore legs, their age. But they looked happy, Joy content, Joy free at last.

Libby fussed over Luna in the makeshift pen and Bisto didn't miss a chance for attention and lost interest in the newspaper he was ripping to shreds. Libby wondered if it was the front page that had dissolved from news to mere facts of lives that had evolved ever since.

Drew came up from behind and pulled her into a hug, kissing her neck. It made her jump, but not as much as Ronald's crow, which sometimes blended in with the surroundings but still had the ability to startle if she was off in her own little world thinking.

'Look at them,' said Libby, nodding towards Samuel and Joy who were laughing about something, not the type of hysterical laugh when something was hilarious, but a gentle laugh that hinted they might just have found the perfect company with each other.

'They look happy,' he said. 'Like us.'

She turned in his arms. 'Joy was wrong to think her secret might come between us. It's shown me what sort of man you are.'

'You like what you see?' he teased.

'Very much.'

It wasn't long before Lauren called everyone together for cake, and the farmhouse kitchen, bursting at the seams, was filled with the same familiar warmth Joy had always wanted and that Libby now knew would be here forever. And when they gathered outside for a group photo beneath the oak tree that had spread its roots to claim its place, a camera balancing precariously on top of Drew's jeep with him running back before the timer took the shot, Libby would forever be glad she'd come home to England.

Everyone who passed through the Farmhouse of Second Chances filled their lives with more love and kindness than they could ever want, and Libby knew she'd got that too.

THE END

Acknowledgements

To my husband, as always, for his support since the day I decided I wanted to be a writer. He never once let me give up thank goodness. And as well as his encouragement he makes the best lunches so that I can get back to my desk to carry on writing.

Thank you to my younger brother Oliver who answered all my questions about the land and what Joy could do with it to raise extra funds . . . he had so many ideas, I couldn't possibly use them all. I've never kept chickens like Joy but Oliver once had plenty of them and so I hope I've created a realistic home for them at The Old Dairy.

When I was a teenager my parents let our dog Topsy have puppies and it is something that will stay in my memory bank forever. Luna's litter in the book was inspired by the experience and the puppy named Buttercup was much like our dog Turvy (yes, the mum was called Topsy and we kept a black lab and called her Turvy!) in that she always, always carried the bowl around in her mouth after the six puppies had finished eating.

Although she has moved on to a new job away from the Orion team, I would like to thank Olivia Barber who I worked with when this book was only at the ideas stage.

Thank you too to Charlotte Mursell who took over from Olivia to work on this story and had me do another round of gruelling edits. Although painful to wade through at the time, it's those expert edits that end up shaping the book into the best that it can be, so that it will sit proudly on my shelf and the shelves of my readers.

I must thank the Write Romantics, my writing family, my tribe, whose support since 2013 when we met online has been solid whether it's about writing or personal life. You girls are all amazing and I can't wait to see you all again soon.

Thank you to the whole team at Orion – in particular thank you to Ellen my publicist whose support is very much appreciated (despite the requests for short stories!), and to Tanjiah who produces beautiful graphics along the way to let all the readers out there know about my books. Thank you also to editorial assistant Sanah for all her hard work getting this book and others ready for publication.

To my daughters for being themselves and for telling me every so often that they're proud – if not in words, by social media likes!

A huge thank you must go, of course, to you, the reader! To every single person who has picked up this book or any of my others along the way. Keep the comments on social media coming, the kind reviews, the emails, all of the contact goes a long way to keeping me going to deliver more of the books you want to read.

And lastly, I wanted to say that with the last couple of years being exceptionally tough, I hope *The Farmhouse of Second Chances* leaves you feeling uplifted and with the encouragement to reach out and ask for help along the way.

Much love, Helen xx

Credits

Helen Rolfe and Orion Fiction would like to thank everyone at Orion who worked on the publication of *The Farmhouse of Second Chances* in the UK.

Editorial
Charlotte Mursell
Sanah Ahmed

Copyeditor
Francine Brody

Proofreader
Laetitia Grant

Audio
Paul Stark
Jake Alderson

Contracts
Anne Goddard
Humayra Ahmed
Ellie Bowker

Editorial Management
Charlie Panayiotou
Jane Hughes
Bartley Shaw
Tamara Morriss

Finance
Jasdip Nandra
Afeera Ahmed
Elizabeth Beaumont
Sue Baker

Marketing
Tanjiah Islam

Production
Ruth Sharvell

Design
Tomás Almeida
Joanna Ridley
Nick May

Publicity
Ellen Turner

Operations
Jo Jacobs
Sharon Willis

Sales
Jen Wilson
Esther Waters
Victoria Laws
Rachael Hum
Anna Egelstaff
Frances Doyle
Georgina Cutler

If you enjoyed *The Farmhouse of Second Chances*, you'll love Helen Rolfe's heartwarming story about family and second chances . . .

Can three sisters stitch their family back together?

Loretta loves running the little village sewing shop in Butterbury. Some of her most precious memories are sitting with her three daughters Daisy, Ginny and Fern, stitching together pieces of material – and their hopes and dreams.

But this Christmas the family is coming apart at the seams: Fern feels like she's failing at motherhood and marriage, Ginny's passion for her job as a midwife is fading, Daisy is desperate to prove she's changed since her wild younger years – and most of all, Loretta seems to be hiding something . . .

As they come together to create a new festive quilt, the bond between the sisters begins to heal. But when Loretta reveals the real reason she's brought them all home, can the sisters mend the quilt, and their family, in time for Christmas?

The smallest things can make the biggest difference . . .

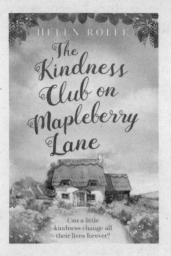

Veronica Beecham's cottage is the neatest house on Mapleberry Lane. A place for everything, and everything in its place – that's her motto. But within her wisteria-covered walls, Veronica has a secret: she's hardly left her perfect home in years.

Then her teenage granddaughter, Audrey, arrives on the doorstep, and Veronica's orderly life is turned upside down. Shy and lonely, Audrey is struggling to find her place in the world. As a bond begins to form between the two women, Audrey develops a plan to give her gran the courage to reconnect with the community – they'll form a kindness club, with one generous action a day to help someone in the village, and perhaps help each other at the same time.

As their small acts of kindness begin to ripple outwards, both Veronica and Audrey find that with each passing day, they feel a little braver. There's just one task left before the end of the year: to make Veronica's own secret wish come true . . .

Come and find love by the sea . . .

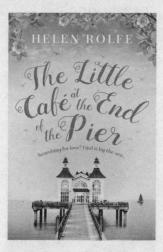

Searching for love?
You'll find it at the little café at the end of the pier . . .

When Jo's beloved grandparents ask for her help in running their little café at the end of the pier in Salthaven-on-Sea, she jumps at the chance.

The café is a hub for many people: the single dad who brings his little boy in on a Saturday morning; the lady who sits alone and stares out to sea; the woman who pops in after her morning run.

Jo soon realises that each of her customers is looking for love – and she knows just the way to find it for them. She goes about setting each of them up on blind dates – each date is held in the café, with a special menu she has designed for the occasion.

But Jo has never found love herself. She always held her grandparents' marriage up as her ideal and she hasn't found anything close to that. But could it be that love is right under her nose . . .?

Welcome to Cloverdale, the home of kindness and new beginnings . . .

Sometimes it takes a village to mend a broken heart . . .

Cloverdale is known for its winding roads, undulating hills and colourful cottages, and now for its Library of Shared Things: a place where locals can borrow anything they might need, from badminton sets to waffle makers. A place where the community can come together.

Jennifer has devoted all her energy into launching the Library. When her sister Isla moves home, and single dad Adam agrees to run a mending workshop at the Library, new friendships start to blossom. But what is Isla hiding, and can Adam ever mind his broken past?

Then Adam's daughter makes a startling discovery, and the people at the Library of Shared Things must pull together to help one family overcome its biggest challenge of all . . .

Step into the enchanting world of Lantern Square . . .

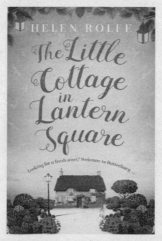

Looking for a fresh start? Welcome to Butterbury . . .

Hannah went from high-flyer in the city to small business owner and has never looked back. She's found a fresh start in the cosy Cotswold village of Butterbury, where she runs her care package company, Tied up with String.

Her hand-picked gifts are the perfect way to show someone you care, and while her brown paper packages bring a smile to customers across the miles, Hannah also makes sure to deliver a special something to the people closer to home.

But when her ex-best friend Georgia arrives back in her life, can Hannah forgive and forget? With her new business in jeopardy, Hannah needs to let the community she cares for give a little help back . . .

Meanwhile, mystery acts of kindness keep springing up around Butterbury, including a care package on Hannah's own doorstep. Who is trying to win her heart – and will she ever give it away?